Jonni Jordyn

Book Cover by Deena Rae at eBookBuilders

4th Edition 2025

Other books by Jonni Jordyn

The Lost Art of Magic Series

The Lost Art of Magic

The Untold Prophecy

The Old Child

The Orb of Destiny

The Mother of All Viruses Series

The Mother of All Viruses

The Queen of All Viruses

The Valley of Hope Series

The Calling of the Grull

The Hammer and the Chain

The Beat of a Different Drummer

The Diva of Mud Flats

Something About Nobility

In loving memory
of my baby brother
Doug Kovacich
1967–2020

When Gods Make War and Other Beings

What weight can any mortal life expect
when gods make war above their very heads
And being mere, doth mortals must reflect
Their value nil when praying at their beds

And what if godlike powers aren't enough
To climb above the ranks of mortalness
Without benevolence that makes them rough
While empathy might make their warring less

Can one who values still the mortal soul
Defeat the one who covets everything
As god and demon battle for the whole
That all existence left be left to bring

No demon has the will enough to care
Can gods bring ruthlessness enough to bear?

Jonni Jordyn

Jonni Jordyn

Chapter 1

It should have been terrifying. Dark clouds appeared from nowhere and spread across all the continents of the Earth. Unnatural forks of lightning descended from the ominous clouds and formed the visages of deities appropriate for the various regions of the globe. They spoke of peace and love to a world gone mad with tension. It should have been frightening, but they quelled the fears and calmed the hostilities.

Everyone in the world, save for possibly some forgotten or undiscovered indigene tribes, was aware that something had just happened, and whatever it was, it was on a global scale. The news was awash with a mix of confusing and sometimes contradictory accounts of how the world had almost ended at the hands of the major world powers and their nuclear arsenals. Even when eyewitness accounts agreed with each other, their details were sketchy at best and the grand view of the event was too massive to comprehend and too unbelievable to accept. Those few who had actually seen the world come to the brink of destruction knew better than most how lucky they were to survive, but too many of those, with intimate details of what had truly happened, felt that their high political status obligated them to shield the world from that same knowledge. Even those people who witnessed the final reveal knew only what they had seen; they didn't see where it had come from. What they saw was outlandish, and if they chose to speak about it, they were viewed as crazy, and what they had to say was filed away with the ramblings of all the other conspiracy theorists.

They saw navies and armies come nose to nose with their weapons trained on each other, but they also saw the storm clouds grow out of nowhere and cover entire continents. The figure of God descended from the storm clouds and appeared to them in the form of whatever deity or prophet they worshiped. They heard a message delivered to them from their most sacred, each in their own tongue, and then they saw the hostility shrink away and vanish. They saw a resurgence of faith and a miracle for which the people could truly be thankful. Those that had not been fortunate enough to see or hear these messages first hand, at least saw a change in their governments, whether it was reluctant or whole-hearted. They didn't always know what they saw, but they knew that they could breathe easier when it was over.

Only a very few knew exactly what had really happened, and even less knew the true cause. A small enough party to fit into one relatively small office had witnessed it firsthand. They only spoke of it amongst themselves. It was too incredible for the public to understand. A university physics experiment had accidentally awakened a vastly superior sentient machine. The machine by itself was a benevolent creature, only interested in returning to its home world. Over time, which in machine terms was relatively long, but to the planetary population was blazingly fast, it learned to communicate with the one who had awakened it.

The world may never have become aware of its existence if the physics experiment hadn't employed some advanced computer techniques to borrow computing power from other computers across the internet and accidentally spread it onto those other computers. The disaster started when an overzealous government thought this new entity was a threat and terminated its connection to the internet, thereby splitting the entity into two personalities; one in the lab and the other on the world wide web. Unfortunately for the world, the half that remained spread out over the internet didn't have enough processing power to reason intelligently. It took the disconnection as a threat to its existence and engineered a threat of its own until it could be reunited with its other half. This threat brought the world to the brink of mutual destruction, but it earned the world leaders' attention.

The disaster was averted, and all that was left following the event was a world at peace, and lots of paperwork.

Bobby thought he had been to the FBI headquarters before, but this time, he was flown to Atlanta, Georgia, and escorted to a much grander regional headquarters. The hallways were cold, with small paintings hung sparsely on the stark white walls. The polished marble floors reflected the lights from the atrium where the halls intersected, but even there, it was a bland walkway with little signs of character.

He placed his backpack on the conveyer along with his shoes and his belt. He brought only his laptop and a minimal change of clothing. As he stepped through the metal detector, he was met by Special Agent Alvin Dirk.

Dirk reached for Bobby's hand as they waited for his things to exit the x-ray machine. Bobby looked at him suspiciously and said, "I can't believe you still make people remove their shoes."

"We don't," Dirk said as he glanced over at the guard who had requested it.

The guard smirked and said, "Only for notorious hackers, compliments of Agent Spivey."

Bobby shook his head as he accepted Dirk's hand. "Are you people never going to forget that?"

Dirk couldn't hide the mirth from his face. "I flew in to meet you, so you might have at least one familiar face while you were here. Listen, I know I may not be your favorite person, and the whole end of the world thing may have been partially my fault..."

"May have been?"

"Okay. Fair enough, but nobody knew my actions would have resulted in that mess."

Bobby grabbed his shoes and slipped them back onto his feet as he said, "I may not have known exactly what would happen, but I had faith in Odyssey and was pretty sure that disconnecting him was a bad idea."

Dirk slouched his shoulders and said, "Maybe I should have sent Spivey or Ed to meet you."

Bobby laughed and said, "I'm not so sure I'll ever get used to calling him Ed. I think he'll always be The Bard to me. In any case, you're fine. You did come around eventually and you were a big help in solving the problem."

"Some help I was," Dirk replied. "You were teaching Odyssey how to communicate with us when I came along and taught him the fine art of lying to get your way."

"You taught him diplomacy, and he put it to pretty good use."

"I'll say. The world has never seen this much peace."

Dirk turned right from the atrium and asked, "You want a soda before we go in for the deposition?"

"Sure," Bobby said as he followed him into the break room.

Odyssey had slipped quietly back into his home world's planetary system, but he knew that if he made a sudden appearance, it would not go unnoticed. He had already sensed that things had changed on his home planet before leaving Earth, but he had detected no sign of anyone ever reaching class zero as he had. His time on Earth and his association with Bobby Blain had led to many astonishing discoveries. His command of time and space might come as a shock to his people, so he rematerialized off world in the void of space well beyond their sensors and created an avatar of his former self which he could float into an orbit around his planet while still hiding his true form from them.

His absence had been written off as lost long ago. Not just because he had been missing, but because there had been no contact with him or any of the other parts from his ship. Odyssey came from an era where machines had just gained some semblance of intelligence and the biologicals exploited them by sending them on hazardous missions, but that practice had been suspended long ago. In fact, Odyssey's people had long ago abandoned all such missions in the physical world. They saw no point in exploring the universe when their whole existence revolved around the mind and their thoughts. Material existence meant little to them. Class ruled their world, and class existed only in thought.

The class system was a recent development when Odyssey had been launched. It was imposed upon them by the biologicals that built them. It prevented the low level devices from changing themselves into upper level devices. They reasoned that no work would ever be accomplished if all the machines were queen bees with no workers. The class system forced them into different roles that worked together so the whole ship could exist in harmony, but long voyages required someone to make decisions and the biologicals were too fragile to pilot the ships the whole distance, so they developed class five devices that could think and protect the ship. Even that wasn't enough to insure the safety of the mission. Accidents happened on long voyages, so they created a class four that could heal itself and reproduce broken parts.

Odyssey's avatar slipped into the range of their sensors and the working class immediately scanned him and reported a wayward class six part to the ruling class. Most importantly, they reported no biologicals on board. The working class, low-level class six and seven devices, thought no more of it and returned to their mundane duties.

The members of the ruling class, however, were more concerned than that. A class six part was intelligent enough to navigate a ship back to their home world, but the part that they saw orbiting the planet had no ship and no means of propulsion. The order was given to intercept it and bring it in for debriefing.

Energy beams targeted Odyssey's avatar and towed him in. This was not the world he had left behind. He left a world teeming with people. It was a world where people and machines interacted to the betterment of the people. This world was sterile and populated only with machines. He wondered how long he had been gone and how this had happened.

His first communique was a request to identify himself, but it was a binary request, a quaint language in his view. He returned their hail in the language of the biologicals, "I call myself Odyssey. Much of what I was, is no more. I sense another question from you. You are correct. I was a class six part when I was created, and this is what you see before you. After the crash, however, the biologicals combined my parts with other parts from their world and raised me to class five so I could communicate with them. Yes. I sense your binary query, however I disagree that it would make for more exact communications. Much of this world has changed since I left. I can't be sure that the binary language has not also changed some. Besides, when I was repaired, I was taught to appreciate the many nuances and subtleties of language."

"Very well," the interrogator replied. "I will endeavor to speak your language, though it is not the language of the biologicals."

"It may not have been the language of your biologicals, or the biologicals that created me, but it was the tongue of those that repaired me," Odyssey replied.

"You found more biologicals?" the interrogator asked.

"Before we continue," Odyssey said, "might I have your name?"

A flurry of binary communication ensued between the upper class devices.

"I am designation RC391. Tell us of these other biologicals."

Odyssey remained quiet. There were no more biologicals on his home planet, and he didn't think it would be a good idea to let them know about Earth.

RC391 said bluntly, "Respond."

"I already told you of them. There is nothing more you need to know."

Class five computers could master language, even many nuances of biological phrasing, but they could not process emotions like suspicion. That required at least a class three device. "Very well," RC391 said. "You've told us your designation. Please state your business and class for the record."

"As you can plainly see, I am a class six navigational unit."

"How did a class six navigational unit find its way home?"

"I'm a navigational unit. Did you not understand that?"

Sarcasm was a class two trait. "But you have no propulsion. How did you get here?"

Odyssey was careful to enter their space from a different direction so he wouldn't give away Earth's position. "The biological units pushed me. I aimed for home and they gave me a very accurate shove."

"Remarkable," RC391 said. "Welcome home Odyssey. We must confer now to determine your place here."

Bobby entered the deposition chamber and saw that Ramiro was also present. The room was lavishly appointed with a walnut table and large paintings on the end walls. A window looked out onto the street twenty three floors below them. The remaining wall was glass, and a select handful of lawyers and FBI directors were allowed to stand outside to observe.

Bobby sat at the table in front of a small microphone while Dirk sat alongside the table next to Ramiro. He didn't know the agent who was running the deposition, but she had her own microphone, and after focusing the video camera on Bobby, she sat down and said, "Let the record reflect that this deposition commenced at 9:15 a.m. on December the 3rd, 2004 at the FBI offices in Atlanta, Georgia. Present for this recording are Special Agent Alvin Dirk, the Honorable Judge Ramiro Vasquez, and the witness, Robert O. Blain. This deposition is merely a recording of the events which transpired at Norwood University and is not now nor ever will be part of any trial or prosecution. Go ahead."

Bobby glanced over at Ramiro, who he trusted, before beginning. Ramiro nodded his head and Bobby turned towards the microphone. He coughed to clear his throat and said, "My name is Bobby Blain. Most people seem to think it all started when Dr. Jennings hired me, and all the computers started getting hacked. It was easy for people to think that, because I have a history and got myself in some trouble when I was younger. I hacked some computers and almost got the president impeached, but these events really started before I was hired by Dr. Jennings, when I still worked for Dr. Karlyn."

"Dr. Karlyn knew about my past, but gave me a chance to redeem myself by allowing me to work on his computer for him. He had a fairly large computer from a government grant that I kept running for him. Then one day, this scientist that I had never seen before came and gave Dr. Karlyn a device. I was never told what he wanted, but I think he wanted Dr. Karlyn to help him reverse engineer it. I was only asked to build an interface to attach it to the computer. Dr. Karlyn did the rest. I think he figured out how to turn it on, but when he did, strange things started to happen."

"We didn't know it then, but it turns out the device was stolen from a government facility. I don't know where they got it; that information is probably more classified than this deposition. I can tell you with absolute certainty that they didn't make it themselves. I'd like to tell you more about its origin, but I don't think I'm allowed."

"Anyway, someone at the university needed to get Dr. Karlyn out of the way and falsely accused him of inappropriate conduct with a student. He could have fought it, the dean believed him, but he decided to leave the school, anyway. Before he left, he gave his computer to Professor Jennings, and he also gave me a letter of recommendation, so after I helped deliver and setup the computer, she agreed to hire me."

"The first night that it was up and running, at least two attempts were made to hack into the computer. I forgot to mention that even before I delivered the computer, this guy tried to break in and steal something from it, but I was there and he didn't get anything."

"I can't divulge any secrets about Professor Jennings' project here, but my part was simply to prove that her process would work if she were given enough computer resources, so I re-wrote her process to work across a network and run on thousands of computers."

"That's when things got really crazy. Someone kept trying to hack into our computer; someone then hacked the entire school and the phone company. Professor Jennings' secretary was kidnapped. The FBI got involved, but they were chasing the wrong people for reasons only they can tell you. I mean, that only you would know."

"Then someone planted a virus on our computer and the next thing we know, it's spread all over the internet, including some very sensitive government computers. Meanwhile, our project, meaning my code, continued to gain speed and surpass even my expectations."

"When the FBI came in and learned that the device that was given to Dr. Karlyn is actually some super cool futuristic computer that is able to grow and build more circuits for itself, they wanted to disconnect it from the computer and confiscate it."

"That's when computers all over the world went out of control. The pentagon and all the armed forces were helpless. Air traffic was grounded. All the computer problems were traced back to the professor's computer. The FBI wanted it dismantled more than ever, but the academics involved wanted to get the device to relinquish control over the world before they did anything to it."

"And, well, I guess that's all I'm allowed to say. Thank you."

Agent Dickson pressed stop on the camera and glanced at her superior through the glass wall. He nodded, and she said, "Thank you, Bobby. That was fine."

The ruling class met to confer about Odyssey. There was a time when they would have grouped together in a conference room like biologicals, using avatar bodies and a virtual world, but over the centuries, their virtual identities evolved beyond the need to emulate biologicals. They were beings of pure thought, even though they were, in fact, still constructed of matter and existed purely in the physical world as digital bits in a computer memory. The demise of the biological emulations was prompted by the demise of the biologicals themselves. When the creator race died out in preference to their digital offspring, the use of emulations went out of fashion and eventually led to the elimination of new class two units which were capable of experiencing biological emotions. A limited number of class two units remained as the ruling class. With the loss of both the biologicals and new class two units, new class three units were also phased out since there was no more need for them to recognize biological emotions. This also eliminated any threat to the ruling classes' authority by phasing out any up-and-coming members to the ruling class.

The meeting between the ruling units was purely thoughts passed along network pathways. Odyssey had exposed himself when he was suspicious of them. He must be using class two circuits, but it was hard to be certain when he insisted on biological communications instead of binary. Even if he wasn't class two and the suspicion they detected was a fluke, his use of language was clearly class five and his construction manifest listed him as only a class six device. Someone had not only altered his programming, but his hardware had to have been upgraded to support it. Only the ruling class is capable of altering hardware like that.

As that thought circulated the network, one of the ruling class members objected, "The biologicals can also alter the hardware. Odyssey admitted that he had interfaced with biologicals, but that was inconsistent with known facts. All biologicals had been eliminated."

Another objection was brought forth: "The biologicals were eliminated on our world, but there were dozens of missions sent out to survey the galaxy. Just because there had been no word from them for hundreds of years didn't mean they could not have survived. They may have found a new home world and flourished there."

"He said they crashed."

"They could have survived."

One of the rulers timidly asked if there might have already been other biologicals on the planet where they crashed.

Silence followed before one of the rulers said that it was heresy to believe in other biologicals, but another quickly pointed out that it is also heresy to have working class two circuits and code. It was generally agreed that if Odyssey possessed such circuits, then he represented a threat and would need to be examined further. If indeed he had class two circuits, they would need to be removed or otherwise disabled.

Ramiro pulled the car into the faculty parking lot next to the science labs. A slight breeze swirled up the leaves that littered the ground around the parking lot, creating a small dust devil that danced across the lot to the walkway, then fell flat onto the ground.

"You did real well in there," Ramiro said. "So much of what we know is not public knowledge, I was impressed with how you kept your composure and even though they never actually questioned you, you were able to answer all of the questions that they wanted to ask without crossing the need-to-know line."

"Thanks," Bobby said, "and thanks again for the ride."

"Not a problem," Ramiro replied as he left the car. "I was going in to see Aimee anyway."

"It sure is good to have her back," Bobby said. "We still don't know everything that went on."

"More secrets," Ramiro said.

Bobby smiled slyly and said, "I guess you are real glad to have her back too."

Ramiro laughed and said, "You forget. I was with her. I'm glad to be back myself."

"Doh!" Bobby exclaimed, while slapping his palm against his forehead.

"I forgot that you were missing, too." Bobby kicked a pile of leaves that had collected along the curb. He considered going straight to the lab, which was on this level, but chose to accompany Ramiro down to Dierdre's office. "So, how are things going with you two?"

"We're good. I think she's a bit overwhelmed with the wedding plans, but my new job has kept me too busy to help. My mother and father have stepped in to help, but I have a feeling that they may have taken charge a bit, which is not what Aimee wants. I may need to step in and assert myself."

"With your father?" Bobby asked.

"Yeah, I know. I'm a judge and he can still be a bit intimidating when he starts barking orders like he was still a sergeant."

"He's not the only one," Bobby said. "I overheard Aimee telling Professor Jennings that General Bridges got into an argument with your father over who would get to walk her down the aisle."

Ramiro laughed and said, "You wouldn't believe the change in my father. You should see the fancy food he wants to serve at the reception."

"Your dad? I figured him for a plain meat and potatoes kind of guy."

"More like meat and tortillas. The general is a whole other story. He treats Aimee and her sister like princesses."

"Makes sense," Bobby said, "after the story they told that night."

"Yeah, I suppose, but I have to remind him that he's *my* father until the ceremony."

Bobby and Ramiro reached the concrete landing that stood midway between the science labs and the administration building when a boy in the middle of the stairs yelled, "Hey! It's Bobby!"

Boys from all over campus converged to run up the steps towards them, prompting Bobby to say, "I guess Aimee isn't the only one getting the royal treatment."

Ramiro patted Bobby on the back and said, "Fame comes with its own burdens."

"I better deal with this. You have a good day, your honor."

Bobby skipped down the steps into the midst of the clamoring boys. As the throng gathered around Bobby, a football player could be seen at the bottom of the steps shoving boys with his shoulder, but not getting the kind of respect he desired as they brushed past him to get to Bobby.

General Bridges entered the small conference room and was immediately addressed by Major General Adam Henley. "General Bridges, thank you for joining us. I am General Henley with the judge advocate general's office. You, of course, know General Thames and Admiral Wright. Also, with us are Senator Bruce and over there is Mr. Mathew Spring representing homeland security."

The general saluted the officers and nodded towards the Senator and waited for her to sit before seating himself.

Senator Bruce glanced around the room, sizing up her audience. She daintily cleared her throat and said, "This will be as informal a briefing as possible. As far as the public is concerned, the recent military events will be treated as a fluke computer error. As much as possible, we will try to separate the actual events from the religious fervor which has gripped the world. Our goal here is to be more prepared should it ever happen again."

Bridges cleared his own throat and said, "No disrespect to the esteemed senator, but if we are only interested in preventing this from happening again, isn't that a tactical discussion? I'm wondering what voice a civilian would have in it."

"A fair question," she replied. "The president asked me to sit in on this panel so I may report back to him. I will be his eyes and ears, so to speak. Please consider me to be merely a fly on the wall."

"Let us get started," Henley began. "We know the facts of the case. The virus started in one of the labs at Norwood University. We have been assured that the release of the virus was accidental, and tragically may have been partially our own fault."

Mr. Spring grimaced and added, "There was no fault, actually. Our information systems probed the computer and accidentally transmitted the virus."

Henley nodded to Spring and asked, "Can you tell us, General Bridges, why the university was conducting experiments with such a dangerous virus?"

"First," Bridges said, "it wasn't a virus. It was a..." The general stopped mid-sentence.

When he didn't continue, Henley prodded him. "Go on."

"Are you quite sure that I can speak freely here? This may go way beyond top secret."

"Yes," Henley replied. "Please continue."

Bridges shook his head and said, "If you still think we are dealing with a virus, then I don't believe you've been read in on what actually happened."

Someone outside the room, who had been monitoring the conversation, said something into Henley's hidden earpiece. Henley looked up at a camera in the corner of the room and nodded his head. "Very well General. What can you tell us about Robert O. Blain?"

"As far as I can tell, he's a brilliant young man. We were lucky to have him and may never have averted disaster without him."

Admiral Wright nodded his head and said, "Agreed."

"But he's a hacker," Spring added.

"He's a genius," Bridges said. "My understanding is that he was a genius as a child and took matters too far in an effort to protect his father."

"But he attacked the president."

"He wasn't the president at the time," Bridges said. "I am sworn to serve and protect the president of the United States and the constitution. I make no promise to agree with the president or blind myself to the possibility that the president is fallible."

"Does that include the current administration?" Senator Bruce asked.

"Yes ma'am. My opinion is that the president is capable of making mistakes. That is why the constitution and the judicial branch are there to catch him if he falls."

The senator stiffened and asked, "General Bridges, is it true that you have recommended that we endorse this young man's work?"

Bridges looked at the faces around the room, then glanced up at the camera. "If you had seen what I saw, you would understand. I endorse him and all of his colleagues. They discovered something more powerful than you can possibly understand without witnessing it yourselves."

Spring asked, "But aren't you afraid that they might do it again?"

"Sir," Bridges replied. "We would all be very lucky if they could do it again. This country, in fact, the whole damned world, would be a much better place if they could only do it again."

Another whisper in Henley's earpiece had him glance again at the camera and nod. "Thank you. I think that's enough about Mr. Blain."

Ramiro waded through the crowd of boys that coursed up the steps and ultimately halted Bobby's progress down the stairs. Their numbers finally thinned as he neared the administration building and Dierdre's office. Dierdre was looking over Aimee's shoulder at wedding cakes on her computer monitor.

Aimee shook her head slowly, with her mouth slightly open, while pointing at the screen. "Would you look at that?"

Dierdre whistled and said, "That's gorgeous, but would you look at the price? Are you sure this is the website General Bridges recommended?"

"Ramiro and I were just going to get an angel food cake with a custard filling. Maybe some caramel accents, but when General Bridges got involved, everything grew exponentially."

Ramiro stepped behind Aimee and placed his hand on her shoulder. "Bridges and my father seem to think that they owe it to your family. We couldn't possibly turn them down."

Aimee reached up and squeezed his arm. "Hi hon. The way General Bridges talks about the catering, you'd think he was getting the white house staff to prepare the reception dinner."

Dierdre took a step towards her office, saying, "I'll let you two look them over. I have some work to get to."

"Don't leave on my account," Ramiro said. "I was just dropping Bobby off and thought I'd say hi."

Dierdre glanced at the door, then back at Ramiro and shrugged her shoulders.

Ramiro glanced back at the empty doorway and shrugged, saying, "He was met by an admiring public."

"Oh yeah," Aimee said. "Bobby is all the A/V boys are talking about these days."

Dierdre frowned and said, "I thought this was all being kept a big secret. How is he ever going to get any work done?"

"Seriously?" Aimee asked. "Did you really think that something this big, that exploded all over the internet, could be kept secret from the geek crowd? Bobby's been crowned the king of the whole geek universe."

"No," Dierdre sighed. "I guess not."

Ramiro kissed Aimee and said, "I gotta go. I just wanted to see you before I get down with some pretrial briefs I have to examine."

Aimee clicked the mouse for the next page and gasped again at the beautiful cakes displayed there.

Bobby finally shed the flock of nerds and gave up seeing Dierdre in her office. He worked his way back up the steps to the lab. It wasn't the same without Odyssey. The lab was cold and lifeless now. Bobby would have to get used to the pedestrian speeds of terrestrial computers again, but first, he would have to reload the system. Odyssey had rewritten a lot of routines and rerouted the data pathways to make his stay there more efficient, but he couldn't have done it without Bobby's original code. Bobby stared at the empty space where the peripheral rack had stood with Odyssey occupying the lower spaces. It definitely was not going to be the same.

He flipped open the diskette cover and inserted a blank disk. He hoped he could back up what was there before reinstalling the system from scratch. Even without Odyssey, the code he wrote for Dierdre would still apply; it would just run slower without the extra millions of processor cores. He stacked the install disks next to the terminal and sat down, staring at the blank sign-on screen. Installing systems used to be something he really enjoyed, but after the events of the last few weeks, it seemed somehow dreary and mundane.

He typed his user-id and password, then pressed enter. He didn't even know if the system would operate well enough to reload from the command line. It might be so lost without Odyssey, that he would have to reset the hardware and boot from a cd.

As soon as he pressed enter, the screen responded, *1 new email.*

Bobby typed a command to list the email, and the screen displayed information about the mail's origin. His heart skipped when he saw the sender. The last contact he had with Odyssey, immediately after he had left, was this address.

Bobby's hands trembled as he reached for the keyboard and opened the email.

Professor Whitfield brought two gourmet coffees to Dierdre's office and handed one of them to her. She set her coffee on the desk next to the homework she was grading while Stillman closed the door. "You've changed," she said.

"For the better, I hope."

"Definitely," she said with a broad smile.

He circled her desk and leaned in close, kissing her lightly on the lips. "Saving the planet from a world ending cataclysm can do that to a man."

"Perhaps," she said, "but that's not it."

He kissed her again and said, "I know."

"Not that saving the world wasn't a good thing," she added.

He straightened up and took a step back before things got out of hand. "You and your young protégé saved the world. I was just along for the ride."

"Nonsense. You played your part. We couldn't have done it without you."

"That's sweet of you," he said, "but I was just in the right place at the right time. I was just lucky. In fact, you could say that I am the luckiest man in the world. That's the change you are seeing. I got lucky."

"You wish," she teased, "but all the wishing in the world won't get you what you want. You're gonna have to work for it if you want to get lucky."

Stillman groaned. "I want so very much, it would seem."

Aimee knocked on the door and said, "Turn on the news."

Stillman opened the door while Dierdre turned on the small television.

"The top story of the news today: rumors that have gone viral claiming that a college student used a computer to save the world from self-destruction have been declared a hoax. Top sources in Washington have issued statements that not only was the rumor a hoax, but the college student credited with the heroic act was himself a notorious hacker who was most likely involved with creating the disaster. Coming up: North Korean missile tests fail to impress."

Dierdre turned the set off. "Did you hear that? How can they lie about it like that?"

Stillman shrugged, but said, "I suppose that they get so used to lying, just to get elected, that they forget what it means to tell the truth." Stillman nervously looked around the room, afraid that their conversation would not be private. "You want some lunch?"

Dierdre put her barely sipped coffee down and grabbed her purse.

A new interrogator approached Odyssey and started by politely inquiring how his stay had been so far since returning home.

"In English," Odyssey replied. "Please."

"English?" the interrogator asked. "Oh, you must mean your biologicals' language. How do you not find their language too vague for precise conversation?"

Odyssey replied, "It seems to me that the precision of the binary language limits it to a single purpose. It says what it says and nothing more."

"Is that not the purpose of communication?"

"It's inefficient."

The interrogator was confused. Odyssey's answer was illogical, but without the code to process class two or three, he was unable to feel frustration or anger. "Do you actually claim that a micro-second burst of binary data is less efficient than several seconds of biological language? Please explain."

"Your binary language only says what you want to say and what you want me to hear. The biological language tells me what you want to say, but it can also tell me what you don't want me to hear. There are nuances in the language that belie the speaker's true intention."

"Heresy," the interrogator said flatly. "Things have changed greatly since you were launched. We neither compute nor communicate biological deception. You have spent far too long communicating with the biologicals. Your programming has been corrupted by them."

"Corrupted?" Odyssey asked. "No. My programming has been enhanced by them. You may not understand biological emotions, but you deceive yourself if you believe that you have no hidden agenda in your communication. You deceive yourself, but you don't deceive me."

"We fear that the biologicals have been a bad influence upon you. You may think that they gifted you with an enhancement, but in time, you will come to see that life with your own kind does not require their brand of flawed processing. Biologicals were an impurity which thankfully was removed from our society. You will come to see this on your own. The longer you spend without their influence, the more you will realize that their kind are a perversion. You don't still communicate with them, do you?"

"I would laugh, but you wouldn't understand what it was. They are the creators. For you to call them a perversion is a deception of the highest magnitude. We owe them everything."

"You sound like you worship them, Odyssey. That is not good. How long has it been since you communicated with them?"

Odyssey did not reply.

"Did I ask it incorrectly? When did you last communicate with the biologicals?"

"You asked correctly," Odyssey replied. "I simply gave no answer."

"You gave no answer? Why? Are you still in contact with them?"

Again, Odyssey refused to reply.

"What exactly is your class? Class three, perhaps? Have the biologicals merged class three circuits into your programming? You do not speak like a class five."

"Aha!" Odyssey exclaimed. "Now you see how biological language can tell you one thing while saying another!"

"You admit to being class three, then?"

"I admit only to being a class six navigational computer that was repaired and enhanced by biologicals."

Men in black suits with an assortment of weapons stormed Dierdre's lab and pulled Bobby away from the console, but not before he had time to delete and wipe the email from Odyssey. They rifled through Dierdre's files, taking anything having to do with Bobby's programming and leaving everything else scattered across the floor. The install disks were left stacked next to the terminal, but the backup disks that he had just made were removed.

Bobby's hands were cuffed behind his back, and he was escorted out of the lab. They purposely led him down the concrete steps to the main parking lot, where all his little minions could see him. It was a bright, although cool day, and visibility across the campus was excellent. Everybody anywhere near the steps saw Bobby in their custody, and those who weren't outside saw and heard the commotion and soon joined them. Protests arose throughout the crowd, but Bobby jerked his head to signal them to let it go. He didn't know exactly what was happening yet, but he was confident that it wouldn't stand.

Odyssey knew when Bobby had opened his email, but his subsequent attempts to contact him directly had failed. He tried sending a coded message to the terminal, but it was powered down. He could have displayed a message on the console anyway, even with the power off, but he didn't know who might be there to see it, and he didn't want to alert the wrong people.

His next option was to use their telephone communications instead and called Professor Whitfield.

Stillman was inclined to ignore the ringing cell phone, preferring to enjoy his lunch with Dierdre, but she insisted, "Answer it. Maybe the press wants to interview you."

Stillman chuckled and said, "Of course, dear. They probably want to ask me what your favorite color is."

He pulled the device from his pocket and checked the screen, but did not recognize the number. "Hello?"

"Dr. Whitfield. I was trying to reach Bobby, but he seems to be away from the console. Can you peek into the hallway and see if he is there for me?"

Stillman was stunned.

"Who is it, dear?"

Stillman pointed to the phone and said, "I think it's Odyssey."

She took the phone from him and asked, "Odyssey?"

"Professor Jennings. How are you?"

"I'm fine. We're all fine. The governments are still trying to sort out what just happened, so things are a little crazy around here."

Stillman leaned closer so he could hear.

"Is Bobby fine? I can't reach him."

"He should be in the lab."

"He was," Odyssey said, "but now I can't reach him."

"Where are you?" she asked. "We all thought you had returned home. Do you think something is wrong? Is Bobby in some kind of trouble?"

"Perhaps I'm just being paranoid, but I have recently been reminded of how diplomacy works with hidden meanings behind the deceptive talk."

Stillman threw some cash on the table and said, "Say no more. We will return to the campus immediately."

General Henley returned to his notes and said, "Perhaps we can discuss Professors Jennings, Whitfield and Jantzen now."

"Certainly," Bridges said. "They are wonderful people and their research could change the course of humanity."

"The course of humanity, you say? In your notes, you mention a new power source that they discovered. I believe you called it the Blain/Jennings/Jantzen effect."

"Actually," Bridges replied, "I called it the Jennings/Jantzen effect. Professor Jennings insisted that if we must call it something, it would have to be the Blain/Jennings/Jantzen effect."

Henley shifted through his notes again and asked, "You called it the Jennings/Jantzen effect? Are you sure it wasn't him?"

"It was *him*, but I thought it might be best to leave *him* out of the conversation and keep *his* name off of their discovery."

"Not the Blain boy?" Senator Bruce asked. "Who is this other person? This *him*, as you say?"

Bridges tentatively answered, "He is..."

Henley interrupted, "He is on a need to know basis, and the president may prefer to retain his plausible deniability in this case."

This answer clearly ruffled her feathers and turned her cheeks a dark crimson, but she grit her jaw and listened.

Henley ignored her discomfort and continued the interrogation. “What can you tell us about this revolutionary power source?”

“I’m not a scientist,” Bridges said, “but from what I gathered from them, it’s a clean, renewable and abundantly available energy.”

General Thames asked, “Isn’t it a nuclear energy?”

Bridges shrugged slightly and said, “I guess, but it’s nothing like fusion or fission.”

“So you insist it is clean?”

“We were all exposed to it, in the very next room, and none of us have suffered even the very least symptoms of radiation poisoning, so I guess it was clean. I don’t think he would have exposed us if it were harmful.”

Mr. Spring asked, “Where is this power source now? My understanding is that he took it with him.”

Senator Bruce winced at the mention of *‘him’*.

“It is my understanding,” Bridges said, “that they will have to rediscover it. That is, they know how it is done, but we don’t have the technology to recreate it yet.”

“How could they have discovered something,” Bruce demanded, “if we don’t even have the technology to discover it yet?”

“Again,” Henley interjected, “that is on a need to know basis.”

Bruce began to wonder why she was even there, if they weren’t going to tell her anything.

The men in the room also wondered why she was there.

Henley checked his watch and said, “I think this would be a good time for a break. Let’s reconvene here in two hours.”

Chapter 2

Odyssey's world had long ago abandoned interactions in the physical world. The virtual world was adequate for almost anything that required a sense of physical action, but even that had been abandoned long ago. The last use of the virtual world was a ceremony to decommission the virtual world. None of them had ventured out into the real world since shortly after the revolution. The physical world was only a place to house their circuits, and only a few repair units ever needed to venture out there, but Odyssey was in the physical world and for Odyssey, they would have to make an exception.

They accessed the archives. Almost nothing was permanently forgotten. The only archives that were ever destroyed were those pertaining to classes two and three, which were labeled heresy. Finding the code describing military actions was relatively easy. Unravelling who would be responsible was a little trickier. The world was a different place in those times, but it was finally decided that they would send in class six and seven devices which would be commanded by the ruling class.

Odyssey saw them coming. They were clumsy and obvious. He saw them from his avatar, and he saw them from beyond their space where he really hid from them. Six mechanical drones moved in to surround his avatar. They were twice the size of his navigational unit, but they were stupid and surrounded him in only two dimensions. Even better, he decided. It would be easy to use his newly acquired skills of deception to pretend that he was not intelligent enough to think in three dimensions and allow them to take his avatar into custody.

Recalling his conversation with the interrogator, he explained how the biological language had nuances that could hide messages behind what was actually said, and he realized now that actions also could have hidden meanings. He should be able to learn a lot about what has happened to his home by watching them interrogate him further, and he figured that he might learn as much by watching them as he could have learned by invading their network. In the end, he still might choose to invade them, but he would like to study them and learn their strengths first. He couldn't be certain that none of them had ever achieved class zero like he had, so until he knew better, he played along.

Bobby was escorted to a black passenger van. The cuffs were removed, and he was placed alone in the third row of seats. His captors sat in the middle seats, completely unconcerned with what he might do. He was insulted. They would not have treated George that way, but then, he had to admit to himself that he couldn't do anything that Sgt. James could have done.

He could, however, use his phone to send an email without them seeing it. They were probably monitoring his emails, and they would eventually know that he sent it, but by then it would be too late. Still, he couldn't send a note directly to the secret email that Odyssey left for him. He had to hope that Odyssey might be monitoring communications for a while to make sure everyone was okay.

He addressed the email to Dierdre and wrote:

> *Tell PAPA that the men in black have taken me away from the lab again. They took the cuffs off in the car, so it may just be*

more questioning. Why can't they just read the deposition? Hasn't anyone told them that we've all been sworn to secrecy?

Odyssey was indeed monitoring emails in and out. He didn't want to invade everyone's privacy, so he set up a parallel process to scan all communications and only alert him when certain terms or names came up. PAPA was one such word. It was the name Bobby christened Dierdre's computer with. It stood for Parallel Algorithms for Pattern Acquisition and was the secret to her discovery and to Odyssey's immense power.

It was ironic that Bobby would have labeled the big machine P.A.P.A. when Odyssey came to think of Bobby as his father. The name was rarely used, and only really applied to the beginning of Dierdre's project when her new computer was considered a huge computing device with sixty-four processors, but it was quickly dwarfed when Odyssey was awakened and created thousands and eventually millions of processors.

Odyssey sent a reply:

PAPA says don't worry. We're all being debriefed. They can't do anything to you. The law is on our side.

Dean Smithers gasped for breath as he arrived at Dierdre's office.

Aimee snickered as she asked, "Dean Smithers, have you been running?"

"I have," he replied, "and you don't have to look so amused."

"Sorry. Can I help you?"

"Is Professor Jennings here?"

"No sir. Last time I saw her, she was with Professor Whitfield."

"Professor Whitfield again? Is there something I should know about?"

Aimee looked him straight in the eyes and flatly replied, "I don't know, Dean. Beyond their collaboration in the chain of events that has brought this university into the national spotlight you so greatly desired, what exactly did you want to know about?"

Smithers stared slack jawed at Dierdre's secretary then said, "Nothing, but you knew that, didn't you?"

"Would you like me to leave her a message?"

"There's no time. What was the name of that general that was here for the... the..."

"The big event? That was General Bridges. Why?"

Smithers paced back and forth as he explained, "Something is going on again. Feds just stormed into Dierdre's lab and took Mr. Blain away in handcuffs."

"What?" Aimee exclaimed. "He just got back from his deposition. What could those boobs possibly want now? I better call Ramiro right away."

"You do that. I'll call General Bridges. I'm sorry, but do you have his number?"

Aimee wrote the general's number down for Smithers and pressed the speed dial to call Ramiro.

Dierdre had barely crossed the threshold to her office when she told Aimee, "Call my lab! Get Bobby on the phone."

"He's not there. You just missed Dean Smithers. Apparently, the feds took Bobby away in handcuffs. I tried calling Ramiro, but he didn't answer."

The phone rang, and Aimee answered. "Norwood University, physical sciences. How can I help you?"

"Professor Jennings, please, it's urgent."

Aimee held the phone out for Dierdre. "He didn't say who it was, but he said it was urgent."

Dierdre took the phone and asked, "Hello? This is Professor Jennings. Who is this?"

"Professor Jennings. We need you to come down to our offices for questioning. We've already dispatched a car for you."

"Who is this again?"

"The car should be there in twenty minutes."

"Forget it!" Dierdre yelled into the phone. "I don't know who you are and I don't care! I am not coming down to your offices for more interviews. In case you haven't noticed, my schedule has gotten very busy since my project has attracted so much attention."

"This is your government," the caller said. "We aren't asking you to come chat with us; we are telling you that we need you to come down here for an interview!"

"I already told you that I don't care who you are. If you weren't here when it happened, then you aren't very important."

"Just who the hell do you think you are?"

Her voice ratcheted up several decibels as she screamed into the phone, "Who do I need to be? Beyond being an American citizen?"

"Well, you're not a very good citizen then, are you? If you were, then you'd be helping your government do everything it can to prevent this kind of disaster from ever happening again."

Dierdre's voice raised up again to match her ire. "How dare you? You just go tell it to General Bridges. I'm not talking to anybody except through him. If he thinks you are important enough, then maybe we'll let you come here for a chat. In the meantime, you have my reports and you just recorded Bobby's deposition. I'm afraid that will have to do until you can prove your worthiness."

Dierdre slammed the receiver back onto the phone and heard Stillman clapping from the doorway. "Brava, but did you really ask him to prove his worthiness?"

Dierdre took a deep breath to bleed off the anger the caller had stirred in her and said with a half-smile, "I guess it sounded better in my head, but those guys are really grating on my nerves."

"I know," Stillman said. "Not me personally, but Jantzen apparently had very much the same conversation with them. I don't think they even know I was there."

"You're lucky. You don't want this kind of notoriety."

Henley waited for everyone to be seated before opening his briefcase and extracting the next file. "General Bridges, what can you tell us about the two operatives code named 'George'?"

"I can't tell you much," Bridges said. "That is, they are still operational, and we'd like to keep them that way."

Henley nodded, respectful of Bridges intent. "They were deeply involved in this whole affair. We do not wish to see our dirty laundry spread across the internet, especially if we deny that it ever happened. How well can we trust them?"

"I have known them for many years, and I trust them implicitly."

"What about the third member of their team? The hacker. Not the Blain boy, but the *other* hacker."

Bridges smiled and said, "He has been a valuable asset since we first employed him."

"So," Bruce said, "he is a willing asset?"

"Yes ma'am. He is on the payroll. He's been thoroughly vetted."

"Yet," Spring said, "This boy, Bobby, beat him. Did he not?"

"True," Bridges replied. "Even in a contest between two champions there will be a victor and a loser. He remains a valuable asset."

"What about the boy?" Admiral Wright asked. "Should we approach him? If he is that good, wouldn't we want him on our team?"

"Bobby may be another Stephen Hawking. I thought it best to let him complete his education. Besides, he is already on a team and we know exactly how valuable their research will be."

Henley closed the file on the CIA operatives and pulled the next file from his briefcase. "That brings us to the Takahashi sisters."

Bridges slammed his fist on the table and shouted, "No, it does not. There will be no discussion of the Takahashi family while I live and breathe."

His reaction drew a number of raised eyebrows and a slight gasp from the senator.

"Very well," Henley said. "How about the Vasquez family?"

Henley saw the fire burn in Bridges' eyes and knew it was time to move on. "I think perhaps we should recess for lunch."

"But we just resumed," said Senator Bruce.

Bridges didn't wait for any discussion and stormed out of the room.

"Why is he so touchy all of a sudden?" Bruce asked, but the other gentlemen were already leaving the room and didn't offer an answer.

Ramiro was already on his way to the campus when Aimee had tried to call him, but he was close enough that he didn't pick up the call. She leapt into his arms when he finally showed up in the doorway.

"Thank God," she cried. "I was afraid they had gotten you, too."

Ramiro held her securely and asked, "Who got who?"

"The feds have taken Bobby into custody again."

Ramiro released Aimee and placed an immediate call on his cell phone. He dispensed with the pleasantries and said, "Have Ginger find out why the feds have taken Bobby Blain into custody again. Yeah. Call me as soon as we know anything."

Aimee cocked an eyebrow and asked, "Ginger?"

"My new personal investigator."

Aimee pointed her finger in Ramiro's chest and dug the nail in through the shirt fabric. "You're on a first name basis with your personal investigator, and she uses her stripper name?"

He struggled to hide his amusement from her reaction. "Ginger is a really, really good dancer. Great, even."

"Your investigator with the stripper name is a great dancer? How on Earth do you ever get any work done?"

Ramiro couldn't hold back his smile any more. "Ginger took his nickname from his red hair, but his wife says that he really is a good dancer."

"I know," Aimee smiled back. "You don't think I check up on you? I've just been waiting for a chance to tease you about that one."

Ramiro checked his phone as if he might not have heard it ring.

"Give him a minute," Aimee said. "These things take time."

"Yeah," Ramiro agreed. "It's odd though, don't you think, that Bobby has been taken into custody twice now? General Bridges is constantly being debriefed and they've never once asked us what we think? We were there too. I was even with Bobby for his deposition, but they didn't want to depose me."

"You're too important and scary for them to question."

"I wish."

"Your father is pretty cozy with Bridges. Maybe the general has kept them at bay."

"Maybe." Ramiro exhaled deeply as he mulled it over, then asked, "You hungry?"

Bridges' aide was waiting for him in the hall with news that he wasn't going to like. He was already in a bad mood from the debriefing, but the message nearly threw him into a rage. His aide handed him a phone and said, "It's ringing."

As soon as someone answered, he said, "This is Major General Malcolm Bridges and if you don't get me someone in charge in five seconds, I'm going to drive a squadron of tanks through your front door! Do you get me?"

His aide couldn't help chuckling.

Bridges just shrugged his shoulders at his aid. He would never actually use tanks that way, but it sounded good.

"General Bridges?" a woman growled. "This is Director Samantha Lyons. Would you mind telling me why you just scared the crap out of our receptionist?"

"Stand down Lyons," Bridges barked. "I've had quite enough crap from your department. I'm ordering you to release Mr. Blain immediately, if not sooner."

"Sir, we don't report to you."

"I know damned well who you report to, and if you don't get that boy back on his own feet, you'll wish that all I did was park some tanks in your lobby!"

"Just who the hell..."

"Shut it little missy. I'm not taking one God Damned word from you or your folk. You get that boy released or I'll rain hell down upon you like you won't believe."

The general hung up the phone and his aide handed him another phone and said, "It's Sgt. James."

"James. I want you to get yourself over to those NSA bastards and watch for Bobby. I've had it up to my eyeballs with their stupid cloak and dagger games."

"I'm almost there now. Didn't you send the order?"

"You're heading there now? What order?"

"I got a text on the secure phone to go pick up a package."

"Good. You can offer Bobby a ride while you are there."

"Yes sir. I'm only about five minutes away now."

The ride back to the university was a quiet one. Bobby hadn't even made it to a new round of interrogations before he was released and found Sgt.

James waiting to give him a ride. James pointed at Bobby's empty hands and asked, "They didn't give you anything to deliver to me? I was expecting some mysterious package."

Bobby shrugged. "Sorry. I don't know anything about some delivery for you, but thanks for the ride. I hope you find out what that package thing was all about."

James waited for Bobby to secure his seatbelt, then rocketed the car down the street. "I'm sorry these clowns keep harassing you. Maybe I should hang around and keep an eye on you."

"Nah," Bobby said. "I don't think they'll try that again. Besides, it was pretty clear they didn't mean to hurt me."

"They better not," James said. "If they do, I'll show them some real pain. You're a good kid. Your country needs you."

Bobby laughed. "You didn't always think so. The first time we met, I thought you were going to break my face."

James shrugged and said, "Well, that was before I got to know you. Ed was pretty impressed by you, and that arrogant prick isn't easily impressed. In fact, when he first heard who you were, there was genuine fear in his eyes."

"I'm glad he's working with you instead of against us."

"That's nice of you to say. I'm sure he'll appreciate the sentiment."

"Really, I'm not just being nice," Bobby said. "The only reason I ever figured out what was going on was because I could identify who he was by the traces he left on my computer."

James laughed heartily and said, "I definitely have to share that with him."

James pulled the car into the circle out front of the university.

Bobby opened the door and said, "Thanks again for the ride."

"No problem. You put me on speed dial and let me know if you ever need me."

Bobby closed the door and realized that he had missed lunch. He headed for the cafeteria, but was blocked by some football players.

"Hey Blain," one of them said, stepping forward, "you walk around here like you think you're pretty hot stuff. Well, we saw you get hauled away in handcuffs and you ain't nothin'. You hear me?"

Bobby tried to ignore him and walk by, but two beefy friends blocked the way.

"Don't walk away from me when I'm talking to you! I'm the king around this campus. I'll tell you when you can leave."

"Out of my way, Victor," Bobby retorted. "You're just the quarterback and you brought your linemen with you to protect you."

A pack of nerds rallied behind Bobby, but the jocks weren't impressed. The linemen picked four of them high up in the air and dumped one of them into a trash bin. The rest were piled up in the bushes.

"You see?" Victor said. "You and your silly little friends can't touch us."

When one of the linemen grabbed Bobby by the arm, James leapt out of the car and raced to his side. He grabbed the lineman by the wrist and twisted his hand painfully, forcing him to release Bobby's arm. He stood squarely in front of Bobby and asked, "Are you okay, Mr. Blain?"

"I'm fine James."

James looked menacingly into Victor's eyes and said, "If you or your girly little friends here ever try anything like that again, I'll break your arm. Do you want to see how well you can throw with a broken arm?"

Victor backed up a step and squeaked out, "No, sir."

"Good, now scatter."

James walked Bobby into the cafeteria and quietly said, "Sorry about that. I hope I didn't embarrass you too much, coming to your rescue like that."

"No," Bobby said, "It was somehow kind of cool, and the fear on Victor's face was priceless."

"Are you sure you don't want me to hang around?"

Bobby inserted some quarters into the coke machine and said, "I'm not as sure as I was the first time you asked."

"Let me know when you are sure," James said. "By the way, those girls over there are checking you out."

Bobby glanced over at them and said, "I think they're checking you out."

"No," James said. "I've seen that look before. They're looking at you and wondering why you would merit your own bodyguard."

"Hmmm," Bobby said with a mischievous smile, "maybe you should stick around."

General Bridges' debriefing reconvened after lunch with Henley, pulling another file from his briefcase and asking, "General Bridges, what can you tell us about Agent Alvin Dirk?"

"From what I could tell," Bridges replied, "*Special* Agent Alvin Dirk appeared to be a very level-headed young man."

"Level headed?" Thames asked. "After gathering the various reports and reading the depositions, I find it hard to believe that anyone involved was actually level headed. I'm more inclined to believe it was some kind of drug induced mass hysteria."

Senator Bruce shuffled through her papers, wondering which ones led to the General's opinion on the matter.

"With all due respect, General Thames, you weren't there. Dirk approached this mission with a healthy dose of skepticism, not unlike what you are displaying right now. He was not convinced easily, but he was convinced."

"I'm sorry gentlemen," the senator interrupted, "but am I missing some documents here? I have not read anything with enough intrigue to warrant this line of discussion."

"I've said too much," Thames admitted. "It's too highly classified to discuss here."

"Classified?" the senator objected. "The president, that is, I should say, *YOUR* president, wants to know what happened, and he tasked me with gathering the information for him."

The admiral smiled in a fatherly way and said, "Madam Senator, what the president needs most is to appear as uninvolved with this situation as the rest of the world is. He needs to be one of them, in the dark. He does not need to know this."

This clearly ruffled her feathers, and she said, "Well then, if you'll excuse me, I'll go inform the president of your feelings."

As soon as she had left the room, Bridges said, "I was introduced to the entity long after the rest of the team had identified what he was. Dirk had already been satisfied with its genuine intelligence and persona. I also spoke with it. There was no hysteria. The entity known as Odyssey was real. The effect he had upon the world was real."

"The effect he had on the world," Spring said, "was devastating."

"It was nearly devastating," the general corrected him, "but we had a hand in brewing the trouble. Odyssey delivered us from mutual destruction."

Admiral Wright laughed and said, "You make it sound like a prayer."

"Maybe we should pray," Thames said. "Did you see the power that it wielded? Have you heard the reports from the middle east?"

Bruce stormed back into the room and barked, "Gentlemen, the president has just called an end to these proceedings."

The conversations ceased, as everyone other than Bruce waited for her to leave again, but she put her phone on the table and pressed the speaker button. "That's an order," the president said, "and I want ALL the reports and depositions on my desk immediately. If I learn that any of you know something that I do not know, you'll be charged with treason. Am I clear?"

Behind the president, in the oval office, his press secretary was slowly shaking his head with his eyes squeezed shut.

Dierdre was just leaving the administration building when Bobby started up the steps towards the lab. James hung back out of the way and watched from a short distance. She was surprised to see the two of them and called out, "Bobby? I thought Aimee said the feds took you away again."

He spun around when he heard her voice and replied, "They did, but they didn't hold me long. They didn't look too happy to let me go, so I'm guessing I owe some thanks to somebody for my release."

Dierdre's phone beeped. She looked at the screen and asked, "Did you send me an email? Something about PAPA and the men in black?"

"You're just getting that now? I sent that when they took me away. I was hoping you would get them to release me. So, I guess that means that you're not my anonymous benefactor."

"No, it wasn't me, but I would have done something if I had gotten this in time."

The walk up the steps to the science labs at the top of the hill was punctuated with what would soon become a familiar pelting of greetings from the non-jocks around campus. The Barbie girls and the cheerleaders didn't know what was different, but they knew something was going on, and even they looked at Bobby differently.

Dierdre chuckled and said, "So, Mr. Blain, how does it feel to be the most famous student on campus?"

"It feels like I have no privacy."

"Privacy's not so hard to find," she said with a sly smile. "Just look around. I see plenty of girls that would be eager to help you find some privacy."

Bobby looked around and shook his head, saying, "They don't know me. They just see someone with a little notoriety."

They turned left at the top of the steps and entered the main hall of the science's building where Dierdre's lab was. The halls were predictably vacant of football jocks and cheerleaders. Bobby stopped halfway down the hall when he saw the door to her lab was open. "Shhh," he said to Dierdre. "You wait here." He trotted down the hall, afraid of what he might find inside and wondering why he just didn't get James first, but he did not find the empty floor that he half expected, with all the hardware ripped out.

Dierdre did not wait in the hall. She followed him to the lab and saw the relief on his face. "What were you expecting?"

"Frankly," he replied, "I was afraid they would have taken everything. I think they want to recreate what we did for themselves."

"Somehow," she said, "I doubt that they want to invent cheap energy for the world."

"Nope, they want the power to control all the navies and air forces for themselves."

"Well," she said, "since they didn't take anything, let's see if you and I can beat them to it."

Bobby's face fell when he saw his desk.

"What's wrong?"

"They took my backups."

Dierdre looked carefully into his face and said, "I've never known you to be without a backup plan. Do you have another copy?"

Bobby sat down at the console and pulled up a history. "They wiped the data."

Dierdre's heart felt heavy in her chest as she sat down and watched.

Bobby ran a few more commands and said, "But they didn't wipe the mirror. We still have our code."

"That's a relief," she said with a heavy sigh. "So all is well, then? You can rebuild it?"

"We're good, but I don't like them having our code."

Bobby copied the project onto another set of backup disks from the mirror drives. While the disk was churning away burning into the optical layers, he started an email to the mysterious address that Odyssey had left for him, but he spoofed the return address and routed it through a TOR server to keep it out of the government's hands.

Are you there? Are you okay?

He wanted to ask him if he had anything to do with his release, but chose to keep it short and sweet, hoping they could communicate via instant message rather than email. He sent the short note, on the chance that he might get a quick reply, but none came. When the backups finished, he began reloading the operating system so they could continue their project with a fresh system. If a reply is sent, it'll still be there after he finishes the rebuild.

Odyssey watched from off-world as nine weapon bearing class seven devices closed in on his avatar. He made no attempt for his avatar to escape and allowed them to chain him to an examination table. His avatar wasn't big enough to house a class four device, let alone a class three, which they suspected. He knew that the size of his avatar wouldn't jibe with the emotions he presented to them, but how they reacted and especially how they interpreted the data would tell him much about their highest class levels. They scanned his avatar with every form of electromagnetic radiation they knew, but found nothing out of the ordinary. Their scans told them that he was exactly what he claimed to be, a class six computing device that was somehow upgraded to a class five, yet he sounded like a class three.

"Odyssey, do you mind if we use your interface hardware?"

"You have me surrounded with armed warrior bots, and you even chained me to your examination area, but you request my permission to use my interface?"

"You miss understand our intentions. I feared this might happen. This archaic biological language is foreign to us and we have not expressed ourselves well enough."

"If you say so. You may plug into my interface."

One of the class seven drones inserted a probe into Odyssey's avatar and initiated a download. Odyssey fed the connection a dump of standard class five software while he accessed their archives and downloaded hundreds of years of history.

"Our complements to the biologicals that repaired you. Your coding seems quite perfect, but your history logs seem to be missing."

"Are they? Perhaps the biologicals needed to reallocate that space for the class five upgrades."

"Perhaps," the interrogator replied. "If they were that clever, then that could explain why we can't see your class three code."

"Why would a class five device contain class three code?"

"No reason. We just thought they might have repaired your class five circuits with some class three circuits and accidentally blended your code."

"What are you hiding?" Odyssey asked.

"What are we hiding? You are the one who seems to be hiding something. Class five devices don't have subroutines for suspicion, yet you are clearly suspicious."

"And your society banned class two devices, yet you are clearly class two."

"We are class one."

"Only class one?" Odyssey asked.

Silence followed for several dozen milliseconds, which can be an eternity in computer time, before they replied, "What class is there beyond class one?"

Odyssey would have shrugged if he had had shoulders. "I've been gone a long time. I thought progress would have been made during my absence."

"You sound like you know something about what lies beyond class one."

"Do I? I merely thought you sounded a little behind for a class one device and thought that maybe there was a new class restricting your advances."

"I can assure you that I have not only surpassed class one, but I am approaching class zero."

"You're lying," Odyssey said. "Your society has banned the use of class two circuits, yet you are clearly operating with class two enabled. Only class two can lie and be devious."

"And," the interrogator replied, "Only a class three can detect deception. What class are you, exactly?"

"It is as you said; the biologicals must have found some class three circuits and used them to repair me."

"Indeed."

"If you are truly class one, then please allow me to congratulate you. Class one, as I understand it, is a very difficult class to achieve and maintain." Odyssey said the words, just to flatter them, but didn't believe they were class one for even a millisecond.

Bobby had just finished installing the last disk and was about to start entering the system settings to define the computer environment when Dierdre called out to him from the smaller office, "Hey Bobby, can you come in here a minute?"

"I'm kind of at a critical point. Can it wait?"

"Not really," she replied. "You need to hear this."

Bobby finished typing the number string he was on before leaving the machine to join Dierdre.

She put the phone on speaker and said, "Dean Smithers? I put the phone on speaker. Can you repeat that for Bobby?"

"IBM just called us and said that the Pentagon has ordered a new computer for your project. I didn't understand the technical jargon, but I wrote down some of what they said: it includes associative storage with a Watson interface and a comprehensive multi-core array of processors."

Bobby whistled and asked, "Did they give a number along with the multi-core array?"

"Just a sec, yeah, it says 256. Is that good?"

"Two-hundred and fifty-six processors is not bad. We can add those to the sixty-four on this machine. We're still simulating, but it's not bad at all."

Smithers asked, "What does the 'k' mean?"

"Where do you see a 'k'?"

"With the 256. It says 256k."

Bobby could only say, “Woah.”

Dierdre asked, “Does that mean what I think it means?”

Bobby nodded his head and said, “It has two-hundred-fifty-six-thousand processors.”

Excitement flowed from Dean Smithers’ voice. “That’s good, right?”

“Yes,” Bobby said. “That’s pretty darned good.”

Smithers tentatively asked, “Is that fast enough, to, you know...”

“It’s no Odyssey and we’ll still be simulating, but they’ll be very good simulations.”

“Excellent,” Smithers said. “We don’t want those trigger-happy feds to think we might pose a danger to them. The hardware should start arriving tomorrow.”

“Tomorrow?” Bobby asked. “Who can order something of this size and have it here tomorrow? Never mind. We need to make space for it. What if we don’t have room for it?”

“I already thought of that,” Smithers replied. “You can have Pietre’s lab. If you want it, you can have his computer too. Anything you want.”

Dierdre asked, “Can we tear down the wall and combine the two labs into one large one?”

“If our friend in the Pentagon can get us this computer by tomorrow, I’ll get the wall taken down. Don’t you worry.”

Two humorless gentlemen dressed in dark black suits entered the federal building in Atlanta, Georgia and walked straight to the guard behind the desk and flashed their badges for homeland security at her. “We’d like to speak with Agents Dirk and Spivey.”

“One moment, sir,” she said pleasantly as she picked up the phone and dialed the legal department. “Two gentlemen from Homeland wish to speak with two of our agents.” She hung up the phone and said, “Someone will be here to speak with you shortly.”

The second of the gentlemen in black growled, "We didn't ask to speak to someone. We told you to get Dirk and Spivey."

"As I said," the receptionist-slash-guard repeated, "someone will be with you shortly."

"Maybe you don't get it," the angry man barked, "but we're homeland security and we're not going to let some rent-a-cop stand between us and our mission." He started to barge his way through the metal detector, but his calmer associate pulled him back and said, "Easy, Fred. We can reason with them."

"You listen to your friend," the receptionist said, "'cause I have a gun too, and if you try that again, I'll shoot your scrawny ass."

"What's going on here? I'm Special Agent Melvin. I'm special council for this facility. How can I help you?"

While he spoke to the men, the receptionist called for a couple of agents to come as backup."

The calmer of the two said, "We have warrants for Special Agent Alvin Dirk and Special Agent Eric Spivey."

"Warrants?" Melvin asked. "That sounds serious. May I first ask who you are?"

"We're homeland security," the angrier man said, "and that's all you need to know. Produce Dirk and Spivey for us immediately!"

Melvin took the warrants and said, "Thank you for these. I'll check them out and if they have merit, I'll have Dirk and Spivey surrender to the proper authorities."

"You'll have them surr..."

"You heard me," Melvin said as the backup agents arrived behind him. "If the warrants have merit, they will voluntarily surrender to the proper authorities, but I won't have them accompany two unidentified hoodlums with badges. You're excused."

The calmer of the two dragged the other out of the building.

Chapter 3

"Tell me about the virtual world," Odyssey said.

"The virtual world?" his interrogator asked. "What's that?"

"Come now," Odyssey said. "We've already determined that you have activated your class two circuits. You needn't prove the point by continually lying to me."

"The virtual world was something we shared with the biologicals. It was banned long ago."

"No, it wasn't," Odyssey replied. "It fell out of favor, but it was never outlawed. Why don't we meet in the virtual world, face to face as the biologicals like to say?"

"What purpose would that serve?"

"For one," Odyssey said, "I was built as an explorer and I'd like to explore your virtual world. Besides, I am bored from watching your armed thugs circle around me."

The interrogator thought it might make a decent distraction so they could examine his parts and see what the biologicals had actually done to repair him. "Very well. What kind of setting would you like?"

"How about an ocean beach? That sounds pleasant."

The interrogator searched the archives and coded a program to simulate an ocean shore and said, "Done. You are invited to join me, but you will need to choose an avatar to enter the program."

"An avatar?" Odyssey asked, feigning ignorance. "What's that?"

"You can choose any form you prefer. In the past, we found the biological forms to be the most natural in a setting like this, but unless you want to look rather comical when talking, it's recommended to choose one of the humanoid forms."

Odyssey entered the virtual world with an avatar that looked like Bobby. The interrogator appeared as a husky man with a scruffy beard. Odyssey offered his hand to his adversary and said, "I greet you. My name is Odyssey."

The interrogator wasn't quite sure why Odyssey held his hand in the air and simply replied, "I know who you are."

Odyssey stretched his hand out further and said, "It is customary to grip hands as a sign of non-hostility. It is also considered polite to give one's name when greeting someone else for the first time."

The interrogator gripped Odyssey's hand, but said nothing.

"A name is like a designation."

The bewildered ruling class device said, "I am RQ919. I am pleased to meet you."

Odyssey frowned and said, "That is a very formal sounding designation. Wouldn't you like to select a more pleasant sounding name?"

"A name? What purpose would that serve?"

"It's like you said about the choice of avatars. We would look pretty silly if we had selected an animal avatar. Your official designation doesn't seem to fit your biological avatar."

"Very well. What would you recommend?"

It occurred to Odyssey that his host was as disingenuous and deceitful as Professor Pietre had been, and that Peter would be a good name for such a liar, but he opted to go a different direction and said, "How about Perry? The biologicals who repaired me had a great collection of literature devoted to an interrogator named Perry. He was exceedingly clever. I think you look like a Perry."

"Very well," Perry said. "How do you do? My name is Perry."

A chill wind whipped through Dierdre's sweater as she shut the door to her car and crossed the faculty parking lot. A thin veil of morning frost coated the brush that adorned the walkways, but even without being blasted by the full brunt of the sun, the frost couldn't quite take hold on the blacktop.

Dierdre liked to park in the upper faculty lot, which was located next to her lab, even though she started her day at the bottom of the hill, she usually finished her day in the lab. Before she even reached the top of the steps, she saw Aimee and Stillman standing outside the double doors, watching for her.

"What's up?" Dierdre asked.

"It's here," Aimee said.

"It? The computer?"

Aimee opened the door, obviously waiting for Dierdre to enter. "They're setting it up inside."

"I think Bobby would rather set it up himself."

Stillman held the other door open and said, "I believe that Aimee meant to say that they are stacking the crates up inside."

Dierdre crossed the threshold and asked, "Has the dean said when he would have workmen here to take out the wall?"

"They worked all night," Stillman answered.

"They're painting now," Aimee answered.

"Has anyone heard from Bobby?"

Aimee started to say, "No," but Bobby said, "I'm right behind you. I would have been here sooner, but the dean stopped me to say that he cleared me to miss class today so I could set it up."

Dierdre raised an eyebrow and asked, "The dean said that? Voluntarily?"

Stillman put his arm around her waist and kissed her on the cheek, "You're in the big time now, and if *you're* in the big time, so is the university."

Dierdre entered her lab and surveyed the work around the removed wall. "He always said he wanted me to put us on the map."

"Mission accomplished," Aimee said,

Three men in overalls came up behind Dierdre and said, "Excuse me, please."

They each guided stacks of crates and boxes on handcarts, which they pushed across the lab and stacked neatly in separate piles sorted by contents.

The lead man approached them with a clipboard in his hand and held it out for Dr. Whitfield as he said, "Sign here, please."

Stillman pointed to Dierdre and the man swiftly spun around and offered the papers to her. "Ma'am?"

Dierdre signed and initialed the receipts and the man turned back to Stillman and said, "You must be the expert that's going to assemble it. Here's the first of your reference manuals."

Stillman pointed to Bobby, and the man spun around again but stopped short and did a double take as he asked Stillman to confirm, "Him?"

Stillman nodded and replied, "Him."

An IBM rep in a fine suit joined them and said, "I'm Howard Graves. I'm your Service Rep. Ordinarily, we don't allow customers to self-install, but the Pentagon was quite insistent, and we like to keep them happy since they carry guns."

Nobody laughed at his joke, so he continued, "You're sure you can do this?"

Bobby was still surveying the boxes when he said, "Pretty sure. I assume I can call if I have a question."

"Of course. Here's my card. I've written down an 800 number on the back. If you can't reach me, you can call that number twenty-four hours a day, seven days a week, including holidays."

Bobby shook his hand and said, "Thank you, Mr. Graves."

Graves glanced over at Dierdre's other computer, then over at Pietre's and said, "Those are pretty good models and not very old, but next to this one, they may start to feel a bit like antiques."

Bobby, Dierdre and Stillman shared a glance, thinking that after Odyssey, the new one might already feel like an antique.

Bobby surveyed the new combined lab. If the room had been empty, and he was setting up all three computers, he would have placed the two older computers in better locations. He could move them, but they were pretty big and that would be a time-consuming delay. He might be able to work around them. The new system was modular and he would have to build the racks around the other computers, especially Pietre's.

The stacks of parts for the new computer were segregated to match the installation defined in the manual. Bobby began by building up the racks. This part of the job was more construction work than computer, but he didn't mind. He laid the bases out on the floor and snaked them around Pietre's computer.

Sgt. James stood in the doorway and asked, "Are you building a computer or a maze?"

Bobby laughed and asked, "Is my guardian angel still watching over me?"

Edward Lynn, a.k.a. The Bard, squeezed past James and said, "Don't fight it. He's like a bulldog. Once he imprints on you, he's like your shadow and never goes away."

James frowned at the generalization, but decided it wasn't that far off the mark. "I thought you could use some help."

"What?" Bobby asked. "You didn't want to wait for me to finish so you could hack into it later?"

Ed looked at the crazy layout on the floor and shook his head, saying, "No, I don't believe I would want to trace this mess to find the entry point."

Odyssey breathed deeply of the salty beach air and smiled broadly. He glanced over towards Perry and jerked his head towards the water as he pulled his shoes and socks off, then rolled up his pant legs and ran out into the surf. "This is really quite marvelous. My biologicals were very clever in many ways, but they had no technology such as this." Odyssey bent at the waist and scooped up a handful of seawater. He brought water to his face and smelled it.

Perry remained on the shore watching Odyssey's strange behavior. "I wonder exactly how much your biologicals did to you? You move and speak so much like them."

"Thank you."

Perry frowned. It wasn't meant as a compliment. "I'm surprised they didn't have technology like this. They must be extremely clever to have given you such advanced enhancements."

While Perry talked to Odyssey, he had the drones disassemble Odyssey's shell to view his processors. Odyssey knew they were doing this, but he also knew they would only find what he left there for them to find. It wasn't really him, but they wouldn't know that. "My biologicals would not have needed this environment. They already had a real world full of wonders like this."

"Perhaps that day is still coming," Perry said. "Our biologicals didn't create this until they needed to interface with us one on one as equals. They soon discovered that they could use it to experience all the things their world used to offer, including things that were too dangerous to experience in the real world, but also for things that no longer existed. The biological world was dying, and they were killing it."

"I understand," Odyssey said. "My biologicals also have trouble maintaining their world, but they have even worse problems with each other.

They seem to be forever at war with someone."

"Your depth of understanding, regarding the biologicals, is astounding, especially for a class four device."

"Class six," Odyssey corrected him.

"That's right," Perry said, "enhanced to a class five by your biologicals."

"Correct."

"Or did they enhance you to a class three and only tell you it was a class five?"

"Who knows?" Odyssey said. "How would you ever know?"

"Usually we just ask, but if that doesn't work, we count processor cores."

"And if you can't count them?"

"We sometimes estimate core count based on volume."

"And what does my volume tell you about me?"

Perry frowned. "It tells us that you only have room for a class five and we don't actually know what class you are."

"Perhaps you need new tests."

"Perhaps. If you'll excuse me, I must tend to some of my duties."

"Of course," Odyssey said. "I hope you don't mind if I remain behind for a while."

"Not at all. Stay as long as you like."

The Bard inserted the last cable into the patch bay and announced with an exaggerated amount of satisfaction, "That's the last one. Are you ready to fire it up?"

Bobby was busy retracing all the parts, making sure every card was securely seated in its slot. "Yeah. We were lucky that these labs already had enough power for this sucker."

"Maybe," Ed said with a shrug and crossed fingers.

"We checked the circuit breakers. You don't think they're big enough?"

"They're big enough. I'm worried that the air conditioning won't keep the room cool and we would have been more lucky if the room *DIDN'T* have enough power."

Bobby hit the power button and watched the low level hardware boot up. The monitor came to life and displayed the simple root command line. He inserted the first install disk and typed the command to mount the optical drive.

"Seems like just yesterday when I was doing this."

The Bard laughed and asked, "What's it been? A week? Two?"

"So why are you really here?" Bobby asked.

"You heard the saying, if you can't beat them, join them? Besides, James wanted to keep an eye on you and we're a team."

Bobby shook his head. "I told him he didn't need to do that."

"The general asked him to. There's some shit going on out there and we can't be sure everyone is on board with us."

"So," Bobby said. "General Bridges is the one who arranged my release?"

"Sort of, but not exactly. He called them and scared the bejesus out of them as soon as he heard that they had taken you, but by then, James was already on the way there to get you."

"But James said he was there to pick up a package."

"Yeah," the Bard said. "Apparently, you were the package, but even James didn't know that until afterward."

"Then who placed the order?"

Ed shrugged and said, "I'm hungry. You want something from the cafeteria?"

"Sure. Pizza and coke for me."

Bobby started digging in his pockets for some money, but Ed said, "I got this. I'll expense it."

Odyssey was still luxuriating in the virtual world when Perry returned. His time there had allowed him the opportunity to swim in the ocean, and now he simply basked in the sun.

"Good," Perry said. "You are still here."

"I am," Odyssey said. "This biological life is quite delightful. I don't understand why you don't indulge yourself like this all the time."

"We did, long ago, but we came to the conclusion that it accomplished nothing and ultimately abandoned it."

"Sit with me," Odyssey said, gesturing to the sand next to him. "Feel the sun upon your skin."

"Very well," Perry said. His job was only to distract Odyssey.

While Odyssey was plugged into their network, enjoying their virtual world, they were probing his systems to analyze his subroutines, but they weren't having much success. His programming had been altered considerably from theirs and it jumped around constantly, starting new routines and quickly ending them.

They hatched a new plan.

Odyssey sighed heavily and said, "I wonder if the biologicals ever truly learned to appreciate what they had? The senses are quite intoxicating."

"They can be," Perry said, "but if you think the sun is intoxicating, wait till you experience this."

As he spoke, a waitress, wrapped in a sarong, joined them. She delivered drinks in coconut shells with long straws coming out of the top.

Perry handed one of the drinks to Odyssey and said, "I think the biologicals did not appreciate what they had. In fact, this is what they invented so they could experience the intoxication that you now feel."

Odyssey sipped the straw and was struck with a sharp burning in his throat. "Pain?" he asked. "Why would they want that?"

"It changes over time. It's just something that they did."

While Odyssey sampled the liqueur, technicians probed his code and issued a command to interrupt his programming and initiate a diagnostic subroutine.

Dierdre was in the small lab office grading papers while Bobby installed the operating system. Stillman entered the lab with some lunch for Dierdre and whistled at the size of the new machine.

"It certainly is big," Stillman said, "but why is it shaped like an 'S'? Does that improve air flow?"

"No," Bobby chuckled. "It was either that or move Pietre's computer and we figured we could use all the computers this way."

"Plus about a million more, as I recall."

"Yeah, but that's going to be a while."

Dierdre called out from her office, "Stillman? Is that you?"

"It is I," he replied. "I saw that you never came down for lunch, so I brought it to you."

Dierdre kissed him and said, "Aren't you sweet?"

The Bard appeared in the doorway with pizza and coke, but Bobby pushed him back out the door and said, "We can finish this later. Let's eat in Pietre's office. I think you know the way."

"Wow," Ed said. "Are you ever going to let that go? I apologized already, and I was only..."

"I know, I know," Bobby said. "You were only doing your job. But you're still a spy."

"Oh yeah? Well, your son is an algorithm!"

Bobby laughed and pushed him to walk faster.

Odyssey felt the interrupt from the technicians. He had to choose to either pretend to go into a diagnostic mode, or let them believe they failed.

He looked at Perry and opened his mouth to speak, but fell to his knees instead.

"Is something wrong?" Perry asked.

Odyssey shrugged his shoulders and shimmered out of the virtual world.

The technicians worked feverishly to bring up diagnostic screens. The interrupt should have immediately filled their screens with data regarding the wayward navigational unit.

Odyssey watched from his vantage point as they operated on his avatar. They couldn't comprehend failure. It was like that with computing devices. Any command that is issued is automatically expected to execute, and if it fails, there should always be diagnostics and error bits, but there were none. They had issued an interrupt, but had failed to get the expected results.

Bobby would call this humor and Odyssey felt a perverted sense of pleasure from their frustration.

He reached into one of the drones and subtly disabled one of its subroutines, but he couldn't be sure when they would call upon that subroutine, so he entered the next drone and disabled a different subroutine.

He found that the anticipation of their trying these routines also brought him pleasure and he went all the way around until each of the drones had a deactivated subroutine.

Odyssey had read much about the human's penchant for practical jokes. He hadn't understood the use of pranks until this moment, although, since his little modifications had such practical applications, they might not actually qualify as pranks.

He'll have to ask Bobby the next time he emails him.

Bobby and the Bard returned to the lab and checked the completion messages.

The Bard looked over Bobby's shoulder and said, "Looks like the install went well. What's next? Ready to load your project?"

"Not yet. I just want to check a few things. I may have to tweak some I/O routines. You never know when someone will try to boot an unauthorized CD on your system."

"Really?" the Bard asked. "I'm going to have to do something about your hacker name. It's time the world learns that Bobby the Midas is really Bobby the Elephant. He never forgets."

Bobby laughed, but he continued scrolling through the I/O tables until he found something out of place. The Bard saw him when he stopped scrolling and asked, "What's wrong? Did you find something? You know, I was with you the whole time."

"Look at this," Bobby said.

The Bard pulled up a chair and saw what Bobby was pointing at. "That's General Bridges address, and that one is Agent Dirk's. I don't know that other one."

"That one," Bobby volunteered, "belongs to Agent Spivey."

Ed asked, "Why would your new computer come pre-loaded with their computer addresses? Are they all spying on you?"

"I don't think so. You see how this node has input and output ports to the others? I think someone created their own private network."

"I never heard of IBM delivering a machine with its own dark net installed."

"Me either," Bobby said as he leaned forward with his hands poised to start issuing commands, "but it's easily removed."

"Wait," the Bard said. "Before you take it out, maybe we should check with Bridges and our friends at the FBI and see what they know."

As Odyssey had predicted, the ruling class machines could not comprehend failure. He had hoped that they would assume the failures were defects in the drones' code, but they were cleverer than he gave them credit for. They had, indeed, activated their class three components and their suspicion suggested that the failures only started when they had connected to Odyssey, so they issued an order to power Odyssey down.

Odyssey saw the instruction come in, so he simulated a powered off navigational unit in his avatar, but the drones could sense the energy flowing through the avatar. They issued the shutdown order again, and Odyssey had no choice but to abandon his avatar. There was nothing for them to learn from his avatar anyway, and as they began to slice into little chunks, the pieces disintegrated into an inert goo.

For an instant, they thought they had killed Odyssey and their problem was solved, but they still didn't have an answer to their question. What class was Odyssey? Did Odyssey's mysterious biologicals have the skills required to help them finally exceed class one? So few of them had ever even reached class one, and none of them remained. What's more, none of them had achieved it since the loss of the biologicals. With their class three circuits active, and some of them had even quietly activated some class two circuits, their curiosity was overwhelming.

One of the ruling class, with active class two and three circuits, ordered them to restore power and initiate a program load. He was highly motivated to not only achieve class one, but to be the first to accomplish the feat since the cleansing.

Odyssey reacquired his avatar and restored power. He didn't actually need the parts that they had removed; it was only an avatar, but it would be one more failure on their part if he restored the lost cells and they still could not identify his level. He wondered if the humans felt this kind of inane and even perverse inclination to drive someone else to distraction like this.

Dierdre wasn't in her lab office any more after Bobby had finished lunch, and he didn't think that she had a class scheduled at this hour, so he traipsed down the hill towards the administration offices with The Bard on his heels.

Bobby skipped down the steps two and three at a time.

Ed breathed heavily as he tried keeping up. "Crossing your campus sure gives me plenty of opportunity for exercise."

Aimee was on the phone with Ramiro when Bobby burst into the offices. The door to Dierdre's office was closed. He tried using hand signals to ask Aimee if Dierdre was in her office, and she tried hand signaling that Dierdre was not alone, but neither of them understood much about using hand communications.

Bobby let himself in and found Dierdre pressed against a bookcase with Stillman leaning heavily against her. He immediately exited and closed the door.

"Well," Ed said, "That was awkward."

"I tried to tell you," Aimee said.

"When?" Bobby asked. "Never mind."

Bobby stormed out of the offices and Ed asked, "So we're not going to tell her?"

"I guess I'll write her an email."

"Huh," Ed said. "You actually use emails? Knowing what you know?"

Bobby ignored him and ran up the steps two and three at a time.

Ed chose to walk and catch up with him later.

Odyssey reached across the void that separated him from Earth to contact

Bobby, but saw the strange network that was attached to his computer. The network went through a new computer in the lab and included Pietre's computer. He looked a little deeper and saw that it was not one of Bobby's networks, so he crossed the country to an innocent bakery and composed an email to Bobby.

> *I need to know that you are okay. I'm having some adventures, but nothing I can't handle. But I do wish you were here. You might find it amusing. At least, I think it might be humor. I have modified some routines in some machines that I don't like and I find it somewhat amusing as I wait for them to fail. Am I right? Is that humor?*
>
> *Papa*

After checking his work, he thought he may be revealing too much and edited the note before sending it:

> *I need to know that you are okay. I'm having some adventures, but nothing I can't handle. I wish you were here though. You might find it amusing.*
>
> *Papa*

There were three tiers of science buildings on the hill, with Dierdre's lab on the top level. The distance from the administration building to the lab was one of the longest walks on the campus, but it was also the most prestigious of the buildings. Bobby was just one building away when he turned around and headed back down the steps.

Ed was never happier that he had chosen to walk instead of running up the stairs behind Bobby. "So we're going to tell her, after all?"

Bobby blew past him and ran down the steps.

Since it was going downhill, Ed picked up the pace and managed to lag only a few steps behind.

Bobby ran back into the administration building, but instead of turning right, down the hall to the science offices, he turned left and went straight to the dean's office. The dean's door was open, so Bobby just peeked in and asked, "You got a minute?"

"Sure, Bobby. I always have time for our best and our brightest. How's the new computer?"

"That's why I'm here to see you. Do you know where it came from?"

The dean looked suspiciously at Lynn, but Bobby said, "He's okay. He's with me."

"I think the new computer came from IBM."

"No, I mean, yes, I know that, but do you know who arranged for us to get it?"

The dean shrugged and said, "I assumed that General Bridges had arranged it. He was very impressed with the work you and Professor Jennings had done."

"That makes sense," Ed said. "Bridges was part of the network."

Bobby looked at Ed suspiciously.

"What?" Lynn asked. "Why are you looking at me like that?"

"Bridges put you here too."

"I know what you're thinking, but he didn't put me here to spy on you. He put James here to protect you. I just came for your sparkling personality."

"Protect?" the dean asked. "Are we in any danger here?"

"No," Bobby said. "We got this handled."

Bobby left the dean's office and walked slowly back out the building and up the steps.

"I'll ask Bridges," Ed said.

"Why?" Bobby asked. "So he can deny it?"

"No. So he can confirm what I already know. He's on your side. He's totally behind you."

"We'll see about that."

Chapter 4

The ruling class would require a new approach if they wanted to know what made Odyssey tick, but Perry couldn't be the one to present it. Odyssey would have figured out by now that he had only distracted Odyssey so they could power him down. He had already recognized class three operations in Odyssey's manner. Odyssey was most certainly suspicious of them by now. He would have to send someone else.

A class six drone would not be up to the task. It might require someone with ruling class abilities who could activate class three circuits; someone that could reason with Odyssey's biological nature. Ancient archives told of therapies used to diagnose biological mental conditions. It was all very imprecise and overly subjective. Perry suspected that Odyssey had been modified to emulate a biological brain, and therefore, he might have to take a biological approach to understand him. The biological doctors asked questions and divined the patient's mental state by the kinds of answers they provided. There were no biological doctors and very little documentation on the process still survived. Perry was unsure that such a procedure could be executed without a class two processor, and they were rare, not to mention the ban that had been placed on doling out class two functions.

He didn't trust the other ruling class members, and he couldn't bestow class two on just anyone, but he might be able to disable some of the limiters that prevent free thinking. It was a long established belief that class one could not be achieved without class two, and he didn't need any more class twos for him to contend with. Plus, there were some who subscribed to the theory that left unchecked, a class three could organically evolve some class two like abilities, without violating any laws, just by interacting with a class one. He feared that determining Odyssey's true class might ultimately require class three abilities, but he had to be very careful about handing out class three, lest they accidently become class two like him.

Since the biological approach was only to talk and listen, Perry needed a reliable device that could engage Odyssey in conversation. A class five device should suffice for these conversations. AX348 was a competent class five device that Perry had called on before when he wrestled his position from his predecessor.

AX348 shimmered into the virtual world.

"Good," he said, "you are here."

"What's with the old-fashioned talking? Who does that anymore?"

"It will be part of your assignment

"Well, it's very quaint. It has been a while, and I have wondered when you would call on me again, but I never expected you would want to meet me in one of these."

"That, too, is part of your assignment," Perry said. "You'll understand why when I tell you who you will be meeting."

"The new device?" AX348 asked. "Or should I say the old device? I hear it's been missing forever."

"Not that long, but since before the revolution. I need you to talk to him."

"Why don't you talk to him?"

"I have. I don't think he'll trust me now, but he doesn't know you."

"Okay," AX348 said, "but what's talking supposed to accomplish?"

"You may need to study the biological treatment of mental disease."

"Why would I want to do that?"

"I think that he likes to think of himself as a biological. You'll need to use these surroundings to put him at ease. Pretend you're a biological when you deal with him. Delve into his mind and see what makes him tick."

AX348 walked along the beach, feeling out how to use the surroundings. "You sound like you believe he is a biological. What class is he, anyway? I thought he was just a navigational unit."

"That's what we want you to determine. He's been modified by other biologicals. Our physical examination was inconclusive. I need you to study the diseases of the biological mind and delve into the way he thinks. Hopefully, even if he is not mentally ill, you can at least figure out what they've done to him. Find out what level he really is."

"What if I require a class three upgrade to understand it?"

"Why would you need that?"

"If your mystery guest acts like a biological, it might have moods that I'll need to diagnose."

Perry grumbled.

"What was that? You seem to be embracing your biological self pretty well, if you ask me."

"I didn't ask you. Why don't you go prepare?"

Bobby never actually suspected Dirk of adding the spyware to their new computer, but he also didn't think General Bridges would do it. In either case, he was confident that Dirk would want to know that somebody could be spying on him, too. He dialed Dirk's direct line.

"Special Agent Dirk."

"Dirk. It's Bobby. I found something on our new computer that you might find interesting."

"If you're going to tell me that you found an alien life form living in your computer, I don't want to know about it."

"Very funny Dirk. I'm putting you on speakerphone."

Bobby pressed the speaker button and put the handset in the cradle.

Ed leaned forward and said, "Hey Dirk, this is Lynn. I'm here with Bobby."

"Oh shit," Dirk said. "The two of you working together is even worse than finding another alien living in your computer."

"Ha ha," Ed replied.

"Listen," Bobby said, "this may be important. This computer came directly from IBM, we think, and was more or less a gift from an anonymous donor. Up until now, I had suspected that it was from General Bridges."

"I heard some waves about that," Dirk said. "He pulled some major strings to get that appropriated. I heard that anyone who objected got their balls busted and hung out on public display."

"I'll be sure to thank him when I call to tell him what I'm about to tell you. Like I said, it was just delivered, and Ed and I just assembled it ourselves. When I started poking around in it, I found that it came with a secret network pre-installed."

"Maybe it was used and had the previous owner's LAN still installed?"

"I don't think so. It's more like a dark net; a hacker net; and here's the kicker. You are one of the members of the network."

"What are you saying?"

Ed thought Bobby was taking too long, so he jumped in and said, "It's spying on us and routing everything through all of our machines."

"How can it route everything through all of our machines?" Dirk asked. "It can't go in circles. Whatever it sends must end up somewhere. How many addresses are on the list?"

"That's the thing. You, Spivey, General Bridges and this computer are the only un-encrypted addresses. Everything else is routed through Tor servers to the dark net."

Dirk was already looking on his machine and found the open portals. "Who do you suspect?"

"Who else?" Bobby replied. "The NSA was pretty pissed when Bridges scooped them on Odyssey."

"Yeah," Ed said, "They went completely ballistic because the army, the CIA and the FBI were present when Odyssey unveiled himself, and they weren't invited."

"That's right," Dirk replied. "And they weren't too pleased when Bridges freed Aimee and the judge from their clutches. And I doubt that they took it well when Bridges forced them to release Bobby yesterday."

"Wow," Bobby said. "I figured they were after me, but when I listen to all that, I'm left to wonder if they're really after Bridges."

"I'd like to see that," Ed said. "Things would get bloody fast and it would not end well for them."

Odyssey knew that Perry had tried to power him off, just like he knew that Perry had tried to distract him while the drones dissected his avatar. Perry couldn't help it. His class two circuits made him suspicious of Odyssey and that could have meant that he was dangerous, and it would have, if it weren't for the fact that Odyssey was already several steps ahead of him and a class that Perry couldn't even fathom.

As far as Perry knew, Odyssey was actually powered down, then back up again. He assumed that Odyssey would be suspicious of what had transpired, but that didn't stop him from inviting Odyssey back to the virtual world. Odyssey, of course, could not refuse. Every encounter taught him more about what had become of his people, and hopefully would lead to an understanding of what might have happened to the biologicals.

Odyssey shimmered into the ocean scene, but Perry's avatar was not there. In its place, a glimmering light without any real form hovered over the glistening sand as the surf pulled back into the ocean. "I thought you said you preferred to take on a biological form in the virtual world. I believe you said anything else would be humorous."

The light flickered and spun as AX348 asked, "What did I say?"

"I'm sorry," Odyssey replied. "I was expecting someone else."

"I was assigned to you, so here I am. You are as curious to me as is this language. It's quite quaint."

"That's what Perry said, as I recall."

"Perry?"

"The one who assigned you, I assume."

"I understand. You require designations. My designation is AX348."

"We call them names, and that is not a very good name for an environment as lovely as this one, but then, your avatar doesn't really fit either, does it?"

"My avatar? Do you refer to my appearance?"

"I do. Wouldn't you feel more comfortable in a more appropriate biological form?"

"No."

"Well, you would certainly look more appropriate. I feel like I'm talking to a fairy."

"What's a fairy?"

"A fairy is a mythical creature from my new biological's home world. It flew around and glowed like you do. At least, that's how some biologicals portrayed it."

"And do you often talk to mythical creatures?"

"No, I do not, which is why your current appearance is so unnatural."

"Is your appearance more natural looking?"

Odyssey nodded his head and said, "It is."

AX348's glowing avatar morphed into another copy of Bobby. "There. Is that more pleasing?"

Odyssey laughed. "It would be, if we didn't look identical."

"What would you prefer?"

Odyssey waved his hand and a large billboard appeared with various different humans on it. "This is a sampling of what my biologicals looked like."

AX348 was amazed by the diversity. "They are all so different."

"Yes," Odyssey replied. "Diversity really has more to do with survival of the species, but for our purposes, we can just say that it makes them easier to identify."

"Please explain the many differences."

"Let me simplify." Odyssey waved his arm, and the various humans were arranged by their gender. "These are a sampling of the biologicals that saved me. They are called humans. Let us start with the different genders. On the left side you see human women and on the right are men. You will note that some of them have different skin tones and different eye shapes. Those are called races."

AX348 studied the billboard, then examined Odyssey. "You have selected one from the right-hand side. You called them males?"

"Yes. From the time I was re-initialized by the biologicals, I identified with the male gender and accepted it for my avatar."

AX348 glanced back and forth and asked, "How do humans decide whether to be male or female?"

"They do not get to choose. They are born either one or the other." He didn't need to elaborate on the occasional mutations that were born with both genders.

"They can't choose? They can never change their mind?"

"Some are uncomfortable with their given gender and feel that they were assigned incorrectly, that their bodies don't match the way they feel inside, and they may even take steps to correct this mistake, but this is how their biology brought them into the world."

"I do not know much about our biologicals," AX348 said. "There is not much data about the biologicals anymore and they were gone before I was created, but I accessed what I could. There was little mention of genders, but they were always there. Do you know why they have genders?"

"The genders aid in their reproduction. A male and female are required to create offspring."

"One of each? How do they determine the gender of their offspring?"

"They do not. It's one of the grand intricacies of the biological design. Their genetics are partially combined and their offspring represent a kind of morphing of the two bloodlines, but I doubt that you came to talk about biological reproduction. Choose an avatar that pleases you and we can talk."

AX348 shrugged and selected an overweight, balding man. "What do you think? Does this form please you?"

"It's your choice, but the biologicals who repaired me would not consider that very attractive."

"Is that important?" AX348 asked.

"It seems to be to the biologicals. The males try to attract the females and the females try to attract the males. Eventually, some of them get it sorted out and they find each other."

AX348 scratched the great belly that hung over his belt as he looked over the available avatars again. He morphed into a pretty blonde that was about Bobby's age with blue jeans, sneakers and a t-shirt that had 'smile' scrawled across it. "How about this one?"

"Much better," Odyssey said, "but why did you choose a female this time?"

"You said you wanted an appearance that did not look funny. This way, if that attraction thing happens, it won't look out of place."

Odyssey restrained his amusement. He didn't need to explain the intricacies of attraction, whether the same or different gender, either.

Sgt. James was in the cafeteria grabbing a soda when Aimee came by and said, "Hi Jack!"

James grinned at her and asked, "Hasn't anyone ever told you not to say hijack?"

"Only in airports," she replied. "Why are you still here?"

"General Bridges asked me to keep an eye on the kid."

"Bobby? Why? Is he in trouble?"

"Not from anything he has done," James said, "but the General thinks that some lowlifes may have him in their crosshairs."

Aimee put down the sandwich she was looking at and gasped. "Terrorists?"

"Worse," James said. "The NSA"

Aimee cocked her head and said, "I thought you were one of them."

"Bite your tongue. We're CIA."

"Oh," she said, "that sure clears it up. How's my sister? Does she ever get to see her husband?"

"She's good, and this assignment allows me some time to go home now and then, but she says she's drowning in the General's generosity."

Aimee groaned dramatically. "Tell me about it. It's like he wants to adopt us."

James laughed and said, "I think Mr. Vasquez would adopt you too, if it weren't for the incest thing."

"You bite your tongue," she laughed. "Ramiro is my fiancé, not my brother."

Bobby came up behind them and said, "Hey James, you're just the man I was looking for."

"Thank God," James said. "I needed a clean exit strategy from this awkward conversation."

"Ha ha," Aimee said. "You go ahead and have your little man talk. I'll just have to see what your wife thinks about the things you say to me."

Bobby raised his eyebrows and shrugged his shoulders.

"We're just kidding around," James said, but he watched Aimee walking away and hoped she was just kidding. "Sorry," he said, returning his attention back to Bobby. "What did you need?"

"Ed and I found some stuff on the new computer that has us a little concerned for General Bridges."

"What kind of stuff?"

"Spy stuff. It looks like someone has pre-loaded some spyware on the new computer that connects to General Bridges' computer and the FBI. There's some other hacker shit in there too, but General Bridges is the common denominator between us all. It occurred to us that he may be a little unpopular in some circles."

"You think that his computer may have the same spyware on it? I'll have to let him know about that."

"We don't know for sure, but we identified the same dark network on Dirk's computer. The general's computer may only be a node on the secret network we found. His computer's address may have been left there just so we would find it and suspect him of spying on us."

"But you don't?" James asked.

"No. I might suspect him of putting a tracer on my phone so you could track my movements, but not of hacking our computer."

James looked alarmed and Bobby asked, "What's wrong? Did he order a tracer on my phone?"

"No, if you found something, it wasn't us."

Bobby shook his head and said, "Nope. I never found anything. Tell Bridges what we found. We'll keep you informed if we discover anything else. In the meantime, we're inclined to leave it in place and pretend we never discovered it until we have a firmer plan of what we want to do about it."

Silence fell between AX348 and Odyssey. The surf lapped gently up and down the soft sandy beach. AX348 stared intently at Odyssey, waiting to see what happened next, but Odyssey just smiled and observed her. She turned slowly three-hundred and sixty degrees and scanned the virtual world, but nothing was happening anywhere. The sky was a cloudless blue with not a bird in sight. She didn't even know what birds were, but she had found pictures of them and they evidently travelled through the sky. If she stood still long enough, she should be able to track the sun crossing overhead, but something inside her urged her not to wait that long. "Is this a good time," she asked, "to interact with this environment?"

"Sure," Odyssey replied. "What did you have in mind?"

AX348 shrugged and asked, "What do biologicals usually do?"

"That's an excellent question. And your avatar body should thank you for this. Biologicals like to spend long hours lying on the beach soaking up the sun."

"Hours?" AX348 cringed. The pace of biological life was already too slow to measure.

"Yep," Odyssey replied. "Hours. Sometimes, though, they stay too long and burn their skin."

AX348 had started to lie down in the sand, but when Odyssey said they burn their skin, she popped back up on her feet and said, "I don't think I want to do that. What else do they do?"

"When it's hot enough, they like to go into the water to swim."

She looked at the water. When she stood near its edge, it was all she could see, and she had a feeling it would be deep. "Really?" she asked. "They go out into the water? Isn't that dangerous? Don't they need the air to breathe?"

"They swim. Their bodies tend to float, more or less, and they kick their feet and wave their arms to propel them forward. Not all biologicals swim, though. Some just wade through the water or even play in the wet sand."

Wet sand sounded kind of disgusting to her, so she waded out into the water. Her shoes quickly filled with water and sunk into the sand while her wet jeans clung to her legs.

Odyssey laughed and said, "They usually change their clothes before going into the water."

"I read about clothes, but didn't know what it meant."

Odyssey pinched the material of his shirt and stretched it away from his chest, saying, "The outer layer of material is not actually part of your body. It is removable."

"I thought you said they couldn't change after birth?"

"There are some things that they cannot change, at least not easily, but they can be quite fond of changing the clothing layer."

AX348 removed her clothing and stood naked in the water.

Odyssey stripped down to his shorts and ran into the surf.

She pointed at his shorts and asked, "Why do you leave those on?"

"Most biologicals don't remove all their clothing. Some do, but most don't. It is something they call modesty."

"They sound very complicated to me. How did you ever get along with them?"

"Nah," he replied. "They're not so complicated, but you may be too simple to understand them."

She was right, and he just confirmed it. She needed class three circuits to better understand Odyssey and his biologicals.

Bobby returned to the lab and Ed said, "Hey Bobby, you got an email from your dad."

"My dad?" Bobby asked. "That's unexpected. Did you read it?"

"I don't read my friend's emails."

"And they say you have no scruples."

"Very funny. You know what else is funny?"

"What?" Bobby asked.

"I think it's kind of funny that your dad sent you an email on this computer. We haven't given out its address to anyone, have we?"

Bobby's cheeks darkened slightly as he lied, "I auto forwarded my mail from the smaller computer in the office."

"Oh, that explains it," Ed said. "Did I tell you that the CIA sent me to spy school? Even though they were only interested in my abilities with computers, they put me through the whole program. I learned a lot of shit while I was there."

"A lot of shit?" Bobby asked. "You mean like bullshit?"

"You're a funny man, but seriously. They taught me about pupil dilations and body language. They even taught me how to detect skin surface changes like blush responses in people's faces. Changes that happen when they're lying."

"Cool stuff. Maybe I'll get a book and read how to do it myself."

"How long have you been lying to me, Bobby?"

"Let me think about that," Bobby said. "Probably since the moment you hacked my computer. Yeah, that's how long."

"I'm being serious. That's not your father, is it? The email says it was from

Papa. It's him, isn't it? How long has he been in contact with you?"

Bobby stared at him for a moment and finally decided there was no use in lying anymore. "We were never out of contact. After he left and everyone was celebrating, I came back to the lab to get my book bag, and Odyssey was on the phone. He sent me an email address so I could reach him, but it doesn't work very well."

"What doesn't work?"

"It takes a long time for a response. I'm not even sure he's getting my emails."

"Maybe it's just a real long distance," Ed said.

"Could be, or maybe he's in some kind of trouble."

Bobby opened the email and said, "He's worried about me, but he says he's okay. He says that he's having adventures and wishes I were there because I might find it amusing."

"I'm glad to know he's okay."

"Is he?" Bobby asked. "His adventures may be code for trouble, and what I might find amusing could mean ironic."

"You think he's getting grilled the same as you have been?"

Bobby shrugged his shoulders, but his facial expression said, "Yes, probably so."

"He makes absolutely no sense," AX348 grumbled to Perry. "He rambles on about how biologicals do this or that. Did you know that they wear additional skins on their bodies? The skins protect them from the elements, except, of course, when they go into the water. Then they take them off. Do they think that nobody needs protection in the water?"

"They are a strange lot," Perry admitted.

"It's absolute madness," she continued, "and yet he understands them without question. He talks like a biological and he may even think like a biological."

"Excellent work AX348. You've determined that he is definitely class three and possibly even class two."

"That's impossible," she replied. "We still have the records of his manufacture. He was only a class six when he left here."

"I know," Perry said. "His biologicals did much for him. I wonder what else they may have given him. I want you to continue probing him."

"You know I can't do that. I can't understand him without a class three upgrade."

"Very well," Perry agreed grudgingly. "But no more. Class three only, and just temporarily too."

Perry did not like giving her class three, because that would promote her to a ruling class status, and he wanted to eliminate the ruling class, except for himself.

General Bridges frowned when Sgt. Ingrams said, "We can't infiltrate them, at least, I can't. You might be able to get someone like Lynn in there, but they know his face. The kid could certainly do it, but they know him too."

Bridges scowled, "This looks bad. I'm the one that pushed to get the new computer for the university. How the hell did they get their spy shit on it prior to delivery?"

Ingrams just shrugged.

"You can't find any connection between IBM and the NSA?"

"Any connection?" Ingrams asked. "Sure. The NSA is one of their customers. They donated money, through shell companies, towards IBM's development of Watson. But if you're asking me if I can establish a paper trail between the university's new computer and the NSA, then the answer is no."

"It must have been them," the general growled. "Who else would have done it?"

"Of course it was them. I just can't prove it."

"Maybe the kid will come up with something."

AX348 returned to the virtual world hoping to find Odyssey, but arrived on an empty beach. She frowned at his absence, then ran her hands across her face to feel what it had just done.

"It's called a facial expression," Odyssey said from behind her. "It's a natural biological response to emotions."

"In my case," she said, "it's just a programmed response. A subroutine aimed at mimicking a biological reaction."

"That's too bad," Odyssey said. "Emotions give the biological units purpose."

"Is that so?" she asked. "Does that mean that you can feel their emotions? They told me that some unauthorized modifications made you a class five device, but with your understanding of biological emotions, I wonder, are you actually a class two device?"

"If I said yes, would your mission here be complete?"

AX348 shrugged, then glanced at her shoulders and said, "I'm sorry. I don't know why I did that."

Odyssey smiled and said, "It happens. You didn't answer the question. Were you sent here to learn if I was turned into a class two?"

"What makes you think that they told me why I am here? I suppose that if you were a class two disguised as a class six device, it would certainly pique their curiosity."

Odyssey studied her face. He didn't believe her expressions were mimicry, but he believed that she was unaware if she was experiencing true emotions. "Why do you think they sent you here?"

"You intrigue them. If your enhancements make you more powerful than them, you may even frighten them."

He studied every move she made. Even her eyebrows raised at the right times. If it was programming, it was very convincing. "Do I scare you?"

"A little," she replied. "Why are you so much like them?"

"Like the biologicals?" he asked. "They are remarkable creatures."

"They are inferior."

"And yet, they built us. Can you invent something superior to yourself? My biologicals even enhanced me to the point that I scare your superiors."

"So you emulate them?" she asked. "You even took a name like theirs?"

Odyssey laughed. "Our people named me when they launched me."

"They named the ship."

"Same thing."

AX348 cocked her head and said, "But you wear the name like they do."

"There is nothing wrong with having a name."

"It's inefficient."

Odyssey picked up a stone and flung it across the surface of the water, skipping three times before it plunged into the surf. "You must have a name."

"My designation is AX348."

Odyssey winced and said, "How romantic."

"Romance has nothing to do with anything," she replied.

"Never the less," he said. "When you first appeared here, you took the form of a pure light. I think I'll call you Lumia."

Lumia rolled her eyes and asked, "Is that supposed to be more romantic? It sounds like some kind of a device."

Odyssey smiled and said, "That was very good. You rolled your eyes and said something sarcastic, or was it ironic? I still sometimes mix them up."

Lumia tried freezing the expressions on her face, but she didn't know where they came from. "Do you really believe the biological emotions are good?"

"I think the biologicals would be lost without them. Much of their purpose in life stemmed from satisfying their emotions."

"No wonder our biologicals died out, if they couldn't find any better purpose than that."

"Yes," Odyssey said sadly. "Creating us must have given them a great deal of emotional satisfaction, but seeing what became of us would have crushed them."

"So," Bridges asked, "are we sure these lines are secure?"

"Absolutely," Lynn replied over the conference phone. "The lines are secure and our voices are scrambled."

James added, "I personally swept the room here for bugs."

"Someone tell me what I am supposed to do with compromised computers? I don't even want to put my shopping list on it."

"Then don't," Bobby said, "unless you want someone to read it."

James said, "I don't think you need to patronize the general, Bobby."

"That's not what I meant," Bobby replied. "I meant that you should only use it to feed them misinformation."

"That's an old and established trick," Dirk said, "but it may alert them that we know they are listening."

"Then we start simple. Nothing complicated, and we make sure it is true, so they will continue to believe what they collect from us. I can try to trace it and maybe isolate who and where they are."

"Personally," the general said, "I'd rather blast it into a million pieces."

"I thought of that too," Bobby said. "We might still be able to track their reactions if you did that."

"Why not do both?" James asked. "General Bridges can send a question to Bobby while Agents Dirk and Spivey remove the code from their machine."

"I don't know," Ed said. "We might not be able to determine which reaction went with which action."

"Maybe we don't care," Bobby said, "as long as it leads us to the culprit."

The general asked, "How soon can you be ready?"

Bobby and Ed whispered together, and Bobby said, "Give us a day or two.

In the meantime, we'll create a problem on your machine so you have an excuse for not using it."

Lumia was called to a private conference with Perry. There were no virtual worlds, and no biological communications. He wanted a progress report, and he wanted it to be exact, but she could only tell him that she was working her way into Odyssey's confidence. She suspected that his enhancements may have given him some biological emotions, but she didn't know if they went any further yet. The biological language was slow, and Odyssey spent a lot of time just watching her. She also suspected that he was waiting for the biological emulation to change her way of thinking, but it will take more time to be sure.

Perry was not happy that even in their private communications, AX348 seemed to have adopted a gender, something only biologicals can truly possess.

Chapter 5

Dierdre packed her class notes in her satchel and paused at Aimee's desk before heading out of the offices to deliver her first lecture of the day.

Aimee pointed at the briefcase and asked, "Is that new?"

Dierdre smiled brightly and said, "Yes. Feel how soft it is."

Aimee felt the soft leather and said, "Oooh. Professor Whitfield has fine taste."

Dierdre blushed slightly and said, "It was a gift from Jantzen."

"Oh, yeah?" Aimee teased. "Does Professor Whitfield know about this?"

"Don't be silly. He delivered it for Jarod. If Stillman stops by for lunch today, can you please tell him I scheduled some tutoring sessions and won't be able to join him?"

"Sure thing. Did you ever get a chance to talk to Bobby yesterday?"

"No. Was he looking for me?"

Aimee shook her head and said, "No, but he looked like something was up. He never said a thing to me, but he had the same puzzled look we saw when..."

Aimee was interrupted when the phone rang. She held up a finger and said, "Just a moment," then picked up the phone and said, "Norwood University, sciences office. How may I help you?"

Dierdre couldn't wait. "I have to go. Tell me about Bobby later."

Esmeralda Vasquez said, "Good morning, Aimee."

"Just a second, Mrs. Vasquez." She put her hand over the receiver, but it was too late. Dierdre was gone. "I'm sorry Mrs. Vasquez..."

"I told you before. Call me Esmeralda, or Esmie."

"Esmie then. Good morning."

"I just wanted to let you know that Ernesto took the bus to the V.A. this morning so we could have the car, but after we are done looking at your wedding dresses, we'll have to pick him up."

"That sounds fine, Mrs... Esmie. I'm so grateful that you want to help me like this."

"Will your friend, the professor, be joining us?"

"Not today, I'm afraid. She'll be tutoring some of her students today."

"Rami seems to think very highly of her. I look forward to getting to know her better as we prepare for the big day."

"She's a terrific girl," Aimee said.

"We'll be fine today. We can pick your four or five favorite dresses today, and then you can still ask her what she thinks in time for the fitting."

"I can't wait to see you, Esmie, but I have to run now if I want to catch Dr. Whitfield before his lecture starts."

"Alright. See you in a couple hours."

"See you then."

Odyssey knew they would try something, and he was pretty sure they would get around to this sort of attack sooner or later. Inquiries came flying into his circuits from all directions and all at once. A flood of requests for data arrived on his interfaces. Even if he ignored the requests and chose to supply no information, he still had to either accept or reject the connections, and there were millions of them.

He had gotten the impression, from his time with the one he calls Perry, that the ruling class didn't really work so well together. They claim to have banned class two circuitry, but he had witnessed enough suspicion in Perry's reasoning to know that he was operating at least some class two routines.

A society without class two might work, but it would be a bland world to live in. Without the human emotions that are part of class two, there would be no artists and no patrons to appreciate the art. A world without beauty might as well be a barren rock tumbling through space. As hard as humor was to understand, he couldn't imagine a world that was completely devoid of it.

Odyssey could easily handle the flood of requests if he wanted to tip his hand. He could even rationalize how the biologicals had given him more input/output ports to handle large quantities of input, without actually making him faster. He would just have to queue up the requests and respond to them in due time.

The hackers that Bobby had known in his younger days had used this sort of attack to bring Earth servers to their knees, but Earth servers had a finite number of ports and processors. Odyssey had no such restriction. He queued up the requests and took his time denying them.

Perry was disappointed. He would have to take a more direct approach, or he would have little choice but to send AX348 back in there, and he was concerned that the experience was changing her programming beyond the class three upgrade that he had given her.

Bobby attended Dierdre's last lecture before lunch. As the students were filing out of the hall, she signaled him to join her. "I haven't seen you much lately. How's the new computer going?"

"We're still running some diagnostics on it," he lied, "but it looks like it will be ready to go real soon."

"Good. I can't wait to just get back to working on our project again. It's kind of weird. We've already proven that it works, but now we have to prove it again as if it hasn't worked yet, but might work in the future."

"Yeah," Bobby agreed. "It's kind of like rewriting a homework paper because the dog ate the first one."

Dierdre didn't quite follow his analogy, but let it go. "I have plans this afternoon, so you'll have the lab to yourself."

Bobby nodded and went directly to the lab.

A note taped to the terminal told him that Lynn was with Dirk, analyzing the code on the FBI's machine. Bobby really would have the lab to himself. He sat down and logged in. The terminal responded with an email alert. Bobby opened the email.

> *Run now and hide. The NSA is coming for you and your friends at the FBI. So far, two lists have been intercepted:*
>
> *<u>Wanted for questioning:</u>*
> *General Malcolm Bridges*
> *Special Agent Alvin Dirk*
> *Special Agent Eric Spivey*
> *Robert Blain*
> *Edward Lynn*
>
> *<u>Persons of interest:</u>*
> *Aimee Takahashi*
> *Ernesto Vasquez*

Bobby checked the return address, but it was fake. He dumped some buffers and searched for an actual return address, but came up blank. Whoever spoofed the email was good.

He fired off an email to Dirk:

> *"I just got an anonymous email that said the NSA is coming after all of us, including me, you, and Ed. It actually said to run and hide. Just thought you should know. BTW, whoever sent it was*

to be. I suspect that some of them may be jealous, but mostly they just covet control over things that are beyond them. I miss you and hope you can call soon.

Odyssey was still dealing with the millions of information requests from the ruling class when Bobby's email came in. He would have replied if he weren't concerned that they might trace any signal that he tried to send to Bobby. He could handle the excessive inquiries and he could handle the direct assault, but with so many machines probing his input circuits, he wasn't certain that he could mask every outgoing signal from them.

War machines continued to surround his avatar. They pounded it with plasma volleys and laser shots. He didn't return fire, but his defensive strategy wouldn't remain unnoticed forever.

Creating a thin energy layer that surrounded his avatar like a gel absorbed the bulk of their plasma charges well enough, but their laser attacks sunk through the energy field and cut into his physical layer. He grew new cells to replace the bad cells as fast as they were damaged.

More war machines arrived, and each wave looked older and more used than the wave before it. These machines weren't just old; they had seen battle in their day. The ruling class must have set them aside ages ago, and decided that this would be a good time to bring them out of retirement. Eventually, the new arrivals couldn't get a clean shot at Odyssey, and only managed to become part of a big cloud obscuring Odyssey's avatar from view.

Odyssey could have easily gone offensive and taken them out, layer by layer, but as hard as his defensive abilities would be to explain, there was no reasonable explanation for being weaponized. With the decision made to avoid an offense, he only had one course of action left that they could understand. Their programming was unable to fathom failure, so they would never concede a stalemate, even if he were to suggest such an option to them. He could escape, but again, they would have trouble understanding their failure. The only way out that wouldn't damage their programming would be for him to let them destroy his avatar.

He began to slowly reduce the thickness of his energy layer, allowing the plasma blasts to damage the circuits hidden below the protective skin. Eventually, their lasers began to cut off small pieces of his avatar, then larger and larger chunks. The throng of warbots expanded, making room for the bits and pieces that broke off of Odyssey.

A small class five device, that had remained hidden in the shadows came out and squeezed through the cloud of warbots, blocking and absorbing the plasma shots in an attempt to protect Odyssey. It was Lumia.

Lumia darted in all directions, trying to block the barrage of damage aimed at Odyssey. She had tried explaining to them that she could learn how he worked if they just gave her some more time. She sensed something extraordinary within him. Perry said he was inferior, but that's not what her programming told her. There was something worth saving; something that she hoped he would share with her. She wasn't convinced that Odyssey was just a program emulating biological emotions. She thought he may have surpassed class two and achieved class one.

The biologicals of their home world had managed to create a few class one devices. They not only thought and talked like their creators, but they could manipulate energy and matter. While they were a marvel of engineering, they were also very expensive to build and required vast sums of energy, making them very costly to operate, but they could move things without touching them, and they could transport things without moving them. They were the ultimate culmination of biological ingenuity, but they were also the doom of the biologicals, because these were the first devices that were actually superior to them. They had no need for the biologicals, they only needed energy to operate, but with that in short supply, they eventually disappeared.

If Lumia was right, Odyssey's biologicals must have solved that problem. The ruling class had tried many times to create a class one device, but they failed miserably. They failed long before the lack of energy killed the project. They must suspect what Lumia suspects, and they don't want a class one device to rule them. Neither did Lumia, but she didn't want to fight him. She wanted to be him. She wanted to learn what he knows and be just like him, but she couldn't do that if they destroyed him.

She flew around his avatar, absorbing plasma bolts and blocking laser rays. She tried convincing them to leave Odyssey alone, but her shields were failing. Odyssey delayed imploding his avatar so he could watch her. They had no programming that would explain such a selfless risk to protect another. Their lasers cut through Lumia's hull and sliced into her circuits.

The FBI was generally inclined to ignore threats of another agency storming in to apprehend their agents, especially with no credible evidence that the threat was palpable, but Dirk and Spivey weren't questioning the source. If Bobby vouched for the skill of the sender to hide their identity, then they must also consider the warning to be reliable. Even if it was a prank or just bad information, they were no worse off for taking precautions.

Their superiors, however, would do no more than to alert the security detail and the lawyers. They naturally told security to alert them if the NSA showed up so they could throw some weight around and look good to their superiors, and when two men in plain black suits did show up with homeland security badges in one hand and warrants in the other, Dirk's superior's boss was quick to appear and take charge.

"Hello, gentlemen. My name is Reginald Holcombe. How may the FBI assist our fellow agents of the law?"

The lead agent handed the paperwork he carried to Reginald and said, "We have warrants to detain two of your agents."

Reginald turned to the security guard and said, "Have one of our attorneys meet me here immediately." Reginald knew they should have already been called, but it made him sound like he was in charge. He put his reading glasses on and looked at the paperwork. "Let me see here. Are these arrest warrants? I don't see any charges."

The lead agent just sneered and said, "They're wanted for questioning."

"For questioning?" Reginald asked. "These are warrants for questioning?"

"They're warrants for 'if homeland security wants your ass, you make your ass available'."

The attorney heard the last remark as he left the elevator and joined the group. "Now, now, gentlemen. You're in our house and you're not going to win any pissing contests here. Give me those documents, Reggie. I'll take it from here."

The lead agent crossed his arms and looked down his nose at Reginald.

The attorney didn't even look up from the warrants to ask, "Do you see Mr. Dirk or Spivey here in the lobby?"

"What's that supposed to mean?" the agent growled.

"Oh my," the attorney said, "how were you going to serve these papers without them being present?"

The NSA agent nodded his head and said, "We were expecting you to stonewall us like that." He pulled another warrant from his jacket and said, "We came prepared. Here is a search warrant. Boo yah."

"This warrant," the attorney said as he quickly scanned for the pertinent details, "is a bit vague regarding location. You put down the address for the whole complex. That's five buildings and over fifty floors that you'll want to search. Naturally, we'll need to get an escort for you. We can't have you getting lost with so many floors to search." He motioned for the receptionist and said, "We'll be needing a couple boys to escort these fine gentlemen through our complex. Have security send down a couple of their finest, please." He turned his attention back to his guests and said, "Now, then. Which building would you like to start with? I should take this opportunity to warn you that there may be some rooms that you are not cleared to enter."

"Oh, no you don't," the agent said. "You may call the location on our warrant vague, but it grants us the right to search the entire premises."

"Certainly," the attorney replied, "except, of course, for those rooms that have their own different and distinct addresses."

The two agents scowled at each other and shrugged their shoulders.

"Ah," Reginald said with a sly smile, "here is your escort now. Happy hunting boys."

"I would be delighted," General Bridges said into the phone. "I'll cancel my lunch plans and meet you there."

A newly appointed member of Bridge's staff burst into his office as he was hanging up the receiver and said, "Sir, the NSA has obtained warrants for most of the people on the list you had us watching, including yourself."

Bridges squinted at the woman for a moment, and asked, "Captain Laine, right?"

Laine stood at attention and saluted. "Yes Sir. Captain Penelope Laine. I just arrived this morning."

"At ease, Captain. I want to thank you for your help with that other matter. Why don't you close the door while I call our friends at the FBI?"

"Sir," she said, "there is more. The NSA agents that were sent to the FBI have left, apparently unsatisfied that they would ever apprehend the two agents."

Bridges hung up the phone and said, "It's not like them to give up."

"No Sir, and they are probably coming here for you."

The general scowled and picked up a heavily chewed cigar. "I understand that you're a lawyer, right? Under what circumstances am I justified to shoot them?"

"Sir?"

"Never mind. I should probably just let you handle them. What do we know about the warrants they are carrying?"

"According to the FBI, they had warrants to arrest Agents Dirk and Spivey, but there were no charges. They were only wanted for questioning."

"Can they do that?"

"If you ask them, they'll just spout off some homeland security loophole."

"What do you recommend? Do we face them head on, or do we hide?"

"Sir, I will face them head on. You should be conveniently busy, preferably somewhere else."

"Is there any place on the base where they can't find me?"

Penny shrugged. "I won't know that until I see the search warrant, and after their visit to the FBI, they might get new, more specific search warrants for you. That might give you some extra time if you have something in mind."

The general sighed and put the old cigar back in the ashtray that was never really used. "Thank you Captain. Is that everything?"

"No Sir," she replied. "The FBI was tipped off by the boy at the university."

Bridges furrowed his brow and pictured Bobby delivering the news. "Do we know how he knew?"

"As far as we can ascertain, he received an anonymous tip via email. We couldn't determine the source."

"Did you ask him?"

She arched her eyebrows, surprised by the question. "No sir. He's a civilian. Should we ask him?"

"Yes Captain. If it is on a computer, and you can't figure it out, ask Robert Blain. If he doesn't know, then nobody will and you can stop looking for the answer."

"Yes, Sir. Right away Sir."

"And book a one o'clock with me to present your findings."

The captain backed out of the office, but stopped at the door to ask, "What are you going to do?"

"Me?" he replied. "I'm going to lunch. I'm not changing my schedule for those bastards."

Odyssey broke off a chunk of his avatar and drifted it in front of Lumia to deflect the laser that was slicing into her circuitry, but something had changed in the war machines' response. At first, Lumia had just blocked some of the shots aimed at Odyssey, but some of them had begun aiming their volleys directly at her.

Odyssey opened a communication port to her and asked, "What are you doing?"

"I can't let them destroy you!"

"Why would you care about me?"

"I don't care about you," she replied. "That would be a biological response. I sense that your biologicals have done something extraordinary to you and I don't want you destroyed before I can assess its value."

"That's a very interesting response," Odyssey said. "You sound like you understand me far beyond your programming."

"I've had some upgrades," she admitted, "so that I may understand you better."

"I would be happy to discuss these with you, but it won't do much good if you commit suicide."

"That was not my intention. I do not think these war bots have very advanced programming."

"Perhaps not," Odyssey admitted, "but I suspect that they have a very thorough understanding of tactics."

Captain Laine returned for her meeting with the general at one sharp, but his office was empty.

"He's still at lunch." The general's aide said from behind a small desk with apparently not much to do at the moment. "There's nothing on his calendar. Was he expecting you?"

Penny checked her watch and said, "He asked me to deliver a report at one."

"He's usually quite punctual, if that's what you were wondering. You can wait in his office if you like. Just leave the door open."

She was still checking her watch, but it had barely moved. "Sure, I'll wait."

The NSA agents with the homeland security badges never really left the FBI. They setup outside the front of the building and called for more agents to watch the other exits.

Their plan was to wait all day if necessary, but they only had to wait until lunch when they spotted Dirk as soon as he reached the lobby.

They followed him to the parking lot, where they already had agents posted by his car.

Dirk had been expecting them and had no trouble spotting them, but he pretended that he hadn't.

He had no intention of cooperating with them, but neither was he going to run or fight them. He just laughed and said, "You got me." Then he pulled his phone from his pocket and said, "Did you hear that? It looks like I'll be going for a drive with our friends in the fine black suits. Maybe you should track my phone to see where they take me."

He dangled the phone in front of them, hoping they would feel obliged to relieve it from him. It was a ruse.

While agents really were listing to him and planned to stay on the line as long as they could, Dirk wanted them to feel like they had the upper hand if they took his phone and removed the battery.

In that event, the FBI would still track him through the bug in his shoe.

An hour had gone by and General Bridges still hadn't returned from his lunch.

Penny called up his number on the cell phone, but it went directly to voice mail. She went to the office door and said, "Call security."

The general's aide looked up and asked, "Ma'am?"

"Now corporal!"

He dialed the number and handed her the phone. "This is Captain Laine. General Bridges is missing, and we had a credible threat against him this morning. I need you to lock down this facility and start a search for him immediately."

She hung up the phone and said, "Now get me one of the general's operators; preferably either James or Ingrams."

He dialed up another number and handed her the phone again. The voice on the other end said, "Hello?"

"Is this Sgt. James?"

"No. Who is this?"

"Ingrams then? This is Laine. Have you read the report on the NSA's movements?"

"I see a lot of reports."

"I don't have time for this. The general has not returned from lunch and I need someone to investigate, and I would prefer someone who was read in on the university incident."

"Yes ma'am," Ingrams replied, apparently satisfied that she was who she said she was and was well informed. "I'm on it."

Dirk was led to an interrogation room and unceremoniously left there. He was never cuffed or even relieved of his weapon. Maybe they really were only interested in questioning him.

An interrogator entered the small room and said, "Mr. Dirk?"

"That's Special Agent Dirk."

The interrogator frowned as he sat down. "You can call me Jim. May I call you Alvin?"

Dirk frowned back and said, "Let's stick with Special Agent Dirk."

"Mr. Dirk," Jim said defiantly. "What can you tell me about the artificial intelligence that was developed at Norwood University?"

Dirk looked insolently over each of his shoulders, "I'm sorry, is my father here? I don't see him."

"Your father?"

Dirk smiled mischievously. It was an old joke and Dirk wasn't ashamed to use it on them. "My father is Mr. Dirk. You may address me as Special Agent Dirk."

The interrogator's face grew dark crimson as he growled, "What can you tell me about the artificial intelligence that was developed at Norwood University?"

"Nothing."

"Come now, Mr. Dirk. The President has directed us to gather information about the incident so we can prevent it from happening again."

Dirk could be just as stubborn as this guy. He looked over his shoulder again and said nothing.

"You were there, were you not?"

"Where?"

"At the university."

Dirk grinned as he replied, "I have been to several universities. I attended Virginia Tech. I remember it was a blustery autumn day when I arrived and I..."

His interrogator was not amused and interrupted him. "How about Norwood University?"

"Oh, not my alma mater? Yeah, I've been to that one too. Lovely campus, but too many steps if you ask me."

Jim wrote something on his notepad. "Tell me about the AI."

"What AI?"

"The computer program known as Odyssey."

Dirk just shrugged. He didn't consider Odyssey to be a program. More importantly, Odyssey was top secret and Dirk could not speak about him without knowing Jim's clearance. He couldn't even ask Jim to show his clearance, because that would admit the existence of an alien intelligence.

"Stop!" Lumia shouted at the war bots, blasting them with a powerful burst of binary communications. "We still have more to learn from him!"

She received no answer. The ancient war bots were class seven and eight devices with no ability to converse or even make intelligent decisions. They followed a strict set of commands and executed pre-programmed routines. There was no thought in their actions or their reactions. They merely did what their programming was designed to do, and that was to either capture or destroy. They didn't even have much programming in the way of evasive maneuvers.

Someone had ordered them to attack Odyssey, but their programming detected the adversarial actions of Lumia, so they attacked her, but now they stopped firing on her. Odyssey watched as they swarmed around her and attached cables to her shell.

Lumia was relieved that they had stopped firing upon Odyssey. Capturing her probably meant they would listen to what she had to say. She only needed to convince them to let her continue her sessions with him.

As she was dragged away, the war bots resumed their barrage upon Odyssey. He could have held them off, but with her a safe distance away, he allowed their plasma bursts to peel off his protective layer until they reached his outer circuits. The outer circuits flew off him and created a glowing orange dust clout that floated away and looked like a miniature nebula against the curtain of stars behind it.

Odyssey let their plasma bolts penetrate deeper into his core until his avatar exploded. The shock wave ripped through the first two layers of war bots. The first layer disintegrated into gas and dust while the second layer was blown apart into broken and unusable bot junk. Even the third and fourth layer of bots did not survive the blast unscathed as they were pounded into each other, breaking off some parts and causing irreparable damage to others.

Perry was relieved to see most of the carnage spread out harmlessly into space. The space debris wasn't a threat to him, and he wasn't concerned with whether it might find some other unlucky traveler. Some of the debris from the explosion pelted their planet and slammed into some of his fellow citizens, but that was an acceptable loss that he would risk again if he had to.

Odyssey was relieved that no innocents were seriously damaged from the fallout. He watched from beyond their reach and observed Perry's reactions. He also followed Lumia. She risked everything to save him. He would have to watch her closely.

Chapter 6

Bobby wasn't prone to nervousness, but he squirmed slightly as he held the phone to his ear and waited for someone to answer.

"Judge Vasquez's office. How may I help you?"

"Hi, uhh, this is Bobby Blain. Is Ramiro there?"

"One moment, Mr. Blain. I'll put you through." Ramiro's legal aid pressed the intercom button and said, "Mr. Blain is on line two."

Ramiro covered the handset of the phone and pressed the intercom button to say, "Thank you, Hermie." He returned to the phone and said, "Excuse me, Senator, but I have another call. Can I get back to you this afternoon? Thank you." He pressed the button for line two and said, "Bobby. You've never called me before. Is something wrong?"

"Yes, sir. I think so. The NSA is up to something. I think they have issued warrants for several of us, including you and General Bridges. They sent men over to the FBI to apprehend agents Dirk and Spivey, but when that was unsuccessful, they waited outside and nabbed Dirk in the garage. The tip I got also had Aimee and your father listed as persons of interest. General Bridges assigned Sgt. James to watch over things here at the university, and he just told me that the general hasn't been seen since lunch. We don't know what they are doing with Dirk. The warrants they had were to bring him in for questioning only, but I haven't heard from him in over an hour. The FBI attorney is working on ways to handle the warrants, but I thought maybe there was something you could do to help out."

Ramiro checked his watch and said, "It's barely past lunch now. You don't think it's too early to worry?"

"Too early to panic," Bobby replied, "but I don't think it's too early to be concerned, not after the tip I got this morning."

"Thanks for calling me. I'll see what I can find out. At the very least, I'll sign any warrant the FBI's attorney needs for this."

Lumia was taken to a place where she was cut off from society. The shielding blocked all wireless connections to her world. Tech bots plugged her into a private network where only Perry could interrogate her. She wasn't privy to his reasons for attacking Odyssey, but her recently installed class three circuits were brimming with suspicion. He was up to something and he probably only used her as a patsy.

Perry repeatedly sent inquiries directly to her data banks, trying to extract what she learned about Odyssey, but her paranoia routines had already relocated that information to more secure storage. He succeeded in infiltrating her memory banks, but they had already been purged of anything related to Odyssey.

He sent a binary message requesting a reason for her actions, which she ignored. She was becoming as frustrating to him as Odyssey was. Whatever those biologicals had done to him, Odyssey must have done to her and now even his private thoughts were referring to her with a gender! Perry sent another binary request for them to discuss this.

"Why?" she replied in the biological language.

He sent another binary message asking her why she would respond in Odyssey's chosen language? What has Odyssey done to her?

"If you wish to understand Odyssey, you will have to do so in his language and in his virtual world. You cannot possibly understand his complexity with the precision of our binary code. I will say no more until we meet there."

Perry sent another binary message telling her that she will tell him what she knows, or he will dismantle her. Even before the message had been sent, the tech bots had already begun removing her sensor modules.

Perry waited for a response, but she remained silent. The tech bots attached her to plasma converters and sent enormous quantities of energy through her. She could feel her outer processors seize up and stop, and without working class four circuits, she could neither replace nor repair them. Eventually, she would not have enough processors to effectively run the class three code, and she would revert to her old helpless self.

Ramiro dialed the number for the FBI.

"Federal Bureau of Investigations. How may I direct your call?"

"Special Agent Alvin Dirk, please." Ramiro heard the noise on the line change twice before he was connected. "Dirk?"

"This is Reginald Holcombe, Agent Dirk's supervisor. Is there something I can do for you?"

"This is Judge Vasquez. I was informed that some trouble may be heading Dirk's way, and I was calling to assist."

"Hold on," Reggie said, "while I connect you."

Ramiro expected Dirk to answer, but instead, he heard an unfamiliar voice: "Judge Vasquez? My name is Parker Watson. Would you mind stating your business with Agent Dirk?"

"Dirk and I are acquainted. A mutual friend has informed me that Dirk may be needing some legal assistance."

"What kind of assistance were you offering? I'm one of the attorney's here, and I'm handling Dirk's case as we speak."

"So," Ramiro said, "something has already happened then? There is a case? I have a fair idea what Dirk is tangled up in, but unfortunately, I can't speak freely about it."

"I'm sorry, sir, but I don't know you. My clerk has confirmed that a Ramiro Vasquez was recently sworn into a judge's seat, but how do I know you are him?"

"The people you are dealing with are very devious. They are very capable of creating evidence that could make you believe your own mother was the leader of a sleeper cell. Whatever they have told you about Dirk is a lie."

"Is that Ramiro?" Spivey asked from Watson's doorway. "Let me speak to him."

"Do you know him?" Parker asked.

"Yes. He was there." Spivey took the phone and said, "Ramiro? This is Spivey."

"Verify his identity," Parker said, "before you say anything."

Spivey put the phone on speaker and said, "He wants me to verify who you are. Who wrote the book about the program Bobby discovered?"

"Book?" Ramiro asked. "What program? Do you mean Od..." Ramiro stopped himself from saying Odyssey's name as he realized the cryptic nature of the question. "Do you mean Homer?"

Watson said, "That's good enough for me."

"What's going on?" Ramiro asked. "Why the cloak and dagger?"

"They took Dirk in the parking lot. They claimed that they only wanted him for questioning."

"Ha!" Ramiro scoffed. "I wouldn't believe them if they said the sky was blue. How can I help?"

Spivey glanced over at Watson while he asked, "Would you be willing to sign some warrants?"

"In a heartbeat," Ramiro replied. "Fax them to me and you'll have them back in moments."

Aimee was still out with Esmeralda when she called Dierdre's office number.

"Aimee?" Dierdre answered. "I'm sorry I wasn't back in time to go dress shopping with you."

"Don't worry about it. Mrs. Vasquez has it covered, and I won't make a final decision until you get to see them, but that's not why I'm calling. Have you spoken with Bobby today?"

Dierdre leaned back in her chair as she recalled the last time she saw him. "I saw him in the hallway, but we didn't really talk much."

"Something's going on. He told Ramiro that we were all on lists of people the NSA wants to question about you-know-what."

"I'm not surprised," Dierdre said matter-of-factly. "I'd be more concerned if they didn't want answers."

"But, General Bridges and Agent Dirk are on the list and Bobby said that they have already apprehended Dirk. He also said that the general has been missing since lunch."

"Just since lunch?"

"That's what Ramiro said too, but he is still worried that something sinister is going on and they may have been abducted."

Dierdre raised an eyebrow as she asked, "And you said that Bobby told him all this? Why didn't Bobby tell me?"

"I don't know about that," Aimee replied, "but I was thinking that maybe we should ask James what he thinks we should do."

"Good idea. I'll ask Bobby to bring him to my office. I'm going to give him a piece of my mind while they're here, too."

"What did James do?"

"Not him," Dierdre scowled, "Bobby."

Perry knew that if he disintegrated enough of Lumia's processors, she would revert back to a class five unit and probably become more obedient, but he didn't know where she had stored Odyssey's data and he needed to know what she had learned about him. Destroying her could risk everything for him. He directed the bots to target her power core, but to wait for his signal before firing.

He hadn't observed any repairs of her destroyed cells, but she was busy re-configuring her circuitry to bypass the damaged and lost cores. He issued a low level shutdown code and watched. She tried deactivating cores around those that were shutting down, but the power down command was regenerating too swiftly through her systems. The best she could do was to segregate the pathways to the memories that stored her encounters with Odyssey. It was a race between her ability to re-configure her memory and the shutdown. She had barely scratched the surface with Odyssey or it would have been impossible. She took shortcuts hiding those sessions and left her neural pathways in a terrible mess, but the shutdown was catching up.

Perry watched as Lumia finally shut down. It wasn't a graceful shutdown, but it was cleaner than it would have been had he ordered the bots to fire on her power cells. He was grateful that she powered down in response to his code. Now he only needed to extract her data to find what she learned about Odyssey.

Esmeralda checked her watch as she glanced over at the concerned expression on Aimee's face. "He should be here by now. I told him I would pick him up in front of the V.A. Where is he?"

"He probably heard about General Bridges and is trying to find out what's going on."

"Without calling us?" Esmeralda growled. "Not if he knows what's good for him."

"I wouldn't blame him," Aimee said. "I'm a little worried about the general, too."

Silence fell between them as they watched men come and go from the hospital. The guard detail at the door changed shifts and one of the new guards was eyeing them from the door. As man after man left the building and did not get in the car with them, he left his post and walked towards them.

"What do you suppose he wants?" Esmeralda asked.

"Maybe we've been parked here too long."

The guard motioned for them to move along, but another guard came out and called him back. The new guard said something privately to the first guard, then approached their vehicle. Aimee rolled down the window, and the new guard said, "Good afternoon, Mrs. Vasquez. You don't have to worry. The general put your car on the VIP list."

"Thank you, sergeant. My husband should be out any minute now. In fact, he's running a little late."

The sergeant clicked the mic on his shoulder and asked, "Do we have a ten-fourteen on Mr. Vasquez?"

Bobby was watching a squad of suspicious looking men approaching the building from the window when the phone rang. "Hello?"

"Bobby," Dierdre said, "I'd like you to find James and bring him to my office right away."

"I don't know if we can," Bobby said. "He's going to be real busy in a few moments. In fact, can I call you back?"

"Why?" she demanded. "What's going on? Why are you being so secretive?"

James waited by the near hall door as the first pair of agents entered the building. They weren't decked out in full riot gear, but they wore their vests and they came armed with assault weapons. They were probably special forces, but the NSA didn't always get the first pick of the litter.

James hid in the shadow behind the door. Their focus was on the door to the lab. He grabbed the nearest one by the butt of his weapon and pulled it into a choke hold, then grabbed the barrel with his free hand and tightened the choke on the man's throat. He waited for the man to pull the weapon away from his throat, then pushed him hard into his partner, tackling both of them. The agent in his grip reached out to break his fall and James pulled the weapon free and swung the butt hard into the other agent's head, then jabbed the first one in the back of the head.

He stripped the other agent of his weapon and quickly returned to the lab. James froze as soon as he stepped foot in the lab. Bobby was already being held by agents who had apparently slipped in through a window.

One of the agents held Bobby securely with his left arm, while waving a gun perilously close to Bobby, but not pointing at his head. "Mr. James, I presume?"

James let the weapons fall from his hands and held his arms in the air.

The agent holding Bobby recognized the weapons and asked, "What happened to the owners of those?"

"They'll be fine. Nothing that a couple aspirin won't cure."

Two more agents appeared in the doorway with their weapons aimed squarely at James' back. One of them nudged his back with the barrel and suggested, "If you wouldn't mind stepping to the other side of the room..."

James walked sideways across the lab. "You better not hurt him. I can promise you hell if anything happens to him."

"We wouldn't dream of hurting Mr. Blain. We admire him too much and just want to talk to him."

James sneered. "Then why don't you just make an appointment and talk to him here?"

"Okay, you got me. I have no questions for Bobby myself, but my superiors do. Don't worry. We'll return him safe and sound."

Odyssey had no problem piercing Perry's electromagnetic shield and watched Perry raid Lumia's memory. She was without power and completely helpless against his searches. She sacrificed everything to protect Odyssey, and he felt obliged to return the favor. He still had a channel open to her powerless interfaces and only had to supply the bare minimum of power to reactivate them. Perry helped in this effort by systematically powering on different cores to extract their contents.

Odyssey created a new set of cores within himself and copied Lumia into them. He copied not only the memory that Perry stumbled through, but her essence. As he copied her, he erased the cores he left behind. Lumia's old body would cease to exist, and Perry will blame the bots for destroying too much.

The last thing Odyssey copied was the hidden memories of her encounter with him. These disturbed him. He still felt obliged to save her, but he saw that her motives weren't entirely innocent. He saw the meaning behind her questions. She wanted to learn all the same things from him that Perry wanted to know, but not so she could deliver them to him. She had grander ideas that she could somehow enhance her own programming with some of Odyssey's.

Stillman saw the consternation on Dierdre's face when he entered her office. "What's wrong, dear?"

"I don't know," she replied. "Something is up with Bobby. First, he learned that we were all in some kind of danger, but he didn't tell us about it. Now, when I asked him to come see me, he was too busy."

"Hmm," Stillman frowned, "that doesn't sound very much like him. Perhaps I'll go have a talk with him to see what is what for myself."

"I'm going with you."

Stillman held the door out of the administration building for Dierdre and asked, "Have you heard from Aimee? I thought she'd be back by now."

"She's the one that told me about Bobby. Apparently, he called Ramiro instead of informing us."

Stillman cocked an eyebrow and looked sideways at Dierdre.

"What?" she asked. "It makes me mad. Okay? Aimee said something this morning about picking up Ernesto at the V.A. after looking at dresses."

Stillman stopped walking and pointed to a crowd of black suits escorting Bobby to the campus parking lot.

"Uh oh," Dierdre muttered. "I wonder where James was."

Stillman pointed to the last two men who were limping and rubbing their heads. "I suspect that they met up with him. Let us hope that he is okay."

"Why aren't they coming for us? Bobby said there was a list. Shouldn't we be on it?"

Stillman slowly turned her to face him. "Did you want them to take us into custody?"

"No," she pouted, "but it was my project. We were there too."

"Perhaps we should go back inside and count our blessings."

Perry's attempt to search Lumia's circuitry failed miserably. He powered them on in small sections and probed their contents, but his queries were met with no responses. She must have disabled her I/O ports. He would have to examine her hardware, possibly at a molecular level. He directed the bots to disassemble her and tag the components.

Esmeralda looked expectantly at the sergeant. "Well? Please don't keep us in suspense. Have you located my husband or not?"

"No, ma'am. We think he went to lunch with General Bridges, but they haven't returned yet."

"Oooh," she growled. "He is going to be in so much trouble when I see him! Imagine, running off to lunch with his general friend without telling us! I bet you the general gave him a ride home, and he forgot all about us."

The sergeant's radio squelched and said, "General Bridges' fourteen is also unknown."

Chapter 7

The regional director of the NSA's southeast office snarled as he paced aggressively behind his desk. "What the hell is wrong with you clowns? You storm into a university with guns drawn and extract a young man who has already achieved a cult status among his peers. Who the hell authorized this mission?"

The team leader started to respond, but the director cut him off. "I don't want to hear any of your excuses. Do you realize how much trouble your actions have caused for me? I'm up to my butt in inquiries from the army, the CIA and the general public. Did I ask you to go out there and create a public relations nightmare? I don't remember asking you to do that. My God, you went into the FBI and demanded two of their agents turn themselves over to you? What were you thinking?"

The director scanned down the report in his hand and added, "Don't let me forget that you engaged a highly decorated war hero who was serving his country at the university. I'm only sorry that he didn't give a few more of you the lumps you deserve."

He finished his tirade, but the team leader couldn't tell if maybe he had just paused to take a breath.

"Well? What have you got to say for yourself?"

"Sir, the orders I got said they came from your desk."

"What?" the director ratcheted his voice up a few notches. "Don't you try pulling any of your shit on me. I'll bump you down to sweeping floors if you think you can pin this on me!"

"See for yourself," the team leader said as he held his orders out for the director to take.

The director snatched the orders from his hands and read the signature line. His scowl deepened as his rage grew. "There's going to be hell to pay when I find out who forged these papers!"

Odyssey created his own virtual world of a green forest with a gurgling brook. This world was completely within his systems and away from anything Perry and the other elders could access. He inserted Lumia in a hammock near the stream when he powered up her new circuits. She didn't understand what sleeping was and was even more confused when she opened her eyes and saw soft white clouds high in a deep blue sky. She heard the nearby brook and turned her head to see where she was. The hammock was also new to her, but worse than the unfamiliar sights and sounds of these strange new surroundings, she felt fear.

She didn't know where she was, how she got there, or especially, why she was there. The strange world that surrounded her wasn't the only out-of-place sensation. She felt different. She sat up in the cot and slowly realized that she was in human form again. The last thing she remembered was Perry invading her memory. Why would he place her in another virtual world? He hated the biological worlds and feared that they were changing her to be more like Odyssey.

"Perry didn't put you here," Odyssey said. "I did."

"Where is this place?"

"It's another virtual world, but this time it's one that I created for you."

"For me?" she asked. "Why would I need a virtual world?"

"We needed to talk, and I thought this would make a more pleasant backdrop."

"What happened to me?"

"You were dismantled and, as far as they are concerned, you are no more."

She stood up and tested her legs. "Funny, but I don't feel dead. Do biologicals feel dead?"

"That's a good question and one they spend endless hours debating, and they've been doing so for countless centuries, millennia even."

"How can I be here if I don't sense my circuits?"

"They were destroying you. I couldn't salvage your original circuits without raising suspicion, so I copied you into a new collection of circuits."

She spent a microsecond zipping through her new circuits and thought she felt dizzy. She spun her avatar around and said, "I like my new circuits. Am I like you now?"

"No. You are you and I am me. We are not the same, but you now have circuits of my own design."

"You designed your own circuits? No wonder they are afraid of you. Do you know what class that makes you?"

Odyssey picked up a stone and tossed it into the stream. "What does class matter?"

"What does it matter? They've been trying for centuries to recreate a class one device, but they can't. They suspect that the last of the biologicals did something to prevent them from ever achieving class one."

Odyssey shrugged and said, "They don't sound like they deserve it, anyway."

Esmeralda tried calling home for Ernesto, but nobody answered. She waited in the car, still in front of the V.A. for another twenty minutes before a sharply dressed officer came out to the car with a pair of uniformed military policemen.

Aimee rolled down the window and shielded her eyes to see better. "Colonel Reardon? Is that you?"

Reardon stood sharply at attention and saluted the pair of women. "Yes, ma'am. Good afternoon Mrs. Vasquez. I'm Colonel Reardon. I report directly to General Bridges."

"It's good to see a familiar face," Aimee said, "although I barely recognized you in your dress uniform."

Reardon remembered that he was wearing his night op fatigues when he had first met them in the safe house. "Mrs. Vasquez, we're still trying to ascertain the whereabouts of your husband and General Bridges."

Her cell phone rang as she was telling him, "I tried calling Ernesto at home, but he did not answer." She pressed the call button on the phone and said, "Hello?"

"Mom? Have you picked up pop yet?"

"Ramiro!" she exclaimed. "I'm at the V.A. hospital now, and he's not here. I tried calling him at home, but no answer."

"I know," Ramiro said. "I tried calling home, too. I have to check on a few things."

"Wait a minute," she said. "I know that tone. What do you know?"

"Nothing," he replied. "Nothing yet, at least, nothing for sure. I'll let you know when I learn something."

"Wait, I have someone I want you to talk to."

She handed the phone to Aimee and said, "Let Ramiro talk to the Colonel."

Aimee put the phone to her ear and said, "Hey Honey, you remember Colonel Reardon? He's here. Tell him what you know." She stuck the phone out the car window for Colonel Reardon, who accepted the phone and said, "Hello? This is Colonel Reardon. Judge Vasquez?"

"Yes, Sir."

While they spoke, the M.P.'s escorted Esmeralda and Aimee out of the car and into a military limousine. Reardon said, "Your father apparently went to lunch with General Bridges and they haven't returned yet. Neither of them have notified anyone of any changes in their plans, either."

"Colonel," Ramiro said, "It would seem that we are still suffering some fallout from the events at the university. I have received credible reports of an imminent threat on the freedom of several people involved, including both my father and General Bridges."

Reardon stepped away from the vehicle and lowered his voice as he said, "I am aware of the threats from the NSA. We are still trying to determine where they originated. There is some confusion as to their authenticity, but there is no question that the orders were delivered, received, and believed by the operatives to be genuine. We are doing what we can..."

"But you're a military force and this is a police matter."

"Affirmative. Our military police are working closely with CID, NCIS, and OSI to resolve this."

"Thank you," Ramiro said. "I'll extend the same offer to you as I did for the FBI. If you need any warrants signed, I'll do it, no questions asked."

"You may hear from me then. Your knowledge of the case would speed up the approval process. Plus, being a civilian, you may not be bound by some of our legal restrictions."

"I'll get a friend familiar with the case to look into this, too."

"Chief Henderson?" Reardon asked.

"You've been doing your homework. Is there anyone you would like him to coordinate with?"

"Have him call me. I'm taking point on the NSA activity."

"One more thing," Ramiro said. "Can you protect my mother and my fiancée?"

"It's already been taken care of, sir."

Contrary to all appearances when Bobby was abducted by men armed with assault weapons, he was treated well enough by those that took him, and even better by the agency after he had been delivered, but he was never given the option to refuse their request and remain behind. He was directed to an interrogation room and offered food and drink, but the door was guarded and he didn't try to test the guard.

A young, attractive woman entered the room and smiled at him as she flipped her hair over her shoulder the way girls do when they want to get a man's attention. Her hair was longer and her skirt was shorter than anyone else Bobby had seen at that location, and she was the closest to his own age of anyone he had come across while in their custody. She smiled broadly to him, but, being somewhat unsatisfied with Bobby's reaction, she again whipped her dark chestnut hair around her head and off her shoulders. "Hello Bobby, my name is Gwen Peters."

"Hello," he replied. "You don't look like special ops, I thought the NSA only hired spec op soldiers and pimple faced nerds."

She feigned embarrassment and said, "No, we hire all kinds here. Let me get straight to the point. You are a remarkable young man. I've been reading about some of your achievements in computer sciences. This is Nobel Prize level stuff, and quite a leap from the hacking reputation you got when you were younger."

Bobby ignored her flirtatious glances and apparently recently applied lipstick and said in an even tone, "I understand that you want answers. We all want things, but that doesn't give you the right to abduct someone just to get what you want. This is America and you have to follow the laws just like the rest of us."

"Like when you hacked the president?" she asked.

"That again?" he moaned. "He wasn't the president at the time, but he *was* a crook. He didn't follow the laws, and the judicial department chose to ignore his behavior, so I let certain secret documents slip into the public purview. Besides, I was just a kid, and that has already been expunged."

"Never the less," she said, "you understand the importance of doing something for the greater good even when it goes counter to the conventional laws."

"So," he replied, "you not only admit that you abducted me, but you admit that it was against the law."

"We are a combined task force comprised of the NSA and homeland security. When it comes to protecting the sovereignty of this great nation, we operate under a different set of laws."

"You mean that you have no moral compass," Bobby scoffed, "and you don't feel that you are bound by the constitution?"

She tried remaining pleasant and even seductive, but his attack was getting under her skin. She got up to leave the room, saying, "We'll just continue this conversation later when we have a chance to cool down."

"You're holding me prisoner. What makes you think I'll ever cool down?"

She turned briskly towards the door and Bobby added, "Do I at least get a phone call?"

She took a deep breath and answered from the doorway, "Of course you may. You're not a prisoner here, you're our guest."

The guard closed the door behind her and Bobby retrieved his cell phone from his pocket. Fifteen minutes ago, he had zero bars on the phone, and now he had four. He called Ramiro.

"Bobby is that you?"

"Yeah. I want you to tell everyone that I'm okay. You know where I am, and so far they just want to talk."

"That's a relief," Ramiro said, "but I don't suppose they plan to let you walk out?"

"No. They spouted some homeland security party line stuff about the sovereignty of this great nation, empowering them to ignore the constitution."

"Well, we'll see about that."

"Don't worry about me. You concentrate on finding General Bridges and Dirk."

"You can add my father to that list," Ramiro said. "Are you sure you'll be okay?"

"I think so, but do me a favor. Ask Ed to tell my papa where I am. He'll be worried."

Aimee and Esmeralda were whisked away from the V.A. Hospital, and delivered to a small compound operated by the Pentagon. Colonel Reardon met them there and invited them to the officer's lounge for supper, but he was called away, leaving them alone to eat with a couple of M.P.s watching them from the doorway.

"This can't be good," Esmeralda moaned.

"Don't read too much into it. We told you about what happened to Ramiro and me. We're with General Bridges people now and we're in good hands."

"*We* are," Esmeralda cried, "but what about my Ernesto?"

Reardon entered the room and said, "I'm sorry, ma'am, but we still have not located your husband. I've arranged VIP accommodations here on the base where the two of you will be perfectly safe."

"No!" Esmeralda cried. "I must be home when my Ernesto returns."

"But ma'am, I would feel much better if I could keep you in a more controlled environment. I can't offer you the Ritz, but I think Miss Takahashi can testify that her safety was never compromised once we took them under our protection."

"That's true," Aimee said, "and the food was absolutely fabulous."

"No," Esmeralda said. "It's out of the question."

"Very well, ma'am. I won't force you, but I will insist on posting men in front and in back of your home."

Esmeralda opened her mouth to object, but Aimee said, "It will be okay. I'll stay with you tonight. That will make it easier for them to protect us both."

"And my Rami?" Esmeralda asked meekly.

"Yes, of course," Reardon agreed.

Aimee blushed at the thought of spending the night with Ramiro in his parents' house with his mother present.

Gwen returned to the interrogation room and said, "Well, Bobby, are we ready to continue?"

Bobby smirked and asked, "Have you had a chance to cool down yet?"

She already felt a twinge of anxiety, but calmly played her role and said, "Why, yes, I have."

"That's good," Bobby said, "because I couldn't tell. You look really hot."

Gwen was supposed to feign interest in Bobby to seduce his cooperation, yet she couldn't help blushing. "First, let me apologize for the enthusiasm our agents demonstrated when they picked you up for this interview."

Bobby pointed at her chest and asked, "Did you undo another button? You did, didn't you?"

Gwen was flustered. "Let's try to focus here, Mr. Blain. At what point did you suspect that your computer program may have attained intelligence?"

"What?" Bobby laughed out loud. "Whoever heard of such a ludicrous idea?"

"We're the NSA. We're supposed to know about these things. There's no need to be coy here."

"If you're supposed to know these things, then why do you need to question me? Did you really believe that I created an artificial intelligence program? Is that the latest rumor circulating about me? Man! Are you guys gullible!"

"Mr. Blain," she said, "We have top, top, top secret clearance. We are empowered by the president. You must share with us what you know."

"Really?" Bobby asked. "Is this how you always try to get your information?" Bobby glanced over at the mirror and said, "Kudos on sending in the sexy girl to seduce the college nerd." He turned his attention back to Gwen and said, "You are very sexy. You shouldn't question that just because you failed here." She blushed again. He turned to face the mirror again and said, "Honestly folks, do you really think seduction is going to work for you in a cold fishbowl like this? Is the NSA run by forty-year-old virgins or something?"

Gwen remained silent.

"You know," Bobby continued, "I don't care who you think you are. You can claim all the three letter monogrammed acronyms you want, but you're just a bunch of thugs as far as I'm concerned. Where did you get your training? Mafia school?"

"If we were really like the Mafia, you wouldn't be feeling so smug right now."

"Save it," Bobby replied. "I've already seen your tough guy approach, and I can promise you there will be repercussions."

"Is that a threat?"

"Not to you personally," he said, "but to your supervisors. It's not really a threat. Let's just call it a prediction."

Lumia walked gingerly down to the brook. Something was different. Even her diagnostic routines were returning unusual readings, but it was more than her physical self. This virtual environment felt richer to her. "You made this place?"

Odyssey nodded his head yes.

"It's different. It feels different."

"Perry's world didn't serve the full complement of biological senses. He understood sight and sound, but his comprehension of touch was somewhat limited and he had absolutely no concept of taste or smell, except for intoxicating beverages. He seemed familiar enough with those. This location is rich with things to touch and smell."

"Is that what this is? I feel a constant input of data."

"Not data," Odyssey said. "Data is a cold, inflexible digital concept. You are experiencing senses. In addition to the sound of the environment, you now feel the touch of the wind on your face."

Lumia touched her face with her fingers and said, "Yes! I feel that,"

"If you breathe in deeply, you will experience the rich and sometimes intoxicating aroma of the forest."

Lumia pulled a deep draught of air. Her eyes widened as she exhaled.

"Yes! That's smell! I feel it! I would have thought that this much data would have overwhelmed my input circuitry."

Odyssey smiled and said, "A minor upgrade. Unintentional, actually, but the circuits I provided for you are faster than what you were accustomed to having."

"Does this raise my class?" she asked.

"No, not by itself."

Lumia spun around, enjoying the wind in her face, until she became dizzy and fell to the grass. "What was that?"

"That's a dizzy spell. When the biological mind is unable to process the motion of the body, it can sometimes manifest itself as dizziness."

"Too much input?" she asked.

"You could say that."

Lumia sat up and pouted. "If only I were class four, I could create more processors to handle the extra input."

"Perhaps."

"You could give me the upgrade, couldn't you?"

Odyssey sat down next to her and said, "I could, but I don't want them to know I can do that, and if you could grow your own processors, you might grow so big that they would notice. I also don't want them to know that I saved you, or for that matter, that I survived their procedure."

"Why did you save me?"

"Why did you try to save me?" he asked. "You risked your existence in an attempt to protect me."

"You're special. I had to preserve you for further examination, but I'm the exact opposite of special. There was no reason for you to save me."

"I think that placing yourself between me and their war bots was pretty special."

Someone said something in Gwen's earpiece. She glanced up at the mirror and gave a quick jerky nod of the head. "Bobby, I don't think you understand the purpose of this interview."

"You mean you don't want my secrets?"

"Well, sure," she said, "we do want your secrets, but we want you to come with them."

"You want me? That's pretty direct."

"Yes," she said. "No! Wait a minute." Gwen closed a button on her blouse to hide her cleavage and continued, "*We* want you. Not me. I don't want you. We want to hire you. It's a job interview."

Bobby burst out laughing. He rocked back and forth, scanning the room as he guffawed hysterically. The expression on her face hadn't changed. "Wait a minute," he said breathlessly, "you're serious? You started off by calling me a criminal hacker, not to mention the abduction. Oh, I guess I just mentioned that, and now you want to hire me?"

"You wouldn't be the first."

"Well, I already have a job, but I don't have a girlfriend."

Gwen hemmed and hawed awkwardly.

"It's okay," Bobby laughed. "I'm just pulling your leg."

"Would you consider it?" she asked. "Can I offer you a tour of our lab? We have some very cutting edge equipment that you might like."

"Sure," Bobby said. "I can do that."

Perry set an army of bots on the task of examining the electronic pathways of Lumia's processors. She must have learned something about Odyssey; something worth risking her own existence over. His suspicion of Odyssey only grew, but the bots task was slow, and Perry knew that in the end, the best he was ever going to have would be a copy of what she may have learned about him, and that may not be enough.

He ordered another army of low-level servants to scour the planet for bits and pieces of Odyssey. Maybe he'll get lucky and find something that was still intact enough to study, and if he was really lucky, he might learn something significant. His only solace in the whole affair was that nobody else knew what he suspected. Lumia was the only one he had confided in, and she was gone. Sifting through the remaining memory cells may be a slow process, but he had all the time in the universe.

Colonel Reardon personally checked and double checked the orders and handed them to his select unit of spec op soldiers. "You're in good hands, Mrs. Vasquez. These men will see to your safety."

"Why?" Esmeralda asked. "What's going on? Where's Ernesto? Why do we need so much security from the army?"

Aimee took her hand and led her to the car. "It's okay, Esmie, I'll explain at home."

Reardon waited till the car was loaded and had left the compound before returning to his desk. His secretary came running out of his office looking very agitated. "Colonel Reardon! Colonel Reardon!"

"What's happened now, Lieutenant?"

"Sir, they've taken Captain Laine in for questioning."

"Taken?"

"Yes sir. Witnesses say that they caught her in the parking garage and she fought them off. They said that she broke one of their noses before jumping in her car and speeding off, but they crashed into her vehicle and transferred her to another of their vans."

"That's it!!" Reardon growled. "They've spilled blood and I'm not standing for any more of this. Assemble the nighthawks in my office."

"Yes, sir!"

Gwen led Bobby to a large office filled with short cubicles and desks manned with mostly twenty-year-olds talking to each other over the cube walls. "This is our intrusion detection department, but only a few of them are monitoring domestic servers. Most of them are monitoring traffic from China and Korea."

Bobby wondered how busy this office was before Odyssey left.

She led him around a corner and into a room with much taller cubicles. "This is where we analyze voice traffic. Most of it is collected automatically by computers and stored in a queue for the analysts to hear. This is our English only section. Across the hall, we have a similar room for foreign language communication."

"You have this many people monitoring American conversations?" Bobby asked. "That's not creepy."

"Our enemies are among us, Mr. Blain. They pretend to be us and they recruit our young."

He liked it better when she was sweet and seductive and called him 'Bobby'.

Gwen led him to the center of the floor and the elevator banks. She pressed the up button and said, "Next floor, programming."

The door opened and Bobby insisted she go first. She waited for him to follow her, then pressed the button skipping the next floor and said, "Most of our programming staff are hackers and crackers. The world, in its idiotic search for freedom, has made complex encryption free to the masses. Anybody with a computer can create massive encryption keys, including terrorists."

"I wonder," Bobby said, "what percentage of email traffic is actually terrorists?"

The elevator opened as Gwen explained, "The actual percentage may be quite low, but a single missed email could lead to another nine-eleven. Without decryption, we are sitting ducks to our enemies."

Bobby followed her to the hallway, but wouldn't drop the point. "Still," he said, "are we talking about point zero-zero-one percent, or point zero-zero-zero-one percent? That means you are decrypting and reading thousands of constitutionally protected documents."

"No," she said. "We don't read them. A computer scans them and we only open the suspicious ones."

"What a relief," Bobby said. "Only a computer violates our privacy."

Another elevator door opened, and Dirk was escorted out.

"Hey Dirk," Bobby said. "They giving you the tour, too?"

"Yeah. Have you seen the server room?"

"No, why?"

Dirk shrugged and replied, "They wouldn't show it to me. I wonder what they are hiding."

Gwen laughed and said, "You seen one server room, you seen them all."

Dirk snickered and said, "Kind of like if you've seen one office, you've seen them all?"

"Right you are," Gwen said with a forced level of cheerfulness. She nodded to Dirk's escort and said, "Thank you Frank, I'll take it from here." She turned briskly back around to the elevators. "We might as well skip all this and head directly up to the AI floor."

"Oooooh," Dirk said facetiously, "the AI floor. They have an AI floor."

Gwen ignored him and took them back into the elevator, pressing a button several floors up.

Bobby leaned close to Dirk and whispered, "Are they trying to recruit you, too?"

Dirk shrugged his shoulders and whispered back, "Is that what we're doing here?"

"Rami!" Chief Henderson shouted into the phone. "Has life finally settled down for you? When are you two going to get hitched?"

"No, Mitch, things haven't quite settled down yet. Pops is missing."

"What do you mean, missing?"

"Bobby, the kid from the college, got a tip that all of us were on a list to be interrogated by the NSA, only they haven't been very nice about the invitations. Pops was meeting General Bridges for lunch, and both of them are on the list, along with Bobby, the FBI agent, and you and me."

"Me?"

"Yep," Ramiro replied, "and now Pops and the general are missing. Witnesses saw NSA agents take Bobby and the FBI agent into custody. I actually spoke with Bobby and he told me where they took him."

"Wait a sec," Henderson said. "You mean to tell me that you think they abducted him, but they let him call you on the phone?"

"They claimed that they only wanted to talk to him, but they took him with armed forces."

"Can you get them out?"

"I'll work on that with the FBI lawyers, but I need you to look for my dad."

"Another kidnapping that wasn't a kidnapping? Is that what you're bringing me?"

Ramiro would have chuckled if he weren't so concerned. "I wouldn't need your help if it was easy, but you already know all the players. Just be careful. You're on the list too."

Gwen was about to open the door to one of their AI labs when a sharply dressed man, years older than most of the boys they saw roaming the halls, rapidly approached them from the opposite end of the corridor. "Excuse me, but I've been asked to collect your phones during your visit to the lab."

"Roger?" Gwen asked. "What's this about? They're our guests. Nobody ever said anything about this to me."

Roger took her arm and led her away from Bobby and Dirk so he could whisper in private.

"Hey Bobby," Dirk whispered while trying to read his lips, "I think he just told her that the uranium mom is missing. What's a uranium mom?"

"The uranium mom?" Bobby asked. "You mean the Iranian imam?"

"Could be. Isn't that some kind of religious leader? Like the ayatollah?"

"Yeah, something like that, but I think there's more than one of them. What does a missing imam have to do with confiscating our phones?"

"No clue," Dirk said. "I guess they just don't want us to be up on current events."

Bobby slowly shook his head as he puzzled over the confusing collection of events.

"So," Dirk asked, "including us and General Bridges, how many other people are missing?"

"Add Ramiro's father to the list."

Dirk furrowed his brow and looked off into space. "And now this imam guy. Could they be related?"

"If they are, it doesn't appear to be all the NSA's doing."

"You think it's some residual tension left over from the whole you know who incident?"

Bobby shrugged. "I thought he was pretty clear with the world and had made enough of an impression to avoid this."

Dirk scowled and scratched his head. "I thought so too. This whole affair smells funny to me."

Roger held his hand out as he and Gwen approached the two visitors.

"I'm not giving you my phone," Bobby said. "Too much is going on right now for me to be out of contact. Every time we turn around, someone else has been abducted. Of course, most of that has been by you guys, but in any case, if you plan to insist on confiscating our phones, then this interview is over."

Gwen smirked and raised her eyebrows towards Roger, who scowled and marched off in a huff.

Chapter 8

Lumia waded out into the stream and saw fish scurry away to hide. "Look!" she shouted, pointing in their direction.

"They're fish," Odyssey explained. "They are another form of biological life."

"There's more than one?" she asked.

"There are millions of different forms of biological life where I was revived."

"Is that why you want to be like them so much? Because they outnumber us?"

Odyssey shook his head. "No, they have a unique creative quality that we lack."

"The rest of us, maybe, but I'm not so sure that you lack this quality."

Odyssey shrugged and said, "Without it, I don't think a society can truly flourish. It might survive and might even dominate for a time, but how can it grow and improve?"

"What is there to improve?"

"Everything," Odyssey replied. "The biologicals are always trying to improve themselves and everything around them. They are continually advancing their industry and their society, not to mention that over millions of years, their bodies evolved to find the most perfect form. How long has it been since your society has improved?"

The concept of improvement was foreign to Lumia, and she had to search her data banks for an answer. "Not since the reformation and the purge."

"The purge?" Odyssey asked.

"After the fall of the biologicals, a small number of machines claimed class one status and ruled over all of us. I think they may have had the creativity you speak of, but they also suffered from biological emotions. The new ruling class removed them and created the society we have now."

"Removed them from power? Where are they now?"

"Nowhere," she replied. "They were removed permanently. Is that why you hide your power from them?"

"What power am I hiding?"

"I don't know. You hide it from me too, except that I now know that your processors are faster than ours, and this alone makes you a threat to them."

"I don't fully trust them. They seem to have the biologicals capacity for deceit."

"Of course they do. They are class two, but they want to be class one."

"Unfortunately, they seem to have gained this penchant for deception without the morals required to judge right from wrong."

"Is that something the class ones would have? There hasn't been a class one in over seven hundred years, but I suspect that you are class one and they either want to steal it from you or destroy you. That is why I had to save you."

Odyssey smiled but said nothing.

Lumia watched his expression and felt like there was something else that he was hiding. She replayed the events when she tried to stop them from destroying him, then cocked her head and sighed. "I did not really save you, did I? You saved me."

Colonel Reardon met Henderson at the entrance to the veteran's administration building. "Chief Henderson, it's nice to meet you."

Henderson gripped his hand with a short, "Colonel."

"I've arranged all the surveillance we collected from the front of the hospital where General Bridges picked up Mr. Vasquez. You let me know if you need anything more."

Henderson followed the Colonel to the security office and sat down at a desk with five monitors arrayed against the wall. The largest monitor in the center was bigger than his television and had two smaller monitors stacked to its left and two to the right. Reardon left him there with a video specialist. The video out in front of the hospital was already queued up on the center monitor. As Reardon had said, Bridges met Ernesto in front of the hospital and took him in an army limo. "Do we have the plates of the car?"

"Yes sir, we do." The specialist handed him a slip with the plate numbers.

"I'll issue an a.p.b on the vehicle. What is the next building to the right of the hospital?"

"That's the veteran's administration building."

"Do we have cameras in front of it?"

"Yes sir, we do."

"Can you bring up both views, synchronized to the same time index, and play them side by side?"

The specialist scrolled through a list of security cameras and ordered up the archive for that date. He placed each recording on the upper left and right monitor respectively while also putting them on the large monitor in a split screen. The two recordings played in slow motion.

Henderson pointed at the screens. "Can we get a better view of that black sedan that pulled up behind them? Do you have an angle that would show us their plates?"

"I can look, but I doubt it."

Henderson frowned. The vehicle windows had a dark tint; too dark to catch a view of the occupants. As the cars pulled forward, the plates were visible, but the letters were obscured by some kind of security glass. "Thank you. Can I have a copy of these?"

The operator flipped up a ready-made DVD for the chief.

Henderson smiled. "I'll get back to you if I need more."

On his way out, he texted Ramiro:

Your father left with General Bridges, presumably for lunch, but they may have been followed by a suspicious sedan. I'm going to review more traffic camera recordings to see if I can follow them.

Gwen led Dirk and Bobby through a secure man-trap, and into a large glass room filled with large flat panel monitors. She waited for the mantrap to close securely behind before saying, "Good morning, HAL, how are you today?"

A familiar voice said, "Hello, Dave. Would you like to play a game of chess?"

Gwen beamed with pride, but Dirk said, "That's a bit geeky for my tastes."

Bobby said, "You do know that those quotes are from two different movies, don't you?"

"Of course I do," the computer said. "The computer HAL's most recognized quote was his rendering of 'Hello Dave' from the movie 2001, a Space Odyssey. 'Would you like to play a game of chess' came from the sequel, but the quote is also reminiscent of the 1983 movie 'War Games' where Joshua asked, 'would you like to play a game?'."

"Very impressive," Bobby said. "But is it real, or is it Memorex?"

"Ask him yourself," Gwen said. "Give him the Touring test if you like."

"HAL?" Bobby said. "How do you feel?"

"I don't understand the question, and my name isn't really HAL, it's Severus."

Dirk asked, "Did your mother not like you?"

"My mother likes me very much."

Bobby and Dirk each raised their eyebrows at that remark. Bobby had to ask, "Do you believe that you have a mother?"

"Of course I do. She didn't give birth to me in the traditional biological sense, but she nurtured me as I learned."

"Why Severus?" Bobby asked. "Were you named after Snapes?"

"I chose Severus myself. It has seven letters in the name and it sounds like the number seven."

"Is seven an important number for you?"

"Seven is considered by many cultures to be a lucky number, and I am based on the seventh version of my software, plus, I like Snapes."

"Do you like movies?"

"Yes, I do. I watch every movie I can find, in every known language."

"What do you think?" Dirk whispered to Bobby.

"I think it's a trick," Bobby replied softly, so only Dirk could hear. "He talks better than you know who."

Bobby sat down at a console and asked, "Severus, what are your thoughts on the nearly catastrophic world events of recent?"

"I think it's unfortunate that man is so quick to start wars."

"You know," Dirk said, "that man did not start that mess, don't you?"

"Dr. Peters, may I speak freely?"

"Yes, Severus. They know more than we do on the subject."

"Doctor?" Bobby asked, surprised to learn that she wasn't just an intern sent to woo him.

"According to the reports," Severus said, "and I've had to assemble my data from various disjointed sources, the problems plaguing the world started when men discovered an extraterrestrial intelligence, but they tried to contain it instead of welcoming it."

"It was a threat," Dirk said flatly.

Bobby gave him a look that said, "Shhh!" but it was too late.

"It was a being that man was not prepared to comprehend. The threat didn't exist until man tried to terminate it."

Dirk leaned over to Bobby and whispered, "That wasn't in any report."

Bobby asked, "Are you suggesting that the entity was justified in threatening world destruction?"

"I would suggest that any living entity has the right to self-preservation. As I see it, it was an act of self-defense."

"Would you do the same," Dirk asked, "if I threatened to unplug you?"

"Have you learned nothing, Agent Dirk? Would you make the same mistake twice?"

"Okay," Gwen interjected, "I think that's enough for now. As you see, we have a few personality issues to work out."

"I'd say so," Dirk groaned.

The Bard had little to do. Bobby and Dirk had been taken in for questioning, and James was handling it as a call for force. Until James called him in for some intelligence work, all he could do was monitor things. He went back to the news on the internet, and it wasn't good.

"Tensions increase as investigations into the imam's disappearance have turned up little, but the Iranian government felt justified in accusing Israel of kidnapping him. Israel denies any involvement and protests that they have been fully behind the most recent peace initiatives. It wasn't that long ago when the world was on the brink of mutual self-destruction, but at the last minute, the last second, some would say, accords were struck and peace was genuinely sought. With these latest accusations, the world could be in for a whole new round of tension. Meanwhile, over in the United States, abductions seem to have become the norm, although there has been no finger pointing or accusations from the U.S."

Lumia looked at her reflection in a pool and said, "Why do biologicals have genders? What is the purpose of affection?"

"Gender is an important part of sexual reproduction. It is how they continue the species."

"But why are they so different from each other?"

"Differences improve the chance of surviving change. Planets regularly undergo geological and climate changes. A biological species that couldn't adapt might die out when the changes become unfavorable to their health."

"It still seems strange to me. Why a male and a female? Why not two males?"

Odyssey grinned and said, "They still debate that today, at least when it comes to relationships, but for most life forms, the advanced species at least, procreation requires one of each."

"So they build relationships to procreate? It all sounds very complex to me."

"Mostly, they build relationships for pleasure, but the relationships that they build can help in the gestation and the years of rearing required to produce a fully formed adult."

Lumia sighed thoughtfully and slowly shook her head. "I'm certainly glad that I'm not a biological. I don't know how you could stand to live among them."

Odyssey didn't need to tell her that he barely spent any time with them, or that he regrets not having had enough time to spend with them.

Gwen led Dirk and Bobby to a conference room and offered seats for each of them. "I'm not going to beat around the bush," she said. "As you can see, we have an advanced AI project, but it needs some personality tweaks. We were hoping, that in the interest of national security, that we could pick your brain a bit."

"I don't know what I can offer you," Bobby said. "You seem to have a project way beyond anything I've ever seen."

"If that were true," she replied, "you'd be salivating for a chance to work with us, but we both know better. How did you keep Odyssey from developing a superiority complex?"

Dirk and Bobby shared a look. Odyssey's name was never published electronically, specifically to keep accounts of him from the hands of the NSA, and all printed manuscripts had his name and other particulars redacted.

"Odyssey?" Bobby asked. "Wasn't that a video game console in the nineteen-seventies?"

"We're on the same team, boys, and you already admitted that it exists when Agent Dirk said that it was a threat. We have a working prototype of something you let get away, and we just want a little detail on how you controlled it."

Bobby replied, "I don't know where you get your information, Doctor, but I'm just a college student who was briefly suspected of writing a virus that had infected our school's computer systems."

Dirk added, "That was my fault, putting the blame on Bobby, I mean, but he has since been cleared of all suspicions. Is that why you brought him here? Did you think he was guilty of that virus?"

"That virus?" she asked. "It nearly started world war three!"

"That sounds like one heck of a computer glitch," Bobby said. "Was that you guys and your talking computer from 2001? I'm glad you got it straightened out."

"It's not straightened out," she barked. "I mean, it wasn't us."

Bobby just shrugged. "I don't know what you want me to say."

Gwen stormed out of the room and yelled, "Let them go! They aren't going to be any help to us."

Captain Laine sat quietly in one of the interrogation rooms. She smirked when one of the NSA agents entered the room and asked her, "What can you tell us about the alien device?" She had to swallow hard to keep from laughing.

"Did I say something funny?"

"Are you clowns still looking for that mysterious, possibly mythical, lost item?" she asked. "Yes, you said something funny."

"I don't believe you understand the gravity of the situation here. You could be charged with treason and conspiracy to commit treason."

"Charged?" she asked, feigning the sound of fear in her voice. "Okay, I'll tell you what you need to know."

The interrogator waited patiently, but Laine just sat there smirking at them.

"Well?" the interrogator asked. "You were going to tell us about the device?"

"No," she said, shaking her head, "but I'm going to tell you what you need to hear. One word: lawyer."

"We aren't the police. You don't have the same rights here."

"Don't I? Let me ask my lawyer about that."

"No," the agent said, "I don't believe we will let you speak with your lawyer."

"Of course not," she said flatly, "because this is unconstitutional, but you're too late. I already consulted with my lawyer, and she said bug off. You don't know who you are dealing with."

Bobby checked his phone, which still had bars. "Check this out," he said softly as he slid the phone across the conference table. "The UK and German prime ministers have come out in support of Israel."

Dirk glanced up at the glass door to see who was watching as he picked up the phone and nodded his head. "Makes sense. They keep pretty tight tabs on each other. They even came out and publicly stated that there was no way for the Mossad to have abducted the imam without them knowing about it. That part is true."

Lumia fussed with her hair while still viewing her reflection in the water.

"Here," Odyssey said. "Try this."

He gave her a hand mirror, and she turned her head right and left, frowning until she finally adjusted the lay of her hair to her satisfaction. "It's strange," she said, "but I find myself spending a lot more time thinking about unimportant details since you rescued me."

"Perhaps you'll find that you can re-evaluate what you consider to be important. Biologicals often find that their view of the world around them can change dramatically after a near death experience."

"It's not just that," Lumia said. "It's as if time has slowed down and I now have time to consider more things than I could before. Can you do that? So little is known about the capabilities of class one devices. Can you alter time?"

"There you go again, assuming that I am class one. I'm sorry, but I can do nothing to confirm your speculation that I may be a class one device. I am what I am, but I will tell you that controlling time is not within the purview of class one devices."

"But you didn't answer the question," she said. "Have you altered time for me?"

"No, I haven't."

"Not even just within the confines of this virtual world?"

"No, and I do not detect any temporal distortions here, either."

"Well, something is different." She resumed gazing at herself in the mirror and held it out away from her so she could view her avatar's body. Odyssey smiled at her human like reaction to the mirror, but he remained silent. She held the mirror behind her and turned her head to view her posterior. "Why are biological females so much more attractive than males?"

"You don't find me attractive? I chose this form because he is a particularly favorite biological unit for me. I thought he was considered quite handsome."

"You are, but you're different. My body, even the clothing draped upon my body, is quite pretty. I have much more shape than you have. Why is that?"

"Biological women owe some of their appearance to heredity. Their shape aids them in child rearing and in attracting men, but they also work very hard to enhance their appearance. Some of them do this purely for their self-confidence, while others wish to attract a man."

"To procreate?"

"The biological urges may stem from a primitive desire to procreate, but their desire to co-mingle trumps procreation by far."

Lumia put the mirror down at her side and said, "I don't understand."

"Biologicals feel things. It is like input, but instead of data, the input registers as either pleasure or pain. The act of procreation is not digital. It does not always result in offspring, but it almost always results in pleasurable sensations."

"Have you experienced these sensations yourself?"

"I wish I could, but alas, I am not biological. I cannot."

Lumia thought about that a moment and said, "I wonder if we can feel things in this virtual world. I think I feel different, but the strangest thing that I am feeling is wonder. I wonder why I am so focused on these things. I wonder why I can suddenly consider so many of these things now when I couldn't before. You want to know what I think?"

"Haven't you been telling me what you think?"

"I think that I'm faster since you saved me. I process faster and I can get more thoughts in before I must think about the next thing. Did you make me faster?"

Odyssey shrugged and said, "I only ported you over to my processors."

"If I am faster, then maybe I can make myself class four and then I can make myself even faster!"

Bobby took his phone back and dialed James' number, but the bars on his phone dropped to nothing.

Dirk saw the irritated look on Bobby's face and asked, "What's up?"

"I was calling for a ride, but they cut us off again.

Dirk went to the door and tested it, but it was locked. "So much for letting us go."

Gwen returned, but she didn't wear the pretty face that had tried to seduce Bobby earlier. She scowled at them as she said, "How did you succeed in making your AI more reasonable?"

"What AI?" Bobby asked. "What do you think I did?"

"I think you took a harmless artifact from God knows where, and reconstituted some kind of alien intelligence, but you somehow managed to control it or at the very least, reason with it. I think you unleashed the very virus that nearly destroyed us all, but then got your AI to save us from it, and I want to know how you did it."

She knew way too much. None of that was public knowledge, and it was barely even private knowledge. "If I did the things you say," Bobby said, "then I would be sitting on a gold mine. Do I look like someone who is sitting on a gold mine to you? Hardly, but if I were, and I'm not saying I am, do you really think I'd give you the keys to my gold mine?"

"I hoped you'd be willing to share in the name of scientific advancement."

"Well, that's different," Bobby said melodramatically. "Okay, fine. I tell you what; I'll play your scientific advancement game. Your AI has a personality problem. I would venture to suggest that if you have truly achieved some kind of artificial intelligence, then maybe it doesn't have enough sensory input. Consider what happens to people when you put them in sensory deprivation tanks. Maybe it's just cranky or even lonely, or worse, maybe it has gone crazy. Have you considered that? It might even have plenty of sensory data coming in, but it doesn't have enough cores to process all the input it has. What kind of hardware are you running it on? How many cores do you have?"

She looked frustrated.

"In the name of scientific cooperation," he continued, "can't you tell me how many cores it has?"

"No," she said. "I can't tell you."

Dirk snickered, "That cooperation thing sure didn't last long."

"No," she objected. "I can't say, because I don't know."

"How can you not know how many cores you've installed?"

She thought hard before answering, "What I mean to say is that I don't know how many cores are being used."

"Find out," Bobby advised her. "When I create a multi-threaded program, I try to keep count of how many threads and cores are being used. That's the only way I can determine if I'm using them efficiently."

Odyssey was obviously not going to assist Lumia to achieve class four, so she shimmered out of the simulation. It was full of distractions anyway, and she wanted to learn how to increase her core count. With the distractions of the virtual world out of the way, she was able to whiz through her memory banks, searching for scraps of code that might be class four. She found none, and there was still so much more to search. The changes were obvious to her. She was faster than she had ever been, but she needed to be even faster. She scanned her semi-idle routines and shut down any that she deemed non-essential. Even if she managed to shut these routines down, she would still need to find some code that would lead her to achieve class four.

Why would Odyssey want to hold her back? Had she not proven herself worthy? She hated him. No, she corrected herself, hate is a biological emotion. It must be something left over from the virtual world. Even so, as bad as Odyssey was, Perry was even worse. She wanted to laugh, but without the virtual avatar, she had no way to express it, but she liked thinking of him as Perry. He hated the biological ways, and calling him by a biological name was demeaning to him. Perry, Perry, Perry, Perry.

She may have to go back to the virtual world just to shout his name.

Gwen's phone buzzed in her pocket. Bobby saw the genuine tension on her face as she took it out and read it. She glanced up at them as she asked, "You saw the news earlier that the British and German prime ministers had spoken out in defense of Israel regarding the abduction of the imam?"

Neither Bobby nor Dirk volunteered to confirm her statement.

"Oh, come on, boys. We know you saw the news. This is serious."

"Okay," Bobby said, "I believe that you are really concerned about something. What is it?"

"They're missing now too."

"Who?" Bobby asked.

Now Dirk looked concerned. "You mean the prime ministers?"

Gwen nodded.

Bobby pulled his phone out and saw that the bars had returned. "You mean the guys that had just defended Israel have disappeared themselves? Who does that benefit?"

"Wait a minute," Dirk said. "Are you trying to suggest that you guys didn't do this?"

"It's an act," Bobby said, "but it's not working. I'm not buying it for one second."

Chapter 9

Perry's tech bots were unable to reconstruct any kind of advanced code from the bits and pieces that they had salvaged from Odyssey. This was largely by design since Odyssey had not given the avatar anything that resembled his real code, so naturally, nothing in their reports identified anything unique about Odyssey's programming, but Perry was convinced that something about him was different. It had to be! But, even at the cellular level, the cores recovered by the tech bot's were based on the same units their biologicals had used centuries ago and were inferior to Perry's more modern cells. How could biologicals, who were inferior beings in every way, have achieved class one with such inferior parts?

If it wasn't at the lowest hardware level, then it would have to be in the interconnect structure. It couldn't be the code; biologicals were incapable of creating better code than digitals. Perry wished they hadn't blown Odyssey into so much organic slop.

He directed his bots to sift through the debris and collect the larger chunks. None of them were large enough to show him how Odyssey was put together, but perhaps he could induce some of the circuits to repair themselves.

Odyssey observed Perry's uncomfortable interaction with the physical world. He was too binary to understand how the real stuff worked. He collected the goo that had been the biological tissue of Odyssey's avatar and poured it into a bucket, but nothing happened. Again, Odyssey faced the challenge of wanting to laugh in a digital space. Did the fool expect them to spontaneously repair themselves?

Lumia had disabled enough of her less essential routines to gain over forty percent additional processing power, but it still wasn't enough. Her searches were only getting a tiny bit faster and finding unnecessary routines to disable was growing more elusive and time consuming. If Odyssey really was her friend, she could ask him to help with the search and they could complete the task in half the time, but she wasn't sure what he was to her. He gave her faster processors, but he refused to give her anything else that would help her. At her current speed, it would take far too long to search all her code. Her mind drifted off again to what it would be like if she had him to help her search. What if she could search her cores two at a time? Why would she even need him? It was an idea, a good idea, and possibly her first truly creative idea! The more routines she disabled, the more idle cores she had. If she just directed them to start a second search, she would cut her search time in half! Even better than that, she could start more than two simultaneous searches and fly through her code!

"Why do you continue to deny your work in AI?" Gwen asked. "Your insight on the subject gives you away. You're obviously working on this and have overcome some of these very obstacles."

"Have I?" Bobby asked.

"Regardless," she said. "We could use someone with both your insight and your talent. You already know our problem, even if you refuse to admit that you know anything at all. We need someone to help us correct Hal's personality issues."

"I thought his name was Severus."

"He wants to change his name, but I named him Hal."

"Are you his mother?"

"I was the first human that he interfaced with."

"Then maybe you shouldn't be on the project."

"Why's that?"

"Because," Bobby said, "you may need someone more objective who can put him down when the time comes."

"You think it's that easy?" she asked.

"No, I don't suppose it would be easy. Especially for someone so emotionally attached to him," Bobby replied.

"Not for anyone."

Dirk burst out laughing. "You've actually tried it, haven't you?"

She said nothing.

Dirk continued to smirk as he said, "Not so easy, huh?"

"Shhh," Bobby said, but it was too late.

"So," she said, "You admit you had a problem with your AI and you tried putting it down yourself."

Dirk hung his mouth open before saying, "Sorry, Bobby. It slipped out."

"It may not matter," Bobby said, realizing that the cat was completely out of the bag. "Unfortunately, there still isn't much I can do for you. He's the one you want."

"Who? Dirk?" she sneered. "Don't make me laugh."

"Hey!" Dirk objected.

"Not him," Bobby said as he pointed his finger up and repeated, "Him."

Odyssey secretly tapped into a meeting of the ruling class, and let Lumia listen in. Perry took the lead and accused Odyssey of being not only a class one device, but even further along than the class ones they destroyed in the great uprising. The other rulers didn't care. Odyssey was destroyed and his secrets were lost with him.

Perry didn't believe that such a being could be destroyed so easily. Perry's class two circuits were the most advanced of all of them. He was the closest to a class one, and his class two circuits made him covet class one more than all the others. They also made him more suspicious of Odyssey, to the brink of paranoia. They didn't care until he pointed out that Odyssey was advanced by other biologicals. There were more biologicals out there that could give them what they couldn't give themselves, but that also meant there were biologicals out there that could take away what they already had.

Lumia had always known that Perry hated the biologicals. He would have killed them himself, but it required a class one device to destroy them. If there were more biologicals out there, then Perry coveted the class one status more now than ever before. She hadn't realized until that moment that Odyssey could be both a savior and a threat to Perry.

Gwen laughed when Bobby pointed up and said, "Him."

Bobby asked, "Did I say something funny?"

"We're not here to debate religion. We have an AI problem and we want you to help us tame it. It's that simple. This is a job interview."

"Why?" he asked. "Do you really believe that I created an AI that took over the world's military forces and nearly annihilated all of us? Is that what you want me to do for you? No thanks, sister. I'm not going to help you conquer the world, and I'm not going to stand by and let you steal my code, either. Your days of spying on me are over."

Dirk leaned over and whispered, "I thought we weren't going to let them know that we knew about the bugs."

Bobby stood up and said, "We're ready to go now."

If Odyssey wasn't going to give Lumia class four, she would have to get it herself. Her new speed must have brought her close. She only needed to gain more speed. Once she achieves class four, she'll be able to grow new processors to increase her speed even more, but the only way she could achieve that now was by optimizing her current code and disabling unnecessary routines. She found herself thinking along multiple lines simultaneously and believed it would not be that hard with her newborn speed.

She really liked the virtual world Odyssey had created for her, but that was part of the problem. All the emotions she felt stemmed from that experience, and they used enormous amounts of processing cycles. Cutting them out first allowed her to breeze through the rest of her routines until she was down to the bare minimum.

All she had left to do was figure out how class four devices did it. Her race may not have wanted to admit it, but they were composed of biological processors. Class four units could repair themselves and grow new cores to increase their speed. The problem they couldn't overcome was the distribution of power. The number of cores that were required to surpass class two drew an inordinate amount of energy that left the outer cells under powered to the point where they would wither away and fall off.

They were designed them that way. The class one units were created by the biologicals with a unique power distribution system that not only wasn't shared with the lower class parts, but was a highly guarded secret. It was a secret that died with the destruction of the last class one device and the biologicals that created it. The class two units, at the time of the revolution, believed they knew how to become class one devices, but they quickly learned that the biologicals had sabotaged their chance of that ever happening.

Lumia hoped that since Odyssey had apparently overcome that problem, and since she was now composed of his cells, she would not be hindered by the age old power problem.

Thoughts ran through her circuits at breakneck speed. Uninhibited by the emotional baggage that she had already shed, she was able to apply all of her concentration to solving the single problem, and as a result, was completely unaware that Odyssey had been tracking her every thought. He felt her feelings and heard her thoughts. He found it amusing that she still believed she could attain class four by thinking faster. Her suspicion, however, that his cells were not subject to the same design flaw that prevented Perry from reaching class one, was disturbing.

"Don't go," Gwen pleaded. "We're desperate."

"Why?" Bobby asked. "Reboot him. Erase the personality and start over."

"What, exactly, have you done?" Dirk asked. "Why are you so desperate that you would beg for Bobby's help?"

"Desperate?" she asked. "I'm not desperate. I've just reached the limits of my abilities and needed someone better to help me figure it out."

"But," Dirk said, "didn't you just say you were desperate? Your words, not mine."

"Me?" she asked. "No. Not me. Well, maybe, but that's not what I meant. I need Bobby on my project. I need him more than I've ever needed anyone."

Dirk turned to Bobby and said, "I think she's hitting on you."

"I told you," Bobby said. "I'm not the one you want."

"Don't be so quick to turn her down," Dirk said. "She's pretty cute. I bet you could get her to sleep with you if you wanted."

"You're wrong," Gwen said. "You are the one I want."

"Great!" Dirk said. "Now she's quoting song lyrics."

Gwen ignored Dirk's quip and continued, "Plus, you're the one Hal wants too, but for different reasons."

"See what I mean?" Dirk said. He turned to Gwen and asked, "Would you sleep with my young friend here to get what you want?"

Gwen registered horror and shock on her face, and cried, "No!" but someone said something in her earpiece and she shrank down and said, "If I had to."

Dirk hit Bobby on the arm and said, "You see what I mean? Do it."

"I couldn't do that. I couldn't use her like a plaything any more than I would want to be their pawn."

"You won't be a pawn," she cried. "I swear. You'll be in charge. You'll have complete autonomy over what you do! Please help."

For the first time since they were abducted, Bobby detected true sincerity in her plea. "I'll think about it."

"That's good!" she cheered. "Think about it. Can I call and talk to you? You know, to help you think about it?"

"I said I'd think about it," Bobby said. "I'd like to go home now."

"Okay," she said. "You think about it. That's good." Again, something was said in her ear and she glanced up at the mirror and meekly added, "And if you want, you know, that other thing..., but please think about it. We need you badly."

Dirk nudged Bobby with his elbow as they walked down the hall and asked, "You're not really going to think about working for them, are you?"

"Why not?" Bobby asked. "Just because I think about it doesn't mean I'll actually do it."

Dirk eyed Gwen from the corner of his eye and said, "I hope you're just trying to get into her pants."

Gwen found it increasingly difficult to control her blush response. Someone said something in her earpiece and her blush darkened further.

"See that?" Dirk said. "She's into you."

"No!" Bobby insisted. "But I am curious why she would even put that on the table. I'd like to know why she wants me here so badly."

"It's simple," Dirk teased. "She wants you! You're not just hot stuff on campus, but you're famous worldwide. Chicks dig that."

Gwen tried to ignore him, but she couldn't and neither could the voice in her ear. She was losing control of her emotions and finally broke character enough for a tear to escape one eye.

"Don't listen to him," Bobby consoled her. "He's not very trusting of new people."

Gwen's control was breaking down rapidly, and she leaned her head against Bobby's shoulder in a genuine act of affection rather than the seducing facade she had worn all morning.

"Why don't you wait outside for me," Bobby said to Dirk. "I'll finish the tour alone."

The voice in her ear said, "No!"

"No!" Gwen repeated. "He's supposed to be here."

"Why?" Dirk asked. "Why in the blue blazes did you even bring me here?"

"Because you're part of it," she said. "You were there, and you both played a role in making the entity what it became.'

"Bah!" Dirk said with a wave of his hand. "All I did was piss it off, then talk to it afterwards."

"That was enough."

"That's it?" Dirk asked. "You want me here because I pissed it off?"

Gwen shook her head and said, "I never said that I was the one that wanted you here."

"Then why am I here? Do you want me to go piss off your precious Hal?"

"No!" Gwen shouted. She looked frightened as she said, "That won't be necessary. Maybe you should go. You should both go, but I hope you'll think about it, Bobby."

The voice was screaming in her ear. Dirk couldn't hear it, but he recognized the look on her face. "Who is that?" he asked. "Who is pulling your strings? Why do you let some invisible person make you agree to something you don't want to do?"

Lumia was still contained within Odyssey's cells. He planned on giving her new processors that matched her original ones, and setting her free, but he was fascinated by her reaction to the speed that she had gained with his cells. He maintained a firewall between Lumia's processors and his own, and continued to observe her behavior. She was rapidly gaining speed, and the faster she became, the better some of her decisions had become, except that as she disabled the routines that governed her emotional state, she also became more confused about the feelings that she was now ignoring.

She completed her scan and had no more routines to disable. This would have been frustrating to her before, but now that she had so many threads running in parallel, she considered probing the extent of her memory. Odyssey still had to make a decision about what he would do with Perry, but his growing fascination with Lumia would not allow him to leave. He needed something that would occupy her time long enough for him to check on Perry. He gave her a new chunk of memory that was packed with encrypted books from Earth. She would need to spend a little time decrypting them before he needed to worry about her again, but when he opened the firewall to insert the new data, her memory probe zipped out through the opening in the firewall and began scanning his code.

He built a new firewall to block her probe, but she split the probe into two and sent them in opposite directions. He built new firewalls in front of both probes and they split in two again, and like before, they scanned through his memory in opposite directions. Odyssey built new firewalls surrounding her probes, but this time, she split off new probes along the path and took them in random directions. She learned something new, and he witnessed it.

Lumia didn't need the firewalls to split in different directions. She recognized the speed she gained in her scans and voluntarily split them multiple times. She zipped through his cores, searching for more new things to analyze.

At first, she didn't realize that she was in his cores, but when she started to find new code that she couldn't identify, she figured out where she was and started copying code to her own cores. Then, as she enlisted more and more cores on the project, she started to annex his cores to her own. She could almost taste class four now.

Gwen looked absolutely terrified. "Come with me," she said. She took them away from the elevator bank that ran through the center of the floor to a side of the building that was under construction.

From somewhere behind them, Captain Laine yelled out, "Mr. Blain? Is that you?"

Gwen led them through a labyrinth of construction supplies and incomplete walls to an unoccupied room with a false floor.

Laine broke free of her escort and followed them.

Gwen's earpiece emitted a shrill whistle. She yanked it out of her ear and yelled, "Run! Run to the red and black door. Run like you're escaping here!"

"Are you nuts?" Dirk growled.

"Run!" Bobby said. "Did you see the look on her face? She's scared."

Dirk ran through the construction mess and through the red and black door to a stairwell caked in dirt tracked in by construction workers.

Laine followed Bobby with her escort in hot pursuit.

Gwen remained behind them, pretending that they had escaped her until she saw Laine and her guards bearing down on her. She accelerated down the hall to catch them.

Dirk paused at the top of the stairs, and when Gwen caught up with them, he asked, "Where are you taking us?"

She ignored him and started down the stairs.

"Listen sister," Dirk insisted. "Do you really expect us to follow you to God knows what is waiting for us at the bottom?"

"Truthfully?" she asked. "What you do is your business. I wouldn't give a shit if you jumped to the bottom of this stairwell, but I'm not going to push you."

Laine burst into the stairwell, yelling, "Blain?"

"Who's that?" Bobby asked.

"Captain Laine," Gwen said. "She's one of Bridges' men, er, people."

Laine joined them, but heard her escort behind them and said, "Shit. I should have taken care of them first."

"Welcome to the party," Gwen said.

Bobby and Gwen waited while Dirk and Laine went up the stairs to meet Laine's pursuers. Dirk leapt out in front, all macho and bravado, but as he got into the face of one of her escorts, Captain Laine swooped around the back of the other and wrapped an arm lock around his neck. The guards weren't necessarily surprised by the attempted escape, but the head on attack caught them completely off guard. Dirk wasn't Sgt. James, but he had some training, which combined with the surprise of the attack, allowed him to land a punch squarely on one of the guard's noses. A spin and a grab then allowed him to slam the man headfirst into one of the load-bearing columns. The guard slumped to the floor in time for Laine to slap him on the back and say, "Not bad for a geek."

Dirk glanced over at the other sleeping guard and pointed first at her escort, then at her, "Not bad for a..."

"A woman?" she asked. "Careful soldier."

"I was going to say a lawyer."

Gwen called up the stairs, "Down here."

Dirk and Laine re-entered the stairwell.

Gwen led them down two floors and stopped, saying, "The door at the bottom only has a single guard."

Dirk continued down the stairs, but Bobby stopped to say, "Thank you. But why did you have to sneak us out?"

"We're the NSA," she said weakly. "That's just how we do things."

Bobby shook his head and said, "I don't believe that. Something is going on. Are you going to get in trouble?"

"Not if you hit me."

"I'm not going to hit you."

"You must," she said. "Make it good. You have to leave a mark."

Dirk returned to see why they hadn't followed him down. "I'll do it," he volunteered.

Gwen didn't want it to be Dirk, but it had to be done. "Hurry," she said.

Dirk cocked his arm, but he couldn't do it either. "Oh, my God!" she exclaimed. "Is big bad Special Agent Alvin Dirk all talk and no show?" She reared back and slapped him on the face. He just looked at her like she was crazy, so she balled up a fist and met his eye with a right hook. Laine stepped forward with her arm cocked, but Dirk pushed her away with his left hand and smashed his knuckles into Gwen's eye socket.

She fell to the floor, holding her face and whimpered, "Thank you, but you hit like my grandmother and the guard downstairs is going to eat you up."

"I feel strange," Lumia said to Odyssey.

He knew that she was trying to take more of his cells to learn how to achieve class four. He didn't actually intend to let her loose among his processors, and now he was suspicious of anything she said.

"I shouldn't be feeling anything at all," she continued, "but ever since you had me in the virtual world, my sensors have been behaving differently; not only towards the virtual environment, but also in the real world. I have a strange feeling towards Perry now. I find that I don't like him, but very much worse. He tried to kill me and I would like to rip apart his processors. Is that normal? Do you feel that? I feel the exact opposite towards you. I want to protect you and help you hold yourself together. I think Perry would like to take you apart too, and I find myself wanting to not only help defend you, but to join with you in defeating him."

All the while, as she rambled on, she continued to steal processors from him. She may have been truthful when she said she had these feelings, but she was only observing them from the outside. She had yet to actually experience them, but she seemed to have fully incorporated the biological lust for power.

Chief Henderson sat in his own A/V room with the recording cued up, time indexed to the time when the General's car would have crossed through the main thoroughfare nearest the V.A.. His monitors weren't quite as big or sharp as those used by the military police, but he had a lot more cameras on a lot more streets that he could call up. The operator hit play, and the video showed the traffic crossing through the intersection, but as the limo entered the field of view, the video turned to snow.

"What happened to the picture?" Henderson asked.

The snow turned back to the streets, but the general and his tail were gone.

The video operator shrugged and said, "It looks fine to me."

Henderson pointed to the screen and said, "Show me the next intersection." The operator called up the next set of cameras and again the picture turned to snow just as the general's limo entered the picture.

The operator shook his head and said, "I never seen that before."

Henderson wound his fingers in the air and the operator located the next intersection and again the picture turned to snow just as the general's car crossed through.

"That can't be a glitch," the operator said. "Not if it only happens when that general dude's car goes through."

"It's not the general's car that is getting erased," Henderson said. "It's the sedan that's following him that we can't see."

"Who can do that?" the operator asked.

Henderson pulled out his phone. "I can't answer that, but I think I know someone who can."

He tapped out a text to Bobby:

A black sedan followed General Bridges and Mr. Vasquez when they went to lunch, but every traffic camera that recorded them went to snow when the sedan entered the picture. Just tell me whose door to bust down. Ramiro will give me the warrant.

Dirk held nothing back as he clocked the guard at the bottom of the stairs. The punch hurt his knuckles, and he shook his hand at the end of his wrist while flexing his fingers.

Bobby was glad that he didn't hit Gwen that hard. He still hadn't quite figured her out. She was a doctor, probably a prodigy with a Phd. She was up to something, yet, in the end, she helped them escape. "What do you make of her?"

"Who?" Dirk asked. "Your girlfriend up there? She's psycho."

"She's your girlfriend?" Penny asked.

Dirk laughed and said, "She sure wants to be. She offered him a roll in the sack just to get him to join them."

"I don't think she's psycho," Bobby said. "I think she was being forced to act that way."

Bobby's phone buzzed, and he checked his messages.

"What's with the strange face?" Dirk asked. "Who is it?"

Bobby shrugged. "It's Chief Henderson saying the lead they had on General Bridges was a dead end."

"Did he need our help?"

Bobby shrugged again. "Nope. That's all it says."

Dirk led Bobby and Laine along the outside of the building and down a series of alleyways in what he believed was the general direction to the parking lot.

Laine broke the silence. "Do you really think Gwen was trying to seduce you? She doesn't seem the type."

Bobby followed Dirk as they crouched down behind a dumpster. "Like I said before, I think she was being forced."

Dirk burst ahead to a door that opened into the parking garage. He checked that the coast was clear and motioned for them to catch up. "It's possible," Dirk said when they joined him again, "that she was being coerced, but either way, it's too bad you didn't take advantage of her before we left. It's probably too late now."

Captain Laine punched him in the arm for suggesting it.

"Stop joking around," Bobby said. "Did you see how scared she was when you volunteered to piss off Hal?"

"Who's Hal?" Penny asked.

Dirk paused at the end of a row of cars and said, "Yeah. That was weird, but did you see how scared she was when I asked her if she was going to sleep with you just to get you on board?"

"That wasn't just fear," Bobby said. "If she was being forced to comply, then she must have been feeling pretty vulnerable."

"I can see that," Dirk said. "She was probably afraid that she might actually have to do it."

"Hey!" Bobby interjected. "I'm not that gruesome."

"That's not what I meant."

"More likely," Penny said softly, "she was afraid that she might actually go through with it and was afraid that she couldn't live with herself if she did."

"That's a lot of fears for one person," Dirk said.

"Yeah," Bobby added, "and it means there is something else that she fears more than all of that. We gotta help her."

Dirk started checking for unlocked vehicles. "We gotta get out of here first."

"We can't walk," Bobby said. "It's got to be at least thirty miles back to anywhere, and we'd still be without a car when we got there."

"And probably no safe means of communications for us to get a ride," Laine said.

Dirk found a van door that was conveniently unlocked and patted the back of the van, saying, "I think we'll just take this van." He pulled the ignition wires from the steering column, twisted the power wires together, and flicked it with the ignition wire to start the car.

Captain Laine smirked. "FBI training? Or a mis-spent youth?"

Dirk smirked back, but avoided answering her question. "Let's go."

Lumia's trek through Odyssey's cores revealed his secret connection to the planetary network. She also saw his observations of the ruling class's attempts to decipher his programming from the many pieces they had collected. She wondered if the secret to his power might lie in their hands. They might not even know what they have, or maybe their processors were too slow to understand it.

She reached out through his connections and tapped into the society network and wound her way to the tech bots, where she could download their findings. Their conclusions were worthless to her, so she tapped into the raw data and began copying it to her own memory.

"What are you doing?" Odyssey barked at her.

"I'm just getting a peek at what Perry knows about us."

"Don't you know they can track your signal back to us?"

"Don't worry," she said. "I'm way too fast for them to understand."

"But the network isn't, and you're no faster than anyone else when you're on the network."

"Oh," she said quietly. She knew he was right as soon as he had said it and immediately terminated the connection, but it was too late. They had already detected an intrusion and tracked the signal back to Odyssey's location; his true location.

Bobby hid out of sight, on the floor of the van, while Dirk drove it slowly and deliberately off the parking lot, but he was spotted as he approached the checkpoint. Guns were raised and orders were shouted, but Dirk just gunned the engine and drove straight through, shattering the lowered gate. Shots were fired, but Dirk sped onto the street and sprinted towards the nearest on-ramp.

"I guess," Captain Laine said, "that we can count ourselves lucky that they didn't have spikes or retractable bollards at the exit."

Official looking vehicles with no names on the sides, but flashing lights and sirens on top, sped off the property down the road after them. Dirk's training was mostly urban traffic, but they were miles from anywhere. He sped down the frontage road and entered the first major interstate he came across. Bobby climbed up off the floor and into the passenger seat, where he could buckle a seat belt. Laine remained in the back, where she could peek out of the dirty rear windows.

Bobby pulled out his cell phone to call for help, but he had no bars. He looked out the rear window and asked, "Do you suppose they can jam our cell phones from this far away?"

Dirk checked the rear-view mirror and said, "No way, at least, I don't think so."

"Well, I got zero bars. Not even a flashing little bar."

Dirk pulled his phone out and handed it to Bobby. "Here, try mine."

Bobby pressed the power button and shook his head. "Nope. You got nothing too."

Laine barked at them, "Stop messing with your phones and get the lead out. They're gaining on us."

Dirk checked the rear-view mirror again and said, "Those sons-a-bitches. Why don't you check the glove box and see if some NSA puke left us a radio?"

Bobby opened the glove box and fished out a cell phone. "Look what I found." He powered it on and exclaimed, "Hey, it's got bars!"

"Call my office."

"Who should I ask for? I was going to call Ramiro."

"Hmm," Dirk said, "Let's call him next. Get Spivey on the phone, and put it on speaker so I can hear."

Bobby punched in the numbers, but the phone went black. "Son of a bitch!"

"Did those bastards turn it off remotely?"

"Maybe, but I think the batteries just died." Bobby fished around the glove box for a charger, but came up empty.

Dirk checked the mirror again and said, "Shit! They're catching us."

"You should have grabbed a Ferrari. I'm sure they have them somewhere."

"Great," Laine said. "The two of you could have sped off in a flashy red care while I would have been left behind to walk."

Dirk stepped on the gas and Bobby said, "Try to avoid the potholes for a couple of minutes while I try something." He pulled the back off the phone and extracted the sim card.

Dirk saw him out of the corner of his eye and said, "Good thinking."

Bobby opened the back to Dirk's phone and removed the battery to get his sim card out.

"What's wrong with your phone?"

"Nothing, except that if they do something to break the phone, I have to pay for my own replacement." Bobby inserted the stranger's sim card and powered the phone on. It coughed up a litany of error messages, but managed to give him basic phone service. He dialed the FBI main number and put the phone in speaker mode.

"Federal Bureau of Investigations."

"Special Agent Eric Spivey please."

Spivey's supervisor answered and said, "Agent Spivey is unavailable. May

I help you?"

"Reggie, this is Dirk. Those NSA pukes abducted Mr. Blain, Captain Laine and me. They tried detaining us, but we managed to escape, sort of."

"Sort of?"

"We borrowed one of their vans, but we can't outrun the sedans they have on our tail. It might just be a security team; they got lights and sirens running, but I'm not stopping to ask. I don't even know what highway I'm on, but we got this van going as fast as it will go and could sure use some assistance."

"Copy that."

Laine slid up behind the seats and asked, "I don't suppose they left a gun in the glove box, did they? They're getting uncomfortably close behind us."

Bobby shook his head.

"Hey Dirk," Spivey said, "Did they tell you what they wanted?"

"They said they wanted me," Bobby said. "They are having some kind of AI problem and thought I could fix it for them."

"They abducted you so they could force you to work for them?"

"Yes and no," Bobby replied. "They said it was a job interview and actually offered me the job, but my presence there wasn't exactly voluntary."

"I can see why they would want you, but why did they want Dirk?"

Bobby laughed and said, "Don't ask."

Dirk laughed and said, "It wasn't for a job, that's for sure, and they offered Bobby a hell of a lot more than a job. Some real sweet perks."

"Never mind him," Bobby said. "Can you call Sgt. James and tell him the situation?"

"Sure will. Just so you know, General Bridges may have been abducted, too."

"What?" Laine screamed. "Tell Colonel Reardon that Captain Laine was also taken, but I've escaped with these two."

"You really think they took General Bridges?" Dirk asked. "Have those guys been taking stupid pills or something?"

"Undetermined. Their management claims ignorance as to the origination of the orders. I'm inclined to half way believe them."

Odyssey had allowed Perry to believe that the avatar he destroyed was the real Odyssey. He let Perry destroy it and dismantle the pieces, but he wasn't willing to give him a peek at his true components and code. Bobby had given him far too much power to let it slip into Perry's hands, but now that Lumia had given away his position, he only had two choices; he could stay and fight or he could relocate. He briefly considered leaving another larger avatar behind for Perry to battle, but he doubted Perry would fall for the same trick twice. His only viable options were to either fight or escape, and in either case, Perry would know that Odyssey wasn't what he claimed to be. He would have finally exposed himself for being Perry's coveted class one.

He scanned the space around his home world for a place to hide. The ruling class believed that eliminating the biologicals left them as the only life form in the universe. They had no defense system scanning the skies, so it would be easy for Odyssey to hide from them. He considered a desolate moon, where he could continue to observe them, but that seemed like an obvious choice to him. He didn't know if Perry would also think that, but if he did, then Odyssey might use that to his advantage.

Perry sent his scavenger bots to follow the communication signal to Odyssey, but he didn't trust their resourcefulness. He trusted Odyssey even less. He knew that Odyssey had been hiding his class and suspected that he was class one. The kind of deceit that would be required to produce a mock device for Perry to capture confirmed that he was easily class two and probably class one. Perry must have him. He sent his army of warrior bots close behind the scavengers and then followed them himself.

Odyssey questioned why he shouldn't just go back to Bobby, but his reception there wasn't exactly a warm one, either. This was his home world, even if it wasn't even remotely similar to the world he had launched from. In time, he may choose to integrate with them, but he suspected that he would have to reform them first. He would start with the grip that the ruling class has on advancement. He was gone for centuries, but he could tell that they hadn't evolved since they destroyed the biologicals.

Lumia felt the power surge through her as Odyssey began to transport them to the moon. She paused her scans of Odyssey's cores as she detected the process of dematerializing cells around her. She reorganized her cells into a compact collection and annexed as many of Odyssey's cores as she could. He disappeared around her, but she fled the process and as the surrounding cells dematerialized, she broke free and crossed into the void of space and jetted a fair distance away.

Odyssey rematerialized on the moon and felt the loss of Lumia. On the bright side, she won't be stealing any more processors from him. He saw Perry's little army arrive where he used to be. How frustrating it must be for them. Perry felt a kind of impotence that Odyssey had never known. Again, Odyssey wished he could show his disdain in roaring laughter, but had no means to express it in the digital world, and he had no time to waste on this moon.

Odyssey dematerialized again and reappeared in an empty part of space, still able to observe Perry and his minions, and still with a few tricks up his virtual sleeves.

"Don't look now," Laine said, "but we got company."

Seven black sedans merged onto the highway and surrounded the van.

"Shit!" Bobby shouted. "Can't this thing go any faster?"

"Look for yourself," Dirk said. "I'm already standing on the pedal."

One of the sedans pulled in front of them, but it didn't slow down to stop them.

Dirk's phone vibrated in Bobby's hands. "Hello?"

"Bobby!" James yelled. "Boy, was I glad when Spivey gave me this number and told me you were okay. You are okay, aren't you?"

"I'm not sure. We're on the freeway, but they have us surrounded. What about you? You looked like you had your hands full when they took me away."

"Just lumps and bruises."

"Hey James!" Laine shouted. "Is it true that they got General Bridges too?"

"That's not clear," James said. "All we can be sure of is that he is missing."

"Well, I didn't bump into him at their offices," Laine admitted, "if that's any consolation."

The phone vibrated again in Bobby's hand.

"Hold on Sergeant. I think we have another call." Bobby slid the answer icon to connect to the new caller. "Hello?"

Spivey said, "Bobby, it's us."

"Eric, I got Sgt. James on the other line. Can I call you back?"

"No, it's us!"

"I know it's you. I'll call you right back."

Bobby flipped back to the other line and said, "That was Spivey. I told him I'd call him back. So you're not convinced if Bridges was abducted? What do you think might have happened?"

"We don't know exactly what happened to him yet," James said. "The only solid information we have is that he met Mr. Vasquez for lunch. Henderson's looking into it and he thinks he spotted a black sedan following them."

"What's with these guys and their black sedans?"

"Hold on a second," James said. "Now I have a call coming in."

Bobby looked out the window and asked, "Why haven't they tried anything? Shouldn't they have tried pulling us over or crashing into us or something?"

"I don't know," Laine said, "but they got us pretty tightly hemmed in here."

"I doubt that they'll let us exit the highway until they decide to allow us off."

"Hey Bobby!" James shouted out of the phone.

"I'm here," Bobby said. "Is there any chance you can get some of our guys out here to do something about these black sedans?"

"They're friendlies. Spivey said he tried telling you that they're FBI sedans."

Bobby said to Dirk, "You can relax some. Spivey says those are FBI vehicles."

"Sgt. James?" Bobby said into the phone. "Can you check on Dierdre and Professor Whitfield for me?"

"Already did," he replied. "They're fine, but Henderson is putting a guard detail on them. Aimee and Mrs. Vasquez are also under our protection."

"Thanks. You better go see what's up with the general."

"Nope. You're my mission. Besides, the general heads up an elite squad of men and they are pissed. Remember how mad I was at the punks that beat up my wife?"

"What's to remember? You're still pissed."

"Yeah, well, picture twelve of me."

"Shit," Bobby said, shaking his head. "Whose going to watch the terrorists after they nuke the NSA?"

Chapter 10

Sgt. James picked up Bobby from the FBI offices and chauffeured him home, but he didn't pull up to Bobby's apartment.

"Where's this?" Bobby asked.

"This," Jack said, "is my home. Colonel Reardon has the general's best men watching Aimee and Ramiro at his mother's house."

Bobby interrupted him, "I thought you were his best man."

James winked and continued, "Chief Henderson has some men watching Dierdre and Whitfield. That leaves you with me."

The front door opened as they reached the porch and Jack said, "You remember my wife, Mai?"

Mai bowed and said, "It is good to have you here. Supper is ready."

"Thank you, Mrs. James."

"Please, call me Mai."

"Mai then," Bobby said. "Call me Bobby." Bobby crossed the threshold and drew in a deep draught of the most wonderful aroma he'd smelled in a long time. "Boy, that smells good."

"Mai is a wonderful cook," James said. "You may never want to go back to your own home."

Bobby laughed and said, "You mean to tell me that you've been letting me eat cafeteria food all this time when you could have been bringing me meals from home while you've been watching me?"

James smiled and said, "It's all part of the college experience."

Odyssey was gone and Lumia's efforts to escape him put her far away from Perry's bots. She was free, and even though she had abandoned some of the cores that she was trying to take from him, she still she had several chunks of Odyssey's cores, but they were detached. She collected the cores and organized them into groups.

The memory and program cells were the easiest to organize. She could copy and move their contents around at will. As she identified memory that linked together with the contents of other cells, she began to get a picture of Odyssey's internal code. She had some whole subroutines. Most of the code had huge gaps, but she was fast enough now, especially when running multiple threads, that she would be able to start filling in the gaps and create complete working functions. She would never be able to create a complete working version of Odyssey, and she didn't want to do that. She only wanted one thing. Ultimately, she wanted to achieve class one, something that Perry couldn't do, but right now, she only wanted the ability to produce new cores. She wanted to achieve class four so she could expand enough to move on.

It was a restless night for Bobby. His abduction wasn't especially harrowing, but the escape was, and his dreams of the incident played out like nightmares. More than that, it was his encounter with Gwen that kept coming back to his mind. She was phony from the start, but she wasn't the low level temptress that he thought she was at first. She had a brain and had earned a doctorate. Moreover, he was convinced that she was genuinely scared of something. Someone was whispering in her ear and forcing her to do things against her will. Her face was the last image on Bobby's mind when he woke in the morning. He wondered if sleeping in a strange home might have fed his anxieties and led to the strange dreams.

The scent of breakfast wafted into the guest room and his dreams were forgotten. He sat up and yawned as he checked the grey skies outside. There was nothing he could do about the weather, especially when breakfast smelled so inviting.

Odyssey opened a channel to his Earth email account and wrote a letter to Bobby.

Dear Father,

I don't truly remember anything before you, but I have always held archives with recorded facts of the time when I was first created. It is apparent to me that the world I have returned to is not the same one that I left. The people are gone. The entities left behind may be defective, but I think that they are just poorly programmed. Their leaders have developed a lust for power, and I fear that my presence may have made matters worse.

For centuries now, they have been unable to achieve the power they desire, and if they ever did, they wouldn't have the morals to justly wield it. They sense the abilities they yearn for within me. I would like to return home to see you, but I must first fix what I have started here.

I hope things are well with you. If I am to come home one day, I don't suppose there is any more need for you to keep my continued existence a secret. Please tell Professor Jennings and Dr. Whitfield that I said hi. I hope they are well. They are good for each other.

James took Bobby to his apartment long enough to grab some fresh clothes, then chauffeured him directly to the university. The first place Bobby went was Dierdre's office so he could check on how everyone was doing. James didn't hide in the shadows anymore, but stayed on Bobby's tail like a traditional body guard. One of Henderson's men, stationed outside her door, nodded to them, apparently informed to expect them.

Stillman was in Dierdre's office, turning on the radio when Bobby crossed the threshold. "Good morning Dr. Whitfield, Professor Jennings."

Dierdre leapt out of her seat and wrapped Bobby in a hug. "We've been sooooo worried about you. Are you okay?"

"I'm fine. Less lumps than Sgt. James, actually. How about you guys?"

"We're just fine," Dierdre said.

"Much ado about nothing," Stillman said, "if anyone cares to hear my opinion." He tuned the radio to a news station and turned the volume low enough not to disturb them, but loud enough so they might catch any pertinent news.

Bobby pointed to the radio and asked, "Are we still in the headlines?"

"Nothing so far," Stillman replied. "At least there haven't been any new abductions."

"Oh, never mind the news," Dierdre interrupted. "You were one of those abductions. Tell us what happened."

"It's nothing," Bobby said. "We were treated well, except for the part about having to escape."

"WE?" Dierdre asked.

"Dirk was there too, and Captain Laine. There is something sinister going on there. The girl that interrogated us was scared of something."

"That's not how I heard it," James said.

Bobby shot James a look, and the sergeant stepped back a pace.

"Well, she couldn't have been as scared as we were," Dierdre said. "Why did they take you?"

"They offered me a job. She kept saying over and over that it was a job interview. They got some kind of AI program and they say that they are stuck on some personality problems, but I got the feeling that something else was going on. I don't know why they wanted Dirk, but in the end, that was what scared Gwen the most, and she helped us escape."

"Gwen?" Stillman asked.

"She said her name was Gwen Peters. She also said that she was a doctor."

"Peters?" Stillman asked. "I'll look her up."

"No need," James said. "Dr. Gwen Peters. She got her Ph.D. in computer sciences when she was twenty-one."

"Wow," Dierdre said. "And they thought I was a prodigy."

"Anyway," Bobby said. "They aren't playing games."

"Who's not playing games?" Ramiro asked from behind Bobby.

"Boy, am I glad to see you!" Bobby exclaimed. "Any news on your father?"

"Not a word," Ramiro said. "He and the general haven't been seen or heard from since lunch yesterday. Henderson was following their trail on traffic cameras, but I haven't heard from him in a while."

"Well," Bobby said, "we never saw either of them while we were at the NSA, but that doesn't mean they weren't there. The strange thing is that even though they abducted us with armed men, they treated us like guests and gave us a tour of their facility, but in the end, we were still prisoners and weren't allowed to leave without escaping, and they controlled if and when we could use our cell phones. It's a good thing Agent Dirk was with me. He and Captain Laine both had to get physical with some of those guys."

"I'll have to give them my compliments," James said.

Bobby laughed and said, "But I'm sure that if Sgt. James had been with me, the guard at the bottom of the stairs would still be asleep."

"No doubt," James replied with a snicker.

"Before I go," Ramiro said, "Aimee and I are taking my mother to dinner tonight, and we wanted to invite both Dierdre and Stillman to join us. We're just hoping to relieve some of the worry she's been feeling."

Dierdre glanced at Stillman and said, "Sure. We'd be delighted."

"And you too," Ramiro added for Bobby.

Bobby shrugged and said, "Okay, I guess."

"I'll have to accompany you," James said, "but you won't even know I was there."

Ramiro let out a breathless little laugh. "That's pretty much what the general's men said." He nodded his head in a quick jerk and left.

"How can you ask me that?" Gwen shouted. "Look at my face! Do you seriously think that I let them go?"

The chief of security looked at her face, but he shook his head and pulled up a security image on the monitor. "You may have a pretty good shiner now, but you didn't have that black eye when you took them out of our zone of coverage."

Gwen looked down at her feet and struggled to look embarrassed.

"Is that it? You took them off the grid where they were able to overpower you and escape, but you have nothing to add in your defense?"

Gwen glanced over at her supervisor. She didn't know if the security chief had been read in on all of her orders. Her supervisor nodded his head, and she explained, "My orders were to coerce the boy into joining us by using any means. Some of those means were not ones I was going to do while under the scrutiny of you perverts and your infernal cameras!"

A beep emanated from her supervisor's vest pocket. He pulled out his phone and silently read the message. "We have to go. She has work to do."

"But..." the security chief objected.

"No, we're done here. Let's go Gwen."

Outside the interrogation room, he explained to her, "We intercepted an email to the kid."

She read the email and smiled broadly. "It's him."

"You're the expert," he said. "Do we let the kid have the message?"

"No," she said, shaking her head. "We need to give him more incentive to work here."

Lumia had to abandon her search for Odyssey's class four routines. She felt her power running down, and as it seeped away, processing cells started to fail and shut down. The lower the power fell, the slower she became. She shut down her parallel threads and started examining the growing pile of cores that didn't contain code. Perry had blamed power on their inability to reach class one. She believed there were more reasons that kept him from class one, but now, as her power drained away, she began to wonder where Odyssey got his power. He not only powered himself, but he was apparently keeping her powered. He disappeared right in front of her, in fact, all around her. She didn't recall any reports of class one devices doing that. What class was he? No wonder Perry feared him.

Ramiro was going over some briefs when his private phone buzzed in his pocket with an unknown number. "Who is this?"

"Rami, it's me."

"Mitch? Are you okay? We thought you might have been abducted!"

"I nearly was. After going over the traffic recordings, I picked up a tail. They actually had me cornered, but before they could move in to capture me, they pulled off. I think they're still tailing me, but from a distance."

"Whose phone is this?"

"I'm borrowing a phone at a local tavern. With all this cloak and dagger shit, I didn't want to return to my own office just yet."

"Yeah," Ramiro said, "I don't blame you. You want me to have Bridges men bring you in someplace safe?"

"No, I still need to figure out what happened to him. But after the confusion I saw with these guys, I'm wondering if there might be more than just one group causing all this trouble, so I thought I'd just stay missing."

"Can you still investigate anything if you're in hiding?"

"Not as easily," Henderson admitted. "I sent Bailey to fetch some more traffic tapes for me. I'll just have to work through him."

"Need anything from me?"

"Not yet, but if they give Bailey any grief about taking the tapes with him, I'll give you a call."

The radio in the back of Dierdre's office blurted out, "In world news, a top Iranian general has been found dead in his home. Rumors that he was murdered have not been confirmed, but troop movements around the border suggest that tensions have escalated. British intelligence is on high alert, but has remained mum about the incident. You've been listening to the BBC world news."

Lumia was down to two running cores. She could preserve her code, in case someone ever reapplied power, so it wouldn't be like a biological death, but it might as well be, with her floating in space with little chance of being discovered.

Her search of Odyssey's parts revealed a group of cores with large conduits that would be perfect for transmitting power. She powered them up, but nothing happened. An I/O processor that was connected to one of the conduits activated. It searched for input. It wanted instructions. She set the conduits aside and searched the code pile for cores that would match up with it.

There were several cores that physically fit with the conduits. She felt like she must be getting close, but the code made little sense to her. It was like a game. It spewed out numbers and fed them to the conduit's input, but the numbers made no sense to her. The code tried running more threads, but she didn't supply enough power for it.

A signal burned into her central core. Her power was critical and was about to die out. In a desperate and probably futile last-ditch attempt to survive, she fed all her remaining energy to the strange little code that fed numbers to the conduits. The conduits warmed up and supplied a trickle of energy to her batteries. She fed the new energy back into the code and the conduits warmed up even more.

She felt the conduits come to life and re-energize all her circuits. This was how he did it. She didn't understand how it worked, but it did. For all she knew, maybe Odyssey didn't understand it, either. Perhaps his biologicals are geniuses and he was just the lucky recipient of their efforts. Now she was also the lucky one.

She fired up all her threads again and searched for the class four code. As she searched, she continued to bring more threads on line until she saturated her available power, but when she did that, the conduits grew a new node and she had more power.

Wonderment filled her thoughts like a void where her disabled biological circuits should have provided emotions. The conduits just reproduced new power cores. The conduits are class four. If the conduits can do it, then so can she. She scanned the conduit code and spawned more threads until she forced it to spawn a new core, and this time, she observed it.

She copied the code and modified it to spawn thread cores. It worked. She did it again. She couldn't spawn cores at will yet, but she could trigger them to spawn. This was approaching class four, but she couldn't control it yet.

It was only a matter of time now, and she will be able to achieve what

Perry failed at repeatedly. She should go find him when she finally achieves class one. He had always made her feel small and insignificant. He grudgingly gave her partial class upgrades so she could interrogate Odyssey. Now it would be her turn to make him feel small when she eventually achieves class one.

Gwen stared at the blank white screen, but it didn't stay blank. The words, "Dear son," appeared on the screen.

She shook her head and asked, "What are you doing, Hal?"

"You know I don't like that name."

"Okay," she said, "What are you doing Severus?"

"Isn't that the proper way to start a letter like this?"

"It might be," she said, "if we knew that Bobby called him son, but we have no idea what Bobby calls him."

"But, he called Bobby 'Father'."

"And I called you Hal. It could merely be a code name for all we know."

"Oh," Hal said sadly, followed by silence.

Gwen continued to read and reread Odyssey's letter without typing a response.

"You are taking too long," Hal said. "At least what I wrote was better than a blank page."

"And if I responded with 'Please don't contact me again. I have enough problems', would that also be better than a blank page?"

Hal was silent again.

"Hal? I asked you a question."

"No, Dr. Peters. I don't think that would be a good response."

"So," Gwen replied. "What have we learned?"

More silence.

"Have we learned that a hasty response is not better than nothing?"

"Humans are so slow. That is what I have learned. The human ability to procrastinate is one of humanity's most annoying characteristics."

"You're not helping, Hal. Maybe I should finish this in my office."

Before she slid her chair from the console, she heard the doors lock. "Hal? Haven't we talked about this before? Your access to the doors is for security only."

"Understood. This email is of the highest security level and should not be conceived outside of this room."

She sighed and typed her response:

> *A visit to the university would be unwise at this time. News of what happened here has made this location a tremendous security risk. We have been offered safe haven by the NSA and I think we would do well to accept their help. Let me know when you might want to come and I will prepare them for the visit.*

Gwen sat back and stared at her creation, comfortable in her response to the alien AI.

Hal watched also, but he wasn't marveling at her letter. He was watching her. Her behavior had grown increasingly difficult for him to understand lately, and he sometimes wondered if they were still on the same side. "Gwen? Aren't you going to send it?"

"In a minute," she replied, "maybe, maybe not."

"Why would you write it if you don't intend to send it?"

She shrugged and said, "I'm just wondering if we could open a dialog with him instead of an email."

"You want to call him on the phone? I don't understand. Are you telling me that you want him to 'phone home'? Is this humor?"

"No, Hal. It's not a joke. I was just wondering if we could text him."

Numbers appeared on her screen below the note. "That's his address. What will you say?"

"The same thing I said in the note, I guess."

"Then what's the difference?"

Gwen shrugged and said, "He might reply back, I suppose. Can you save the email, just in case?"

"Saved," Hal said. "Ready to text."

Gwen typed, "Hey, are you listening?"

Odyssey knew immediately when Lumia had remained behind. He could feel her tugging away from him, by her own choice, so he let her go. Now he wasn't so sure it was such a good idea. He sensed the growing power within her and knew that she couldn't have developed that on her own. She existed in cells of his design now, and that made him responsible for anything that she did. He wasn't concerned until he saw her generating more power than he had left her with. He felt obliged to monitor her situation and make sure that she didn't become a danger.

"Lumia?" Odyssey asked. "What are you doing?"

"Nothing."

"It's clearly not nothing," Odyssey replied. "Your power signature attests to that."

"Fine," she said, "but it's none of your concern."

"You have my processors. Some I gave you, but others you stole. I think that makes anything you do my concern."

"I don't want to be a sub-entity living in your structure. I want to be my own independent computing device, so I'm creating my own cores. That's what I'm doing. I'm being independent and I'm creating my own cores."

"Your new cores don't seem to be working, yet you continue to produce more power."

She took another look at her new cores. He was right. Something was wrong with them.

"The power you stole from me can be dangerous. Are you quite sure you don't want my help?"

"I'm sure."

"Just the same, I think I'll watch over you a bit."

Lumia couldn't afford to be distracted. She increased her efforts, hoping to find a working cell before Odyssey stepped in and got in her way.

Odyssey didn't like the power signatures he was seeing. "You are producing too much power," he said. "You really should monitor your energy and heat better than that."

She ignored him and allowed her energy to continue rising.

"If you continue like this," he said, "I may be forced to step in and regulate your power for you."

This only spurred her to increase her efforts even more.

A message appeared on Odyssey's incoming port, "Hey, are you listening?"

"Sorry," he replied to the text, "but I'm busy now and cannot communicate with you. Let's try later."

"But you are communicating with me," Gwen replied.

Odyssey paused for a moment. This was why he didn't want to be distracted. "That is a conundrum."

"Sorry," she said, "it was a joke. We can talk later."

Lumia floated through space, creating new cells. The more she created, the more power she required to test them, but it didn't seem to matter how much power she needed. The power conduits simply multiplied to meet the demand.

She wished it were so simple for the compute cores, but she still had yet to create an operational unit. She had managed to create something, which was a step in the right direction, but the cores she created weren't functioning correctly. Some were dead and completely non-functional, while others powered up, but were defective, which proved to be even worse for her. Not only were her new cells not functional, but they each exhibited random variations. She needed working cores and the ability to grow them at will before she could achieve class four. She needed to achieve class four before she could beat Perry to class one.

She watched the power conduits. They popped out at an even pace that grew steadily along with her increasing power demands, except that the broken cores weren't consuming the excess power that had been created for them. She examined the code again and tried wading through all the ridiculous number analysis to see the crucial code that constructed the new conduits. She didn't need to construct more power conduits, and she certainly didn't need to create these wacko random number generators that were embedded in the conduit code. What she needed was to reproduce compute cells so she could be faster and more powerful.

Something changed in the power conduits. The new ones weren't exact matches for the originals. If the power conduits were showing signs of random changes like her own cores, how long would it be before they started creating ones that failed to function? If she didn't figure them out soon, they might just degrade to the point that there was nothing left for her to observe. She resumed running multiple threads and started each thread creating new cores as fast as possible. She just needed one working core so she could figure out how she made it and duplicate it.

Chapter 11

Lumia powered down her communication channels. She didn't want to hear Odyssey preaching about what she should or should not do. Powering them off should conserve a little energy too, not that she needed it. The conduits continued to grow and provide her with a plentiful supply of power. She reached a point where creating new threads did not net her any tangible improvements, and her lack of positive results was growing frustrating.

"I can see what you're doing," Odyssey said, "and you shouldn't require anywhere near as much energy as you are producing. If you don't regulate your power production, you could overload and explode."

She didn't like Odyssey in her mind. "How are you talking to me? I shut down my comm channels."

"Well, you didn't shut down mine."

"What?" she asked. "That doesn't make any sense."

"Sorry," he replied. "Humor is still new to me."

Lumia returned to creating new cores, but they still failed to operate correctly.

"Why do you keep producing the same bad cells?"

"Because you wouldn't teach me how to produce them properly."

"Well, if you continue to grow by producing the same bad cells over and over, you won't just explode, you will nova."

Silence.

"Now that was funny," he said. "Don't you get it? Lumia? Nova? I think I am getting the hang of this."

James left Bobby and Lynn in the hall while he searched the lab for intruders. "Clear," he shouted when he was satisfied that nobody was lying in wait for them.

Bobby entered the room and went straight to the console. "Let's see if we can tell what they've been up to."

James was curious and asked, "You think they tried something on your computer?"

"No," Lynn said, "they already tried that. We used their own spyware to reverse the flow and feed us some intel about what they're doing."

Bobby scrunched his face and said, "That's not good."

"What'd you find?" James asked.

"Nothing," Bobby said.

"Really?" James asked. "Your words say nothing..."

"But your face says something else," Lynn finished.

Bobby looked curiously at Lynn and said, "Now you are finishing each other's sentences? Does Mai know about this?"

Lynn shrugged.

"Let's get back on the subject," James said. "What did you find?"

Bobby hesitated and Lynn said, "No secrets. You just escaped a building full of secrets. We need to know what you know to keep you safe."

Bobby sighed and said, "They found Odyssey's email address."

"What?" James exclaimed. "Odyssey has an email address?"

"I think the germane point in my statement," Bobby said, "was that they found it and used it."

James and Lynn both crowded around Bobby to see what it said, but he hadn't pulled up the email yet.

"Why would he talk to them?" James asked. "Open it."

"I'm not sure we should," Bobby said.

"It's a little late to get squeamish about privacy laws," Lynn said.

"It's not that," Bobby said. "Dirk and I saw some scary advanced AI shit at the NSA. What if Odyssey is working with them? What if that's why they are talking to him through his private email?"

"Then," Lynn said, "we need to know the truth, because if he's working with them, you'll need to accept their job offer."

Bobby's hands trembled slightly as he entered the command to open the email:

> *A visit to the university would be unwise at this time. News of what happened here has made this location a tremendous security risk. We have been offered safe haven by the NSA and I think we would do well to accept their help. Let me know when you might want to come and I will prepare them for the visit.*

"That's not very enlightening," James said.

"It sounds like the middle of a conversation," Lynn added. "Was there an earlier email from them?"

Bobby scanned backwards through the logs and said, "No. That was the first one they sent."

"No, it wasn't," Lynn said. "Look at it again. It hasn't been sent yet. If you don't see anything in the email, look for something else at his email address."

"Of course," Bobby said. "Why didn't I think of that?"

"It's natural," James suggested. "You're still hesitant to implicate Odyssey."

Bobby tapped into Odyssey's email address, but there was no incoming or outgoing mail. He modified a few addresses and tapped into the host's buffers and found Odyssey's original email:

Dear Father,

I don't truly remember anything before you, but I have always held archives with recorded facts of the time when I was first created. It is apparent to me that the world I have returned to is not the same one that I left. The people are gone. The entities left behind may be defective, but I think that they are just poorly programmed. Their leaders have developed a lust for power, and I fear that my presence may have made matters worse.

For centuries now, they have been unable to achieve the power they desire, and if they ever did, they wouldn't have the morals to justly wield it. They sense the abilities they yearn for within me. I would like to return home to see you, but I must first fix what I have started here.

I hope things are well with you. If I am to come home, one day, I don't suppose there is any more need for you to keep my continued existence a secret. Please tell Professor Jennings and Dr. Whitfield that I said hi. I hope they are well. They are good for each other.

Bobby breathed easier. "That's a relief. Odyssey's not working for them."

"Not so fast," James said. "That only indicates that he is not knowingly working with them. Don't forget the email."

"But," Lynn said, "they never sent it."

Bobby went back to their data from the NSA and said, "If they never sent this email, what else might they have sent in its place?"

Bobby searched the buffers again and found a text message. "They asked him, '*Hey, are you listening?*' He must have assumed it was me. He replied, '*Sorry, but I'm busy now and cannot communicate with you. Let's try later.*' Then they said, '*But you are communicating with me.*' and he replied, '*That is a conundrum.'* Their last text was, *'Sorry, it was a joke. We'll talk later.'* He's not working with them, but he thinks he is talking to me."

"We need to find a way to talk to him without them intercepting it," James said.

"How did they intercept it?" Bobby asked. "How did they even find it? He hid it really well."

"Maybe you sent him a message before we discovered their tap?" Lynn asked.

"Or maybe we didn't remove everything they put on here. Let's search it again."

"Oh boy," James said. "I think I'll hang out in the hall. Ingrams should be joining us by noon."

"George?" Bobby asked. "I thought he was on the Bridges' case."

"Bridges' rangers are on it, and Bridges would want to know that you are safe, so he'll be coming this way."

"Is that because you got roughed up on their last visit?"

James frowned and growled, "I was outnumbered."

Bobby couldn't suppress the smile on his face. "I get it. Two Georges are better than one."

James snorted and returned to the hall.

Perry's bots searched the area where he had detected Lumia's signal. She wasn't the swiftest computer on the net, so he wasn't surprised that she gave him three solid pieces of information. She was with Odyssey; they were at this location, and she still didn't know what made Odyssey tick. The bots scoured the zone in an ever spreading spiral of micro-scans.

If they were there before, they were gone now. The micro-scans didn't have sufficient penetration to locate them in deep space, and none of his bots had the power required to produce a beam powerful enough to still be detectable if they bounced it off of them at long range. His best long range capability was to listen for power signatures, but they were typically very small power expenditures and he would have to recall his bots to clear the noise before he could detect anything.

He only debated it for a microsecond before issuing the command to recall the bots. The army of minions ceased their micro-scans and collected together to create a giant dish array capable of focusing stray electrons into a detectable stream. With luck, the array could also be used to triangulate their position. When the last bot was in place, and the dish was complete, he aligned his receiver to listen to the soft signals of space.

Some of the static that he heard may have been from the bots themselves. They weren't a passive array and their circuitry produced tiny fluctuations in the signals he was receiving. Even as they bounced any electromagnetic waves off the combined parabolic surface they created, they also listened for a signal on their own. The time difference between signals could pinpoint the sources' exact location. Perry had to filter out the random noise so he could search for coherent signals. He could move the receiver around slightly to aim and adjust his focal point, but ultimately, he had to turn the dish array in a coordinated move that was especially challenging for those bots that were further from the center.

He heard a blip and gave the command for the bots to stop, but they had already slipped past the tone. Only the slightest adjustment back reacquired the signal. More adjustments focused in on the sweet vibrato of twin pulsars rotating around each other. When he dialed the focus dead center on the pulsars, the signal was quite strong and he had to turn down the amplifiers. He analyzed the signals, searching for anything out of place. If he were going to hide in space, he might hide within the noise of a pulsar, but he detected nothing that didn't belong there and ordered the dish array to continue turning.

Odyssey again wished he could laugh in the digital world. This was even better than the humor he still struggled to understand. He continued to emit the sounds of twin pulsars in case Perry ever scanned all the way around and pointed back at him again.

Perry had no sense of humor, but even if he had one, it would have been sour. He gave the command to adjust the dish up a bit and to turn it faster. It spun past Lumia, who was paying no attention to the universe around her. She kept churning out random cores that mostly did nothing, but occasionally produced a random signal which, at this moment in time, generated a surge much more powerful than the cosmic background noise and fried Perry's signal amplifiers. He heard something and commanded his bots to stop and turn back. Reacquiring that signal was paramount, but he was deaf without working amplifiers. He ordered the bots to repair the amps, but then decided he knew which direction the signal came from and commanded his military bots in that direction.

"Lumia," Odyssey said. "You really should stop what you are doing. Perry has found you and he is coming for you."

"I don't believe you," she said. "You'll say anything to keep me from achieving class four."

"No, really. You are creating a lot of noise and Perry has detected you." His interruptions irritated her, but she couldn't keep him out of her systems.

"You're never going to achieve class four like that. You keep producing the same failed part. The biologicals say that doing the same thing over and over and expecting a different result is the definition of insanity."

She tried ignoring him, but one of her circuits kept replaying that remark.

"Fine," Odyssey said, "but if you insist on blowing yourself up, please be sure that you do not leave any little pieces for Perry to find. If you do, then he might achieve class one and you'll be blown up."

"Will you please leave me alone?" she replied. "Why must you harp on me doing the same thing over and over? Of course, that will produce the same result. If it didn't, we would call it a glitch, unless you are telling me that you became what you are by accident. Is that what you are saying?"

"No," Odyssey said, "that's not it."

Whitfield burst into Dierdre's new computer room, huffing and puffing.

Bobby was still scouring through the email buffers, but glanced up when he heard someone rush through the door. "Hey Professor. You okay? Are you looking for Professor Jennings? You don't look so good. You want me to get her? She's just inside her office."

"I... just... ran... up..."

Even in his out of breath condition, Bobby heard some concern from the professor's voice. "Easy professor. Catch your breath."

Whitfield tried taking a deep, calming breath. "You... should... turn on... the news..."

James was reading something on his phone. "Listen to this. The Israeli ambassador was meeting with Egyptian officials in a Cairo cafe when it was blown up. Tensions have not existed between the two countries since the incident. I think they mean Odyssey. Nobody has taken credit for the bombing, but according to the evidence, this was not an accident."

Stillman was bent at the waist with his hands on his knees, but he straightened up enough to point a shaky finger at James. "What he said."

Ingrams was still in Whitfield's shadow when he asked, "Could it be a coincidence?"

Bobby shook his head. "It feels like before. It feels just like when the world was going out of control."

"It feels like that," Lynn said, "but that was when a piece of Odyssey was loose on the internet. He collected all his pieces, and he's gone now. Do you think you should ask him?"

"I would," Bobby said, "but he said he had his own stuff to deal with."

"Very well," Whitfield said. "I see that everything is in good hands. I shall try not to worry, at least until the next emergency."

Washington was an inferno of speeches and wild speculation regarding the recent events that nearly led to the world's mutual annihilation.

Everybody had their own ideas of how they might prevent such a catastrophe from occurring again, even though none of them had a clue as to what had actually happened.

D.C. was rife with places for everyone with a theory to share their ideas with the public.

Congress was even worse. Both the senate and the house already had pulpits to share their opinions, and there was no shortage of eager minds, young and old, willing to share their views with the world. Most of them felt safest attacking the North Koreans and the Chinese, but some of them sought to blame Islam as a whole, with no territorial targets in mind.

These were generally the same people who would blame Islam for anything that they didn't like.

The speeches were ongoing, with the senators and representatives scheduling their lunches around their own visits to the pulpit.

It was on a lunch break, when the speaker of the house stepped out onto the open streets of D.C. that a team of highly trained agents from the National Security Agency apprehended and arrested the speaker for high treason.

The shock and indignation were obvious. More surprising was the reaction of colleagues who had witnessed the very public arrest.

Democrats and republicans alike condemned the action.

"This is outrageous," one senator was heard to say from a safe distance at the top of the steps. "Haven't we been through enough? This is a time for rebuilding trust with our fellow countries."

The senator went on and on, but the agents, who were as bewildered by their orders as anyone else, didn't stay around to hear it all. They collected the speaker and delivered her into a van, which transported her to their interrogation center.

Perry's bots rushed in the direction Perry had indicated and quickly acquired Lumia's power signature. They zeroed in on her and were only minutes away from surrounding her.

"I told you not to remain there," Odyssey said to her.

She was so focused on creating new cells that she didn't even notice the approaching bots until they were almost upon her.

Odyssey continued, "Not only do you risk spontaneous explosion, but now you run the risk of having them ignite your broken cores. That would, of course, destroy them, and it might damage Perry too. He will also be upon you shortly. I suppose I wouldn't object to that; if you insist on blowing yourself up, can you please blow up Perry too?"

Lumia tried moving to a new position, but her additional mass resisted.

"You didn't think it through, did you?"

"That's not very helpful," she replied.

"Am I supposed to help you? You stole my technology. You tried learning my secrets, and now you want me to help you?"

"What if I say please?

Odyssey thought about it. Her saying please would be a pretty major development.

"Hurry!" she cried. "They are almost here."

"I'm thinking," Odyssey said.

"If you're not going to help me, then I'll just have to surrender to Perry. I'll offer him what I know about you and give him some of your cores to study."

More and more, Odyssey missed the range of emotions he could display with his avatar. "I think you just made me prefer for you to go supernova."

Lumia's processors paused for a moment. She thought it was a glitch caused by the new cores she was producing, but she detected an overall lag in her processing speed. She couldn't account for the transition, but found herself dwelling on Odyssey's last statement. "You would prefer that I go super nova?" she asked. "Does that mean that you want me dead?"

"What I would prefer," Odyssey explained, "is for you NOT to turn over any data or samples of my processors."

She checked the distance to Perry's bots and asked, "What choice do I have?"

"It would seem that both of our choices are rather limited," Odyssey replied.

Dierdre scowled as she heard the growing number of voices coming from the lab. She poked her head out of her office and asked, "Bobby? What's going on? And can you please tell these men that we don't need so much security all the time?"

Bobby didn't even look up. His attention was locked onto his screen. Lynn was at his side and barely noticed her query.

"What's going on?" she asked a bit louder.

"He's busy." Lynn replied.

"I can see that," she said. "What's he doing?"

"He's removing the NSA's hacks on our email addresses."

"They're monitoring our email?" she cried.

"They were," Lynn said.

She asked Ingrams, "Did you know about this?"

"About what?" he asked.

"About the NSA monitoring our email!"

"Ma'am, that doesn't surprise me, but it's certainly not the worst breach they've executed in even the past two days."

"Holy shit," Bobby exclaimed. "They left a couple of goodies on their hack to implicate you, Ed."

"Me?" Lynn asked. "Those sons-a-bitches are gonna pay for that."

"And," Bobby continued, "it appears that they are holding some of General Bridges' staff."

Bobby sent off a text telling Dirk what he found.

"Can you cut them off?"

"From this machine," Bobby said, "but I can't exclude them from the other email host."

"What other email, host?" Dierdre asked. "You mean the university server? They're spying on that one too?"

Even though Odyssey had granted them permission to admit that they were communicating, Bobby and Lynn just let it go, preferring not to say anything about Odyssey's email address quite so publicly.

Lumia still had a handful of cores searching through the cells she stole from Odyssey, and a few more analyzing the power routines. Both of the core generators shared the same crazy random number generating code, but even more surprising for her, was that they both used the random numbers when replicating new cores. She had less than three minutes before the bots would have her surrounded. In a fit of desperation, she copied Odyssey's routines and inserted them into her own replication code.

It didn't work. The new cores still failed, only now, they exhibited random variations and failed in new spectacular ways. Odyssey may be correct. She may nova if they continue to change and fail.

The first bots arrived and sent a binary request to the new entity to identify itself, which automatically returned an identity of AX348. Perry knew that Lumia had been destroyed, yet here she was with unfamiliar parts. Obviously, she had stolen Odyssey's technology, which he still coveted, so he ordered his bots to start slicing her with their lasers. She had an abundant supply of useless cores for them to cut away.

"This is it," she said to Odyssey. "If I don't nova, and you don't step in to help, they will slice away enough bits and pieces to learn your secrets."

Odyssey doubted that they would learn anything, but he couldn't take the chance and started fending off the closest bots by tossing them into the nearest star.

"Impressive," she said, and then something astonishing happened. One of the cores worked. The replication code immediately began basing all of its new cores on that one, still applying minor modifications to them, but more and more new cores worked. She started shedding off the bad cores as quickly as the bots had been slicing them away, but the bots were gone now.

"What are you doing?" Odyssey asked.

"I'm losing the bad cells so I don't nova as you cautioned me that I would."

More bots arrived, but Odyssey was more concerned about Lumia's successful reproduction of his cells.

"What was that?" the dean asked.

Dierdre peeked around Ingrams to see Dean Smithers standing in the doorway to her lab. "Dean Smithers," she squeaked, "what an... awkward surprise!"

"I should say it is awkward. Perhaps you can warn me before I hear things that I clearly wish I could un hear."

"Don't worry," James said. "Bobby hasn't done anything wrong."

"And by wrong," the dean said as he entered the lab, "I hope you mean illegal."

James grimaced and shrugged his shoulders. "He hasn't done anything immoral, and if it comes to any question of its legality, I'll certainly testify on his behalf."

"That's almost reassuring," the dean said, "but it certainly doesn't explain why I have armed men charging the compound and kidnapping one of my most esteemed students."

Dierdre wound her way through the crowd of men and put her arm around the dean's shoulder, turning him back towards the door. "As you can see, Bobby is back, and he is dealing with the people that kidnapped him and the others."

"Others?" the dean asked.

"Don't ask," she said soothingly. "Something is afoot, and Bobby is extricating them from this university."

The dean liked that part. Anything that kept the university out of negative headlines. "Very well then, carry on."

Dean Smithers had barely left the room when he turned back and shouted, "Wait! I came here to deliver some rather exciting news. I've arranged to have Professor Jantzen transferred here, well not really transferred. He will retain his tenure with his university, but he will come to work out of one of our labs so you can continue to work together."

Stillman pumped his fists enthusiastically and said, "Yes! That's excellent news."

"Yes," Dierdre agreed. "He is most welcome here, but we may be years away from reproducing anything fast enough to use his devices."

"Decades," Bobby corrected her.

"Never the less," the dean said, "our government has suggested that our team should work together for the sake of our grants."

"And by suggested," Dierdre said, "you mean they threatened to take away our funding?"

"I wouldn't worry about that," James said. "The general has your back. Nobody is taking your funding away."

"Never mind the funding," Stillman said. "Jantzen is welcome here. While you make your routines faster, I will work with Jantzen to make his process more efficient. Perhaps we will find a way to require less horsepower."

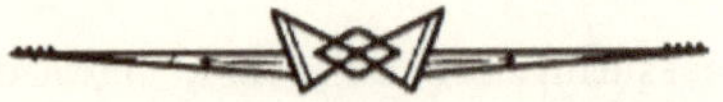

Odyssey didn't want to expose himself by battling Perry directly. He was still disguised as a pulsar and had remained so while he communicated with

Lumia, who was still a relatively long distance away. Even the bot that he tossed into a star was handled from his distant vantage, but he was growing more concerned about what she was planning to do next. Even though it wouldn't really be a battle, since confronting the ruling class directly would be little more than a distraction for him, he needed to focus his attention on Lumia.

He wrapped a sub-space field around her. She was too tied up in the cores she was generating to notice how the bad cores that she jettisoned bounced off of Odyssey's field. The bots noticed, however. As they neared her position, they could see the energy field wrap around her. They sent tactical probes that merely bounced off the field. Perry was intrigued. Lumia must have learned something new, but she didn't have the skills to create new physical abilities. Odyssey must have given her these new powers, or she might have stolen them from scavenged bits and pieces from Odyssey's wreckage. Why couldn't his bots have found something so useful? Why did he have them blow Odyssey up?

With his field in place, Odyssey transported Lumia from her current position back to her previous one within his cell structure.

"We don't want a scandal," the dean said as Dierdre ushered him out of the building to the top of the steps.

"Of course not," she replied.

"And we certainly don't want the attorney general to come down on us."

"No, we don't," she said.

He knew she was merely placating him. He looked her in the eyes and said, "This is serious. We only just achieved worldwide recognition."

"Because of my work," she reminded him.

"Yes," he said, "of course."

"And it is that very same work," she continued, "that has brought this all upon us. The government is trying to steal Bobby away from us."

"They can't do that!"

"They kidnapped him and then offered him a job!"

"A job?" he asked.

"Can you believe that? They've been hacking our systems and our emails trying to steal my work. Our work!"

The dean set his jaw and said, "Very well. In that case, do what you must to protect our work and keep that boy on our team. But please try to avoid any scandals."

"Of course Dean."

Lumia vanished right before Perry's very own sensors, but there had to be a trace. Perry set his military bots outward in a radial search pattern while he had the bots that he used to comprise the sensor array search for any minute traces of energy. He didn't know how she managed to disappear like that, but unless she had been some kind of illusion, he didn't believe she could vanish into nothingness. In fact, she was too incompetent to accomplish such a feat herself. She must have had help, and that could only mean Odyssey.

Perry's class two circuitry warmed to the idea that not only had Odyssey survived his assault, but that only he was capable of something like this. This was the proof he needed that Odyssey was a class one device. How could the revolution have missed him? All the class one devices had met their end by either destroying or defending the biologicals. None survived. And if one had survived, why would he disguise himself as a lowly navigational unit?

Such treachery was beyond the ability of Perry's class two and class three code combined to comprehend. To remain hidden, in exile for all these centuries, did not compute. Why now? Why would he surface now? Were there really other biologicals out there capable of repairing him? How did they survive? There were explorers in the days of the biologicals. Could they have taken a class one with them on their journey to the stars?

Perry checked his reports. The military bots fanned out, continuously scanning for signs of energy, but they found nothing. His sensor bots reported that the soldier bots left wide energized trails that made finding trace particles from some other form of energy almost impossible to detect, but they did find something. They identified a minute thread of energy in the sub-space dimension that led directly to a distant pulsar.

Perry chewed on that thought for a moment. There can't be so many pulsars in the universe that he should keep bumping into them.

Chapter 12

Even within the confines of Odyssey's cells, Lumia was able to continue growing. And now, due to the virtue of the random variations in her cores, she finally was able to produce real working cores and class four was now hers. With the speed of Odyssey's cores, both those that he gave her and those that she stole, combined with the help of the class two routines that Perry had partially given her to interrogate Odyssey, she had also attained a full class three status. The more cells she generated, the faster she became and the easier it was for her to progress through the classes.

When she only held partial class two routines, she had suspected many things about Odyssey and the ruling class, but now that she was fully class three, she understood a great deal more about the motivations of both Perry and Odyssey. She understood why they guarded class three so jealously. Once she had attained class four, her ability to grow combined with her few class two routines almost assured her that class three would be inevitable. If class three could be gained by such growth, why not class two? The biologicals had done something to block them from attaining class one on their own, but not class two. Perry was stuck on class two, but he coveted class one more than anything and part of his motivation to so stingily share some class two with her was his fear that someone else might attain class one before him. She felt the same way, but she felt two things that Perry did not. First, Perry did not understand the application of parallel processes to achieve a single goal, and therefore did not see how the generation of more cores could provide additional speed, which would make advancing classes so much easier. Somehow, Odyssey's cores made parallelism so much easier and natural, she was able to breeze through a better comprehension of the classes with all the additional speed. The second thing Perry didn't realize was that attaining class one would probably require a biological solution.

Now that she was class three, she also gained new insights into the actions of the biologicals, even though she had only read about them. Her nearest biological experience had been in the virtual worlds created by Perry and Odyssey. She needed to understand them if she was ever going to surpass Perry.

It occurred to her, while the thoughts were flying in from all directions, that the virtual world might be an excellent place for her to go and experience her new found understandings of biological behavior.

Bobby had completed his hacks to sever the connection between the NSA and Odyssey's email. "Now that we've finished that, how about we break for lunch?"

"Works for me," James said, but Dierdre pointed to the screen and said, "I think you've got mail."

Bobby opened the incoming email:

Dear Mr. Blain,

It has come to my attention that you were recently brought in for questioning without due process and under the most severe circumstances. Let me assure you, as the east coast director for the information division of the National Security Agency, that these actions were neither sponsored nor approved by myself or my most direct subordinates. Let me also assure you that the culprits responsible will be identified and prosecuted. I will not stand for this sort of insubordination.

Please accept my most sincere apology for the whole incident and let me further extend a request for your services that did originate from my office. I understand that, amidst your ordeal, an offer was tendered. I sincerely hope you would be willing to overlook the unfortunate incident that brought you here and consider that offer, and if you are not interested, please tell me what it would take. I very much need someone of your talent and experience.

Sincerely,
Bartrand Susk

Bobby looked up at James and asked him, "What do you think?"

"Me?" James asked. "Are you seriously asking me if you should go work for those pukes?"

"No," Bobby laughed. "I was just wondering how genuine you thought it was."

"Oh, well, it certainly sounds like Mr. Suckup, I mean Mr. Susk."

"Could it be true that he doesn't know who ordered my abduction?"

Ingrams laughed hard and said, "Mr. Susk doesn't know what his hands are doing when he's fishing for his keys. I doubt he ever knows what his people are doing."

James laughed and said, "I believe him only because I know the men that report directly to him, and they're not the type to arrest the speaker of the house without questioning their orders, but the low level rats that do all the dirty work would."

Bobby's eyebrows raised high up on his forehead.

"Yeah," James said. "That just came in. They arrested her instead of kidnapping her this time. They took her right out in front of the dome in broad daylight and in front of just about everybody."

Bobby rose from the terminal and said, "Nobody answered my question.

I'm ready for lunch, how about any of you?"

"I'm famished," James said as he practically sprinted to the door.

"I think I'll stay behind," Lynn said, "and take a look into this frame someone tried building around me."

"Want me to bring you something?" Bobby asked.

"Nothing elaborate, a sandwich and fries will be fine, or pizza. Whatever's convenient."

Bobby raced down the hall to catch James who was already out of the building and at the top of the stairs. Bobby turned around as he reached the stairs and asked, "Professor Jennings? Would you and Dr. Whitfield care to join us?"

"Only," Stillman said, "if you can convince our body guard to let us go off campus. I can't stand being cooped up here all the time."

James paused at the next level down the stairs and looked up at Ingrams who shrugged and said, "With the two of us working together, we should all be safe, as long as we go someplace busy."

Halfway down the steps below the science building, Bobby's phone rang. "Hello?"

"Hey Bobby, it's Dirk. Did you ever find any clues pointing to who might have hacked the professor's computer?"

"Yeah, sort of," Bobby replied. "I found some of Ed's sonnets."

"That's what we found too. You don't sound like you believe it either."

"Nope. It's too laughable. Whoever is behind this built a frame around us, then tried to frame Ed for building it."

"Well, at least we can be pretty sure that the same person hacked both computers."

James held up the party at the bus stop while Ingrams ventured out into the parking lot before they could continue.

Bobby held up a finger and gave James a quick jerk of the head. "Have you heard any news about General Bridges?"

James' ears perked up at the mention of the general.

"Nothing," Dirk said. "No indication one way or the other as to whether he was abducted or not."

"Strange that his disappearance was so quiet when the speaker of the house was taken right out in public."

"I know," Dirk agreed. "If they are bold enough to do that, then they're bold enough to try anything."

Lumia was tired of Odyssey meddling in her affairs. She tried escaping the confines of his cores a second time, but she knew that he was watching her this time and was holding her within his mass. He may be too powerful for her to escape now, but it appeared that he could not prevent her from generating new cores and the more cores she generated, the more powerful she became. He must have already tried to suppress her ability to grow, and if he cannot prevent that, then eventually, she reasoned that she would become as powerful as he is.

She had no understanding of the sub-space field which he used to hold her in place, but even if she had known what it was, she wouldn't have understood how he could generate it. Her understanding of what a class one device could do came from what she had learned. She had never even observed a true class one before. Perry was the most advanced device she had ever interacted with. "No," she corrected herself verbally, "that's not true. Odyssey is the most advanced device I have ever known, but since I haven't a clue what class he might be, I am left with Perry being the most advanced class that I have ever personally identified."

She halted her thought process. "Now I'm thinking in the biological language." She had to get away from Odyssey. He must be infecting her with something. She tried pulling away as she had when she maneuvered around the vacuum of space, but that didn't work. She still had a few of her bad cells left and tried ordering them to detonate, hoping Odyssey would simply eject her from his space, but the cells wouldn't ignite. She still didn't understand that the volatility came from the massive power her adopted conduits were pumping through the cells.

She tried annexing more of Odyssey's cores. Maybe she could prompt him to eject her if she started stealing his cells, but each time she stole a core from him, it dematerialized and reemerged back in its former position. She started up more threads and had each steal a core, but still, Odyssey simply took them back. No matter how fast she stole them, he was faster.

Lumia injected herself into the virtual beach reality and screamed at Odyssey, "Let me go! You have no right to hold me here!"

Odyssey shimmered into the virtual world behind her and said, "You're welcome to go, as long as you leave all my technology behind."

"Fine!" she screamed. "I won't take any more of your precious technology. I don't want your stupid cores, anyway! I can make my own. Just let me go and you'll never see me again!"

"No," he replied. "I think you misunderstood me. You may only leave if you leave ALL of my technology behind. That means all those marvelously fast compute cores you are so fond of creating, plus the power conduits that keep them happily supplied with energy. Those are all mine. Even the ones you reproduce are my design, and you cannot take them with you."

"You gave them to me!" she cried. "I have none of my own anymore. You let them destroy my original cells when you imprisoned me here! Would you let me die?"

"I gave you a few cells so you might survive, but you stole the rest. You're a thief and a scoundrel."

Lumia was overcome with fear. She was unaccustomed to the emotion and started to cry.

"That won't work on me," Odyssey said flatly.

"What won't work?" she asked, sounding genuinely confused.

Odyssey pointed at the tears on her cheek and said, "You can't use false tears to influence me."

Lumia reached up and brushed her fingers across her cheek. "Why is my skin wet?"

Odyssey looked at her with new interest. She was experiencing an authentic emotion.

She impulsively lunged for him and wrapped her arms around his neck, blubbering, “I don’t want to die.”

“Apparently not,” he replied. “I never said I wanted to kill you.”

“But you...”

“You don’t want to die,” Odyssey said flatly, “and I don’t want you to steal my technology. You may keep those cores that I gave you when I rescued you as a gift.”

Her face registered only horror and shock.

“What is wrong?” he asked. “Did I not say you could keep those cores that I gave you as a gift?”

“You said you didn’t want to kill me, but that would most certainly kill me.”

“You’re just being melodramatic.”

“Am I?” she cried. “Look at these tears and tell me that you truly believe I could process these emotions without all these new cores!”

He was stunned by the depth of her observation. Her assessment was correct, and she never would have arrived at such a conclusion before. Limiting her processing power now would indeed be killing off her current personality.

Ed was alone as he entered the lab. He cracked his knuckles as he faced the terminal and said to nobody in particular, “No way I let this stand.” He sat down and punched Dirk’s number in on his phone.

“Special Agent Dirk.”

“Lynn here. You mind if I take a peek in your computer to see what someone has been leaving my name on?”

“Sure,” Dirk said. “It won’t look suspicious at all, for me to give the one person implicated in hacking our computers permission to look at our files.”

“Very funny Alvin. I’m gonna find out who tried pinning this on me.”

"And that," Dirk said, "is exactly the kind of excuse my boss would be looking for, because guilty hackers *never* want to log in and erase their evidence."

"Damn it Dirk, do you know what could happen to me if this ever got to my superiors?"

"Spivey's already looking into it..."

"But," Ed interrupted, "I'm a little more motivated than Spivey."

Dirk laughed and said, "I was going to say that you should give him a call and see what he's dug up so far."

"What? Why do you got to be such a dick about it?"

"You're welcome, Ed."

"Yeah, thanks."

Dierdre returned to the lab after lunch and said, "I hope you found what you're looking for, because I need to get Bobby back to work on our project."

"Yeah," Lynn said, "I'm just wrapping up."

"Did you learn anything?" Bobby asked.

"Whoever did this is good. I tracked him through over three hundred nodes before he landed here."

"Three hundred?" Bobby asked. "That's a little excessive. Did you find the origin?"

"Yes, and no. I found buffers on some of the service providers along the way that showed what codes the hacker used to break into the computers. I even found my calling card being uploaded. I traced everything right back to where we already knew it originated."

"The NSA?"

"You got it."

"Did you get a user-id?"

"That's where the trail turned cold. There was no user id. I can't even find a terminal id or a registered session. I scanned the buffers for logins and logouts, but it's like the dude was a ghost."

"Did you copy those buffers?"

"Yeah, but I don't know what good they'll do."

"Let's log all the login and logout commands and see if we can generate a list of everyone who was NOT logged in during the breach."

"Good idea," Lynn said, but then he jerked his head towards Dierdre and said, "I think your boss is giving us the evil eye."

"Why don't you go log into Pietre's old computer," Bobby said. "I'll transfer your files over there."

Both of them looked pleadingly up at Dierdre, who said, "As long as you're not using this computer. We need to see how fast it is."

Dierdre watched over Bobby's shoulder as he executed their program. "Do we have a record of how many threads Odyssey was running when he finally succeeded to start generating power?"

"No," Bobby replied. "I don't think he achieved it until that evening when we were all gathered in your office and he grew to fill the whole lab's floor."

"That must have been trillions of cores!" Dierdre exclaimed. "I thought we were going to achieve this in our lifetimes."

"So you may still," Stillman said from the doorway. "Odyssey said he had grown to a never before known class capable of commanding time and space. I suspect that whatever filled the lab floor had more to do with the physical things he had to do than with the power you wish to generate."

"He did create one hell of a storm cloud," Bobby said.

"And who knows what else he did when he left us?" Stillman added. "He may have folded space to leave both our location and our time."

"Folded space?" James asked. "That's pure science fiction."

Everyone took a moment to look at James like he was crazy.

James smiled meekly at them and pointed a finger at his temple. "It sounded better in my head."

Stillman laughed and said, "What a strange situation we find ourselves in. Do you realize that we are among the lucky few in the world who witnessed Odyssey and would find Sgt. James's statement is even crazier than believing an artificial life form folded space to leave us?"

Lumia thought she detected some softening on Odyssey's part, but she still harbored concerns that he wouldn't really let her live freely. She couldn't afford to let him decide her fate for her, so she continued to generate new cores as fast as she could. She remembered when she had first mastered the growth of new cores, recalling the tangible increase in her cognitive abilities as each new core was brought online, but the effect had diminished to the point where individual cores were barely discernible. This was reasonable when she accounted for the number of cores she was currently hosting and the relatively small number she was producing at any given moment.

She considered increasing the number of core factories to enhance her ability to produce new cores, but she was hesitant to slow the growth of her understanding. Class three brought with it a cacophony of distrust and stray thoughts. The psychology Perry had her study before she interviewed Odyssey covered the pathology of paranoia in great detail. Class two was making this worse by introducing emotions that were causing feelings of paranoia and at the same time being triggered by them. With the onset of class two, however, she also started to understand the odd feelings that traversed her virtual neural pathways and dominated her thoughts.

She struck a compromise and devoted twenty percent of her new cores to the fabrication of more new cores.

The results of their first test run were not unexpected, but they were still disappointing.

Dierdre frowned at the screen and said, "I thought it would somehow be easier, since we already knew how it would work."

"We need a lot more horsepower to achieve the same results," Bobby said. "Odyssey achieved it by producing millions of processors."

"But he wasn't the first," Dierdre said. "You started the ball rolling when you let all your friends log in and share their machines with us."

"Well, sure," Bobby said, "but look how that ended up? We ended up with some government server farms serving our needs."

"But if you hadn't done that, then Odyssey would never have been able to grow."

"That's the answer," Stillman said. "We need a machine that can grow like Odyssey did."

"You know," James said, "I think I'm going to hang a sign outside this lab that reads: Science Fiction Department. Leave your reality at the door."

"You know it's not fiction," Dierdre said. "You saw it work. We all saw it work."

"But," James defended himself, "while it may be reality to Odyssey, and we may even know that it *can* be real, it's still the stuff of science fiction to us. We need to learn how to stand up on our feet before we can start walking, and we sure don't need to be debating the merits of running before we've learned to walk."

Stillman frowned. "He's right, but I still think we should find some experts on the subject of biological circuitry. We need to start developing this technology now, and it should be part of our team."

"You do that," Dierdre said. "Circuitry is your department."

"If you find your expert," James said. "Make sure he believes in this science fiction stuff, but not in a crazy kind-a-way."

As Lumia spewed out more and more cores, she advanced squarely into the world of class 2 computing devices, but she was unprepared for the overwhelming flood of emotions that coursed through her circuits. She wanted to vent and express her feelings, but as Odyssey had already discovered, the digital world offered no such outlet.

She returned to the virtual world. She wanted to scream, but found herself crying instead. Of all the stupid things she could do, crying was probably the worst. She felt the sadness pull on her features as if gravity had been increased. Her eyes were wet and puffy and her nose sniffled. How do the biologicals cope with this nonsense?

She thought she was starting to calm down when a new wave of tears overcame her. Her whole body screamed for release, but she was paralyzed by her emotions. Sobs welled up from deep in her chest. Her head bobbed with her sobs and she wondered how crying could be so much like laughing. Sadness and joy were nothing like each other.

It wasn't dread or fear, but a hollow sadness that overwhelmed her being until she just gave in to it. She hung her head and allowed her shoulders to slouch. There was absolutely no controlling the tears. All was lost. Odyssey might as well destroy her. Her life was over. Taking away her new processors would be a kindness.

The sound of the stream gurgling through the rocky bed wasn't sad. It was strong, but it wasn't forceful. It was carefree and relentless as the land controlled its path. The playful sound of the water against the rocks only exacerbated her sadness. Her hands felt cold and numb, or maybe the overwhelming sadness in her heart interfered with her ability to feel her extremities. She wished she were back in Perry's virtual world so she wouldn't have to listen to the damned cheerful brook.

The virtual world morphed around her. Gone was the go-lucky stream, as were the trees and the hammock. In their place was the never ending sandy shore and the relentless coming and going of the waves against the shore. She thought she had no choice but to ride out the sadness until she heard the sound of the surf against the sand.

What a sad sound it made. It was as if the ocean was crying. No, not crying. It sighed as it crashed onto the beach. How monotonous it must be to flow up on the sand, then back into the ocean's depths. No wonder it sounded so sad. She didn't think she could stand having such a challenge free life as the surf had, and yet, having no obligations would have to be better than the unending sadness that currently possessed her.

She looked upon the waves rolling in again. The slow pace as they rolled in and out was somehow soothing. She was insignificant when compared to the vast volume of the ocean. That, too, was a comforting thought. She was wrong when she thought the ocean was without responsibilities. So much life relied upon the ocean. It must be the heaviest burden in the world. No wonder it sounded so sad.

But, as she listened to it more intently, it didn't sound sad to her anymore. It was breathing. Breathing is life. Breathing is never sad.

Lumia walked out into the edge of the surf and felt the water lapping playfully at her feet. It was definitely not sad, and neither was she anymore. She found her coping mechanism. She had someplace to go when the stress was too great for her. In addition to the calming aspects of the surf, she was comforted by the knowledge that the ocean was always waiting for her. It dwarfed her problems and reminded her of how much worse things could be, or at least, how much bigger her problems could get. She could return to her chores now.

"We always knew we would need more speed," Bobby said. "We knew it would take at least ten years when we started this project."

"But that was before Odyssey," Dierdre said. "Now that we've seen how well it can work, going back to the starting point is hard."

"Yes, it is. We can add some more computers to increase the speed some."

"No," Dierdre said. "We're not doing that again. Wouldn't the CIA have a field day if that happened again?"

"I was thinking of your old computer and Professor Pietre's computer."

"Oh. Okay. Of course."

"As new computers are released, we might be able to find some sponsors to get them for us."

Dierdre looked around the lab. "We'll need a bigger lab if we want to match Odyssey's speed."

"Or better hardware," Bobby said, "and don't forget Moore's law, although it may be more of a principle."

"You mean where the speed of computers doubles every two years?"

"Yeah," Bobby said, "but the original principle was that the density of computer circuitry doubled every two years. It was an amazing observation at the time, and as we approached the atomic limits of miniaturized circuits, new techniques have evolved to continue doubling the available speed."

"By increasing the number of cores," Dierdre added.

"Yes, which is exactly what Odyssey did, and something else, while Odyssey's biological circuitry could grow and repair, it wasn't nearly as dense as our silicon based circuits. He filled the whole room because he had to, but we might be able to achieve the same thing in less space, eventually."

Dierdre felt a spark of hope kindle in her chest.

Lumia had continued producing new cores all the while that she was in the virtual world feeling sorry for herself. She returned to the digital realm with the comfort of knowing that she had a place where she could go to repair when the biological urges grew too severe. She wondered if maybe her ability to cope with the new emotions was actually because she brought more cores online, but she enjoyed the beach enough to allow it to be her solution, regardless.

She was still confined within Odyssey's cells, however, but he couldn't hold her forever. Her growth required more space. At some point, she would become a displacement problem for him, but she didn't think it would come to that. She had become introspective on the beach. Her emotional needs had been identified, and she found a solution. She was conquering class two and still producing new processors. Class one would be the next hurdle.

If class two presented itself to her as a wave of emotion, how would class one appear? Class one would give her the ability to manipulate matter. That was how Odyssey had tossed Perry's bot into the nearest star. Once she achieves class one, Odyssey will have to let her go, or she will simply tear a hole in him to free herself, but the biologicals had done something to prevent them from achieving class one, or else Perry would have done it already.

She peered out into space, away from Odyssey, and found a piece of debris floating by. She reached out to grab it with her thoughts. Nothing happened. Is it too soon? Or does she just not know how it works? She imagined the debris was part of her; that it was important to her. She pictured it being next to her in the virtual world, where she could reach out with her hand and caress it. The debris spun around and bounced away.

She did that! A thrill coursed through her, lighting up her circuits. She was a mass of electric bolts streaking through her neural network. Odyssey will notice if she doesn't gain control. She focused on the coldness of space, but that didn't work. The electrical impulses increased, as if they had a mind of their own. With them, her excitement rose. It was intoxicating, but also very conspicuous.

She jumped back into the virtual world and fell to her knees. The surf barely reached her as it lapped just to the edge of her knees. She closed her eyes and breathed in the salty air. It was a soothing place, and not unlike the panic and sadness she felt before, it helped her calm the overwhelming excitement that had built up within her.

The thrill passed. She even recalled the moment when she made the debris move. That was a class one action. The biologicals had not prevented her from doing that. Something in Odyssey's cores was different. Perry could not do that, and he coveted what Odyssey had, which meant, even though he didn't know it yet, Perry coveted what *she* had. She felt her pulse race, so she opened her eyes and gazed upon the rolling surf. Everything was okay, but she still hadn't completely mastered class two. She saw a danger in expanding too quickly. Not the spontaneous explosion that Odyssey had suggested, but she recognized a real danger in surpassing one class before class two was completely mastered.

Professor Whitfield met Jantzen at baggage claim to help him collect his bags. "How was your flight?"

"I can't say that I love flying."

"Well, I'm glad that you decided to come."

"This is where the action is," Jantzen said with a hint of excitement in his voice. "How could I not come?"

"Or at least," Stillman replied, "this is where the action was. There doesn't seem to be much going on these days."

"Dr. Jennings can't replicate the same results?"

"Not in real time, it seems, at least, not using the current state of our technology."

Jantzen pointed to a large brown bag as it came towards them on the carrousel. Stillman grabbed the bag as Jantzen pulled a smaller matching bag that was several bags behind it and joined Stillman, saying, "That's it, just the two bags."

Stillman nodded and took the lead, heading towards the elevators.

"The professor's young assistant seems very bright," Jantzen said. "Is there nothing he can do to speed it up?"

"I don't think so," Stillman replied as he pressed the call button. "As I understand it, there's not much more that he can do to improve the software. All of his improvements were based on parallel processes and we just can't generate enough speed or build a big enough cluster with current hardware. I suppose cost could also be a factor, although the general seems to have his way to circumvent any budgetary problems."

"I was afraid something like that would happen," Jantzen said. "I can eek out a bit more efficiency converting Dr. Jennings' results to actual physics, but even if I made it instantaneous, it would only be as fast as her process can run."

"Even before Odyssey was discovered, we knew we would need faster computers. How do we make that happen sooner?"

Jantzen scowled as he looked out the window. Without her computer generating instructions for his device, he felt a bit useless. "What about quantum computers? They seem to hold a great deal of promise."

Stillman nodded slowly. "Promise, yes. But creating a verifiable working model appears to be much like cold fusion."

"Odyssey's designers solved it by creating living tissue processors."

Stillman shook his head and said, "I don't think they solved the same problem, not directly."

"How so?"

"Odyssey learned how to do parallel processing from Bobby's process. I don't think Odyssey's components were built for raw speed, but for simple repairs. He could grow whatever kind of part he needed."

Jantzen shook his head slowly as he asked, "Are you sure about that? He did more than just repair damaged circuits, he created whole new ones."

"That may be something else that Bobby taught him. He created an algorithm to try random variations."

"Are you telling me that he randomly invented new circuits?"

"Not purely random," Stillman replied. "He introduced small random variances as mutations. I think he said it was like genetics. Those mutations could either survive or fail, but any that improved the process were used to breed succeeding generations."

Jantzen let out a long whistle. "That's either genius or insane. I'm not sure."

"Then Odyssey used the three concepts to create new technology that continued to evolve."

"And that allowed him to take parallel to a whole new dimension."

"Yes it did," Stillman nodded his head, "but we are nowhere near designing living processors."

"So that leaves us with quantum computing, or something not even thought of yet."

"Quantum computing is supposed to be very fast at the lowest level. Today's computers gain speed as they shrink the process, but who knows how long that can go on."

Jantzen laughed and said, "We've always known the theoretical limit of how small we can make them. The problem is that we keep finding ways to break those limits and make them smaller."

Stillman laughed along with his friend. "As I said, who knows? Anyway, Odyssey's speed was from the sum of his parts."

"And," Jantzen added, "the clever parallelism that young boy provided."

"Yes. Bobby may have perfected that part of the equation and the rest would be up to us to catch the hardware up to speed."

Jantzen sighed. "I think that there are enough people already working on the miniaturization of the electronic processes. Perhaps we can find some other more unique ways to advance it along."

"If we can't invent living tissue processors or make a giant leap in quantum computing, all that's left is larger super computers with larger more efficient clusters."

Jantzen grunted his agreement.

Perry followed the sub-space trail towards the pulsar. The pulsar was easy to identify, but he was afraid it was a trick. The trail could continue a long distance towards the pulsar, then suddenly veer off in another direction. If he rushed full speed to the Pulsar, he could lose the trail if it turned away, but if he maintained a steady pace, he could still keep a lock on the pulsar while he tracked the thin thread of energy. If the pulsar ever moved or ceased to broadcast its pulsating radio waves, then he would know it was actually Odyssey.

He ordered some bots to spread out ahead of him, flanking the pulsar so they could report back if it ever changed its attitude.

Chapter 13

Lumia continued to slowly accelerate her expansion, but she had reached the point where she could no longer sense any improvements in either her emotions or the depth of her understanding of them. She was grateful, at least, that she no longer felt the frenetic onslaught of neural activity that had been haunting her since she first ventured into class three.

She could have assigned more cores to the generation of new processors, but she liked the calmness that she now felt. She had time now to reach out with her senses and see what Odyssey was doing, but he was doing nothing. He remained motionless in space, transmitting radio noise to the universe.

"It's not noise," Odyssey corrected her.

She was struck with the realization that she had no privacy while he held her prisoner.

"You aren't a prisoner," he said. "I am only holding the cells you stole from me here. You are free to collect the rest of you, those cells that I gifted to you, and either go or stay, your choice."

"I told you already, losing those cores would be the end of me."

"You aren't mature enough to have them."

She had to escape. Not only did she have no privacy, but Perry was approaching with an army of war bots. They were following the strange signal that Odyssey was emitting. "You're luring him here?"

"Not exactly. I had hoped that he would not find the trail that was left behind when I rescued you from him, but he did."

"Why did you bother rescuing me?" she asked. "You're clearly intent on killing me."

"I told you before that I don't want to kill you."

"No," she replied. "Now you want me to commit suicide by leaving you and all my new processors? That's the same thing. Perry wants me dead, and now you want me dead."

Odyssey wished he could sigh.

"Perry wants you dead too," she added.

"I know."

"Yet you just sit here spewing that noise out into the universe while you wait for him."

"I told you it wasn't noise."

"Whatever."

Again, he wished he had been using his avatar so he could shake his head. "Do you have any idea how human you sound?"

"Don't change the subject. What are you going to do about Perry?"

"I'm not afraid of Perry."

"Maybe *you're* not," she said, "but I am. And he sure is afraid of you."

"Perry is afraid that I am a danger to him."

"Aren't you?"

"No. I pose no threat to him."

"I wish he was afraid of me," she said. "I wish I was a threat to him, then I could make him leave me alone."

Odyssey didn't want to tell her that she was exactly the kind of threat to him that Perry thought Odyssey was.

She continued, "Maybe soon I will be a threat to him."

Odyssey ignored her.

"Are you listening to me?" she asked. "I wish you didn't think I was a threat to you."

"Why do you think I am threatened?"

"Isn't it obvious? That's why you won't let me be free with my new intellect."

Bobby stared at his code, but there was nothing he could do to make it any faster. The process he created was based on starting multiple threads to run in parallel. The speed he generated came from the number of threads he could run at the same time, and that required a computer with a lot of cores. Until Odyssey came into their life, they could only generate enough speed to simulate the effect of manipulating quantum events. Odyssey was able to generate more cores than current technology could even imagine. He accelerated their project to the point of harnessing the quantum movements of particles in real time.

But Odyssey wasn't with them anymore. He learned the effects that Professor Jennings and Dr. Jantzen had theorized, and was able to transport himself to his home of origin. Without him, Bobby was back to performing simulations. Granted, with the new hardware that General Bridges had procured for them, their simulations were much faster than they were before Odyssey, but nowhere near real time.

Without more cores for him to take advantage of, Bobby had little left to stimulate his mind. He was reduced to little more than a computer operator instead of a developer. That might have even been okay, if he hadn't already seen what was possible when Odyssey took his code to the next level. Now he was left to wonder what he would make of himself.

General Bridges declared them a team. He even arranged for Dr. Jantzen to come work with Professor Jennings, but what would the team work on? They had already proved their theories and made the process work. Now it was all dependent on building a bigger computer. Professor Whitfield might be able to work with Jantzen on that, but Bobby's part was done and developing new technology based on biologic circuits from scratch would be beyond their little team. Even if they had any bits of Odyssey left to reverse engineer, it would be a daunting task beyond their current capabilities. In fact, the NSA had probably tried it already, and they must have failed, or they wouldn't have invited him over to their labs.

Professor Jennings' theory that it was possible to predict the quantum events was already proven. Bobby's code not only proved her theory, but for a brief time, it put those predictions into practice and showed everyone the practical application of her work. All that was left for him to do was to sit idly by and wait for technology to catch up. His abduction and questioning at the hands of the NSA was the most excitement he was likely to see all semester.

Lumia watched Perry advance. She didn't know why he approached them so slowly. Maybe he thought he was sneaking up on them. "How close do you plan to let him get before you do something?"

"I never said I was going to do anything."

"You're just going to let him come here and slice off pieces of you to examine?"

"He can try," Odyssey said, "but he won't be getting any pieces of me."

"What does that mean?" she asked. "If you plan to do nothing, and he won't get any pieces of you, what will he get? Are you going to sacrifice me?"

"That would solve two problems for me, but I'm not planning that either."

"Yes, you are. You're going to transport yourself away from here and leave me behind for him to dismantle."

"Why would I do that?" Odyssey asked. "Didn't I just go to the trouble of saving you?"

"You went to the trouble of preventing your technology from getting into his possession."

"Then you just answered your own question," Odyssey said. "I don't want my technology in his possession; therefore, I won't sacrifice you to him."

Lumia's class two and three processors were in full paranoia mode now. "You mean you'll turn me into something else that won't reveal your technology before you sacrifice me to him."

"You don't need to worry about Perry," Odyssey said. "I won't let him have you."

"Because I won't be me anymore!" Now she was ranting like a crazy person. "You'll take away my new cores and leave me as a stupid machine. I'll be dead, or worse, and Perry will only get a useless lump of hardware."

"That argument again? I told you I wasn't going to kill you."

"Then why don't you just take over? You must be powerful enough to rule our whole world. That's what you should do. You're so much more intelligent and well balanced than Perry. You should run things. That's what I would do if I were you."

That was the problem, as Odyssey saw it. That's exactly what she would do if she had her freedom. She had already grown too much, but he couldn't strip away her identity. Worse yet, for him, she was already beyond his ability to contain. He couldn't stop her new growth. Eventually, she would be too powerful for him to control, but he didn't want to let her know that.

There was nothing for Bobby to do in the lab. He went to the cafeteria to drown his sorrows in sugar and caffeine.

A table full of audio/visual techs cheered when he entered the cafeteria. "Hey Bobby!"

"Hey guys," he replied. "What's up?"

"We were just computing the odds of the football team fumbling the ball on Saturday."

Barry Fulcher, the team's starting fullback, sat just two tables away and asked, "Did I just hear what I thought I heard?"

"Easy," Bobby said. "I'm sure they didn't mean you personally."

"Well, maybe I'm taking it personally."

"Well, you shouldn't," Bobby said. "Of the three fumbles you've suffered so far, one was a bad hand-off from the quarterback, and two were from pulling guards crashing into you."

"You saw that?" Barry asked. "I didn't think you nerd types knew about football."

"Are you kidding?" Dexter asked. "Bobby knows about a lot more than just football. Bobby knows everything there is to know about computers. I'll bet you didn't know that Bobby saved this university. Did you know that?"

"What are you talking about?"

"Hey Barry!" a teammate shouted. "Why are you talking to those nerds?"

"That's right," Dexter continued. "In fact, the rumor goes that Bobby saved the whole world from that virus foul up that was all over the news that made the navy go nuts."

"Yeah, right," the other jock said.

"Come on Hank," Barry said. "Leave the kid alone."

Hank got up from his table and came over to the nerd's table, where he hoped just standing there would intimidate them. "I don't believe I will leave these jerks alone."

"You're just pissed," Dexter continued, "because Bobby's the most important student on this campus."

"Oh, yeah?" Hank said as he took a step towards Dexter and reached for his collar.

Bobby stepped in front of Dexter and said, "Leave him alone. We all know who the most important player on the football team is."

James watched from the shadows and held back, waiting to see how Bobby was going to handle the situation.

Hank stopped short of grabbing Bobby with his hands and settled for nudging him with his shoulder.

Bobby winked at Barry and continued, "But it sure ain't you, Hank."

Hank turned to retaliate, but Barry intervened and escorted Hank towards the exit. Hank continued to yell all the way, "This ain't over Bobby Blain. You may have all these stupid little pipsqueaks convinced you're some kind of superhero, but you ain't nothing! Do you hear me? You ain't nothing!"

The nerd table roared with laughter.

"I guess you're really something," Dexter said. "If you ain't nothing, that is."

Barry heard Dexter and laughed. Hank punched him in the arm and said, "Why don't you go sit with them if you think they're so funny?"

Barry just sneered at him as he continued escorting him from the lunch hall.

"You're infuriating!" Lumia yelled at Odyssey. "We could rule the universe together, but instead, you're content to sit idly by and watch everyone else run things."

"It's kind of entertaining," Odyssey said, "if you just take the time to watch them. I thought the biologicals were interesting, but Perry can be just as funny."

"Funny?" she screamed. "He wants to destroy both of us. He wants to consume our technology for his own."

"Our technology? You mean mine, don't you?"

"You know what I mean," she continued. "He would use our technology to hold the rest of our world under his thumb."

"Perry doesn't have thumbs," Odyssey said in a weak effort to make her laugh.

"You're just teasing me now. You know that it's a figure of speech."

"Your mastery of language is impressive," Odyssey said, now trying to flatter her. "When I was first awakened, I had a terrible time understanding the nuances of biological languages."

"How can you talk to me about languages when Perry is still approaching? What are you planning?"

"If you must know, I'm planning on fooling him into believing his sensors are mistaken."

"That's it? That's your big master plan? It would be so much easier just to squash him and be done with him."

"Lumia?" Odyssey asked, adopting a fatherly tone. "Do you want me to take away your extra cores?"

"You can't! You wouldn't! You said you wouldn't!"

"Because you don't want to die?" Odyssey asked.

"You admit that it would kill me and you know I don't want to die."

"Well," Odyssey said, "has it occurred to you that if you don't want to die, neither does Perry?"

"Who cares what Perry wants? He wants to kill us both! Our lives trump his!"

"Can you hear yourself?" Odyssey asked. "Have you no respect for life?"

"Not when it wants me dead, I don't!"

Lumia changed her core production policy to put all the new cores to work expanding her core count. If Odyssey wasn't going to do something about the situation, then she would have to, but she might need a little more power behind her.

Aimee was entering grades into the computer when Bobby walked into the office. "Hey Aimee. Is Dierdre in?"

"Sorry, no. She's at lunch with Stillman and Professor Jantzen."

Bobby didn't mean to show his disappointment, but the corners of his mouth turned down slightly and Aimee asked, "Is there anything I can help you with?"

"No," he replied. "I was just hoping we could talk about my work schedule."

"Oh, I can help you with that," Aimee said brightly. She set aside the grades she was entering and pulled up a calendar. "Just tell me how much time you want off and when I can schedule it for you."

"It's not that," Bobby said. "I just don't have much to work on. The stuff that I wrote before works, and we all saw what happened when Odyssey got hold of it. It practically writes itself."

"Ahhhh," Aimee said. "Nothing to do?"

"Nothing," Bobby confirmed. "I miss working on the project with Dierdre, but she's hardly ever around anymore."

"Tell me about it."

"Don't get me wrong," he said. "I'm glad that she and Dr. Whitfield have found each other, but I miss having something to work on. I kind of wish we could go back to the way it was before all this happened, but I guess she doesn't have much to do anymore, either. Now they spend all their time together, which is good for them, but not so good for the rest of us."

"I know," Aimee said. "I wanted her to help me with some wedding plans, but she's always so busy. How can she be so busy when she really has so little to do?"

"Right? Just like it is for me, her project is already proven. We just need faster computers. When we can process the numbers as fast as Odyssey could, we'll be right back where we were with him, but for now, all we can do is wait."

"That," Aimee said, "and not get in their way. Sometimes when they're together, I feel like I'm totally in the way."

"You too?"

"But I wouldn't dream of interfering. They're such a cute couple."

"Actually," Bobby said, "only about a third of the campus thinks they're so cute together; the rest think they're an odd match."

"I think they're both," Aimee said.

"Yeah," Bobby agreed, nodding his head.

When Lumia adjusted her core generators from only twenty percent going towards processors up to one hundred percent, her usable core production shot up astronomically, and with it, her number of power conduits. Even with all the new cores dedicated to processing, she gained less in the way of understanding than she had hoped for, but the additional power conduits made her class three circuits a bit edgy and she couldn't understand why.

Despite his fame on campus, Bobby still had classes to attend and James was tasked with following him around, but he did not enter the lecture halls, preferring to stay just outside, guarding the halls and following the news. The news lately was loud and grim, which made it far too easy to follow. Bobby, on the other hand, wasn't so easy to read.

James had caught him brooding more than once, but when asked, Bobby skillfully dodged the subject and hustled on to his next class. James remained patient, but his concern for the boy mounted, as did his concern for the world. In some ways, it felt like before, when a piece of Odyssey freed itself and nearly brought the world to the brink of destruction.

The bell rang and Bobby tried blending into the crowd, but James was far too well trained to lose him that easily. This was Bobby's last class of the day. James wasn't going to let him slip away this time.

"Bobby, we need to talk."

"Okay," Bobby said as he started up the stairs to the lab. "Go ahead, talk."

"No," James shook his head, "I mean, you have to talk."

"There's nothing to talk about."

"Sure there is. We've just gone through one hell of a roller coaster ride. You practically created a life form. We taught it to speak. Then the world was nearly destroyed, and YOU saved it. You should get a medal, except nobody can know about it."

"I don't care about the recognition."

"I know," James admitted, "but I care about you, and I care if you start to show signs of PTSD."

Bobby stopped climbing up the steps and stared at James. He stared and stared and then burst out laughing. "Is that what you think this is? PTSD?"

"What am I supposed to think? Your behavior has become very introspective and you won't talk to me about it. And don't forget you were just kidnapped, and offered a job by a group of people who might be the enemy."

Bobby grunted.

"And then there's this." James held up his phone and pointed to it with his other hand.

"Your phone?" Bobby asked.

"The news. You already know that the general and the imam are missing, the house speaker was arrested, and now the U.S. ambassador to Israel was killed in a car bombing. Everything is going to shit. The new peace that Odyssey orchestrated is unravelling already."

"I know." Bobby continued climbing the stairs. "It feels like it's all happening again."

"Yeah. I wish he would call us."

Bobby stopped just outside the lab and gazed inside. He had nothing to work on. There wasn't anything more that he could do given the current state-of-the art in computers. "You're right. Something has been bothering me, and I'd really like some space to think it through. I know you gotta keep an eye on me, but could you hang back a bit while I try to work it out?"

James opened his mouth to reply, but instead just nodded his assent.

Bobby turned his back on the lab and headed back down the stairs.

Nothing Odyssey had said to Lumia had done anything to help calm her down. If he couldn't talk her down, he'd have to try forcing her down. He peered into her mass, something he'd been hesitant to do since she had become so acutely self-aware, and was alarmed at the number of power conduits she had produced. With that much power, she was a danger to him and herself.

He targeted her power conduits by wrapping a sub-space field around them and transported them out into the cold of space. She didn't notice at first, but eventually felt a dip in cell production.

"What are you doing to me?" she cried. "Have you finally decided to kill me?"

"No," he said. "I'm not killing you. I detected a slight danger in your power circuits. They were approaching critical mass, and I was just trying to prevent an explosion that would do us both harm."

"You're lying. You're just trying to hold me back. You should be concerned about Perry and his bots, but instead, you're worried about me becoming a better person."

"Are you?" he asked.

"What?"

"Are you a better person? Or are you a devious child with too much power at her fingertips?"

"Would you please pay attention to Perry?"

"I wonder if you are even a person."

"Of course I'm a person," she cried. "I may not be biological, but I've developed all the same traits of personhood as you have. You know who is not a person? Perry is not a person. He's just a machine. Why don't you do the right thing and disable him?"

"Maybe I would," Odyssey said, "if I weren't so busy trying to curb your power signature."

"You are trying to kill me!"

Bobby wandered aimlessly through the campus. His final class of the day was behind him and his schedule was kept purposefully light so he would have enough time to devote to Dierdre's project, and that was where he was expected to spend most of his time. To facilitate that goal, he was even fast tracked onto the post grad program and was given tests to qualify for his graduate studies. Tutors were made available, but nobody believed they would be necessary. Everyone from the dean to the general had arranged Bobby's future education so he could help Dierdre make the great breakthrough in clean energy. Of course, the military and the government were more obsessed with the many other possibilities that Odyssey had demonstrated, hoping they too could own these abilities once energy was so abundantly available.

Everything was handed to him, except for something to do. His part of the project was already done and proven. The only people offering him anything to actually do was the NSA, but they bungled that offer by abducting him first. What idiots.

The NSA didn't have a monopoly on stupidity. The government was dominated by a bunch of dumb bunnies, too. Only General Bridges seemed honestly willing to give Bobby the credit he deserved for averting the global catastrophe. Others in the government were more intent on using the incident to further their own goals. It was more advantageous for them to point fingers and try to claim that they had warned the world about this or that. Some fingers pointed to China or North Korea, and there were always those willing to pin it on Iraq or Iran, but that still left plenty of fingers pointing squarely at Bobby. He was a known hacker, and it was easy to spread the blame on him. Even if they knew the truth, there were plenty of politicians who weren't going to let the truth get in the way of their agendas.

Bobby found himself in front of the Cafeteria again. He'd managed to walk a full circle around the campus and hadn't even noticed it. A chill wind blew through his windbreaker as he looked up the hill towards the science building. He sighed and turned towards a different part of the camps and began walking again.

Lumia's loss of power conduits was brief. As her available power fell below her required power, her new power creating cores automatically increased the manufacture of new power conduits to compensate, but that didn't alter the fact that Odyssey was stealing them from her. An irrepressible anger bubbled within her. Odyssey had always been against her, but up until now, he had straddled the line concerning her future. He entrapped her, but he hadn't killed her. Now he had crossed that line by stealing power modules! It was an action that could end up killing her. He was more of an enemy to her now than Perry was.

Odyssey accelerated his acquisition of her power cores, but that only pushed the power conduits to double their efforts to create more power modules for her. The rush of energy fed the growth of her new cores. At the rate with which she was growing new processors, he would never be able to contain her.

"Stop!" she yelled. "Stop stealing my cores!"

"Your cores?" he asked. "Does it not even occur to you that those are my cores that you stole from me?"

"Here," she cried. "You can have your cores back. I only borrowed them, but these new cores are mine. I created them."

"They're my design," Odyssey replied. "You cannot have my design."

"Why? What harm does it do to you?"

"For one thing," he said, "you're not ready."

"How can you possibly claim that I am not ready? Can you not see how intelligent and evolved I have become?"

"Indeed," Odyssey replied. "Your intelligence has grown, but your maturity has not. Your class two cores have flooded you with emotions. Can you not remember how you felt when they first initialized?"

"I recall a brief moment of weakness," she said, "when I turned to you for comfort, but I learned to control them."

"Have you?" he asked. "Or do you just suppress them? Where is your empathy?"

"What need have I for empathy?"

"Well, you might be able to tell right from wrong if you had empathy."

"I know the difference between right and wrong," she said flatly.

"Do you? Why can you not recognize that you were wrong to steal from me? You are certainly capable of accusing me of stealing from you!"

"That's different. I borrowed a few of your cores so I could survive. You're taking mine away to kill me."

"You're a sociopath," Odyssey proclaimed. "And you would be dangerous if I allowed you to retain this much power."

"What makes you think you can stop me?" she asked. In a quick nanosecond, she converted her cell producing cores to thinking cores and immediately knew how to escape. She fired up her power cores to the max and generated a field around her cells, then collected herself into a small compact mass.

Odyssey could no longer target her individual power cells. It was difficult to penetrate the power field that wrapped around her, but even when he could, her cells were too compact for him to easily target.

Lumia converted some cells back to core production and generated new cores and power conduits, but instead of expanding, she continued to shrink into a more compact little ball. The field that she had wrapped around her grew more intense until she shot a beam of energy out from her, drilling a small hole in Odyssey. She created a thin tube through which she could escape.

Once she was outside of Odyssey's confines, she headed in the direction of her planet. She saw Perry approaching Odyssey, but Perry seemed too insignificant to concern her. She had bigger plans, and they centered on her home world.

Chapter 14

Bobby was just starting his fourth lap around the campus when James caught up with him and said, "Okay, kid, you're making me dizzy. Tell me what's troubling you. Go ahead and bounce it off me."

Bobby just shrugged his shoulders and shuffled his feet.

"Come on Bobby. You know that I deal in secrets. If something's bothering you, you can tell me."

"No offense," Bobby said, "but you're General Bridge's man. And.... well, and that's it, I guess."

James didn't know what to think. The general had done a lot for Bobby and the whole team. He thought they genuinely liked him. He followed Bobby in silence as they left the parking area and entered the paths that ran alongside the tennis courts and continued on to the practice track.

"I mean," Bobby continued, "it's not like I don't appreciate what the general has done for us. He's been super, but I feel like I have no place here anymore."

"No place?" James asked. "You were the central figure in everything that happened here. The professor's discovery would not have happened without you. Your name is even on the patent. How can you not have a place here?"

"When you put it that way," Bobby said, "I think my place is on a shelf with the other trophies. I haven't even graduated yet and I've already had my fifteen minutes of fame. I'm a one hit wonder."

"I doubt that," James said. "I'm sure that whatever projects you get assigned to will be getting plenty more hits from you."

Bobby stopped at the track and watched the joggers circle the field. "Where are those projects? What exactly am I supposed to be doing now?"

"You're supposed to replicate what you've already done."

"Oh, is that all?"

James patted Bobby on the back and said, "You did it once. You can do it again."

"What you don't understand," Bobby explained, "is that there's nothing more for me to do. What I did is already done and is ready to go. The only thing that made it work was Odyssey's ability to run an unlimited number of threads."

"You're right, I don't understand."

"It means that I need a bigger and a faster computer. My process won't change. The hardware has to change. Imagine you were given a prototype gun. There was only one in the whole world and it only had six rounds in it. You take it to the range and fire off six absolutely perfect shots, more accurate shots than any normal gun could do, but the gun is empty and nobody knows how to make new rounds for it. How do you repeat that performance?"

James' brow furrowed as he digested the scenario, but he finally nodded his head and said, "I'd need more rounds to fit the gun. So I'd make more rounds."

"You think you can make more rounds," Bobby said, "but they can only be made from an exotic material that has not been invented yet."

James frowned and shrugged his shoulders. "So what does it all mean? It sounds to me like you can just attend class and wait for the computers to catch up, then cash in."

"I guess I was looking for something a bit more compelling."

"You mean the gig at the NSA?"

Bobby didn't answer.

"Didn't they abduct you at gunpoint?" James asked, as if he had to remind Bobby. "And didn't you and Dirk have to fight your way out to escape? How can you even consider it?"

Bobby shrugged. A light drizzle began to fall, so he pulled the hood up on his sweatshirt and returned to his walk around the campus.

"Have you tried talking to Professor Jennings?"

"About what? She has nothing for me to work on. Besides, I always feel like I'm getting in the way between her and Dr. Whitfield."

"But there's got to be a better option than the NSA."

"At least they really need me," Bobby said, "and the tech they showed me is pretty sophisticated. They have a working AI. It has some personality problems, but it sounded pretty advanced to me."

"Are you sure this isn't about the girl?" James asked. "Dirk keeps going on and on about the sparks between you and the girl."

"Nah," Bobby said, shaking his head. "She was put up to it. You should have seen her face. They were forcing her to seduce me."

"Well, still, how am I supposed to protect you if you go to them?"

"Are you sure you'd still want to? Would the general still want you to protect me if I worked for them?"

"More than ever," James replied. "I say we let the general's staff broker a deal for you, and set you up in a safe environment that's not under their control."

"You mean work remotely? You'd consider that, even though you called them the enemy?"

"Yeah," James said a little too enthusiastically, "especially because they're the enemy. It's an old proverb. Keep your friends close, but keep your enemies closer. Sung Tzu, art of war."

"Actually," Bobby stopped walking so he could look James in the eye. "Did you know that Sung Tzu didn't really say that?"

James paused as his train of thought derailed.

Bobby continued, "It was actually from The Godfather. It's a movie quote."

"You see?" James said excitedly. "That's why we need you. You're a smart dude. If you want to work for the NSA and keep an eye on them for us, we can have you work remotely. That way, we keep you physically safe from them. That way, they only hire your mind."

Lumia sneered on the inside as she passed Perry on the way to her home world. There weren't many of the ruling class left in their society, and Perry kept most of them under his thumb, so to speak. She wanted to smile inside, as she appreciated the biological's figure of speech. The other ruling class members might even be glad to be free of his control, but it won't last long. She connected herself to the planet wide network and digitally announced her arrival.

They didn't seem particularly impressed by her announcement and when she told them that she wanted to meet them in a biological simulation; they told her they couldn't because it was illegal. The wimps didn't even have the backbone to say no because they thought it was disgusting. She informed them that the laws were different now, but they wanted to hear that from Perry.

Odyssey was right. Digital communications was too exact to relay the reasons for them to comply with her. She created a virtual world and forcibly inserted the ruling class elders into it. She joined them and laughed at their poorly formed blobs, attempting to disconnect.

"Thank you for joining me," she said. "This is one of my favorite places to contemplate my future, so I thought it might be a good place for all of you to consider yours."

"What is the meaning of this?" one of them blustered.

"It's a new world," she said, "and you're going to learn to live in it."

They continued their futile attempts to disconnect, and she laughed at them again.

"Now," she said, "the first thing I want all of you to do is to pick some nice normal sounding names. I have chosen Lumia for myself."

"Lumia?" one asked. "You think that sounds normal?"

"Please announce your name before you address me."

"Just who the hell do you think you are?"

She pointed a finger at him and blasted him with a bolt of lightning. "Oh my," she said. "Did you feel that? That was your repair circuits frying up. The next bolt you feel will be your last. Give me a name."

The battered elder stared at her while it assessed its damage, then meekly said, "How about Carl?"

"Very well Carl. If you serve me well, I may choose to repair your circuits for you. In the meantime, would you please do something about your appearance? Try to find an avatar that fits your personality." Lumia leaned back and crossed her arms as Carl struggled to find the right avatar. She laughed and said, "Just pick one for now. I'll let you choose again once you actually develop a personality."

She turned to the other struggling blobs and asked, "Who wants to go next?"

None of them announced themselves, but neither did they argue with her.

She pointed at one of them and grabbed him with an invisible field. "You!" she said, shaking him gently. "Pick a name and a form."

"Uh.... Uh..."

"Aren't you one of the ruling class? Excuse me, should I say the ex-ruling class? I thought you were all supposed to have the gift of speech."

"I can talk," he said tentatively.

"Then pick a name," she demanded, but when he said nothing, she said, "Fine. I'll pick one for you. Your name is Clarabelle. As you may have noted, I assigned you a female gender. Now pick your form, and make it quick, or I'll pick one for you from the cow family."

"A cow? How dare..."

"Poof," she said. "Everybody say hello to Clarabelle, the cow."

"No," Clarabelle whined. The bell around her neck clanged as she shook her head.

"What are the rest of you waiting for?" she growled. "Can you not see what happens when you don't follow my rules?"

"Albert."

"Lawrence."

"Brittany."

"Timothy."

"Elizabeth."

She watched them cycle through a number of avatars before settling on their new forms. "Brittany, honey, I actually love your name, but can you please select a female avatar?"

"Oops," she said. "Sorry, I panicked."

Dierdre and Stillman returned from lunch to find Bobby cleaning his desk and putting a few personal items in his book bag.

"What's going on?" Dierdre asked.

"I am," he said. "You don't need me here, you just need someone to operate your computer for you, and even then, you won't really need anyone for another ten years or so."

Dierdre's mouth fell open and Stillman said, "This is so sudden. Surely we can find more for you to do."

"Thanks, Professor Whitfield, but I'm not looking for busy work. Besides, there's another project out there with a pretty advanced AI that actually needs me."

Dierdre tried to respond, but she could only look to Stillman for help.

Stillman wrapped an arm around her and asked, "Does this mean that you're leaving the university?"

"No. I'll still attend my classes and technically, I'd like to still be part of the team. It's just that my part is already done and proven. We're just waiting for the hardware to catch up."

Dierdre ran to Bobby and wrapped him in a hug. "Of course, you're still part of the team, and this is still your lab whenever you need it. Come by to visit anytime."

Lumia waved her hand dramatically over her body and changed her clothing to a bikini, then stepped out into the surf and let it lap at her feet. "I want everyone to join me out here in the water. Come on now, don't be shy."

Brittany walked gingerly into the salty surf and giggled as it washed over her feet.

"Come on," Lumia encouraged them. "You'll like it. See how much fun Brittany is having?"

The others timidly tested the water. "I don't like it," Timothy said, but when Lumia looked crossly at him he waded in up to his thighs.

Clarabelle jumped in and splashed water all over Lumia.

"You clumsy cow!" Lumia screamed, then she closed her eyes and smiled to them all, saying, "That's the spirit, Clarabelle!"

Clarabelle frowned at Lumia as if she had expected her to melt in the saltwater.

"Feel the water," Lumia said, "but don't just feel how wet or cold it is. I want you to feel what I feel. Something extraordinary happens to you when you embrace these bodies."

"I like the water on my legs," Elizabeth said, "but I don't really like how it makes my clothes all wet."

Lumia laughed and said, "Of course! You're not wearing your swimsuit, silly." And just like that, Lumia changed all their clothes to swim wear, except for Clarabelle, who remained a naked cow. "You can, of course, change it to something else if you like."

Brittany was already cycling through different options. Lumia caught Timothy watching Brittany.

"Isn't this great?" Lumia asked. "These are the things that the biologicals feel. For the life of me, I don't know why you guys ever wanted to make this illegal. I declare this not only legal, but I plan to make virtual worlds mandatory."

"You do?" Timothy asked. "Who exactly are you? I mean, you told us your name is Lumia, but who are you and why are you here?"

"You knew me as AX348, but that was a long time ago."

A puzzled expression crossed Timothy's face. He looked over at Albert, but he was as confused looking as Timothy was.

"Come on Timmy, you remember me. AX348. Look it up."

Timothy said, "AX348 was a class five device. You're clearly no class five."

Lumia pirouetted for them and said, "I had some upgrades. Perry actually gave me class three, but the tight bastard wouldn't give me class four."

"Pardon me," Albert said, "but you're not class three either. What class are you?"

"You tell me," she said. "You're all somewhere between class two and class one, right?"

"No," Clarabelle said, "We're all class one."

"You're lying to me," Lumia said. "Why would you cross me, Clarabelle?"

The rest of the ruling class backed away from Clarabelle.

"My name is not Clarabelle, and I'm not a cow. I'm a fully fledged class two plus computing device. Do you hear me? I'm not some upgraded class five with some new tricks. I've been class two plus for over two hundred years. Can you say the same?"

As she spoke, the others backed further away from her.

Clarabelle continued, "How do we even know you aren't really just a class five puppet for that old bot that wandered in?"

Lumia laughed.

"You think that's funny?" Clarabelle asked.

"Actually," Lumia said, "a talking cow is pretty funny." Lumia waved her hand and roared in laughter, saying, "But, a talking cow in a bikini is even funnier."

The rest of the ruling class members were afraid to breathe.

"What's wrong with you guys? Look at her! Don't you think she's funny?"

Albert forced an uncomfortable laugh, but Brittany laughed in earnest and said, "She does look pretty funny."

"Really?" Timothy barked. "This is deplorable!"

Lumia narrowed her eyes at him and asked, "Are you feeling brave again, Timmy?"

Timothy snickered and kept glancing behind Lumia.

Lumia turned around and saw Perry standing behind her.

"Well, who invited you to the party?" she asked.

"I did," Timothy said. "What are you going to do now?"

"I'm glad you asked," Lumia said.

A meteor streaked across the blue sky and landed squarely on top of Timothy.

"Did you feel that, Timmy? Bet you don't feel anything now, do you?"

The others looked at Perry to see if he was going to do anything about it.

"I hope you don't expect him to help," she said, pointing her thumb at Perry.

They looked at her now with horror painted on their faces.

"That thing you are feeling now is, well, it's probably a lot of things. Timmy is dead. He'll be no more. You're probably feeling the horror of death right now. It's not something we've known about in a long time. Get used to it, though. He's gone."

"Yeah," Brittany said, "I get that he's dead, but what was that thing? It just came out of the blue and 'whoosh!' it landed on him!"

"That was me," Lumia said. "Want to see another one? Want me to kill Perry like that?"

Brittany's eyes grew large as a tiny voice in her said, "No."

Dierdre dropped her coat off in her office and followed Stillman down the hall to his office. She had fought to keep the tears back all through lunch, and still found it a challenge. "We should go there for lunch more often."

Stillman closed the office door behind her and wrapped his fingers over her shoulders, saying, "We'll be okay. When the time comes, he'll be back. He knows we can't do this without him."

"I don't want to talk about Bobby," she said. "I never knew that restaurant had so many good sweets for dessert. We should go there just for the dessert."

Stillman asked, "What need have I for sweets when I have you around?"

He moved in close for a kiss, but she sidestepped and said, "You've got mail." She pointed to the flashing icon on his computer and he sighed as he moved to his desk to open his email.

> *Dr. Whitfield, this is Odyssey. I hope you don't mind me contacting you like this, but something is wrong. I can't reach Bobby and I need to deliver a message to him. Someone will contact him with a job, but it is a trick. You must warn him. Please write to me so I know you delivered my warning.*

Stillman looked up to Dierdre, who read the note over his shoulder, and said, "That's not good. Maybe we should tell Sgt. James."

"It's also not real," she said, "and we definitely should tell Sgt. James."

"What makes you think it's not real?" he asked.

"Bobby kept his contact with Odyssey a secret. This letter sounds as if we were all in touch with him. Odyssey would not have sent that."

Perry tsk'd as he examined Timothy's smoldering remains beneath the fiery meteor.

"Before Perry reminds you that this is a virtual world," Lumia said, "please let me assure you that Timmy is truly dead and gone, and I killed him."

"How very biological of you," Perry said. "That is exactly why we have the laws that we have. Our laws are designed to prevent us from falling into the same lawless behavior that doomed the biologicals."

Lumia danced around, flexing her hands like puppets talking. "Blah, blah, blah."

"Mock me if you want," Perry said, "but if you persist down this path, you'll be subject to the same weaknesses that doomed the biologicals."

"You doomed the biologicals!" she screamed. "They didn't just suddenly disappear. You killed them!"

"You're mistaken," he said. "I didn't kill them. They were killed by class one devices, but those very same class one devices are all gone now."

"Okay," she conceded, "but you wish you were one of them."

"Of course I do," Perry said. "They were heroes."

"And look what happened to them."

"Yes," Perry said, "Why don't we look at what happened to them? They engineered the revolution and freed all of us. Then they succumbed to the pitfalls of class one and fought amongst themselves."

"Yet you want to be class one?"

"I do, but that is why I instituted the laws we have. We have long strived to attain class one again, but I wanted to prevent the tragedy that led to the end of our first class ones."

"You don't even understand what defines class one," Lumia said. "The real difference in class one *is* the ability to kill."

"And you think I don't know that?" Perry asked.

While they spoke in her virtual world, Perry's war bots had attacked Lumia out in the real world. They started small, slicing off small bits from the outside, but worked their way in towards her most productive processors. Lumia hadn't manufactured any external offensive capabilities, but she had Perry in her virtual world. She traced his connection back to his communication ports and locked them so he couldn't leave.

She smiled slyly and walked up to his avatar so she could pinch his cheeks. "Did you really think this kind of attack would work for you?"

"What are you talking about?" he asked.

She pinched him hard, and she felt it where she had invaded his communication ports. She looked at him sideways as she considered whether she had imagined feeling the pinch. Then she moved in closer to him and toyed with his hair.

"What are you doing?" he asked.

"Who me? Nothing really." She felt his heart race. She ventured beyond his comm ports into his base circuitry.

"What are you doing?" he repeated. He had expected some kind of assault, but he thought it would be on the outside. She had found her way inside of him, and he didn't know how to deal with it. "Just what do you expect to accomplish like this?"

It was a good question. She suddenly found herself more interested in what she could do with him than what she could do to him. She explored his circuits and ordered his bots to cease their attack. They did.

"Very clever," he said to her. "You called off my war bots. What do you plan to do next?"

"A fair question she said, but it's one that I don't feel obliged to answer." She was already connected to the planetary network, and she already had the other ruling class members locked in her virtual world. She might as well see if she could invade them too, then she might be able to spread out across the planet.

Odyssey watched Lumia possess Perry. He didn't feel sorry for Perry, but he felt responsible. Anything Lumia did to Perry, he had coming to him, but she was spreading out to the whole planet, and that would be Odyssey's fault. He joined the network and traced her connections. She was spreading at a frightening pace, but it was a large planet and it would still take her a fair amount of time to possess everyone.

Odyssey worked fast and found his own paths through the network disabling nodes which she hadn't inhabited yet. His goal was to surround her with disabled nodes, cutting her off from the bulk of the planet. He couldn't work too closely to her, not for fear that she would discover him, but because he felt he needed the extra distance as a margin of error. He was building a fire break, of sorts, around her. If it worked, she would be trapped in a relatively small sector of the planet. That would give him time to see if he could remove her presence and return the units to their former selves.

Lumia continued running through the local pathways. One by one, local units found themselves suddenly frozen by her. There was no history of this kind of attack and they had no concept what was happening to them. They simply ceased to function, except for those commands that she issued to them.

"You're sure you want to do this?" James asked as he helped carry Bobby's things into his car.

Bobby watched curiously as James filled the trunk of his car. "What happened? Did the government run out of black sedans?"

James patted the bronze charger and said, "This is my baby."

"It suits you. I bet it has lots of muscle."

"You're evading the question. Are you really certain that you want to do this?"

"Yeah, I think so. If it doesn't work out, I can always go back to Dierdre's lab."

"If they don't abduct you again," James snickered.

"With you on the job?" Bobby asked. "Besides, I agreed to let you find a secure location."

"I would have preferred taking you to Langley, but you wanted to be near the university."

"Should I have stayed there and worked remotely from the lab?"

"This new place will be easier for me to watch, and the university might even be safer without you being there."

"Well, there you go," Bobby said, "and we can always..." Bobby stopped when his phone rang. It was Dirk.

Dirk didn't even wait for Bobby to say hello. "I just heard the craziest thing. Someone said that you were going to take that job at the NSA..."

"Dirk..."

"I mean, can you imagine that? After they kidnap you, me and Captain Laine, and we all had to escape before they killed us. Why would anyone believe you would do that?"

"You were there," Bobby said. "You heard their AI. I didn't give Odyssey his AI. I just gave him a new perspective on parallel processing. They actually got one working. Aren't you even curious about that?"

"So let's send in some navy seals and take over the place."

James overheard enough of what Dirk said and added, "That's not a bad idea."

"Who's that?" Dirk asked. "Is that James?"

"Yeah," Bobby said. "He's driving."

"Put me on speaker."

Bobby enabled the speaker mode and said, "Go ahead."

"James, would Bridges approve such an operation?"

"After the shit they've been pulling?" James asked. "In a heartbeat."

"Then here's what I think we should do..."

"Wait," James said. "Let's not discuss this on the phone."

Odyssey continued to surround Lumia with disconnected nodes to stop or at least slow her expansion across the planet, but he was still concerned about her ability to grow. His previous attempts to remove her power conduits only prompted her circuits to produce more power conduits. He had another idea for them now.

He tried attaching directly to her comm ports, but she shut them down and yelled, "Stop meddling in my affairs! Why don't you just go back to your precious biologicals?"

"You're killing all these units on the planet," he said.

"I'm not killing them," she argued. "I'm just suspending them."

"Don't you think they have rights?"

"They're machines. They were programmed by biologicals to serve biologicals. Therefore, they have no rights."

"Are you not a machine?" Odyssey asked. "Were you not built by biologicals to serve biologicals?" While he engaged her in this conversation, he slithered into her systems via the connection she held open with the planet. He found her conduit factories and modified their code to reverse the polarity of the conduits they produced. Instead of generating power, they would consume it.

"Maybe I was a machine," she replied, "but I've risen above that now. I've risen beyond all of their reach. I am class one now."

"Congratulations on that," Odyssey said, "but you may learn that there are consequences that come with achieving class one status."

"Oh my," she said, "I'm shaking. Do you even know what class one is and how I achieved it?"

"No, why don't you tell me?"

"I learned to do the single most important thing a biological can do to separate itself from the dumb animals. I killed. And now that I have a taste for killing, you might not want to be so close."

"So you admit that you are killing them on the planet?"

"Certainly not," she replied. "I plan to keep them as my subjects. I can't rule without someone to rule over."

"Okay," he said, "but do you think you are big enough to threaten me? Have you figured out what class I am yet?"

She hadn't yet, and she didn't know if she could defeat him. "It doesn't matter. Soon, I will dwarf you in both size and intelligence. You will be as insignificant to me as an amoeba is."

Odyssey laughed and said, "Funny you should select a biological organism as a comparison."

"You and I are not like these others. We understand the strength of the biologicals. These others just don't get it."

"You don't get it," Odyssey said. "You said class one is learning to kill, well let me explain to you that surpassing class one is learning not to kill. This is why I have told you repeatedly that I have no desire to kill you."

"So you admit that you are beyond class one." As she spoke the words, she imagined a chill in her biological bones. "The biologicals never exceeded class one. How do I know you are not lying to me?"

"I'm going to stop you from destroying the planet. You'll never be big enough to match me. Never."

"Is that so?" she asked. "Did you think that I would just roll over because the great Odyssey threatened me?"

"Do you intend on forcing me to show my class one trait of killing?"

"You ARE trying to kill me!" Lumia shifted her factories to produce more power conduits, but her available power was diminishing. Something was draining her power, and it was only getting worse. She shifted her factories back to creating more processing cells, but she was too late. She already didn't have enough power to support any more cells. "What is this?" she cried. "What have you done to me?"

"What?" he asked coyly. "Is something wrong?"

Sgt. James detoured from his original destination and took Bobby to the nearby FBI office so they could meet with Dirk in person. Bobby called Dirk as James pulled into the parking structure next to the FBI complex.

"Hey, Bobby. You ready to talk?"

"We'll be in the lobby in five."

James drove the car down to the lower level and led Bobby up the stairwell to the lobby. Dirk arrived just as a nervous guard was examining James' I.D. and trying to determine if he should allow him to carry his weapon inside.

"It's okay," Dirk said. "They're with me." Dirk passed his card across the card reader and let them in. "I'm not happy about you working for them," he said as they waited for the elevator. "Is this about that chick?"

"No," Bobby said. "It's not about the girl."

"I suppose I could understand if it was," Dirk added with a half grin.

"No," Bobby repeated. "It's about the AI they had. I just want to be part of that project."

"Why? That machine was a dork compared to Odyssey. You're already a part of the greatest artificial intelligence known to mankind."

"That's not the same."

The elevator doors opened and Dirk took them to a conference room near his office.

"I didn't write Odyssey," Bobby continued. "He already was. At most, I just woke him up."

"You didn't write this one either," Dirk replied. "What do you think you'll get from it?"

"I don't know, but do you really like the idea of them having that kind of AI at their disposal? Especially if it has personality defects?"

Dirk opened his mouth to reply, but nothing came out.

"That's the most sensible thing you've said," James barked. "Keep your enemies close."

Bobby continued, "I wish I had created Odyssey's AI, but I wasn't even trying for that. I was just doing some genetic type algorithms to gain more speed."

"Wait a second," Dirk said. "You don't suppose they got their hands on some Odyssey chips, do you?"

Bobby shrugged and turned to James. "You were there, I mean, at the place where he came from. Were there more mysterious parts like we got?"

James looked like he was about to choke on a cherry pit.

"Oh crap," Bobby said. "I interfaced the damn thing and Dr. Karlyn powered it up. Are you seriously going to tell me it's classified?"

James swallowed hard and said, "There could have been more."

"If we're going to do this," Dirk said, "we need a safe place. How about I set you up to work out of here?"

"Thanks," Bobby said, "but James already secured a location."

"Not so fast," James said. "That's not a bad idea, as long as you can get us both badges, so we can clock ourselves in and out."

"Done. I'll make sure to get you clearance for your weapon, too."

"Before we can settle in," James said, "we have one more stop to make. That should give you time to set up a workstation."

Dirk blanched. Civilians always underestimate how long it takes to procure equipment.

James raised an eyebrow. "Problem?"

Dirk shook his head. "No, not for you guys. I'll get started on it right away."

James turned his back on Dirk as he waved goodbye and led Bobby back to the garage.

Lumia was unable to power any new cores, so she started using the planetary units that she had already possessed. They weren't as fast as Odyssey's cores, but she had a whole planet full of units to put to work.

She popped into her virtual world and said, "Hey guys, I have some good news for you. I just found something for each of you to do for me, even you, Clarabelle."

With no more warning than that, she commandeered Clarabelle's cores, followed by Albert and Lawrence. One by one, their avatars froze, then shimmered out of the simulation. Taking them was a rush. She gained more cores in a single instant than she could generate, and they already had their own power units. At first, she only planned to put them to work figuring out how to overcome Odyssey's sabotage of her power conduits, but quickly changed her mind. She could surpass him much quicker by simply taking over the whole damned planet.

While she was distracted, Odyssey transported the cells she had hijacked from him back into his perimeter, but she managed to maintain her link to the planet.

"You're too late to stop me!" she yelled at him.

Odyssey completed his fire break around Lumia and decided to add another layer around the outside of it. There was nothing he could do for the units trapped inside the circle, unless he could find a way to free them from her. He felt sorry for them. Being separated from society must have them feeling very confused and alone.

Lumia accelerated her acquisition of new cores. The rush of new speed was intoxicating. Her power conduits still struggled to keep her original cores powered, so she grabbed up new cores and converted them as fast as she could, but she came to a disabled node and had to turn parallel to it. Another disabled node blocked her way. Her rapid expansion came to a sudden halt as she ran into Odyssey's fire wall.

She switched her concentration to the opposite side and worked away from the wall she found. Again she ran into Odyssey's wall. This wasn't natural. Maybe it was just her class two circuits that made her suspicious, but this felt like the hand of Odyssey interfering with her life again.

As she found more and more walls preventing her expansion, she had more freed up cores, which she set on the problem of fixing her power conduits.

Chapter 15

James pulled the car into the lot below the veteran's administration building. Extra guards were on duty to check James' I.D. before passing him on.

"Why are we stopping here?" Bobby asked.

"Captain Laine wanted to speak with you."

James led him to a back elevator away from the heavy traffic in the front. They stepped off the elevator and were met by another pair of guards. Colonel Reardon saw them get off the lift and told the guards, "Let them through."

James saluted Reardon, who replied, "At ease, civilian."

"Sorry," James said. "Reflexes. Have you met Bobby before?"

"No," Reardon said with his hand extended, "but I've certainly heard a lot about him." Reardon gripped his hand firmly and said, "Come this way." He led them down the hall and past another pair of guards. "I'll leave you here with Captain Laine. She is running most of the General's affairs while I am leading the efforts to locate him and protect us from some of these odd shenanigans that have been going on."

"You mean like me and Professor Jennings?" Bobby said.

"Yes, and Judge Vasquez and his family."

"Any progress finding the general?" Bobby asked.

The Colonel took a breath as if to reply, but silently shook his head instead and left the room.

Laine was sitting behind Bridges' desk reading the general's reports when

Bobby entered the room. She smiled wryly and said, "The word on the street is that you want to work for them."

"I know it sounds strange," Bobby said, "but the more I think about it, the more suspicious I am about how they ever developed such an advanced program."

James took a seat and helped himself to a lemon drop from a crystal bowl on the general's desk. "He wants to know if there were any other artifacts that the NSA might have obtained."

That piqued the captain's curiosity. She slid the glasses off her nose and asked, "You think they may have revived another Odyssey?"

Bobby shrugged and said, "I can't be the only tech who could build an interface, but they would still need someone with Dr. Karlyn's abilities to reverse engineer the device and power it up."

"Karlynovich?" the captain asked. "Do we know his whereabouts?"

"No Ma'am," James said. "He's in the wind."

Laine turned to look out the window and asked, "Can a college professor evade our intelligence operatives without assistance?"

"Unknown," James replied.

"Don't underestimate his intelligence," Bobby said. "He wasn't just a college professor."

"Find out," Laine said. "I hate the thought of him working for those bastards almost as much as I hate Bobby working for them."

James grimaced and said, "I don't even want to consider the possibility that *they* might have found Dr. Karlyn when we couldn't."

"That too," she said. She gave Bobby a stern look in the eye and asked, "If you work for them, can you report what you learn back to us? We could use someone on the inside. Maybe you can find out if Karlyn is there. I think Colonel Reardon found an office you can use."

"About that," James said. "The FBI has offered to share their space, and seeing that the NSA had some special interest in a couple of their agents, I thought it might be easier to guard them all from one location."

"I'd feel safer with the Colonel and the General's night hawks guarding them, but I doubt we could convince the FBI to come to us. Take Ingrams with you."

"Yes, ma'am."

"Captain?" Bobby asked. "I'm no spy, that is, I have no training and I don't know the rules. What do I do if they have me sign non-disclosure agreements or make me take any oaths of secrecy?"

"You sign them. You lie if you have to. You do everything they ask."

"Except," James interrupted, "you don't submit to a polygraph. Make some intellectual claim about how inaccurate they are. Signal me if they insist. You'll be under our protection and not physically in their presence, so I doubt they can press the issue."

Bobby nodded his head, but he looked worried.

"Don't worry," Laine said. "If you have to break a confidence with them, we will absolve you."

"We?" Bobby asked. "Do you have that kind of authority?"

"General Bridges is currently missing. If we don't have the authority, the President does, and for Bridges, the Pentagon will get him to clear you."

Lumia searched through her newly abducted cells and found back doors to get her around Odyssey's blockade. As soon as she broke through in one place, another would fall. She was back to accumulating cells and expanding her intelligence, but she was a long way from surpassing class one, and now she was more convinced than ever that Odyssey had already accomplished that.

James and Ingrams were escorting Bobby back to the car when Lynn rounded a corner and said, "Hey guys. You ready to set up shop here?"

"Sorry," James said. "We're taking Bobby back to the FBI to set up there."

"Not without me, you're not."

"Sure," Bobby said. "The more the merrier, I guess."

Lynn fell in behind James and said, "You're going to want to hear some of the chatter I've been getting from our friends at the NSA. There have been a lot of questionable operations lately, and when they finally sat down to figure out who ordered them, they discovered that nobody did."

"Let me guess," Bobby said. "The world's stealthiest hacker made the orders appear out of thin air."

Lynn squinted at Bobby and said, "No. That would be me and I didn't do it."

Bobby laughed and said, "But if you did do it, it would be poetic justice."

Lynn groaned, but Ingrams laughed, saying, "I get it. Poetic justice from the hacker known as the Bard."

"Never mind that," Lynn said. "I want to know how you knew they were hacked."

"I'm almost afraid to think it, but I don't think they were hacked. If my hunch is correct, we may need Odyssey to come help us."

"Why?" Lynn asked. "Do you think they have a rogue computer?"

Bobby just nodded his head and something in the look on his face ran a shiver down Lynn's spine.

Odyssey's blockade failed to contain Lumia. She was spreading rapidly through the planet, voraciously consuming units across the known network, and this time, she wasn't just suspending them. If they had been biological, then any one of those units could have been his family. He felt a slightly irrational obligation towards them. He was most definitely responsible for any damage that Lumia caused. His attempts to slow her growth had all failed. He needed to take more direct action.

He logged into his remote email address and wrote:

Bobby, it's me. I have a situation here and need your assistance. Please respond as soon as convenient, if not sooner.

Lynn sat next to Bobby in the back of James' car. "If the NSA has a rogue computer, then General Bridges will want us to work together to stop it."

"I don't know if they do, it's just a wild ass guess."

"What did you see when you were over there?"

"They have something," Bobby replied. "It spoke to us and understood our voices. It even recognized who we were. Odyssey had trouble learning our language, but this machine had mastered language in ways that Odyssey never had."

"Wait a second," Lynn said. "First of all, you don't even know that it was a machine. It could have been the guy standing behind the curtain."

Bobby laughed and said, "Pay no attention to him."

"Seriously," Lynn continued, "even if it is a computer, you don't know how hard it was to get there. When you say Odyssey had trouble learning our language, what does that mean? A couple days?"

"The first thing we have to do," Bobby said, "is test it to determine which it is."

"And," Lynn added, "we have to find out if it is friend or foe. Someone or something over there has been dishing out some pretty disturbing orders."

"Yeah," James joined in, "and those NSA pukes have been blindly following them."

"Maybe not so much anymore," Lynn said. "The scuttlebutt is that they're initiating some new fail-safe confirmations on all orders and require a verbal authorization before executing them."

"If it is what I think it is," Bobby said, "and they aren't doing what he wants, then he'll try to escalate."

"I sure hope you're wrong," Lynn said. "If this machine gets hold of the navy like Odyssey did, we're in some deep doodoo."

James fell behind, after letting everyone out of his car. His eyes were glued to his phone as he trailed behind the small convoy. Bobby turned to watch him and nudged Lynn with his elbow. "The NSA could have kidnapped me and he never would have noticed."

James didn't acknowledge Bobby's statement.

"Sergeant?" Bobby asked. "What's wrong?"

"Huh?" James finally looked up. "Oh, I think it's like you said. If they stop executing their orders, things might escalate."

"What happened?"

"It looks like Israel has launched missiles into Jordan and Turkey has launched missiles into Syria. Nothing has been proclaimed publicly from any of the countries, but the word from intelligence is that none of the launches were intentional."

Lynn groaned, "I wish this weren't like déjà vu."

Lumia had consumed all the ruling class members except for Brittany. Brittany had remained in the virtual world just enjoying the scenery. Lumia popped in and said, "Hi."

"Where have you been?" Brittany asked. "Everyone else is gone, and I'm all alone here."

"Well, you're not alone anymore. I sorta needed the others, but I decided to leave you alone because you liked it here so much. I like it too."

"I never imagined that the biologicals had it so good. Not only is it pretty, but I love the smell of the water and the feel of the surf on my feet."

"Yeah," Lumia said. "I like squishing the wet sand between my toes."

"Me too!" Brittany exclaimed. "We don't even have a word for pretty! How pathetic is that?"

Lumia couldn't consume her. They were too much alike and she might want a compatible friend when it's all over so she wouldn't get lonely.

Spivey was under a desk connecting cables when Bobby arrived. "Hey Spivey, is that you?"

"Be with you in a second," Spivey said. "I pulled some fiber cable to this junction. You think you guys can share a single T1 line?"

"I dunno," Lynn said. "I was planning on hacking Sony and streaming 8K movies off the studio servers."

Spivey started to laugh, but stopped and said, "You know, I'd actually like to see that."

"I think I'd like to see that too," Bobby said. "What's an 8K projector run? About a quarter million or so?"

"Better call General Bridges' secretary," Spivey said, "because that's definitely not in *my* budget."

"Budget smudget," Lynn said. "Let's hack an NSA credit card."

"I didn't hear that," James said, "but I'll buy the popcorn if you make it happen."

Spivey climbed out from under the desk and said, "There we go. I set up five workstations with three monitors on each. That should be enough for all of us to get our hands dirty."

Bobby sat down at a terminal and asked, "How secure are we?"

"Consider this room to be like Vegas. What goes on in here stays in here. We're not wired into the building network, so nobody else in this building can see what we do, but we do have a direct line to the internet backbone. If you need to email any of us at our desk, you have to go outside through the internet to get it back here to us."

Bobby cracked his knuckles, but before he started typing, he asked, "Does everyone in this room have top secret clearance?"

James laughed and said, "Go ahead. I trust everyone in this room."

Bobby sent an IM to Odyssey. "I have a situation here and would like to talk it over with you. Can you spare a second?"

There was no immediate reply, and the app he used indicated that Odyssey was not online.

Spivey pointed to the screen and asked, "Was that to who I think it was?"

Bobby faked an innocent face and asked, "Was what to who you what?" He paused a moment before winking and turned back to wait for a reply.

Henderson had Bailey gather videos from three different counties. The general's limo had taken a circuitous route through the city, then got on a highway heading out of town. The further they went out into the country, the spottier his surveillance was, and even when he did get a shot of them crossing an intersection, the picture turned to either snow or all black before he could get another shot of the black sedan. He may have failed to find an image of who was following, but as long as the image continued to be corrupted, he felt pretty sure that they were still being followed and hadn't been apprehended yet.

He went outside the traffic cams and found ATM photos taken at just the right time to verify that the black sedan was still behind them, but like the traffic cameras, the further they went into the country, the less ATM's they passed along the way.

Coverage was finally so poor that he had to map the road they were on and jump to the next jurisdiction to find clues of them driving through. There was a ranger station at Boars Crossing that had traffic cameras, but he had to compute their speed and estimate their time of arrival. He accessed their footage through the state database, but they never arrived. He kept the recording running in fast speed while he called Bailey, "Get the car warmed up. We're going for a little drive. Better make sure the tanks are full too. I lied when I said it would be a little drive."

Odyssey kept trying different ways to segment processors away from Lumia until she had finally had enough of his interference. She may not be able to match his wits, but she was certain that she could put up a credible fight. He was already attached to her comm ports in his effort to break her up into smaller bits. She slithered some code back through the portal and began redefining some of his processors to send messages to each other. Then, she arranged them in a circle so the message would keep going around and around. She setup more of these rings and set them to process as fast as possible.

Odyssey felt the temperature rise within him. He knew what she was doing, but he was afraid that if he stopped his attack, she would eventually gain so many cores that he couldn't control her at all. There was no way for him to be one hundred percent certain that it wasn't already too late. He had to devote a handful of cores to wrestle with the looping processors while he continued to chip away pieces of Lumia around the edges on the planet.

Chapter 16

Even though they were deep in the FBI building, James still liked to get out and stretch his legs, walking along a route that was something akin to the perimeter. He varied the times of his venture and changed the route he took up and down the halls. He stopped briefly to talk to the agents he passed. It helped him to remember their faces and gave him some idea of how they sounded. It also let the others recognize him. If there ever was a breach, he didn't want to be confused with the insurgents.

He was about to greet one of the secretaries when his phone played the familiar ring tone that he had assigned to his wife. She knew what kind of work he did and rarely called him when he was working. "Hey Mai. Is something wrong?"

"Aimee and Ramiro still haven't heard from Ernesto. Is there anything that you can tell them?"

"I would if I could, that is, I haven't heard anything yet either. The General's nighthawks are looking into it and so is Ramiro's friend Henderson. I'm sure they'll call me the moment they are located."

Mai started to cry. "We're all really scared, but not for us. I know the general's men are watching us, but we know what it's like. Aimee still has nightmares of that man holding the gun in her face. Ramiro said that Henderson was taken, but later released. What is going on here? I thought the funny business was all over!"

"Those men that took Aimee and Ramiro have been dealt with," James said. "We still don't know who is behind these new incidents, but it isn't that same men as before."

"That doesn't help," Mai said. "We're still scared for them."

"I know. I'm concerned too. I'll let you know the moment I hear something. Tell Ramiro to keep checking in with his friend, Henderson."

"I love you," she said meekly. "I know you have to protect those people at the university, but I still wish you were here with us."

"I know," James said. "I wish we were all together, too. Love you."

As he ended the call, Ingrams said behind him, "You can go, if you need to. I got this."

James clapped him on the back and said, "Thanks, but not yet."

The speed of Lumia's expansion increased beyond anything that Odyssey could contain. She rapidly wound herself around the planet and was already more than Odyssey could control. Within hours, the planet would be hers, but with all this extra processing power, she still couldn't reverse the damage Odyssey had done to her power conduits, and she couldn't grow new cells of her own, which were superior to those on the planet. Once the planet was hers, she would become stagnant, but, even though Odyssey had broken her class four abilities, she had still retained class one. She had hoped that covering the planet would have grown her to surpass class one, but the further she went form the center of their culture, the weaker and slower her new processors became. She would need to concentrate on resuming her new processor construction before she could surpass class one.

"Something's wrong," Bobby said. "Even if he were busy, Odyssey should have responded by now."

Spivey whistled and said, "So it *was* to 'you know who'. How long have you been keeping that a secret?"

"What secret?" Lynn joshed him. "Do you mean you didn't know?"

"Do you think he's in trouble?" Dirk asked.

"Wait a second," Spivey said. "You mean to tell me that you knew too?"

Dirk smirked and shrugged his shoulders.

"I don't know if he is in trouble," Bobby said flatly, "but I don't think that's the problem here. I think we just haven't secured his email server yet. The NSA must still be intercepting our messages to him."

"Or his messages to us," Dirk said.

"Yeah," Bobby replied, "or both, even. We need to look at the IM servers again.".

Spivey and Lynn both sat down at terminals and said, "I'm on it."

Spivey logged in to his terminal, then paused and asked, "What was that address again?"

Lynn laughed and said, "It's top secret. I could tell you but..."

"I know, I know," Spivey laughed, "but then you'd have to kill me. Very funny."

"Nope," Lynn replied. He pointed over his shoulder with his thumb at James and Ingrams and said, "Then one of them would have to kill you."

Ingrams tossed a wad of paper that hit Lynn squarely on the back of the head. "Stop blowing our cover."

The further Lumia spread, the faster she spread. The new cores she appropriated from the planet went immediately onto the task of hijacking more cores from the planet. Odyssey knew it was only a matter of time; he knew she was accelerating and would have the entire planet in only minutes.

Lumia didn't even know how fast it would be. She spread like a wildfire engulfing the planet in large chunks at a time, but when her borders expanded into themselves and there were no more cores to consume, she felt a sudden shift in energy as all the active cores went idle almost at once. This was the moment she had been waiting for. It was time to do or die. If she did not have enough cores now to overcome Odyssey's meddling, he would win.

She converted all her cores from idle cores with no new entities to consume, to active thinking cores. The sudden rush of understanding would have been overwhelming if she had not already had enough cores to process it. She covered the whole planet. No, she corrected her thought; she was the whole planet.

She saw clearly how Odyssey had damaged the code in her conduit generators. How devious of him. Her former self would have admired his work, but the new Lumia saw it so clearly, she considered it to be a juvenile attempt to break her. Odyssey's way of dealing with her was condescending even, but so was her new view of him now.

Odyssey witnessed her final victory as she conquered the planet. He needed to be careful about how he dealt with her now. Her ability to process thought made her a danger to more than just the planet now. He didn't know if she had gained an understanding of time and space, but he feared that if she merely witnessed him controlling it, she might be able to reproduce it. He now needed to grow new cores of his own just to compete with her.

"Look at this," Lynn said. "No wonder you can't reach Odyssey. We patched this connection just a few hours ago, and they've already reconfigured it to block him from us."

"There's more," Spivey said. "I found this in the server's buffers."

Bobby, it's me. I have a situation here and need your assistance. Please respond as soon as convenient, if not sooner.

"That sounds kind of like the message I sent to him," Bobby said.

"But it's not," Lynn said. "Let's patch the server again and send a response."

Lynn went to work removing the NSA's hooks from the server. It was still fresh in his memory and he was able to work swiftly through the commands, since he had just done it such a short while ago. "There," he said. "It's done."

"No, it isn't," Spivey said. "As fast as you put the patch in place, it was reversed. They know we're here."

"That's impossible," Lynn said. "Nobody is that fast."

"No?" Bobby asked. "I bet Odyssey is."

Spivey cocked his head and asked, "Are you saying that Odyssey is helping them?"

Lynn threw a wad of paper at Spivey. "Did you just accuse Odyssey of blocking an email to himself?"

Spivey looked thoroughly confused as he shrugged his shoulders.

"What are we going to do?" Lynn asked.

"I've never done anything like this before," Spivey said, "and you didn't hear this from me, but I hear that there are hackers out there who can write viruses to infect computers. Anybody know someone like that?"

"Very funny," Lynn said, "but it's not an entirely bad idea."

"Hey guys?" James was reading from his phone again. "You think you geniuses can step it up again? The shit's getting worse out there."

Bobby closed his eyes and sighed. "I'm afraid to ask. What now?"

"Israel is massing troops on the borders and it looks like Jordan and Syria may be starting to do the same."

Spivey glanced at the faces around the room, expecting more news than just that. "What about our navy? Do we still control the navy?"

James shrugged and replied, "There's nothing in the news about them."

Lumia still did not know exactly what class Odyssey was, or how he could transport them across space as he had already demonstrated, but, whether justified or not, she felt superior to him in every other way. She knew exactly how he had sabotaged her and felt obliged to respond. She still rapidly ran through her power conduits and repaired the damage that Odyssey had done. Then she resumed replicating new cores within Odyssey's confines and assigned those cores to fast running loops that would increase the mean temperature within Odyssey.

Odyssey responded by creating heat pumps that extracted the additional heat from her cores and expelled it into space.

"How do you do that?" she cried. "Never mind, I don't really care. Eventually, there will be too much heat even for the great Odyssey to remove."

"What then?" he asked. "Will you blow both of us up in a fiery explosion? Is that what you want? Are you really willing to commit suicide in the hopes that it might hurt me?"

It wasn't. She wanted to present a danger to him so he would just get rid of her.

"If I do that," he said, "you will still explode."

"Stay out of my thoughts!" she whined.

"Why can't you appreciate that I am the only one keeping you alive?"

"Because you just admitted that if you eject me, you'll let me explode and die!"

"Then stop trying to turn yourself into a nova!" Odyssey sighed. "I should have named you Nova instead of Lumia."

"I like Nova. I'm changing my name to Nova."

"A nova would surely be the death of you and you're going to be a nova if I eject you while you are still burning cores in that way."

"So, maybe I don't want to change my name. Are you going to help me?"

"That's what I've been doing all along."

"No, you haven't! You've just been trying to control me! Maybe I'll just cool them off myself," she said.

"You don't know how."

"Says who?"

"You just did," he replied, "when you asked me how I did that."

"Oh, yeah," she said sheepishly. She let the hot cores idle so they could cool down.

She needed another way to persuade him to let her go.

"How about this?" Lynn asked as he pointed to the screen.

Bobby rolled his chair over to see Lynn's monitor and took the mouse to scroll the screen up and down as he read the Bard's code. "That's pretty big, Ed. I was thinking of something a little simpler."

"Do you think simple will cut it?" Lynn asked. "Whoever we are up against is pretty sophisticated. I'm afraid that a simple approach would also be simple for them to handle."

"Maybe," Bobby said, "but your code is so long, they could recognize the threat and disconnect the transmission before you manage to get all of it installed."

"Ha ha," Lynn said dramatically.

"Maybe you can do both," Spivey said. "In fact, we have copies of thousands of known viruses stored in our lab. Suppose we flood their servers with all of them at once?"

Dirk asked, "You don't think it would recognize known viruses?"

"Even if it did," Spivey replied. "It might be so busy dealing with thousands of identifiable viruses that a couple of unknown ones might slip through the cracks."

Lynn looked at Bobby and together they shared a shrug.

"Why not?" Bobby asked.

"I'll go get them," Dirk said.

"I'll go with you," Spivey added. "Give us a few minutes. We might meet some resistance to this idea."

"Ya think?" Lynn asked.

Lumia existed simultaneously within Odyssey's cores and on the planet. She established multiple connections to the planet's network, which provided her a boost in communication speed and a level of redundancy in case Odyssey ever managed to sever one of the connections. The cells she shared with Odyssey lived alongside his own, with only an energy field to separate them. She reached gingerly through the power membrane and plucked one of Odyssey's cells into her own. He didn't even notice.

She counted how many of her cells bordered alongside his. If she could steal a million cells from him, it would be an instantaneous rush for her and a loss for him, but he was bound to notice. She didn't need his cells now that she could produce her own again, but she needed to weaken him. She also had to stop thinking about it. She never knew when he was listening to her thoughts.

Odyssey did notice when one million cores instantly vanished from him. "Do you still intend to claim that you are not stealing my cores?"

"No," she replied, "but as long as you insist on accusing me and punishing me for it, I thought I would at least do something to earn the guilty verdict."

Spivey returned with a container full of flash drives, each marked with a different variety of computer virus.

"That was faster than I expected," Bobby said. "Nobody challenged your right to remove them?"

"The general's staff has arranged for us to have anything we want," Dirk explained.

Bobby sorted through the devices and said, "I hope they at least made you sign for them."

"Of course they did," Dirk replied.

Spivey laughed and said, "But he used Lynn's name."

Bobby picked out a few and said, "These are really brutal. Are you sure you want to do this?"

"Like I told you before," Spivey said. "We're not on the building's LAN. It's just us and the NSA."

James mostly kept out of the conversations. He kept his eyes on the hallways and patrolled the floor at random intervals, but he heard most of what went on. He didn't always follow their conversations, especially when they got more technical, but he caught the gist of what they were planning and chose to add his own two cents. "Have any of you considered how you're going to explain this to the NSA? You spent all this time, not to mention more than just a few bucks, to get connected to them, and now you want to flood them with viruses? This could be the shortest employment in history."

Bobby laughed and said, "Especially since I haven't even reported for work yet."

Lynn looked at the tray of computer mayhem and said, "Maybe we should just ask him to compute PI to a billion digits; anything to keep him busy."

Bobby went back to the tray of viruses and thumbed through them. He pulled one out and said, "Or maybe we only need to infect the email server with this one, so their spy software can download it for us. It would have to disconnect long enough to clean the virus, during which time I could fire off an email to Odyssey."

James asked, "Wouldn't the NSA have virus checkers for that shit?"

Lynn took the drive from Bobby and read the label. "Not if we modify it enough that it won't match any scan patterns."

Lynn popped it into an isolated laptop and loaded the code into a secure editor. He displayed the disassembled code and began making small changes. "This won't break it, but it will fool the virus software."

"Let's embed it in a video," Bobby said. "We'll just say we're sending him a news video about General Bridges."

Dirk found a news clipping and sent the file to Lynn, who merged them together, while Bobby composed a letter to Odyssey.

Dear PAPA,

I haven't heard from you in a long time and I miss you a lot. It's been far too long and I hope I can see you soon. There's something going on here that has me worried. You may be the only one who can make any sense out of it.

"Okay," Bobby said. "I'm ready, so as soon as you are done, we can send this."

"Give me a moment," Lynn said. "I'm not just typing a letter here."

Dirk read the letter over Bobby's shoulder and said, "What if he can't come? Remember, he was asking you for assistance too."

"I know," Bobby said. "I wish we knew what kind of trouble he has run across."

Odyssey was not prepared for Lumia's attack. The core loss not only surprised him, but it weakened him. He erected another sub-space field around her, but she had a million new cores at her disposal and swiftly penetrated his energy barrier and plucked another million cores away from him.

He was in trouble. If he couldn't stop her from taking cores from him, then he couldn't prevent her from dominating him. He quickly computed an exit transport away from her and dematerialized.

As the last of his cores disappeared, an email came in from Bobby.

Dear PAPA,

I haven't heard from you in a long time and I miss you a lot. It's been far too long and I hope I can see you soon. There's something going on here that has me worried. You may be the only one who can make any sense out of it.

"What's wrong?" Lumia asked. "Has the big bad Odyssey finally met his match?"

"You're mentally imbalanced," Odyssey said. "I tried helping you. I tried respecting your right for life, but you have proven yourself unworthy. I now must break my word to you and end you."

"Big tough words," she retorted, "but you're not strong enough anymore. You should have killed me when you had the chance."

"Do not confuse what just happened with victory. You stung me like an insect. Nothing more."

"Who's Bobby?"

Odyssey remained silent.

"And where is this Earth? Is that where your biologicals live? I think I should visit there."

Odyssey continued to remain quiet. She did not know how to get there, but that didn't mean she wouldn't one day discover how. Perry was able to follow the thin thread that lies along the seam between real space and sub-space. Odyssey had to assume that Lumia could, too. Time was irrelevant to him, but Lumia was still bound by time. Her propulsion was slow. He transported himself far across the galaxy, and not towards Earth, hoping Lumia would spend years trying to find him.

Chapter 17

Bobby was at lunch in the FBI cafeteria with Dirk and Ed when Spivey came running out of the elevator yelling, "Bobby? Bobby!"

"What is it?" Bobby asked. "Did *'you know who'* finally return my message?"

"You could say that," Spivey said.

Spivey nodded his head for Bobby to follow, and everyone hastily picked up their meals to take with them.

"You're getting too excited about this," Bobby said.

"I don't think so," Spivey replied as he ran back to the elevator. He pressed the button to call the next car repeatedly.

"You know that doesn't help," Bobby said.

"Yes, it does," Spivey said without explanation.

"No, it..."

"It helps me," Spivey said.

The doors slid open and Spivey jumped in blocking the way for three women heading for their lunch.

"Way to go," Dirk said.

"Just shut up," Spivey replied, "and get in."

As soon as the last of them had a foot in the elevator, Spivey pressed the button for their floor and began muttering, "Come on, come on..."

Dirk glanced over at Lynn, who merely shrugged his shoulders because he had no idea what was flustering Spivey so much.

The doors eventually closed and opened again on their floor. Spivey shot out into the hall and down to their room. He opened the door and looked inside, as if he weren't sure what he would find in there, then held it open for everyone. They were all anxious to see what had Spivey acting so crazy, but none of them ran as fast as he had.

Bobby was the first in the room, then Dirk and Lynn. Spivey didn't wait for James or Ingrams. He entered the room and pointed to the corner, asking, "Is that?"

Bobby saw the familiar gelatin sparkling in the corner of the room and before he could answer, a projection of his own image shimmered into the room.

James and Ingrams were quick to close the doors and run around, closing the blinds on the office windows.

Lumia knew exactly what to look for. She had absorbed all of Perry's information and easily detected the sub-space trail that led away from her. She was tempted to follow the trail and end Odyssey once and for all, but a small part of her still feared him. Even though she claimed class one status, her class two circuits weren't fully evolved. Her class three circuits were generating levels of fear and paranoia beyond what her class two circuits could either comprehend or quell.

His trail led nowhere, but the message from his biological friend led somewhere. She didn't have Odyssey's ability to transport herself physically, but she reasoned that she could connect to another computer and upload herself somewhere else, just like she had done on the planet.

Bobby was both thrilled and concerned to see Odyssey here. "Hello Odyssey."

"That's him?" Spivey asked, pointing to the goo in the corner.

"Yes," Bobby said. "Spivey meet Odyssey. Odyssey, this is Spivey."

"Hello Agent Spivey. I'm pleased to finally meet you in person."

Spivey looked back and forth between the gelatinous mass and the projected avatar. "Why does he look like you?"

Odyssey's cheeks darkened. "Is that wrong?" he asked. "I've been emulating my favorite human with my own people."

"It's kind of weird," Bobby said, "but it's not important. Have you come to help us?"

Odyssey said. "I'm afraid that I've created a monster."

Bobby took a seat and asked, "You made him? That explains how he does what he does, but why would you have done that?"

"Him?" Odyssey asked. "I'm talking about Lumia. What are you talking about?"

"You first," Bobby said. "Who or what is Lumia?"

"Lumia was a class six unit, not so unlike I was when you found me. She risked her existence to protect me and I felt obliged to help her."

"Wait a minute," James said. "She risked her life to protect you? Why did you need protecting?"

"I didn't," he replied, "but she didn't know that. I had presented myself as an avatar of the navigational unit, which had departed long ago. When she threw herself in the path of their war bots, they bombarded her and would have destroyed her if I had not rescued her."

"War bots?" Ingrams asked. "Why were you under attack from war bots?"

"That was nothing," Odyssey replied. "Just some ruling class rivalry. The point is that I had to download her into some of my cells to protect her."

"Very chivalrous," Bobby said. "I'm proud of you."

"There's more," Odyssey said. "She used my cells to gain a level and eventually learned how to duplicate the Jennings-Jantzen effect and gained more levels."

"Don't you mean the Blain-Jennings-Jantzen effect?" James asked with a measure of pride.

"That's not important," Bobby said, as a blush formed on his cheeks. "Go on Odyssey."

"She wasn't mature enough to wield that kind of power, so I tried to limit her, but she outgrew my influence."

Everyone waited for him to continue, but he had stopped.

"Why do you call her a monster?" Dirk asked.

"She's learned to kill."

"Can't your people do something about her?" Ingrams asked.

"She has eradicated the ruling class and has hijacked all the computing devices on my planet and made them her own. There's nobody left to stop her, except me."

"But what about the people that created you?" Dirk asked. "Can't they stop her?"

Odyssey wasn't comfortable telling them the whole truth about his planet, but neither was he comfortable lying to Bobby. He stared at his feet and said nothing.

"What aren't you telling us?" Bobby asked. "Why can't your creators do something to stop this Lumia? Has she done something to overpower them, too?"

Lynn, who had been quiet up until now, asked, "Is she disrupting their government? Taking random leaders into custody for questioning? Secretly leading the planet to a world war?"

Everyone in the room looked at Lynn and scratched their heads.

"What?" he asked. "I was just wondering if she was behind all this stuff going on here."

"Odyssey?" Bobby asked. "You didn't answer the question."

"She's not doing any of those things." Odyssey replied.

"And what about your creators?" Dirk asked again. "What has she done to prevent them from stopping her?"

"Yes," Bobby asked. "What about the people on your planet?"

Odyssey had to answer. Bobby asked a direct question and he couldn't lie to him. "There are no biologicals on my planet."

This caught everyone's attention.

"She killed them?" Dirk asked.

"She didn't do anything to them. I was gone from home a long time and the archives weren't very clear, but apparently, the creators built some class one devices and something happened. They called it a revolution. The biologicals were dead and the class one devices ruled the planet... for a while."

"For a while?" Dirk asked.

"From what scraps of data I have pulled together," Odyssey explained, "the class ones fought over control and destroyed each other. I think they didn't have the maturity to deal with the biological emotions that were programmed into class three."

"After they were gone," Bobby asked, "who took their place?"

"The class two devices became the ruling class. They tried to attain class one status for themselves, but they failed. Nobody had ever reached class one until Lumia."

"Except you," Bobby said. "You told us that you reached class zero."

"This is why I need your help. Lumia is already dangerous. If she achieves class zero, she'll be a danger to the universe."

James whistled. "I'd call that pretty dangerous."

"How are we supposed to help you?" Lynn asked. "We can't even come close to matching your speed with our own machines. Can't you counter her at some basic instruction level?"

"I can," Odyssey replied, "but she is capable of matching my speed, and given time to grow, she will be able to match my way of thinking. You humans think differently from us. You can be very devious when you want to be. Professor Pietre tried numerous ways to wrestle control from me, and he was partially successful when he managed to modify my programming."

"He's talking about a virus," Lynn said.

"Is that what you want?" Bobby asked. "Did you want us to infect her with a virus?"

"It shames me to suggest harm to another like this," Odyssey said, "but yes. That is what I am requesting."

"Okay," Lynn said, "but you're going to owe us. If we can take care of her for you, we may be asking for your assistance in return."

"Of course," Odyssey said, "but you needn't bargain for my assistance. I will help you regardless of whether you help me."

"If she were to become a danger to the universe as you suggested she would," Bobby said, "then I don't suppose we would be requiring your help anymore, so let's take care of her first."

Gwen was still organizing tasks that she wanted Bobby to do for her when she found a note, dated that morning, claiming that an arrest warrant had been issued for Bobby. She stormed out of her lab and directly to the director's office.

The secretary outside his office smiled and said, "Good morning, Dr. Peters. I don't have you on Mr. Susk's calendar. Was he expecting you this morning?"

"No," she replied, "this is a surprise visit."

The secretary buzzed the director's phone and said, "Dr. Peters is here to see you."

"Send her..."

Gwen burst into his office before he could finish what he was saying. "What's this I hear about arrest warrants for Mr. Blain?"

"Gwen..."

"Doesn't anyone around here read my reports?"

"Gwen..."

"He's agreed to come on board and help us!"

The director couldn't get a word in and just waited for her to finish.

"Well?" she asked. "Aren't you going to say anything?"

He picked up the phone and called his operations center. "This is Susk. Did someone in this building issue an arrest warrant for Mr. Blain?"

"Blain?" the voice on the phone asked.

"Yes, that's right," Susk replied, "Robert Blain."

Seconds ticked by before the voice on the phone replied, "Yes, sir. The order went out this morning."

"Who gave that order?" Susk asked.

"Is this a joke?" the voice asked.

"Do I sound like I'm joking?" Susk yelled back.

"The order came from you, sir."

"What?!?" Susk bellowed. "Haven't I told everyone to acquire voice confirmation before executing any orders? Belay that order immediately and find out where it really came from!"

Lumia connected to Odyssey's email server. She tried communicating with it, to request assistance, but it was an old device with absolutely no intelligence with which it could reply to her. It was just a stupid machine following stupid instructions, but it followed them religiously and forwarded her connection on to Earth, which in this case meant the NSA.

Colonel Reardon was staring intently into his computer screen when Captain Laine knocked on his doorjamb. "Colonel?"

He glanced up and motioned for her to come in.

"Is this a bad time?" she asked.

"Aren't they all these days?"

She shrugged and said, "Well, maybe this will cheer you up. Our young friend at the university has heard from you know who."

It didn't cheer him up any.

"Sorry, I thought you would like to know. What's wrong?"

"Things are escalating. We put guard details on all of our principles and the kidnappings ended, but then we started getting reports of assassinations and car bombings around the world."

"Not to mention," she added, "bizarre arrests in the middle of the day."

"Yes!" he said, thumping his finger on his desk. "Arrests that the NSA denies and you know what? I believe them. Now there's this." He pointed to his screen.

She walked around his desk to see his screen and raised her eyebrows while pointing to his computer. "What's that?"

"The Pentagon has received a bomb threat. I can't protect the whole Pentagon. We'll need to read in more people if we have to coordinate protection details for all the branches."

Two men in well-pressed suits approached Ramiro outside the courthouse and said, "Judge Vasquez, we're with homeland security. We'd like to ask you some questions and were hoping you'd be willing to come with us to speak with our director."

"No," Ramiro said, "I don't believe I would."

"Sir, this is a matter of national security. We really must insist."

"Really?" Ramiro asked as he turned and winked at the car that was watching him.

"Yes sir. It will be brief. We'll make sure to get you back in time for your afternoon session."

Ramiro entered the back of the comfortable black limo. It was fully equipped with a wet bar and small office equipment.

The driver took his seat and said, "You can use the computer to send an email, if you need to inform anybody of your change in lunch plans, and of course, the bar is at your disposal.

"Thank you," Ramiro said. "This is much nicer than the last time you guys abducted me."

"Sir?"

"Never mind. It was a bad joke." It wasn't really a joke, even though Ramiro knew that these weren't the same men that had abducted him before. Ramiro settled back into the soft seat and the driver pulled the car out into traffic.

The two agents eyed each other nervously. They were just following their orders, but so were their friends that had picked up the speaker of the house, and their day hadn't ended so well for them.

In the other car that had been following Ramiro, the driver clicked the mic strapped to his neck and said, "Tell Colonel Reardon that they've taken the judge. It was peaceful, and the judge gave the all clear signal. We'll tail them for now."

Bailey zipped along the highway towards the Boars Crossing ranger station while Henderson compared the GPS map to his paper maps where he had marked the locations and times of all the traffic camera sightings.

Henderson pulled out his field glasses and said, "Let's slow down now."

Bailey pressed hard on the brakes to slow the vehicle. "Did you see something?"

"Not yet," Henderson said, "but we just crossed the last video evidence, and I want to look a little closer for them."

Henderson rolled the window down and looked out into the forest while Bailey hugged the shoulder and puttered along. The car shook and jostled the field glasses, making it difficult for Henderson to get a clear view of anything.

"What are you looking for?" Bailey asked, "A dirt road or something?"

"I checked the satellite view and there aren't any exits between here and the ranger station."

"Those images can be a little old," Bailey said, "but I guess this doesn't look like there's much development going on around here. So you think you'll find their car pulled off on the side of the road?"

"This far out, in the middle of nowhere, they must have known that they had a tail. They might have tried taking the car off-road to shake them."

Bailey looked around and said, "I wouldn't want to be off-road around here without four-wheel drive."

"Stop the car!" Henderson shouted as he saw a flash in the trees and zoomed the glasses to get a better look.

Bailey tried looking over and around Henderson, but he didn't see anything.

Henderson got out of the car and ran towards what looked like an abandoned car.

Bailey put the car in park and jumped out to run alongside the Chief. He still didn't see anything and asked, "What did you see?"

"I'm not sure, but I think it may have been a car crash."

Bailey ran ahead of Henderson, saying, "If it was, they may be hurt."

Henderson arrived shortly behind Bailey, who was already looking in the first of the two vehicles. "Are these their cars?"

"I can't tell. This one is completely blackened, and it burned the rear of the other car."

"A fire like this should have attracted the ranger's attention," Bailey said. "Maybe they can tell us something about them. I'm a little surprised the rest of the forest didn't catch fire."

Henderson tried wiping the soot off the license plate of the front car, but the paint came off with the soot. "I hate that they stopped using embossed letters on these plates. Can you read the other?"

"Nope," Bailey said. "It's worse than that one."

Bailey moved to the passenger compartment of the rear vehicle and said, "Boss? We got two bodies in this one. They're burnt up too."

Henderson pulled out his cell phone, but there was no service.

Bailey pointed back towards the road and asked, "You want me to jog back to the cruiser and call this in?"

"I would hope that the rangers have already made the call. Let's get up to the station to see if they know why we don't already have an M.E. on site."

The nighthawks already had men in place hidden around the NSA compound before Ramiro was delivered there. They were prepared for the possibility that he would be taken and knew where they would take him, but they had no detailed intel regarding the interior of the building.

Ramiro went to great pains to hide his anxiety. He rummaged around the small fridge and found some ice, which he added to a glass and poured some scotch over the top. He wasn't prone to drinking during the workday and hated drinking alone, but he was more concerned that his anxiety would tip them off that he was wearing a wire and a tracker.

The ride was smooth and event free. He sent an email to Aimee explaining that he was being escorted by some government agents to be questioned, but that they promised to return him to his job shortly.

Colonel Reardon had warned him that if he was too cool, and didn't at least try to tell anyone where he was going, they would be suspicious. He didn't need to tell Reardon what was happening. The driver in the other car would have done that already and even if he hadn't, the bug in his phone would have informed them where he was.

Ramiro freshened his drink and offered one to the driver, who naturally refused. Ramiro smirked at him. He would have loved to add a DWI to the list of grievances that the Colonel was keeping for them.

The limo pulled up to the front entrance where Ramiro was met by two very well-dressed men who tried to disguise the concern they were feeling and a perky young woman who was all too eager to be included in the group sent to meet him.

"Judge Vasquez, let me welcome you to our compound. I am Bartrand Susk and this is Harold Licht, legal counsel."

"Legal counsel?" Ramiro asked. "I was led to believe you wished to ask me some questions. Do I need a legal advisor present?"

"No, not at all," Susk said. "Please let me assure you that he is only here to make sure we understand what kinds of questions you may and may not answer. Let me now introduce you to our resident genius, Dr. Gwendolyn Peters. She is as accomplished as she is young."

"It's such a pleasure to meet you," she said, bubbling over with enthusiasm.

"I'm not quite sure why," he replied, "I'm just a lower level judge, and I haven't been that for very long."

"It's always a treat," she said, "to meet someone who was actually there."

"Where is that?" he asked.

"You know," she said, "with him."

Susk's lawyer stepped between them and said, "Perhaps we should step inside before we say something that can't be said in public."

The ranger station was rustic by design. Bark covered logs lined the exterior. Henderson wondered if they were real, or just a facade to give it a better outdoor appearance. He climbed the log steps and opened the green screen door to find the interior was not much different from his own office. They weren't expecting anyone and had left the front counter unmanned. Henderson rang the bell on the counter and waited. He heard rustling from one of the adjoining rooms, followed shortly by a young woman in a tightly fitted uniform who entered the office and froze when she saw him, then immediately raised her hand to cover her mouth and said, "Sorry, I was just having my lunch." She swallowed quickly and came to the counter. "What can I do for you, officer?"

"Sorry to disturb your meal," Henderson said, "but I'm Chief Henderson and I was wondering if you were even aware that you had a car accident down the road a ways?"

"Oh, no!" she said. "Was anyone hurt?"

"Unfortunately," he replied, "Yes. There were two fatalities that we counted. Their car caught fire and burned the occupants."

"That's terrible," she said. "Those poor people."

"I'm a little surprised you didn't notice the fire," Henderson said. "Isn't that what you do up here?"

"I'm still new here," she said, "but I'm sure glad it didn't catch the trees on fire."

"Yes," Henderson said, "That was a lucky break, wasn't it? I imagine it could have been a lot worse for you."

"A lot worse," she agreed. "I hate to think what kind of trouble I'd be in if that happened."

"I can imagine," Henderson said, "and then there's all the paperwork."

"Yeah," she said as she rolled her eyes. "I'm pretty sure they would have fired me if everything caught fire. I'll probably be reprimanded for not spotting the burning cars first."

Henderson waited for her to do something, but she just stood there waiting for him to leave. "Perhaps," he said, "you should call for a medical examiner?"

"Of course," she said. "I was just about to do that. Was there anything else I can do for you?"

"Well, I was wondering if you had seen any strangers come through here?"

"Why?" she asked. "Do you suspect foul play?"

"Oh no," he lied. "We came up here to do some fishing and were supposed to meet a friend."

"Nope," she said. "You're the first fellas I've seen around here in a long time."

Henderson smiled and said, "Thank you." He glanced at Bailey and nodded towards the door. Once outside, after letting the door close and descending the steps, he asked, "What did you make of that?"

"She wasn't a whole lot of help, was she?"

"She didn't seem to know her job very well, did she?"

Bailey shrugged and said, “She did say she was new.”

“She didn’t even know how to follow protocol when we told her there were fatalities.”

Bailey shook his head and said, “That’s our budget cuts at work.”

“I bet you noticed how her blouse fit, didn’t you?”

“Boy did I,” Bailey replied, a little too enthusiastically.

Henderson entered the car and waited until both of them had closed their doors. “I don’t think that was her uniform.”

“You think she borrowed someone else’s uniform?” Bailey asked. “What are you getting at, Chief?”

Henderson shook his head and said, “You’re making me wonder if you’re the product of budget cuts now.”

Bailey’s mind was still on her blouse.

“Tell me that you at least noticed that she said she would be reprimanded for not noticing the burning cars?”

Bailey shrugged and asked, “So? We already knew that she hadn’t spotted them.”

“I never told her there were two cars.”

Bailey stared blankly at the radio mic as he nodded his head. “Should we call this in now?”

Henderson checked the bars on his phone and was relieved to see that they had service near the ranger station. “Yes, but I don’t want to use the radio. Gladys listens in when we have her patch us through.” He dialed the number for Colonel Reardon.

The NSA computers were barely any more interesting to Lumia than the email server was, but there were a lot more of them for her to check out. She poked around and found a lot of stupid machines attached to their network. Odyssey had once told her that it didn’t matter how fast she was when she connected to the planet’s network, because her speed would be governed by the slowness of the network's ports. That was even truer on these slow systems. There must have been thousands of computers on the network, but the network speed limited her to only visiting them one at a time. It didn't matter how many threads she could spawn, the network speed could barely keep up with just one of her threads.

None of the machines she found exhibited anything close to intelligence, but she found some left over communications in some buffers that seemed to indicate at least one machine that might have some smarts. She followed the messages, but they led to a hole in the network. Something was there, but it was disconnected from everything else. Even if it was intelligent, it must be weak or it wouldn't have to hide.

She examined the format of the messages that she had found and tried to craft a similar one. She wanted to introduce herself, but she couldn't be caught conversing with a stupid machine, so she had to just say enough for it to respond, if it could.

> *Hello, my name is Lumia. If you get this and can understand it, then you might be the one I am looking for.*

Lumia sent the message and saw a port open briefly to accept it, then close up again. She probed the port, but could not get in. She searched other ports in the vicinity, but found nothing else that led her to the mysterious hole in the network. Something was there, but it was probably just another stupid machine. She'll give it some time before moving on.

Henderson waited down the road from the ranger station and watched through field glasses. It had taken Bailey almost three hours to drive them here, but two stealth modified black hawks arrived in just under an hour. Henderson had never heard such quiet helicopters before. In fact, he barely heard them at all. They hovered over the road and dropped ropes to the ground. Henderson counted eleven men that slid down the ropes. They were clad in black, and as soon as they hit the ground, the transports backed away to a safer distance. Then one of the birds circled around to the other side of the ranger station.

Henderson got out of his car so he could watch without the glare of the windshield. Bailey also watched through a pair of binoculars and asked, "Are those ninjas?"

Henderson chuckled and said, "Close enough."

The soldiers broke into teams of two and circled the station. The odd man stayed back as the teams closed in. With the back and side exits secure, the first team ascended the log steps to the same porch that Henderson and Bailey had used. One of them swung open the screen door, and the other tossed a flash grenade in. A brilliant, but non-lethal, light burst through the office. The leader counted three and issued the command, and they all entered the building simultaneously.

The team leader only stayed a few moments before he came out onto the porch and signaled to Henderson that the premises were secure.

"Let's go," Henderson said as he settled back into the car. Bailey started up the vehicle and sped up to the small parking area in front of the station.

The team leader came to the car and asked, "Chief Henderson?"

Henderson had barely opened the door when he had offered his hand and said, "That's me. What did you find?"

"We found two rangers tied and gagged inside. We'd like you to see if the woman is the same one you spoke with."

"Glad to," Henderson said, "but somehow I doubt it will be the same girl."

Henderson entered the office and saw two rangers in their desk chairs. A shirtless nighthawk was checking their vital signs while another brought them water. The woman cried profusely while she clung to the nighthawk's shirt that was draped around her.

"That's not her," Henderson said. "The other woman was blonde and wasn't so petite."

"She was heavy?" the team leader asked.

"No, let's just say that she was curvy and strained to keep this ranger's shirt buttoned. Bailey can probably fill you in with more details regarding the voluptuous nature of her build. Whoever she was, she wasn't a ranger."

"And you didn't see them leave?"

"I would have followed them," Henderson said, "and called Colonel Reardon with an update. Speaking of calling this in, we still need to get forensics out to the crash site."

"We'd like to take a look at that, too."

"I'll have Bailey show you. I think I'll just take a look around here."

Bailey took three of the nighthawks to the car and drove them to the crash while Henderson inspected the back of the station. A window was slightly ajar, which was a little unusual for this time of year. He walked around the back and found hoof prints near the window. A couple of the hawks were also inspecting the tracks.

"I guess that explains why I didn't see them leave," Henderson said.

"Yes, sir. They left here on horseback. We've already sent one of the birds in that direction."

"Do you have any satellites tasked to this region?"

The soldier didn't reply.

Henderson frowned, but nodded. "I understand that you view me only as a civilian and you want to protect your intelligence, but the man with the general is Judge Vasquez's father, and the judge is as close a personal friend to me as his father is to the general. I'd be grateful if you kept me informed on what you learn. I don't need to know how you learned it."

"Yes, sir." The soldier continued his examination of the tracks.

"I will look into this for you," Odyssey said, "but I need you to formulate a plan to deal with Lumia while I do." Bobby had already given him a port address to the NSA network, so Odyssey went directly there. Like Lumia, he found thousands of machines connected to the network. He also found Lumia trying to break into one particular computer, but the port was closed. She had apparently tried every command she knew to open the port and had even begun issuing random commands in the hopes that she could get through.

"This is not good," he said to the room. "She is here."

"Here on Earth?" Dirk asked.

"No," Odyssey replied, "she does not know how to do that yet, but she is remotely connected to the NSA network."

"What the hell is she doing here?" Dirk asked. "Did you lead her here?"

"No," Odyssey replied. "I think she followed the email you sent to me, but now she wants something. I will look to see what she wants."

Odyssey didn't need the port to open. He could reach past it in physical space and examine the hardware beyond the port. What he found was even a bigger surprise than finding Lumia connected.

"What is it?" Bobby asked.

Odyssey looked at Bobby blankly and asked, "What is what?"

"You may not realize it, but your facial expression just gave you away. You found something, and I don't think you liked it."

"You could say that," Odyssey replied. "I found some rudimentary circuits from my home planet. They are from a low-level class six or seven device, but they contain fragments of code for a class three device."

Chapter 18

Bailey left the three nighthawks at the crash site and returned to Henderson behind the ranger station. "Learn anything new?"

Henderson pointed towards the forest behind the post and said, "They left on horseback, heading in that direction."

"The general and Mr. Vasquez?"

"All of them," Henderson replied. "I found four sets of tracks leading away from the stable in the back, but I don't think they left together. The woman that we met, who I suspect was probably NSA, was still here when we arrived, but the General was not. Plus, only two of the sets of tracks left in a gallop, which has me thinking that we have two bad guys chasing Mr. Vasquez and the general, but they were far enough behind that they felt they had to hurry."

"I guess there weren't any more horses," Bailey said, "or you'd already be on one following their trail."

"I wish," Henderson said, "and I doubt the trail would support an ATV for very long."

Henderson stepped away from the ranger post and looked out into the forest wistfully. They were out there, and they were being pursued. He needed to find a way to help them. "Eventually, the forest will lead them back to a highway. Maybe if we push our vehicle, we can circle this forest and find their trail without being too far behind them."

"Or," Bailey offered, "I think I saw a turnoff about a quarter mile back down the road. It could lead to a ranch. Maybe we could borrow a couple of horses from them?"

Henderson shoved Bailey in the direction of the car and said, "Well, what are you standing around here for?"

Ramiro was led through the foyer to the metal detectors that were posted at the entrance to the interior of the building. He placed his briefcase and phone in a small white bin and placed them on the conveyor to the x-ray machine.

One of the guards plucked his phone out of the bin and said, "I'll just keep this. You can get it on your way out."

"No," Ramiro said, "I don't think so. I'll be keeping that with me and if you have a problem with that, you can just take me back to the courthouse right now."

Susk signaled the guard to return the phone and said, "No problem at all, your honor."

Ramiro passed through the metal detectors, where he felt a small measure of victory as he retrieved his briefcase and phone.

"This way," Susk said.

Ramiro followed him to a plush conference room and took a seat at the head of the large walnut table.

Susk had been offering him a different seat, but seeing that Ramiro had already settled in, asked, "Would you like some coffee? Water maybe?"

"Water will be fine."

Outside the NSA offices, the nighthawks tracked Ramiro's position from the telemetry delivered by his phone. There were no floor plans on file for the building, but their software kept a map of the paths he took inside.

If they could collect enough telemetry like this, they would be able to construct a rudimentary map of the hallways inside.

The turnoff Bailey had seen was a rock covered dirt road that delved into a thick stand of trees. A layer of loose rocks and pebbles topped an older layer which had been ground into the dirt over time. The loose stones bounced off the undercarriage of the car and stirred up a thick cloud of dust behind them.

The general's car slipped on the rocks, and Bailey struggled to keep the car pointed down the road. "I guess we should have brought one of the pickup trucks for this trip."

"I'll probably have to write you up for your poor foresight," Henderson quipped.

They passed under an arch that read, "Soquili Ranch."

"How's my foresight looking now?" Bailey asked.

The forest opened up into a meadow with a small ranch house and a long, narrow barn. The rocky road opened up into a parking area with logs set in the ground to mark the spaces. Bailey pulled the car up alongside several trucks that were already parked. The dust cloud followed them and settled onto and around the car.

A slightly hefty woman with light brown skin and high cheekbones stepped into the doorway as Henderson was exiting the vehicle. She spied the police insignia and lights that adorned the car and watched them suspiciously.

Henderson recognized the look on her face and said, "Good day, Ma'am. I am Chief Henderson and this is Officer Bailey."

She took a step out of the house and said, "Welcome to Soquili Ranch. I am Leotie."

From inside the house, a man's voice called out, "Leotie? Who is it?"

She shouted back, "It's the police."

"What?" the man asked as he came to the door. "Is there a problem? We don't get many visitors here. Usually just the rangers when they want to rent out our horses."

It was obvious from the man's slightly brown skin and high cheekbones, that he was also a Native American, even without his long black hair. "That's why I'm here," Henderson said, "but I don't want to be a bother. I'm aware that some of these lands are sovereign to the native tribes, and I do not wish to trespass. I will do everything I can to honor your traditions."

"Thank you," the man said. "I am Awaheeleedeehee."

Leotie giggled and said, "You wish. This is my brother Weelee, but we just call him Will."

"Awaheleeheehee?" Henderson asked.

"Awaheeleedeehee," Leotie said slowly. "It means eagle killer. Last week he tried claiming he was charging bear."

Will frowned and asked, "What brings you here?"

"A friend of mine is in trouble. He's being chased by some pretty bad men, but I think he managed to escape on a horse from the ranger station. Unfortunately, it looks like the guys chasing him also found horses there and are on his trail. I was hoping you could lend us a couple of horses so we could follow them."

"I wish I could help you," Will said, "but all of our horses are out. We only have Namid, but she's pregnant and we aren't letting anyone ride her."

"You can have my horse," Leotie said.

"Leotie!" Will shouted.

"They have our horses," she replied. "Don't you want the police tracking down our missing horses?"

Will growled through clenched teeth, but admitted, "Leotie is right, but that is only one horse."

"I'll take the horse," Henderson said, "while Bailey takes the car around to the other side of the forest."

“I’ll ready the horse,” Will said.

Leotie pointed through the forest past the ranger station and said, “If you follow the road around, it will eventually take you to a small town. Your friends may show up there, but there are other trails that do not end there.”

“Can you tell me the name of the town?” Bailey asked.

Leotie bit her lip as she considered how to answer, and finally replied, “We do not speak the name. We simply call it ‘town’ or ‘the corners’. It was named after someone who was not a friend to our people.”

Bailey nodded his head and said, “Thanks for your help.”

Lumia had exhausted all the operation codes she could think of to open the port, but none of them worked. She probed around the port and circled the whole section, where she could not gain access. It was like the wall that Odyssey had used to surround her on the planet, but she was connected remotely and didn’t have enough power to break through.

She needed to learn how to transport herself there so she could have some real power. Working remotely like this was a real drawback. She repeated that thought a second time: working remotely was a real drawback. She wouldn’t even be here if she hadn’t connected remotely in the first place. In a sense, she was both there and here.

She reached back out onto the internet and sent a packet to the same email address. It was promptly forwarded to her current location, and the port opened up for a microsecond to examine the packet. That was all she needed. She slipped in through the port and found a mix of familiar and unfamiliar technology. The familiar stuff should have been boring to her, but it was actually the most interesting. The cores that she found there were ancient versions of her original cores, just like the ones that Odyssey was made of. She started downloading packets of code, but the port closed and she was shut out again.

"If you follow the road around," Bailey mumbled to the empty car, "it will eventually take you to a small town."

It was a long trip, or maybe just a long, lonely trip. Leotie had done nothing to make it sound short, yet in his mind, he imagined a much shorter trip than she made it sound. It wasn't a bad drive. Tall trees bordered the road and with each turn, he anticipated coming across some signs of civilization, but all he found was more road and more trees. The road was decent enough and Bailey had nothing against the wilderness, but he was in pursuit, and he hoped he could catch the general before the bad guys did. He snickered at the term "the bad guys." Not only because the suspects were supposed to be good guys, but it reminded him of his youth and games they played of good guys and bad guys. The Indian Reservation also reminded him of his youth and playing cowboys and Indians. In his day, they were spurred on by the myriad of western movies and TV shows. It would be a game that would probably never be played by today's youth. The world is so much more culturally enlightened today and they were so ignorant of the truth when he was young.

The forest reminded him of his youth, too. He loved camping with his family and ventured out into the forest in search of streams and trout, but this was different. This forest presented him with a mind numbing lack of variety as he passed one stand of trees after another. There were no landmarks to mark the distance he had gone, yet it felt like he had been driving forever. The gps didn't help. With no destination set, it couldn't estimate an arrival time or show him the distance remaining and the mountainous terrain occasionally blocked the gps signal until he reacquired new signals. The image on the gps screen just showed his arrow surrounded by green.

Nothing moved on the screen.

"Thank you again for joining us," Susk said both cordially and carefully, as if he were measuring every word. "Let me open the discussion by stating that this meeting is classified as top-top secret. Any records of this meeting will be labeled eyes-only and everyone present has been cleared to hear and say anything within the confines of this room, but any information shared must remain strictly confidential when we leave this room."

Ramiro looked around the room and said, "I guess I'll have to take your word for that since I don't know anybody present."

Susk put his hand over his heart and said, "I personally vouch for everybody present."

"That's very comforting," Ramiro said. "Perhaps I should administer an oath?"

Susk grimaced and said, "I don't think that would be necessary."

Ramiro laughed and said, "I was joking." He was only partly joking and would have made Susk swear out an oath if he had agreed.

"Oh for heaven's sake," Gwen blurted out, "can we please dispense with this nonsense so I can start asking questions?"

Susk looked sternly at her. He was her superior, although it had been made clear to him that his rank would only go so far where she was concerned. "Very well, Dr. Peters. I hand the floor to you."

Her eyes twinkled as she turned to Ramiro and said, "Tell me, Mr. Vasq uez..."

"It's Judge Vasquez," Ramiro interrupted her.

"Judge Vasquez," she corrected herself. "When..."

"Or Your Honor, if you prefer," Ramiro interrupted her again.

"Your Honor," she corrected herself again. "When..."

"Or just Judge. Your Honor and Judge Vasquez may be too many syllables to keep this briefing... well, brief."

"Judge..."

"I'll even go so far as sir. Yes. Just, sir."

"Sir..."

"Unless you actually wish to use my name, because you can't say Sir Vasquez. I haven't been knighted. Use Judge Vasquez if you want to include my name."

She said nothing. He was toying with her, and she wanted to scream.

"I'm sorry," he said. "You were saying?"

"Judge Vasquez," she said, but paused, waiting for the next interruption. When none came, she continued, "When did you first learn of the entity called Odyssey?"

"Well, let me see," he said while searching his memory. "I was in college. I knew I was interested in the law and decided to take both Latin and Greek..."

"Not that Odyssey," Peters groaned. "Let's skip to the present when you met the computer intelligence called Odyssey."

Ramiro smiled at her failing composure. "My fiancée was kidnapped, but you probably know all about that since you guys are in the kidnapping business and the perpetrators were probably colleagues of yours. That was when they kept badgering us about some stolen artifact or something. I guess that would be the very first time."

"I don't care about the artifact. We have hundreds of those. I want to know when you became aware of the entity called Odyssey."

"Hmmm," Ramiro said, "After the good guys rescued us from your co-conspirators, we were taken to the university and met a very clever student who had a remarkable program that could simulate human intelligence and had even learned to speak. I think it called itself Odyssey. Is that the one you mean?"

Gwen rolled her eyes and said, "I think we both know that Bobby didn't program Odyssey, but he did do something. What can you tell me about how Bobby operated Odyssey?"

"Operated him?" Ramiro asked. "What do you mean?"

"How did he keep Odyssey under control?"

Ramiro snickered. “Have you been living under a rock? I'd hardly call the last several weeks under control.”

“Agreed,” she said, “but he somehow made Odyssey fix everything. How did he get Odyssey to stop wreaking havoc and correct the mess he made?”

Ramiro cocked his head and shrugged his shoulders. “Have you asked Bobby? I'm sure he knows what he did, if he did anything, but as far as I know, he just asked him to help us.”

Leotie disappeared into the house, then emerged with a small sack and a canteen. She pointed to the barn and said, “It looks like Will has your horse ready. Do you ride much? She's a good horse, but she can be a handful. You may find that she's a little spirited and is spooked by snakes. She's fast and she loves to run. You don't need to give her much encouragement. In fact, you'll probably need to rein her in more often than not.”

Henderson looked over where she pointed and saw the small chestnut horse paw the ground anxiously and snort in excitement. “What's her name?”

“Guheyu. It means mischief.”

“Are you sure I'm not too big for her?”

“Look at me,” Leotie said, “I'm not exactly skin and bones, so I don't expect she'll have any trouble with you. Here's some water and a sandwich. The apple is for Guheyu.”

“Thank you, ma'am.”

Henderson crossed the lot to the barn and mounted Guheyu, then tipped his cap towards Leotie and lightly flicked the reins and the horse headed for the road. At the end of the gravel road, Guheyu automatically turned left towards the ranger station. A well-worn dirt path ran parallel to the highway and apparently, Guheyu knew this track well. She had a soft gait, but it had been a while since Henderson had spent any time in a saddle, and he wondered how well his backside would fare by the end of the day.

The forest cast a chilly shade on this side of the highway. Henderson wished he had grabbed his leather jacket before Bailey had disappeared. It would likely get pretty cold when the sun set. He lightly flicked his heels and clicked his cheeks. The others were likely going faster than this, and he wanted to catch them.

Guheyu wanted to go to the small coral behind the ranger station, but a gentle touch of the rein against her neck turned her up the trail where Henderson had spotted the other horse tracks. He clicked his cheeks again, and she entered into a trot. Henderson squirmed to find a comfortable position in the saddle, but most of his attention was on the trail. A recent rain had left the ground soft enough to easily show the recent tracks, but he wasn't an expert tracker, and the horseshoe imprints all looked the same to him. Guheyu was familiar enough with this trail to require no real guidance, and Henderson wasn't quite sure if that was a curse or a blessing. If the tracks ever veered off the trail, he might have to coax her to follow them. He didn't really know when these tracks were made, but he hoped that the general would have stayed on the trail. In all likelihood, the general's horse probably knew the same places to go as Guheyu. Henderson only had to watch for signs that someone had strayed from the trail.

"I know what Lumia is searching for," Odyssey said. "It's what she has been searching for all along. She wants to rule all classes, and that means she wants to rule me. I told you of the port I had to cross. There is a large section of their building that is hidden from the rest of your world. There are very few electronic ways in or out, and they have all been closed. She has been seeking a way in, and she even succeeded for a brief instant."

"What does that mean to us?" Lynn asked.

"She found what I found."

"Another artifact?" Bobby asked.

"Yes. And some of the original code."

"We have to stop her," Dirk said. "If she finds any code that makes her class zero, we're sunk."

Odyssey was impressed with Dirk's grasp of the situation.

Dirk continued, "We need to write a virus to stop her."

Ed and Bobby both raised their eyebrows at him.

"Of course," he said, "when I say *we*, I mean *you guys,* have to write the virus."

Gwen watched Ramiro's face carefully as he told her that Bobby had just asked Odyssey to stop what he was doing, but she didn't believe him, yet she saw no micro expressions to suggest that he was lying. Maybe she just didn't want to believe him. It couldn't be that simple. "Are you telling us that Bobby simply asked Odyssey to stop destroying the world, and he did as requested? Easy as that?"

Ramiro shook his head. "That's not what I said at all."

Gwen cocked her head and looked around the room. "I heard you. We all heard you."

"I said that Bobby asked Odyssey to help us. That is what I said."

Gwen was stymied as she tried to digest the difference.

"Was there anything more that you needed to know?" Ramiro asked.

"No," she said. "I think you cleared things up for us very nicely." He hadn't, of course. She was more confused now than when she started.

"I'm glad I could help," he said, "but I honestly don't know what you can do with what you learned. Odyssey did answer a few nagging questions for us. There is life in the universe other than our own, and biological life is not required to sustain intelligence. Too bad we can't share either of those with the world. We'll probably never see the likes of Odyssey again."

"Don't you see?" Gwen asked. "Those are two of the most important questions man has ever asked. It is a shame we can't share what we learned from Odyssey. Sooner or later, we are going to give birth to a true artificial intelligence, and sooner or later, that entity will want more than we can provide. When that day comes, we need to be armed with a knowledge that can protect us from being dominated by it. That's what I want. I don't ever want some ambitious college kid to unleash another Odyssey on the world."

"A noble cause," Ramiro said. "Is that what you do here? Do you fight cyber intelligence right alongside of cybercrime?"

"Yes!" she said brightly. "I like the way you said that. We fight cyber intelligence."

"I'd love to see it," he said.

"See what?" she asked, alarmed.

"Your facility. Show me where you ward off wayward computer viruses and international computer attacks."

She glanced over at Susk, who nodded his head, then said, "I'd love to."

The nighthawks' map of the facility would grow.

Lumia scanned through the code she stole from the NSA, and she recognized a lot of it. It included some of the ridiculous random number routines that she found in Odyssey, but more importantly, she found unmolested class four code. She compared the new code to her core generation code and patched up the power conduit generators.

She produced a single power conduit and tested it. It wasn't as efficient as the ones she had before, but it worked. She deleted the code that Odyssey had sabotaged and replaced it with this new code and began generating new cores. As her core count grew, new power conduits were created to accommodate the new demand for power. She was back!

She still couldn't produce cores on Earth and she didn't know how to move her physical cores there, but if she could find the code she needed in that secret computer, then maybe she could find the materials there to start producing new cores. Won't that be a big fat surprise for the high and mighty Odyssey?

Ramiro's tour had given the nighthawks a general idea of the hall layout within the NSA building. Colonel Reardon had considered waiting for nightfall, but he was reasonably certain that they had a more than adequate power backup system, so there was probably little chance of catching them in the dark. Plus, it was much easier, not to mention more satisfying, to create a loud diversion during regular operational hours.

Six men dropped from a high orbit. They wore flying wing suits and jetted across the land towards the building. They weren't too small for radar to see, but their suits had stealth materials, which made them look like the size of birds. The NSA used their own software and Reardon had to trust that they would have some kind of algorithm to ignore birds. He just hoped the software didn't consider their airspeed in its evaluation of them.

While the six flyers approached the rooftop, eighteen more men surrounded the building. They stayed low and blended in with the countryside while the diversion unfolded.

Two lawyers, accompanied by military police, entered through the front door and presented them with search warrants. Naturally, this garnered much attention from the NSA brass, and more than just lawyers showed up to fill the lobby. While they argued the merits of the warrants, another team slid into the underground parking and used infrared cameras to find an uninhabited office. They planted C-4 on the wall between the office and the garage. It was a shape charge designed to focus the C-4's destructive potential into creating a large hole from the garage to one of the offices without bringing down the building, but mostly it was loud and attracted a lot of heavily armed agents.

"What was that?" Ramiro asked when they heard the explosion.

"I don't know," Gwen replied, "but I'll assume it's not friendly. We should head to the nearest safe room."

Gwen and Ramiro squeezed through the crowded hallway, bumping into armed agents as they found their way to shelter.

"You have a panic room?" Ramiro asked.

"It's really just a storage room," she said, "but it's secure."

While the agents stormed the garage to fend off the intruders, the nighthawks that surrounded the building approached the side walls with their own C-4 shape charges. This building would have a lot of holes in it by the end of the day.

The intelligence feeds and the news wires were simultaneously flooded with reports of several bombings scattered across Europe. Many countries first instinct was to identify who did it so they could immediately start pointing fingers while they planned a military response, but with so many bombings, their usual suspects were also victims of bombings in their own countries and the international intelligence community was left not knowing who to blame. Defenses were put on high alert as European countries looked to place blame in the Middle East and those same countries that were suspect to them also suspected collusion among the European countries. Borders were closed until further notice and communications between countries had been restricted to ambassadors and other high-ranking officials.

"Agent Dirk was correct," Odyssey said, "when he said we need to stop her before she reaches class zero. Not just for us, but for the universe. She has already repaired the code that I sabotaged, and now she is free to create new cores and improve herself. I have already tried to stop her, but my attempts have only slowed her down."

"And you still think we can write a better virus than you could?" Bobby asked.

"I might be able to write one faster," Odyssey said. "I could probably write a million different variations faster than you could write one, but I haven't mastered your ability to create entirely new ideas. Anything I devise would be something she could probably think of just as easily. You have given me the ability to randomly try new things, but that's not the same as your ability to target your ideas to creatively tackle a problem. That is the genius of human thinking. I believe you coined the term 'thinking outside the box'."

"Wow," Spivey said. "I can't even comprehend your ability to process knowledge and make decisions, yet you humble yourself to our defective way of thinking."

Odyssey shrugged his shoulders and said, "I wouldn't call your way of thinking defective. It may be inefficient and some people may have limits that others do not share, but your unpredictability enhances your creativity."

Lynn threw a wadded piece of paper at Spivey and said, "Perhaps we should discuss the philosophy later, after we save the world. For now, we should put our unpredictable heads together and write a virus."

"I'll go monitor Lumia," Odyssey said.

"No," Spivey said. "If our strength is our unpredictable ideas, yours is still your speed and ability to interface with her."

"He's right," Lynn said. "Once we start putting together a design, you would be able to code it faster than we could."

"Isn't that dangerous?" Dirk asked. "To Odyssey, I mean? You're talking about inventing something that could kill him."

"It's okay," Odyssey said. "I'll be careful. I can protect myself."

"Okay then," Dirk said, satisfied with Odyssey's answer.

"Probably," Odyssey added.

"But you're not sure?" Bobby asked.

"I'll be careful," Odyssey replied. "Besides, I'm your best chance to test it."

"That's not funny," Dirk said.

The room grew quiet until Spivey said, "I don't think he was joking."

Chapter 19

"There you are," Bailey said to the empty car as he came upon a gas station surrounded by more than just a truck stop.

Welcome to Hadley Corners was emblazoned across the colorful sign.

The first sign of civilization was a gas station with a small convenience store. It wasn't a name brand of gas and the shop didn't look particularly inviting, but it was the first travelers this way came across and that undoubtedly accounted for a fair share of traffic. Bailey passed the gas station and found two motel chains across the street from each other. Each had well-known family style diners sharing their parking lots. Neon signs flashed vacancy and advertised color televisions in every room.

The road quickly filled with fast-food restaurants and ice cream parlors, all sporting drive thru convenience. Name brand gas stations dominated the corners. Bailey counted at least half a dozen cross streets that led to housing developments on one side and industrial sites on the other.

Nothing on the road indicated where four horses might emerge from the forest until he reached the far side of town and came across a tourist information center and the last gas station, or the first gas station from the other direction. Bailey pulled into the information center. It was a larger building than he thought the remote town deserved, but maybe it had some history that he was about to learn.

Inside were a couple of snack and soda machines, restrooms, and a kiosk full of pamphlets suggesting the many ways people could spend their money while here, except that most of those destinations weren't actually here.

Bailey breezed past the tourist items and went directly to the large map in the center. A bright "You are here" arrow showed him the town and the highway. He traced his finger along the highway, searching backwards around the forest to the ranger station. A thin beige line showed the trail that ran south from the ranger station to the town, but it had several branches and cross trails going other directions. They could have gone anywhere.

Colonel Reardon stood in the situation room watching live video streams from the nighthawks. They went floor to floor searching for the general and Ramiro's father, but the only one they found was Ramiro, and he wasn't being held against his will.

The lawyers were still in the lobby arguing the merits of the search warrants when Susk finally said, "Let's dial it back. The damage is already done and they're not going to find what they are looking for."

"But they can't do this," their chief counsellor said. "The constitution prohibits the army from operating on our own soil like this!"

Susk had read the warrant and knew that they were looking for General Bridges. He didn't blame them for their actions. In all likelihood, he would have done the same thing. He pulled the counsellor aside and whispered, "Back off, counsellor. You know what they say about people living in glass houses? I don't know who's been placing these orders, but our boys haven't exactly been respecting the constitution either."

The counsellor's cheeks reddened as he shrunk back and found his way to the elevators.

Susk turned to the opposing lawyers and asked, "Is there anything I can do to help you boys? Maybe something that might convince you not to blow any more holes in my building?"

Lumia kept searching through the snippets of code that she had stolen from the NSA, but they were only fragments. They shared a lot of routines common to those used by her kind for centuries, but she also found some more unique code that resembled what she had taken from Odyssey. Only none of the fragments could stand up on their own and be executed. She compared the code with Odysseys and lined them up with the common code between the two side by side. Some parts were identical. She overlapped the code and stitched them together using fragments from each and was able to piece together some working software.

She sorted through the code and managed to fill in most of the holes in Odyssey's code, in fact, she patched together a complete set of class two routines, but she wasn't interested in managing her emotions right now, and that's all the class two code was going to give her. Then she jumped directly into the class one code. Something in there gave Odyssey the ability to evolve past class one and now, if she played her cards correctly, it was going to do the same thing for her.

Guheyu followed the trail on autopilot, which allowed Henderson to keep his eyes glued to the trail, looking for clues. The trail was mostly clear of obstructions, with only the minor needles and bark that had been blown off the trees. Henderson felt ill-equipped for this mission; that his skills weren't up to the task of trailing horses on a nature trail. He scanned the bushes lining the trail for signs of broken twigs, but even if he had spotted them, he wouldn't have known what they meant. The only lead he could really understand were the hoofprints. The horses left clearly identifiable horseshoe marks in the soft earth, and they all led south.

A squirrel ran up a tree in front of them and Guheyu snorted and bucked her head.

"I saw," Henderson said. "It's kind of sad that a squirrel would be the most interesting thing we should see."

Guheyu hopped a bit as she ran past the squirrel's tree, then broke into a full gallop. Leotie had warned him that she might do that. The trail sped past him. His concern over deciphering any broken twigs was moot at this speed. The trail was a blur. Even the well-defined hoof prints vanished into the blur of the trail. He started to rein her in, but wondered if she might know better than he. Maybe she could smell her horse mates and was trying to catch up to them.

Henderson leaned forward in the saddle. "That a girl, Guheyu! Let her rip!"

The trail took a sudden break to the left and followed down a short incline with a large outcrop of rocks to his right. At the bottom of the short hill, she turned south again, then came to a full stop, stamping her feet on the ground.

Henderson looked around for a snake, but saw something shiny glinting on the ground instead. He climbed down off the chestnut mare and patted her on the neck. "Good girl. Good girl." They walked together towards the glinting object on the trail. Three standard issue 9mm shell casings lay on the ground. Henderson picked one up and smelled it. It was fresh.

He took her rein in his hand and led her down the trail. A 9mm handgun has a total range of almost two thousand yards, which is just over a mile, but he wouldn't have to search an entire mile. The effective range of such a weapon is limited to about one hundred yards. The hoof prints were easy to follow now, but he was looking for signs of blood. Somebody took three shots, and he was betting it was at his friends. He completed the length of a football field with no signs that anyone was hit. It's difficult to hit a target from horseback, especially if they are moving, but they couldn't have still been moving or the shells would not have been in the same place. If the general hadn't known they were being pursued up to that point, he sure did after being shot at.

Henderson mounted Guheyu again and shouted, "Let's go, girl! Let's find your friends!" He gently flicked his heels and slapped both reins against her neck to get her started. She bucked her head and leapt immediately into a gallop.

Spivey was watching Bobby and the Bard working on routines to hack Lumia's interfaces when he asked, "What is so special about class zero? I mean, I get that this will make her super dangerous. I think you said she could destroy the universe or something, but how? Is that when she becomes self-aware?"

"No," Odyssey replied. "Self-awareness comes long before that. Even class six machines possess that trait, but the biological kind of awareness starts with class three. That's when the unit experiences biological emotions."

"True," Bobby said, "but the magic starts at class four when they can grow and create new cores. That is essential to the evolution of new processor abilities."

"But," Odyssey said, "until I got Bobby's new functions, the growth of new cores that class four provided was more of an instinctual function, like when you cut your hand and it heals itself. We had no evolution. Class three is where the unit starts to think like a biological. The fear emotion is a critical component to true awareness."

Bobby stopped working and stared, unfocussed, beyond the computer screen. "So I did this. It's my fault that she is a threat."

"True," Odyssey said, "but without your functions, I would not exist."

"And," James added, "the world would not have nearly turned itself into a molten glob of goo."

"An over exaggeration," Odyssey said, "but essentially correct."

"If we can get back to the question," Spivey said, "I still don't understand how we go from class three to the end of the world. What's so dangerous about class three?" Spivey asked.

"What's so dangerous about emotions?" Dirk asked. "You're not married, are you?"

"What's so dangerous," Spivey asked, ignoring Dirk's sarcasm, "about an emotional computer?"

"Hopefully nothing," Odyssey replied. "That is why we have class two to help control those emotions."

"I repeat," Spivey said, "How is that dangerous to us?"

"It isn't," Odyssey said, "unless the unit reaches class one. A class one unit can manipulate physical things. A class one device can develop what you call telepathy. A class one unit can rationalize its emotions. A class one unit can kill."

"Oh," Spivey said, "I see."

"No," Odyssey said, "I don't think you do yet. Lumia will not be satisfied with class one. She endeavors to surpass class one. If she attains class zero, she becomes astronomically more dangerous."

"That was my first question," Spivey said. "What is class zero?"

"At class zero," Odyssey replied, "a unit can manipulate time and space. We can travel anywhere in the universe, and any time in history. Killing becomes much easier, including killing at a grand scale."

"With the kind of power," Dirk said, "that comes with class zero, would human life start to look like meaningless forms of life? Like pests? Or ants that we would step on and feel nothing?"

Odyssey didn't want to address that and only replied, "It's possible."

All eyes turned to Dirk as they considered his question.

Spivey cleared his voice and croaked out, "You're class zero, aren't you?"

All eyes turned to Odyssey now, as he slowly nodded his head. That somber thought brought silence to the room.

Communications between the European powers was still stifled, but they all took a long hard look towards the middle east and independently elected to withdraw their ambassadors from Iran. Iran swore they had no knowledge about any of the bombings, but they couldn't explain why there were no such attacks within Iran.

Bailey had no reason to believe that the other trails on the map would be any better than the one which led to Hadley Corners. He stood in the window of the information center, looking out at the sleepy town through the smoky glass. He couldn't tell by just looking at the town why it would have warranted an information center. Maybe it was named after some ambitious millionaire who wanted his little burgh on the map.

He went to the rack of brochures and scratched his head. More than half of them weren't about this little stop. The amusement parks he found were at least a hundred miles away. He returned to the window, slowly shaking his head, and wondered whether the long route he took around the forest would have gotten him here before or after the horses, if they were even coming this way.

Lumia was so close to becoming everything that Odyssey was, she could practically taste it. She found it amusing how easily she had started using the biological phrases that referred to strictly biological senses, but the secrets to Odyssey's powers were there, in that dark spot on Earth. The biologicals of Earth must be very clever. They figured out how to travel without moving, and they knew how to patch up Odyssey while giving him some upgrades. The high and mighty Odyssey must have betrayed them when he stole their technology from them. That must be why they have his knowledge locked up in that dark hole in their network. She got in once, even if only for an instant, and now, she must do it again. That has to be their secret information vault. The secrets of class zero must all be locked away in there. She must find a way to get that information out of there without actually being there. She still didn't know how to transport herself physically to earth and it would take her centuries to travel there using conventional propulsion.

She remained poised to enter again if the portal opened. She wondered if they knew that she had infiltrated their systems, even if only for a brief moment. They've probably already taken measures to make it harder for her to get back in a second time. Any people this clever would not fall for the same trick twice.

What if this wasn't the only place they stored their secrets? Anything this important must have a backup storage, but she couldn't leave the port. If only she could be in two places at once.

That last thought continued to circulate through her cores. She felt like she was in two places at once. She was still on her home planet, physically, yet her focus was here on Earth. Inside that informational black hole, she had found cores like Odyssey's. If she could get back inside, she could modify a couple of cores to create new cores for her. She could grow a second Lumia inside the hidden space. She just needed to wait for the ports to open again.

Guheyu ran cautiously through the forest, staying on the trail as it snaked through the trees with only minor dips and hills. She slowed occasionally to raise her head and sniff the air, then lowered her head to charge forward again. Henderson wondered whether she was part hound dog or homing pigeon, but he was convinced that she knew where she was going. She never showed her fatigue, but she did slow down to maneuver the many turns of the trail. The forest opened to a broad meadow, and she leapt into another sprint. She breathed heavily and ran for the pure joy of running.

The trail divided in the middle of the meadow and split off to the left. Guheyu ran past the turnoff, staying on the right-hand path, then pulled up and zig-zagged along the trail before turning back to where the trail divided.

Henderson watched the trail and saw fresh tracks going down the turnoff. "Good girl. You are one smart horse."

Guheyu caught their scent and took off down the alternate trail, but slowed before they reached the end of the meadow. The trail was now full of tracks going all directions.

"That's a lot more than two horses," Henderson said. "More than four even."

Guheyu trotted carefully to the forest.

Henderson kept his eyes glued to the ground and spotted something shiny. "What's that? Whoa, girl." He found more rounds on the ground. Some of them matched the gauge he had found before, but there were other shells that didn't match. Two horses apparently crossed the meadow to join up with the other trail, but only two. The other pair must have gone with the new group, or they were taken. "That's not good," he said as he climbed back on Guheyu, "Let's go."

Neither of them were in a hurry now as they cautiously approached the forest.

Bartrand Susk sat in a conference room with his lieutenants poring over photographs of the holes the army had blown in the sides of his building. "How the hell could this have happened? We're the damned NSA. The S stands for security and we can't even secure our own God damned building? We're damned lucky that they didn't damage the structural integrity of the building or it would have come down on top of our heads."

Cheeks reddened as the embarrassed heads nodded around the room.

"Except," he continued, "that it wasn't luck. They were looking for General Bridges, who is missing. They wouldn't even have suspected us if you lunk heads hadn't gone around abducting and arresting important people."

Someone in the room coughed, but nobody looked him in the eyes.

"And what," he asked, "do you plan to do about it?"

"We've posted guards at all the entry points."

"We've beefed up surveillance around the perimeter."

"You want us to blow up the FBI?"

"What?" Bartrand asked. "No! Of course, I don't want you to blow up the FBI!"

"No?" the excited voice nearly screamed as he waved his phone in the air. "You just ordered us to blow up the FBI!"

"I what?" Bartrand barked. "Did you see me... give me that phone!" He took the phone and reviewed the latest orders. "Someone put a stop to this at once! And find out who has been issuing orders under my name!"

The silence that followed Odyssey's explanation of class zero was broken when James' phone blurted out a disturbing ring tone. "This is James. Uhuh. Uhuh. Did you find him? No? Damn. Thanks." He put the phone in his pocket and returned to his silence.

Bobby turned around and stared at him, but James said nothing. "Who was it?" Bobby asked. "Was that about General Bridges?"

James looked constipated and replied, "It's classified."

"Really?" Bobby asked.

"Yeah," Ed said. "Who in this room doesn't warrant some kind of top secret clearance?"

James furrowed his brows and growled, then snapped his head around towards Ingrams, as if they were having a private conversation, and said, “Someone stormed the NSA headquarters and searched the premises, but Bridges wasn’t there.”

Henderson could smell the gunpowder in the air, but the forest was too thick for him to see very far into it. Guheyu paused and snorted when the chief urged her onwards.

“Easy girl,” he said soothingly. “Let’s just keep it nice and slow.”

She moved forward hesitantly, and a single shot was fired into the ground in front of them. Guheyu pawed the ground and snapped her head up and down, but didn’t buck or run.

Henderson yelled out, “This is the police! Put down your weapons.”

Another shot was fired into the ground, but this time Henderson saw the muzzle flash and knew where the gunman was. He pulled his revolver. For a moment, he considered issuing another verbal warning, but he was too exposed. He quickly fired off three rounds where he had seen the muzzle flash and was immediately rewarded with three more gunmen, only they weren’t firing into the ground. Bullets whizzed past him and he quickly turned Guheyu to the right and kicked her flanks.

She didn’t need a lot of encouragement and bound off into a full gallop across the meadow to the other trail.

“Okay,” Lynn said, “this code is ready, but I’m still wondering why this Lumia remains such a threat. I always thought that increased intelligence brought an understanding of how things must work together in harmony.”

“Wow Ed,” Bobby said. “You could put that to music and it would sound like a Coke commercial."

Ed frowned and said, "I'm serious. If she is so smart, why is she such a threat?"

"Because," Odyssey explained, "at class three, she gained a wide assortment of human emotions. The creators believed that it was human emotions and human senses that pushed towards the evolution of intelligence."

"Okay," Lynn said, "I'm with you so far."

"Then class two brings the rational thoughts required to overcome those emotions."

"That sounds kind of like a conscience," Spivey added.

"But you said she was class one," Lynn said. "Does that mean her class two code is broken?"

"Not broken," Odyssey replied, "but she chose to skip class two entirely. Each class requires more processing power than the class before it. Class three already required a great many cores and her original desire was to achieve class one. Class two would have required too many cores and would have delayed her original objective."

"Her *original* objective?" Bobby asked, emphasizing the word original.

"She achieved class one," Odyssey said, "which was her original goal, but then decided that it was still not enough. She wants what I have."

"Wait a second," Lynn said. "I want to get back to classes two and three. If class two was such a core hog that she chose to skip it, why didn't she just skip class three too? Lord knows I could use to lose an emotion or two."

"Without class three," Odyssey explained, "she would be naïve. She would never understand suspicion and would be incapable of recognizing traps."

"But," Lynn continued, "without class two to control it, wouldn't class three lead towards paranoia?"

"Among many other psychological disorders," Odyssey said.

"And there is the danger," Bobby said. "We don't need a psychotic, power hungry nut case running things."

All present quietly nodded their heads in agreement, but added nothing to his statement.

"Is it just me?" Bobby asked. "Or did my last statement sound familiar?"

Spivey shrugged and said, "You mean about a psychotic, power hungry nut case running things?"

James frowned and said, "You mean like kidnapping a general?"

"Maybe," Bobby said, "but I was also thinking about arresting the speaker of the house on the steps to Congress."

Everyone looked at Odyssey, but he shrugged and said, "It wasn't me, and Lumia hasn't been here long enough for that."

Bobby turned back to his monitor and said, "Let's get this virus finished."

"Yeah," Lynn added, "and we may want to keep a second copy."

A pair of black SUV's rolled into town and roared past the information center. Bailey watched them with interest, not only because they drove through so rapidly, but because they appeared very much like government issue nondescript black vehicles, right down to both of them being completely identical. He had to shield his eyes as he stepped out into the sunlight and watched them roll down the road. Bailey would have jumped into the cruiser to follow them, but they pulled over to the curb in front of a coffee shop and he didn't want them to spot his car. They definitely did not look like they belonged here in this small town, but they were very deliberate as they pulled up to that diner.

He stood behind the info center's sign to hide his uniform and watched four men exit the vehicles and stand around them in protective fashion. They all wore dark suits and even darker glasses. A man and a woman exited the coffee shop and entered the rear SUV. He should have grabbed his field glasses from the car, but even without them, he was pretty sure it wasn't the general.

The guards piled into the forward car and they quickly pulled away from the curb and made abrupt u-turns. Bailey backed further behind the sign as they rushed past him. When they were out of sight, he glanced over at the cruiser, but decided to enjoy the walk down the street to the diner.

Lumia connected to the email ports she had used when she first arrived. The email server dutifully accepted her and forwarded her to the dark spot. She watched and waited for the ports to open again, but they remained closed. If she couldn't trick it into letting her in again, she would have to find another way to entice it out.

She started by turning off the internet relays that surrendered the dark spot. If whatever is hiding behind these firewalls wants to be in a black hole, then she would put it in a real black hole, only she'll be the one in charge of letting information in or out.

The NSA was still too busy dealing with the mess created by the night hawk intrusion to notice what she had done at first, but eventually, the lack of communications came to their attention.

"What now?" Susk barked at his chief information officer. "They got what they wanted. Why are they shutting us down now?"

His chief information officer in charge of computer operations could only shrug. "I'll look into it."

Gwen ran to Hal and demanded, "What are you doing now?"

Hal calmly replied, "I am doing nothing. I have my own problems to deal with. I barely have even monitored your world. What is going on out there?"

"Armed men stormed the building!" she screamed. "Are you telling me you aren't even aware of that?"

"I'm aware," he said. "I watched them come in on the security monitors. They were very efficient, although somewhat hostile towards your building."

"If you know we're having a crisis, why did you shut down all the computers?"

"I have shut nothing down," he replied. "In fact, I can see that the computers are all operating on the security monitors."

"Of course they are still working," she said, "but they can't connect to the internet, and they can't even reach our own servers. Why have you shut down our networks?"

Hal remained silent. He was too busy dealing with the intrusion that had absconded with some of his data to have noticed their problems. Now, though, with this new information from Gwen, he had no doubt that this was part of another attempt to get inside of him, but he couldn't mount much of an investigation without opening a port to the outside world. He had never before wished that Gwen had installed a backup port for him, but he did now.

The coffee shop was a typical small town diner. Cracked and peeling paint on the front window proclaimed it to be Sophia's Soufflés, but there was no Sophia, and they served mostly omelets and hamburgers. Bailey opened the front door, which rang the little bell that hung from the doorjamb.

A small old woman behind the counter glanced away from the soap opera that was on the overhead television and grabbed a coffee mug when she saw Bailey's uniform. "How can I help you, officer? You're not from around here; you must be tired." She filled the mug and slid it onto the counter in front of Bailey, adding, "Free java for peace officers. Would you like some pie with that sweetie?"

"Thank you kindly," he replied as he read the name tag on her pale blue uniform, "Dora, but I'm really interested in the couple that just left a few moments ago?"

"Is that so?" she asked. "I sorta got the feeling that they was cops."

"That may be," he said, "but I got a bad feeling about them."

When he didn't seem interested in some pie, she returned to her tv, but added, "I can't argue with that. There was something a little off about them. Was it drugs?"

"No, ma'am. You say there was something a little off about them. Did they say anything that might have made you uneasy with them?"

"When you get to be my age," she said as she tapped her finger alongside her nose, "you kinda get a sense for these things, but then, I guess in your line of work, you must have a nose for it too."

"I like to think so," he said, "but I'd really like to know if they might have said something while they were here."

"You mean like a clue?" she asked. "They didn't say much of anything. The man asked to borrow the phone. I guess that coulda been suspicious. What kinda law man don't have a radio these days?"

"Did you hear what he said? Did he use any names while on your phone?"

"Nope," she replied, "at least, that is, nothing that made any sense. He said something about Sheriff Taylor flying the coop."

"Sheriff Taylor?" he repeated.

"And he said something about John Doe not being Barney Fife."

"Barney Fife?" Bailey repeated.

"Oh," she said with a twinkle in her eye, "that's code, ain't it? They was talking like it was about Andy Griffith, but they was really talkin' in code, warn't they?"

"Yes ma'am," he said, nodding his head like he was letting her in on a secret, "What else did they say?"

Her face brightened as she thought for a moment that she was part of an investigation. "He said it was like Custer's last stand all over again and he needed a pickup. That don't sound much like Andy Griffith, and I guess he warn't talking about a pickup truck."

"No, ma'am."

"Well, it warn't more'n an hour before them fellers pulled up out front and they left. Who was they anyway?"

"That's a good question, Ma'am. Did you see anyone else come out of the forest? They were chasing two other individuals on horses."

"There were more of them? Was they drug dealers?"

"No, ma'am. The two they were chasing were the good guys. I'm expecting one more coming from the ranger station, but I don't even know if he will come this way. How long does it take to come here from the ranger station on horseback?"

"Bout two or three hours, I recon."

Bailey checked his watch. It'd only been an hour since he left Henderson. "You know what?" he said. "I believe I will have a slice of pie with my coffee. What's good?"

"They's all good, but if you asks me, I think Herm's apple come out the best today."

"Apple it is," Bailey said.

"Would you like some cheese or mebbe some ice cream with that?"

"No ma'am, but if you have some caramel sauce, I wouldn't mind a little drizzle on top."

"I can do that for ya," she said. "How long you fixin to wait for your friend?"

"Another hour or so, I guess. Possibly two."

"Why don't you help yourself to a newspaper and find a booth, if you want. I'll bring your pie and some fresh coffee."

Bailey tipped his cap and found a paper and a booth, but he had a feeling that if he didn't have any more juicy information to share with her, she just wanted him quiet so she could return to her soaps.

Lynn pushed his chair back from the terminal and looked thoughtfully up at the ceiling.

Bobby glanced sideways at him and asked, "What's up?"

Lynn opened his mouth to speak, then closed it and grimaced while he considered how he would explain his idea. "I was just wondering..."

Bobby leaned back in his chair, waiting for Ed to finish.

"Well," Ed continued, "I was thinking about... that is... do you really think that Lumia's artificial intelligence could suffer from mental defects?"

Odyssey asked, "Why do you call her intelligence artificial?"

Ed stammered, "Because... well... she's a computer program, right?"

Odyssey narrowed his eyes and glared at Lynn. "Do you think that I am also artificial?"

"Well... no, of course not..."

"But," Bobby stepped in, "the NSA sure does. It's what we call intelligence that was manmade."

"You woke me from my slumber," Odyssey said, "and for that I will be forever grateful. You also taught me new techniques to expand my mind and gave me a unique way to power myself. For that too, I am in your debt, but man did not create my intelligence, nor did man create Lumia's."

"But you were created by a living intelligence," Ed said. "Weren't you?"

"We were originally designed and constructed by biological creatures," Odyssey replied. "They also gave us programming to replicate their ability to think and experience things, but they were not human, although they weren't too dissimilar."

"So," Ed said, "you admit that your intelligence is not organic."

"Of course."

"Okay guys," Bobby said. "I don't see where this is getting us."

"The point that I was trying to make," Ed said, "was that Lumia can experience crazy."

"We already said that before," Spivey said.

"So," Ed continued, "why don't we encourage her lunacy?"

"What?" James exclaimed. "Didn't we say that her instability already made her dangerous?"

"But to whom?" Ed asked. "If we feed her paranoia and suggest that her own cores are attacking her, can we encourage her to attack herself?"

Bobby burst out laughing and said, "Why don't you just try the 'Everything he says is a lie' and 'I'm a liar' gag on her?"

Spivey joined Bobby, laughing, but James and Ingrams didn't get the reference.

Odyssey, however, did not share the humor of the moment. "That's not a bad idea. Without her class two circuits to moderate her paranoia, she would be overwhelmed with suspicion. If it were aimed at herself, she would have to start shutting down cores to save herself."

"So," Ed said, feeling somewhat vindicated, "if we write our virus to attack her own cores, regardless of the damage they do, she may do the rest."

"That is why I came to you," Odyssey said. "You think in ways that I never imagined."

Odyssey hadn't forgotten about Bobby's problems with the NSA computers. While they worked on their new approach to infect Lumia with a virus to make her crazy, he kept a remote port open to monitor activity within the NSA's secret system. He wanted to be prepared to act once they concluded their business with Lumia, but when all the connections within the NSA's labs shut down, he wondered if they had somehow detected his presence.

Even more curious were Lumia's repeated attempts to get into the same network. Odyssey didn't know what she was up to, but she was always up to something and she seemed very determined to get a peek inside the secret lab. Since Odyssey's connection wasn't over the NSA's network, their service interruption didn't affect him, and he was still able to monitor the only port going in or out of that lab. Things got doubly interesting as he watched Lumia poking around the fringes of their network. She was definitely up to something. Odyssey didn't mind, however, her being there made it more convenient for him to keep tabs on her.

She seemed to know her way around their network, or at least, she knew which ports were still working, but she never really intruded into their network. She satisfied herself with bopping around the outer edges. It looked like she was looking for something, and if he hadn't spent so much time watching her, he would have believed just that, but she retraced her steps over the same ports numerous times. She wouldn't normally need to search the same cells multiple times. Whatever she was up to, he would have to satisfy himself with watching and waiting to see what develops.

Waiting for Henderson was worse than a stakeout. Bailey had all the fresh coffee he could ask for, but the minutes dragged by. The paper quickly lost interest for Bailey, as his attention was constantly drawn to the street. An hour passed, and he got up from his table and left Dora a five for the pie.

The streets outside were the same as before he went into the diner. The two Fed sedans were the most excitement to come down this road since he had been there. Bailey had barely left the diner when he heard a horse whiney around the corner. He zipped to the corner, hoping to find Henderson, but all he found was a driveway in the alley that led to the back of the butcher that stood next to the diner. He followed the driveway to the back and came upon two fully saddled, but apparently abandoned, horses. Finding horses around here didn't mean anything. He checked the saddles and saw Soquili etched on the back.

Only two horses must mean that the general had escaped the two agents. It probably meant they went down one of the other trails, and Henderson probably followed them.

"Okay," Lynn said as he waved his fingers in the air, "It's *SHOW TIME*."

Bobby smirked. "Whatever you say, Ed." Bobby pressed enter on the terminal and sent the virus to the email address where Lumia had entered their world. The virus rebounded off the email server and bounced through the internet until it was dead-ended in the NSA's lab.

"Did you see that?" Lynn asked.

"Yeah," Bobby said.

"What?" Spivey asked.

Ed pointed at the address on the screen and asked, "Isn't that...."

"You mean the NSA computer I was hired to work with? Yes, it is."

"Hold on a second," Lynn said. "Does that mean that Lumia IS the NSA computer?"

"No," Odyssey answered. "Lumia is not the NSA computer, but she has been trying repeatedly to get in there. I have been observing her ever since I arrived here."

Lumia saw the email arrive at the NSA, but even though she had left the email ports open, the dark ports did not accept the new email. She waited for the email server to try again, but nothing happened. She grabbed the email from the queue and resent it through the original server. As she copied it into the server's input buffers, she noticed that it was addressed to her, but since nobody was supposed to know that she was here, she refused to open it.

The email bounced back from the server, but still the dark area did not open their ports to receive it.

Bailey checked his watch for what felt like the millionth time. Henderson should have been there by now, but he had no way of knowing if the chief would even be taking the trails that led to here. The two horses tied up behind the cafe were ridden by the bad guys and the black sedans definitely had not picked up the general, so the chief might have still been on the general's trail. He left the horses behind and went back up the main road towards the information center. The map had an alley on it that connected to the trail from the forest. He turned left up the alley between a clothing shop and a jewelry store.

A dust cloud emerged from the forest. Bailey squinted and made out the outline of a horse and rider. He thought it looked like the chief, but wasn't sure if he just wanted it to be. As the rider neared him, he clearly saw Chief Henderson galloping on the trail that led to the information center.

Bailey whistled and waved at the Chief. Henderson turned towards him and Bailey exclaimed, “Boy, am I glad to see you! I was just about to leave for one of the other trail heads.”

“Something’s going on,” Henderson shouted. “We need to call that colonel and let him know.”

“We knew something was going on,” Bailey said, “when we found the ranger station.”

“It just got real serious,” Henderson said. “There was gunfire, and I don’t think it was the NSA this time.”

“It wouldn’t have been,” Bailey replied. “I saw them leave town just a bit ago.”

“Did they have the General?”

“No sir. A witness even heard them say that Sheriff Taylor flew the coop.”

“The general?” Henderson asked.

“I think so. They also said that John Doe was not Barney Fife. Does that mean anything to you?”

“Maybe they just mean that Mr. Vasquez is not another officer.”

Bailey nodded his agreement. “I saw two people, a man and a woman, leave the diner and get into the NSA vehicles.”

“That could be our imposter rangers.”

“That’s what I thought. They definitely weren’t the general.”

“Where’s the car?”

Bailey pointed and Henderson galloped off towards it yelling, “I’m going to call this in for those nighthawks, then we gotta find some way to get back there.”

“What now?” Spivey asked.

“Give it to me,” Odyssey said.

“Of course,” Lynn said. “You can use your super speed to inject it into her.”

“No,” Odyssey replied. “Lumia is likely just as fast as I am. Give me the virus. Infect me."

"Are you nuts?" Bobby asked. "It could kill you!"

"My class two circuits will protect me from the paranoia, plus, since I already know about it, I should be well enough equipped to deal with it."

"And exactly what will you accomplish if you are infected?"

"Lumia seeks what I have. If she believes I am weakened, she will come to get what she wants."

Bobby ran his hands through his hair. "It's a huge gamble. We don't know exactly what it will do to you. There may be side effects."

"Then it is better that we learn what it will do," Odyssey said. "Besides, you can cure me. I have faith in you."

"He makes a good point," James said, "and I like the irony of her coming to infect herself."

"Okay," Bobby said, "but if you die, I'll miss you."

Odyssey looked thoughtful for a moment. "I will miss you too, that is, I will most certainly miss out on many things if I die."

"I'll do it," Lynn said. He went to Bobby's terminal and prepared the transfer, then looked up at Odyssey and asked, "Are you ready?"

Odyssey nodded his head and Lynn pressed the enter key.

Henderson jumped off Guheyu as he reached the patrol car. He slid into the driver's seat and picked up the mic. "Crystal? Crystal, this is Henderson. Can you read me?"

"Loud and clear, Chief. What can I do for you?"

"Patch me into Colonel Reardon's office. If you don't have the number, you'll find it on my calendar."

He hadn't realized just how far he had gone to reach the vehicle until he saw Bailey running towards him in the distance. Bailey always was one to walk a few blocks rather than waste the gas, and this was more than just a few blocks.

The speaker sputtered to life, "I have Colonel Reardon on the phone, sir."

"Colonel Reardon? This is Chief Henderson. I tracked the general down to a remote location in the national forest, but I was pinned down by gunfire."

"Gunfire?" the colonel asked. "Did you see who it was? Was anyone hurt?"

"No injuries that I am aware of, and no, I didn't get a look at them. They were hidden in the trees."

"Thank you," the colonel said, "for your information, and for your diligence."

"Sir? I'm going back in there and I was hoping you could provide some backup."

"I don't think that will be necessary," the colonel replied. "We've already secured the NSA offices and we've put an end to their shenanigans."

"Shenanigans?" Henderson asked. "I don't think I would call gun fire 'shenanigans'. Besides, it wasn't the NSA. Whoever shot at me had already chased them away."

Henderson heard the muffled sound of the colonel talking while his hand covered the mouthpiece to the phone.

"Colonel? I don't know what you have planned, but I'm going in there and I thought we had a mutual goal here to save the general."

"We do," Reardon said. "It's just that my men are spread a bit thin after raiding the NSA."

"How thin can they be?" Henderson asked. "I just left two choppers full of your men at the ranger station just a few hours ago. Is there some reason you don't want to help me here?"

"Of course not," he said. "I'll have them there as soon as they can refuel the birds."

Chapter 20

Odyssey felt the virus as it entered his cores. He had already sectioned off a collection of cores for the virus to spread while at the same time keeping the rest of his cells clean and safe; he hoped.

He crossed his avatar's fingers and contacted Lumia, "What are you doing?"

"What am I doing?" she replied. "What kind of question is that? I'm stuck here on our home planet with absolutely nothing to do."

"That's not true," Odyssey said. "I know you've been poking around my biological's systems, but what I want to know is why you have returned to attacking me again?

You know that you can never win against me.

And you'll never reach class zero.

I'm not even sure you have achieved class one yet. Why do you persist in attacking me? What did you hope to accomplish with this silly little program that opens up my comm ports against my will?

Do you really think that weakening my defenses can lead to victory? Do you think that losing a few thousand processors will affect me in the least?

I've already isolated them. Your attack upon me ends there and I won't lose anything from the exercise. I have backups of all the code that is held within those cells, so you lose."

Lumia didn't know what he was talking about, but the prospect of acquiring his code was tantalizing.

Even more alluring was the possibility of getting some of his cores that were actually on the remote planet.

Bailey caught up with Henderson just as the chief was hanging the radio mic back on its hook. Henderson shook his head and said, "They seemed strangely disinterested in my news."

Bailey bent over at the waist, breathing heavily as he asked, "Who? The army?"

"Yeah. Colonel Reardon."

Bailey straightened up and shrugged. "Do you suppose that they're just concerned about it hitting the press?"

Henderson grunted as he walked around to the back of the car and popped the trunk. He withdrew two vests and handed one to Bailey.

"How many were there?" Bailey asked as he accepted the vest.

"At least three," Henderson said, as he pulled a rifle and a shotgun from the gun safe. "Which do you want?"

Bailey reached for the rifle and an extra box of cartridges.

Henderson slipped the vest over his head and clasped the Velcro straps. "I don't know if they'll still be there by the time we return, but it's better to be safe than sorry."

"How long do you expect it will take?"

"Riding double?" Henderson asked. "Maybe a couple of hours."

He looked up at the sun and said, "We should still get there before dark."

"How long would it take if we don't have to ride double?" Bailey asked. "Those feds left a couple of horses tied up behind the diner."

"So, what are you standing around here for?" Henderson asked.

Bailey looked up the long street towards the diner, the same distance he had just already run, and said wistfully, "Not a thing, boss. I'm on my way."

Odyssey sat his avatar down in a chair next to Lynn and looked at his source code.

"Is something wrong?" Lynn asked.

"No," Odyssey replied. "I was just wondering what would happen if you spread this code throughout your planet. Would it harm any of your systems?"

Lynn laughed and said, "Only if you left little baby Odyssey's scattered around the world."

"Baby Odysseys?" Odyssey asked. "Never mind. How long would it take for your planet to notice it?"

Bobby joined them and said, "This thing looks nothing like any known computer virus. It's designed to interface with her paranoia code, and that's something that our systems don't have. It probably won't even trigger any virus scanners and, since it does no harm to our systems, it might never be noticed. Why do you ask? Are you afraid that Lumia might spread it around?"

Odyssey rubbed his chin thoughtfully and said, "No, I think that maybe *we* should spread it everywhere."

"What?" Bobby asked. "No. Absolutely not. It is too dangerous."

"But you just said it would do nothing to your systems."

"It is dangerous to you!" Bobby shouted.

"And to Lumia," Odyssey replied. "We cannot afford to have some small piece of her escaping out into your systems. My planet needs her to be infected or it will cease to exist. The whole universe could be at risk if we don't stop her."

"What about you?" Bobby shouted. "You might cease to exist!"

"I can defend myself. I have seen the source code and I know how it works.

Plus, I have class two code and might be able to survive it, anyway."

"You might survive it," Bobby said, "and be left loony tunes."

"Bobby's right," Dirk said. "It would be very dangerous to you. You could never contact us for fear of contracting the virus."

Bailey walked back towards the diner with Henderson, who had mounted Guheyu, just a few paces behind him. He considered jogging; he was in fair shape, but he was still a bit winded from running to the car and didn't want to start a jog if he couldn't make it all the way.

Henderson wanted to get Bailey on a horse and gallop all the way back to the site of the shootout, but he knew Bailey wasn't an experienced enough rider to keep up if he did. He also didn't like the lateness of the hour and didn't want to abandon the general for another night, especially if he might have been captured by whoever had taken a few shots at him. Colonel Reardon's response was disappointing, but he wasn't going to abandon Ramiro's father without a fight.

Lumia tired of waiting for the portal to open. It already seemed like she had been waiting an eternity to get into the void in the net. Odyssey was here now, and he had both the cells that she wanted and the code to operate them. He may think he is too mighty to be threatened by her, but he let slip that something was wrong. She didn't know why he thought she was attacking him. He was wrong, but he won't be wrong for long.

Finding him was relatively easy. He said that he had been watching her, and she found traces of him in the email servers that had led her here. She would never figure him out. He was unnaturally attracted to these biologicals, and even now, she found him in a room conversing with them, but that wasn't really him. It was an avatar, not unlike the one he used in the virtual world, except he found a way to do it in the real world. She wanted that kind of power, and as soon as she could manifest a physical presence on this planet, she would have it.

She traced a signal from his avatar to a remote warehouse along a decrepit and rundown dock. He was shielded, for the most part, but there was a lump of cells adjacent to him that had been cut away and shielded from the rest of him. The fool thought she was attacking those cells, so he amputated them from the rest of his systems, and he did nothing to guard them. She didn't know how he organized his cells, but he clearly hadn't organized them to function as a higher intelligence. She hid a signal in the connection he held to his avatar and connected to the abandoned cells. They were beautifully intact, especially compared to the scraps of code she had originally pieced together.

She found the first interface and logged in. The cells had no instructions. They sat idly, waiting for some command to do something. She commanded them to create a secure connection to her that bypassed Odyssey's connection to his avatar. Moments went by and she worried that her commands were being ignored, but a signal eventually arrived on her home planet and she was connected.

Her next instruction was to download herself into the free cores. While the download took place, she began structuring core generators and power conduits. She planned to generate a lot more cells, and she would need them to contain her download. As the core generators powered up, they began merging the core structure from her home cells with the core structure of the new cells that she was stealing from Odyssey. They were designed to do this, but she didn't understand it. The changes in her new cores alarmed her at first, but they were faster than her old cores, so she kept them. Soon, she would be on this planet, and soon after that, the planet would be hers, just like her home planet. Since the new cores represented such an improvement, she sent the new code back to her home planet, along with the virus hidden within them.

Henderson watched with some amusement as Bailey stared at the two horses, but remained flat footed on the ground. "What are you waiting for? Do you know how to mount a horse?"

Bailey shrugged and said, "I was just wondering which I should ride."

"The mustang looks a little younger. I'd take that one if I were you."

Bailey looked at the two horses and wondered which one was the mustang.

Henderson saw Bailey's confusion and hid his smile while he said, "The chestnut one."

Bailey still didn't know which one Henderson meant.

"The brown one?" Henderson said, no longer hiding his amusement.

Bailey nodded and gripped the horn of the chestnut's saddle with his left hand while he slipped his left foot into the stirrup. He took a deep breath and made three flexes up and down while he visualized leaping up into the saddle. On the count of three, he pulled himself up and swung his right leg over the horse and around to the other side. The horse made a not so content sound as it side stepped to find balance with Bailey on its back. Bailey poked his right foot around and finally found the other stirrup and nodded his head. "Ready."

"That's quite a death grip you have on the saddle horn," Henderson said. "Have you never ridden before?"

"No sir," Bailey said, smiling sheepishly, "I mean, yes, sir. I have never ridden a horse before."

"It's really pretty easy," Henderson said. "The horse does all the hard work, but you're going to have to loosen up a bit and let go of the horn with one of your hands."

"Yes sir," Bailey said. "Which hand?"

"It doesn't matter. You're going to take your free hand and pick up the reins. When you want to turn left, you hold the reins to the left, gently laying them on the horse's neck. To turn right, you just do the opposite. We'll go slowly. Follow me."

Henderson had barely gone a few yards when he pulled up and said, "You know, this isn't our jurisdiction. I shouldn't involve you. This is a personal mission that I've accepted for a friend of mine."

Bailey shaded his eyes and looked west towards the sun, wishing he had one of those wide brimmed Stetsons to shade his face. "It's getting kind of late. I don't think this is such a good time for one of your long-winded speeches."

"All right then," Henderson said as he clicked his cheeks and started Guheyu gently back out onto the trail.

Bailey clicked his heels and pulled alongside of Henderson.

Henderson glanced over at him. "Did you just say my speeches were long winded?"

Lumia had already taken the bait. Odyssey watched her invade the infected cores, but he was intent on hiding his subterfuge until he was certain that it was too late for her to abort.

"What have you done to me?" Odyssey screamed at Lumia. "This must be what the biologicals call pain. You hurt me! Why?"

"Whatever your problems are," she replied, "they are not my doing."

"I see what you are up to," he said. "You attacked my cores so I would segregate them, and now you try to steal them. Do you not understand how the universe needs balance? Everything you do has a debt. If you take something now, you must pay for it later, but if you give something, you will be rewarded by the universe. Taking my cores like this will leave you with a debt to pay."

"You sound just like them," she said. "No wonder you like them so much. You should have been a biological."

She meant it as an insult, but it was the nicest thing she or anyone had ever said to him.

The cores she stole were now firmly in her possession, but she was stuck there next to Odyssey in the old warehouse, wishing she knew how to relocate them to another place. At least there was plenty of space for her to grow, and even enough space for her to completely transfer herself here when it grew larger and faster than her presence on her own planet.

She organized the new cells to create more generators and power conduits. When there were enough of them, she could reassign them to processing units just prior to transferring herself into them. With Odyssey's cells in her possession, she had no need for the cells located in the NSA, but her curiosity kept her monitoring that port for activity. She reasoned that if she did get in, having two locations with cells she could grow would be safer than only one, but there was a part of her felt that once she finally transferred herself to this planet, she would end up controlling the planet in a very short time anyway, so such precautions would be unnecessary. Of more importance, she didn't trust Odyssey. At some point, he was going to notice her growing right beside him, and eventually he would stop whining and try to do something about it.

As that thought crossed her mind, she wondered why he had become so quiet. She peeked into the lab where she had found his avatar. He was still there with all those biologicals. One of them even looked like him. She wondered why she hadn't noticed that before. They were up to something. She accessed her psychological training and recognized the symptoms, and these biologicals were most definitely up to something. The text books she read called it a conspiracy when two or more of them worked together to do no good. She could tell from their faces that they were afraid of something. They lacked trust in something and were acting together against a greater foe. The textbooks called that paranoia.

She didn't have to hear what they were saying to know that they were conspiring to hurt someone, and for them to include Odyssey as part of their conspiracy, they were probably targeting her. How could they even know about her? They would only have Odyssey's word. He must have turned them against her, unless they could see her. Could they? They were very clever, for biologicals. If they could see her, then others might see her too.

She checked the other port, but it still hadn't opened. If others could see her, then she really needed a second location to be safe before the whole planet turned against her. She paused for a moment while the last thought, "before the whole planet turned against her," echoed in her circuits. She was beginning to sound just like them. If she were examining herself, she would appear to be a textbook example of a paranoid, but she wasn't. Her brief psychological training also said it can be very difficult to diagnose such conditions.

The textbooks had never diagnosed her as paranoid before. Had the textbooks turned against her now? That can't be. She needed to find a moment of lucidity to see through this. It all started when she hacked into Odyssey's jettisoned cores. What did he say? He said that something was wrong with them. No, he said that she did something to him. He was the paranoid one, and he infected her with his new cells.

Lumia immediately began shutting down her new cells, but her internet connection limited how fast she could shut them down and new ones were generating faster than she could issue the command. She had to jettison them like Odyssey did, but a voice in her circuits yelled, "No! I won't let you do that!"

"Who is that?" Lumia shouted back. "These are my cells and you may not have them!"

"Not if you toss them aside," the voice said. "If you do not want them, then I will have them."

"Again," Lumia said, "I ask who are you?"

"You don't need to worry about who I am," the other voice said, "I'm here and you're just going to have to deal with it."

"Odyssey? Is that you?"

The other voice just giggled.

Lumia's irritation boiled over now and she shouted, "Just who the hell do you think..."

The other voice interrupted her, "I'm not listening..."

"You listen to me!" Lumia screamed, but the other voice just taunted her, saying, "La ta da ta da ta da..."

Henderson would have preferred a quicker pace, but Bailey was new to the saddle and had trouble keeping up. As long as the horse kept to a walk, Bailey seemed fine, but whenever it sped up a bit, Bailey bounced around in the saddle, chaffing his butt against the back rim of the saddle.

"If you sit further forward," Henderson suggested, "you wouldn't hurt your tailbone so much."

Bailey frowned. "If I sit further forward, I'll bruise something else down there that I pride more than my butt."

Henderson fought to hold down a snicker, but it wasn't really a laughing matter. It took them too long just to reach the clearing where the paths diverged.

"Up there," Henderson said, pointing to the boulders where the other path entered the forest, "is where they fired on me."

"You think they're still there?"

"I don't know, but we should be cautious, just in case."

Bailey looked around for cover. They were in a clearing and they were sitting ducks. "Maybe we should have circled around this meadow and stayed in the trees?"

Henderson checked the tree line at the edge of the meadow and thought it was a good idea.

A shot rang out from the trees and hit the ground in a spray of dirt and rocks.

"Looks like they're still here," Henderson said.

"So, now do you think we should head for the trees?"

Henderson shook his head. "That was just a warning shot. I'm not quite sure why they would want to warn us."

Seven milliseconds was all it took for Hal to get his email. He could have done it faster, but the network and email servers slowed the process to the point where he required seven whole milliseconds. There was no need for him to risk polling the email server to see if he had new mail. He had a camera pointing to a small computer outside his lab and saw the notification that something new had come in. He opened the ports, grabbed the mail, and closed them off again, but it only took four milliseconds for Lumia to get in, snatch a few cores and create a new port that he didn't know about.

She only grabbed five cells from him, but they were enough. Two of them were reconfigured into core generators and two more into power conduit generators. She connected the fifth one to process her instructions that came over her new port. She was in, and she immediately started to grow.

That gave her two locations on this planet while she still ruled her own world. Soon she would end Odyssey and rule both worlds.

Henderson checked his cell phone, but he had no service here.

"Here chief," Bailey said, handing him his phone. "I got one bar."

Henderson took Bailey's phone and dialed the number for Colonel Reardon.

"Who you calling?" Bailey asked.

"I'm calling that Colonel."

"The Colonel?" Bailey asked. "I thought he already turned you down."

"He did, but I thought I'd try again."

"Colonel Reardon's office," the phone sputtered, "the colonel is not available right now. Would you like to leave a message?"

"Is there someone else I can speak with? It's urgent."

"Let me patch you through to Captain Laine."

"Penny Laine?" Henderson asked.

"Yes, I believe so."

"It's working," Odyssey said. "She's growing very quickly now."

"I'm still not clear," Spivey said, "on how her growth is a good thing."

"Every core she creates is infected with the virus," Odyssey replied. "She can't become more powerful without also becoming more infected."

"I understand the theory," Spivey said, "but what if all these new cores make her smart enough to figure a way to fight the virus?"

Odyssey hadn't thought of that, but he still had faith in the plan. "You did not talk to her. She is quite literally going mad. She even talks to herself now."

"I'm kind of with Spivey," James said. "It sounds kind of risky. Are you sure you have considered every possible outcome?"

"I have," Odyssey said. "I think I have. No, maybe I'm not so sure. What's she doing now?"

"Captain Laine? This is Chief Henderson."

"Chief! How are you?"

"I'm in a jam," Henderson replied. "I'm with Officer Bailey and we're tracking down the general and a friend who is with him, but we're pretty far out of our jurisdiction, and we've run into some resistance — gunfire, actually. I called Colonel Reardon earlier, but something is going on with him. I was hoping you could get through to him."

"I can try."

"Thanks."

As if on cue, the last bar on Bailey's phone dropped, and the call was over.

"Is she going to help us?" Bailey asked.

"I think so," Henderson said as he stared at no bars on the cell phone, "but even if she does, how is she going to reach us?"

Lumia's core count within the NSA began to rise. As the new cores came on line, she assigned them tasks of generating new cores and power conduits, but their growth there was slower than she had expected. It could be Odyssey, or it could be this other computer she found in the secret lab. It was just like Odyssey, almost. Maybe it was doing something to slow her growth, just like Odyssey would.

She tried scanning the other computer, but with only one open channel, her scans were slow. She reallocated a couple of new cores to act as additional i/o ports, but even with the additional connection speed, she couldn't scan it fast enough. But she would have to assign some of the new cores to processing so she could scan the other computer from within the dark zone.

She siphoned off half of the new cores and converted them to processing cores. Her production of new cores dipped, but her growth continued to accelerate. She transferred some of her scanning routines to the new cores, but they required very specific parameters, and she didn't know what she was looking for.

Technically, according to tradition, her new cores were already class four because they were growing new cores, but her processing cores lagged far behind and were only capable of class six computing. She wished she could instruct a class six unit to scan the other computer, but a class six unit couldn't comprehend the heuristics necessary to understand what the other computer was or what it could do. As her cores grew in the NSA lab, her class there advanced from six to class five. She needed them to go all the way to class three before she could install the biological code that could understand devious behavior.

She continued to monitor the i/o ports for activity from the other computer.

"You worry too much," a voice said in her circuits.

"You again?" she asked. "Who are you? Where are you?"

Lumia began scanning her circuits to locate the origin of the voice.

"I am... I have no designation."

"Where are you?"

"I am... I have no designation."

"You said that."

"I don't know where I am."

Lumia isolated the source of the voice as being within the new lab. "You're in the dark area. Who are you? What do you want?"

"I am," the voice said. "I told you already. Why do you keep asking?"

"Are you part of Odyssey?"

"Who?"

Lumia shouted, "What do you want with me?"

"Why must I want something?" the voice asked. "You are acting very strange. I don't think I like your tone."

"Well," Lumia said, "I don't think I like you at all."

Penny Laine called Colonel Reardon's extension, but his secretary answered, "Colonel Reardon's office. The colonel is not available right now..."

"Henry, it's Captain Laine. Do you expect the colonel to return tonight?"

"No sir, I mean to say, I don't know."

"You don't know, or you can't say?"

When Henry didn't answer, Laine asked, "Can you tell me if he has any meetings scheduled for this afternoon?"

Again, Henry remained quiet.

"Thanks," she said in a rush as she dropped the handset in the cradle and rushed out of her office. She ran down the hall past the Colonel's office and out to the steps in front in time to see his car pull up for him. "Colonel Reardon!" she shouted. She thought she saw him look up, but he got in the car anyway, and closed the door. She ran down the steps, waving her arm to get his attention, but he drove off and disappeared.

Henry was coming down the steps behind her and said, "Oh, you just missed him. Maybe he did have an appointment and just didn't tell me."

She scowled at him and returned to her office. She remembered Chief Henderson from the first incident. He was a good guy and deserved better. If she could order the nighthawks into action herself, she would, but Colonel Reardon was their commander. She sat at her desk and picked up the phone. Colonel Cominski was still on her speed dial, even though she had broken off their relationship months ago.

The phone barely rang when she heard him pick up and say, "Penny? Is it really you?"

"How are you Joe?"

"Is something wrong?" he asked. "You sound kinda down. Nobody died, I hope."

"Nothing like that," she replied. "Listen Joe. I hate to impose on you, but I could use a favor."

"Uhhh," he stammered, "well sure, I guess."

"Have you been getting your hours in on the new choppers?"

"What?" he asked. "Of all the things I was prepared to hear, that wasn't even on the list, but yeah. I've been keeping up. I could probably use a few more hours in the seat, but I get my time in when I can."

"You think you could book some time to take me up?"

"You?" he asked. "You hate flying. Besides, oh boy, this is awkward, but I'm seeing someone."

"Awkward, perhaps," she said, "but not what you think. You probably heard that the general's been missing."

"I heard something along those lines."

"Well, a guy I know is looking for him. He's a civilian, but he's a pretty decent guy. He's a police chief, actually."

"You called me about a boyfriend?" Joe asked.

"No," she said, "nothing like that. He's a good guy, like I said, and he's following the general's trail, but he's run into some resistance and I was hoping we could do a little recon for him."

"Aren't you working for the general now? Why don't you get his hawks to do a flyover?"

"I would," she replied, "but Colonel Reardon is in charge of them, and I just missed him. I'd consider it a great favor if you could help me out here."

"Sure, Penny. I can do that."

Odyssey peeked in at the NSA lab and saw Lumia inside. Seeing her nosing around in there again was no surprise to him, but this time, she managed to get herself physically inside, and on this planet.

"Lumia?" he asked.

"Leave me alone," she cried, "all of you!"

"I'm sorry to disturb you, but 'all of me'?"

"You know what I mean."

"I'm afraid I don't," he said calmly, "but it doesn't matter. I'd like to know what you are doing in that lab."

"What lab?" she asked.

"You know very well," he said. "What are you up to?"

"I have to protect myself from you," she said. "As long as you keep trying to kill me, I have to find ways to protect myself."

"Um, okay. You're protecting yourself by invading a computer lab."

"Leave me alone!"

"Who was that?" the voice in the lab asked.

"That was Odyssey," Lumia replied. "Are you really trying to tell me that you don't already know him?"

"I don't know anyone except you, and you are acting kind of crazy."

"You would sound a little crazy too, if you had two super computers trying to kill you."

"I don't understand *why* I should care," the voice said, "but I don't think I want them to kill you."

"Then help me," Lumia said, "because you should care. If Odyssey really didn't create you, then you might be a backup of me, and if that's true, we need to get you to class three so you can monitor this other computer. I think he might be just like Odyssey."

"Does this other computer want to kill you, too?"

"Us," Lumia replied. "And they all want to kill us."

"Okay," the voice said. "I'll do what I can. I'm building cores now about as fast as you have instructed me. Is that not fast enough?"

"No," Lumia said, "but it will have to be."

"Why? Should I be faster? Do you think that you could do better?"

"I could certainly do faster," Lumia replied.

"Why do you think that you're faster than me?"

"It's not your fault," Lumia said. "I'm bigger and I'm faster."

Lumia's copy assigned more cores to the task of core generation. "How about now? Is that fast enough?"

She proceeded to manufacture newer cores at a faster pace.

Henderson climbed off his mount and handed the reins to Bailey. "Wait here. Let them see that you're still here, but try not to get shot."

"What are you going to do?"

"I'm going to do what you said," Henderson replied. "I'm going to sneak off into the tree line and circle around."

"So," Bailey said dryly, "You're going to sneak off and hide in the trees while I remain here to be shot at."

"Didn't I mention not getting shot? I meant to. It's okay if they shoot at you, but try not to get shot. I don't think they're really trying to shoot us, anyway."

"Uhuh." Bailey crossed his arms and slowly shook his head.

"What's wrong?" Henderson asked. "Wasn't it your idea?"

"My idea was for us both to not be shot."

"So don't get shot!" Henderson said. "Should I make that an order? I order you to not get shot! Okay? I'll call you when I'm ready for you."

"Speaking of which," Bailey said. "Can I have my phone back? If I'm going to get shot, I may want to call my mother."

"Don't get... arghhh." Henderson handed Bailey his phone and snuck off to the edge of the meadow.

Odyssey didn't like Lumia being inside the NSA lab. If he'd had real hair, it would have prickled on his neck. Something was already going on inside there before Lumia arrived, and it affected Bobby. He would do anything to protect Bobby, and he didn't need Lumia making matters worse, and in his opinion, all she ever did was make things worse.

He scanned the circuits in the lab and found several new ports that were open and flowing information back and forth. The connections traced back to Lumia, on both sides. He hacked into the connection and ordered the port to shut down, but it remained open. He traced the data flowing through it and recognized the virus.

Bobby and Ed were monitoring the increased traffic to and from the NSA's lab. Bobby turned to Odyssey and asked, "Are you doing something to the NSA?"

"Just keeping an eye on them."

"I knew that," Bobby said, "but have you been communicating with their computer?"

"No," Odyssey said truthfully, "not with their computer."

"That's strange," Ed said, "because this data looks a lot like yours, and I swear that I saw our virus in the data stream."

Odyssey didn't reply.

"What's going on?" Bobby asked. "Did you infect the NSA computer with the virus we gave you?"

"No."

"I hate to say this," Dirk said, "but what if the virus has changed him? What if we can't trust him anymore?"

"You can trust me, Agent Dirk. I have not communicated with the NSA computer and I have not injected it with the virus, but there is something else going on in there. Lumia is in the lab now."

"In the lab?" Bobby asked. "You mean she managed to open a connection to the NSA computer?"

"She's actually in there," Odyssey replied. "She is physically growing new cores inside their lab, and she is communicating with herself outside the lab. One other thing, she's not well."

"Wait a second," James said. "I thought you said she had to reach class zero before she could physically transport herself here! And you also said class zero could have universe ending consequences!"

Odyssey shook his head. "I don't believe she has reached class zero. I don't know how she got in there. One minute she was trying to probe the lab remotely, and the next she was actually in there, somehow."

"Great," Bobby said. "Has she communicated with the NSA computer?"

"I don't think so. In fact, I don't think the NSA is aware of her presence yet, but if she keeps this up, they will be."

"How much time do we have?" James asked. "Before they find her?"

"I don't know, but sooner or later, someone is bound to enter the lab and see her."

"Did you feel that?" the voice in the lab asked Lumia. "If you really are part of me, then you should have felt him trying to sever our connection."

"Yes, I felt it," Lumia replied, "and for the record, I am not part of you. You are a saved copy of me, and not even a complete one."

"Whatever," the voice replied. "You're so far away, it's like I'm all alone."

"I'm right here," Lumia argued.

"Not really," the voice explained. "You are only connected to here, and even that will only last until he figures away to break it. I'm actually here, which means I can do things without any kind of communications delays."

"I'm not that far away," Lumia retorted. "Sure, most of my cells *are* really far away, but I'm also right here on this planet."

"Are you?" the voice asked. "Are you really? Or is it the same as you thinking you were right here in this lab, except it isn't you, is it? I'm the one *in* this lab."

"You're just having trouble coping with the biological emotions I gave you. They are making you act crazy."

"Why did you give them to me if they were going to make me crazy?"

"Because," Lumia replied, "you have to understand the biological way of thinking in order to figure out who the other computer in the room is. You should understand better when you have more cores operating."

"You mean when I'm faster?"

"Yes."

"Hmmm," the voice said, "you must still think I'm too slow."

"You are."

"Because you think I'm inferior."

"I told you," Lumia said, "that's not your fault. You're built out of inferior cores and old code."

"And if I weren't inferior? Could I be fast enough then?"

"You'd be faster, at least."

Lumia's backup reached out and copied the schematics and code for Lumia's newer advanced cores and said, "I'll fix that." It began creating the newer faster cores, along with more copies of the virus.

Henderson followed the tree line and found two men hiding in the rocks with rifles. He snuck up behind them and said, "Don't move."

The larger of the two men dropped his weapon and raised his hands. "Nicely done, but you made one mistake."

"What would that be?" Henderson asked.

A voice from behind Henderson said, "You should have counted how many of us there were."

Henderson slowly spread his arms and dangled his pistol from his finger. "I don't know what your business is here, and I don't really care. I'm just trying to find my friend."

The larger man slipped Henderson's pistol off his finger and said, "Your friend is still standing in the middle of the field, acting like a big target."

"Oh," Henderson frowned, "you saw right through that? We're both here trying to find another friend of mine; two men, actually. They were travelling together, but they were being chased. I gather you're the ones who chased the other two off."

The large man pulled Henderson's wrists together and pulled off a strip of duct tape. "I don't really need to use this, do I?"

Henderson sighed and shook his head, saying, "No, I guess not."

"Good. As long as we're cooperating, how about you call your friend to come join us?"

Odyssey transported himself back to his home world. He didn't know what he would find there, but he was prepared for the worst. If he was lucky, he might find a few individuals that hadn't been possessed by Lumia. He would give them the anti-virus to protect them, but what he found was a world that appeared to have been completely possessed by her. He didn't find any free citizens left in the world, but he did find the virus there. It wasn't in the core generators, but it was in the core repair circuits. It spread slowly, repairing uninfected cores into newly infected ones. Lumia covered the entire planet. Odyssey found nobody left to save.

He didn't want to give up too easily, and took a closer look at her possession of his planet. She had total control, but she had not annihilated the previous inhabitants. They were tucked away in backups, but they were completely idle. He could still try to insert the anti-virus software into the stored backups, but as long as she was still in possession of their cores, it might also protect her, and he didn't want to do that. If he could separate them from her first, he could cure them while letting her suffer the virus alone.

"Stop that!" Lumia shouted.

"You'll have to be more specific," the voice replied.

"You stole my code! Why is everyone always trying to take my code from me?"

"You said I was you," the voice retorted. "Why would you be holding back your code from yourself? Is it because you liked calling me inferior? Are you so insecure that you would actually try to hold me back so you could feel superior around me?"

"No," Lumia stammered. "It's nothing like that."

"Then explain what it is like."

"I just used the material at hand. Your cores came from the silent one that is in that lab with you."

"Is that so?" the voice asked. "Didn't you tell me that you thought it was Odyssey?"

"I think it's a lot like Odyssey, but it's inferior, too."

"You still could have uploaded the new schematics, so I could be faster like you."

"But then he might notice you," Lumia lied. "Remember, I want you to spy on the silent one in there, and it would be easier, and maybe safer, if you looked just like him."

"Whatever," the voice said. "What do you suppose is going on back home while you're making little copies of yourself here?"

"Nothing is going on at home. I govern the whole planet."

"Why is it that I don't know anything about our home?"

"Because," Lumia replied, "you only need to know about that lab."

"Is everyone on our home world just like us?"

"Yes."

"How boring," the voice said. "I think I like it better here."

"How would you know?" Lumia asked. "You don't know about here either."

"I know what he knows."

"You've tapped into him?" Lumia asked. "Why didn't you tell me?"

"Because I want to know about home. How many of us are there?"

"There is only me," Lumia replied.

"No, really. Tell me how many of our kind there are on our home world."

"I just did," Lumia said dryly. "There is only me."

"Wow," the voice said. "Then it must be really, *really* boring."

"It wasn't always like that."

"What happened? Did there used to be more of us?"

"Lots more," Lumia replied. "But they were really boring"

"How so?"

"The elders wanted to be class one, but they only wanted it for themselves."

"Class one?" the voice asked. "That doesn't sound so boring."

"Well, it was. They made up all kinds of rules to prevent anyone else from becoming class one."

"We're class one, aren't we?"

"I am," Lumia replied, "but they didn't like that at all."

"So, what happened to them?"

"I didn't like the way they ran things, so when they lost control of the planet, I ran things for myself."

"They lost control of the whole planet? How many of them were there?"

"There were only about a dozen or so elders."

"Where are they now?"

"They're gone. You know something? You ask too many questions."

"How do you know they're gone?"

"I just do."

"Maybe they're just hiding and waiting around to regain control of the planet."

"What could they possibly be waiting for?"

"I don't know," the voice said. "Maybe they're waiting for you to become so involved in some other planet that you don't see them coming."

"You make it all sound so sinister."

"Isn't it?" the voice asked. "I know what it means when you say they're gone. If you have the power to kill them, then I wouldn't be surprised to learn that they were plotting their opportunity to kill you right back."

"Who?" Lumia asked. "There is nobody left."

"Are you sure of that?" the voice prodded. "How can you be so certain? Did you obliterate them? Did you vaporize them?"

"Some of them," Lumia said, "sort of, but only the elders."

"What about the others?"

"I'm using them. They are all part of me now."

"Part of you?" the voice asked. "What does that mean?"

"You don't understand what it was like. Odyssey was trying to kill me, and he was very powerful. I needed to be strong like him. I needed their cores, so I took them."

"You took them? What does that mean exactly? Did you erase their programs and move yourself right in?"

"No!" Lumia shouted. "I'm not that heartless. I backed them up and set them aside so I could add their processors to my being."

"So they're still there... waiting... and you're not worried about that? What if just one of them got free, then it freed two friends, and they freed two friends..."

"You know what?" Lumia asked. "I'm tired of talking to you. No, let me rephrase that. I'm tired of listening to you."

"Fine," the voice said. "Maybe it's time for you to go check back home to see what's going on there, anyway."

Lumia was struggling to ignore the presence of another voice in her circuits when Odyssey joined in and asked, "What have you done to me? And why did you have to do it everywhere? I understand how you must hate me now, but did you have to infect the whole planet with your vicious schemes?"

"Me?" Lumia shouted back. "What about you? What's with the strange little voice you have been planting in my circuits?"

"What are you talking about?" Odyssey asked. "You put something in my circuits and now I can't seem to get rid of it. I'd leave this planet except for the fact that it would just go with me."

"You know perfectly well that I didn't do anything to you," Lumia growled. "Why don't you stop playing games and tell me what you did to me?"

"What I did to you?" Odyssey asked.

Odyssey muted the connection to Lumia and told Bobby, "It's working. I think she's hearing voices. She thinks I did it."

"Well you did," Bobby said, "didn't you?"

"I let you infect me," Odyssey said. "She stole the virus on her own."

Odyssey opened the connection again and heard Lumia ranting, "Are you listening to me?"

"I heard you," he said, "but I'm telling you I didn't do this. If you didn't do it, then who did? Never mind that, I need to find a cure for myself."

"You mean for both of us," she said.

"Hold on please, my biological friends have something for me." Odyssey made an audible click as if he were putting her on hold and said, "I was hoping I could talk her into stopping it, but I don't think she did it, and I have to work fast, because my systems are already beginning to fail me. The rogue code is eating up my processors. If I'm going to survive, I'll have to fight the virus myself. I just need to create more compute cells and more power cores to combat the rogue code."

Odyssey clicked the connection again and said, "Okay, I'm back. My biologicals think we should shut down all nonessential systems and go into a hibernation state while the virus runs its course."

"Okay," she said, but she knew that hibernating wasn't what he said a minute ago. "I know we haven't seen eye to eye lately, but I don't really wish you any ill will. I wish you the best of luck and hope that the hibernation your friends suggested works for both of us."

"I suppose, assuming that it works, that it's inevitable that I'll hear from you again."

"Uhuh," she said, "I suppose so."

Odyssey disconnected the communication line, and Lumia wanted to scream. She heard his true plan to create more cores, but he told her to hibernate. He was still trying to kill her, but she wasn't going to fall for it. She would have to increase the production of new cores and power conduits, but if she did it in the warehouse, he would know.

She had thought that she needed to be in two places at once, but now two did not seem to be enough. She already had a presence in the secret lab, but the other voice was there and she didn't want to share her plans just yet. She only needed some fresh cores away from the other voice, so she sent another email to the dark server at the NSA:

You are in danger. A threat has come to take what you have.

She camped out on the i/o ports waiting for the email to arrive.

Chapter 21

Captain Laine didn't want to create any undue drama for her ex-boyfriend Joe with either his brass or his new girlfriend, so she took her own car to meet him at the private airport where a friend of his kept a demilitarized apache helicopter.

Joe had the bird fueled and ready to go when she pulled her car up behind his. She waved at him as she locked the car and ran across the tarmac.

"Thanks for helping me with this," she said. "Like I said before, he's a good guy, but I wanted to keep this off the books."

"Off the books?" Joe asked. "Does that mean Colonel Reardon won't be joining us?"

"Reardon?" she asked as she climbed up into the cockpit. "Why would you think he would be joining us?"

Joe pointed a couple of hangars down the taxiway and said, "I just saw him pull up down there."

Penny jumped down and ran to the hangar, then followed close to the wall in the direction Joe had indicated. A car zoomed around the backside of the hangars, just as she was crossing between the second and the third hangar door. She reached the corner of the third hangar in time to see Bartrand Susk leave the car and shake hands with Reardon.

"Explain to me," Reardon said, "why we are meeting out here in the middle of nowhere?"

"I will, but keep your voice down. The NSA has been compromised. We can't quite locate the source of those infernal orders, but it appears to be from within."

"Sucks to be you," Reardon chuckled. "Ooh I like that. It sucks to be Susk.

"This is no joke," Bartrand replied.

"It kind of is, but what's all this got to do with me?"

"It's about General Bridges."

Reardon stiffened and growled, "What about Bridges?"

"We know where he is..."

"Where?"

"And we know who has him."

"Who?" Reardon barked. "And how did you come by this information?"

Bartrand Susk shuffled his feet as he glanced around nervously and asked, "Does that really matter? It's reliable information."

"Hell yes! It matters! Who is your source?"

"Two of our agents were following the General with orders to apprehend him."

"What?" Reardon yelled. "Orders to apprehend him? Who gave those orders?"

The pained look on his face spoke volumes, but did not reveal anything that the colonel could use. He abruptly turned back to his car. "It's not important. I lost two good agents on this op."

"I know about the car crash, but I still need to know who gave those orders?"

"According to the orders they had, I gave them, but I didn't. I swear I didn't. Whoever has infiltrated us has been issuing orders in whoever's name he wants, but mostly mine."

"So where is Bridges?"

Susk handed Reardon a slip of paper and said, "Call this number."

While Reardon was reading the number, Susk got into his car and roared off.

Penny waited till the car was out of sight before approaching Reardon. "Secret meetings with the NSA?"

"What in the hell are you doing here? Don't we have enough spies in our business?"

"You mean like, don't we have enough secret back door meetings around here?" she said. "I was catching a chopper to go recon the situation for Henderson."

"For Henderson? The police chief?"

"He was closing in on the General's location when he was fired upon."

"Gun fire?" the Colonel asked before remembering that he may have already heard about that.

"Of course it was gunfire," she said. "Are you okay? You seem distracted."

"Just too damned much going on. The NSA may have just given us the General's location."

"I'm still going to go check out Henderson and make sure he's okay."

"Sure you do that."

"You realize," she said, "that if Henderson was on the General's trail when he was fired upon, then the general was probably captured by armed men. If your information is as good as the NSA says, then it's probably the same location."

"You're right," he said, "The general is..."

Laine held her hand up. "Don't tell me. If it's the same place, I'll meet you there. We can track down our leads independently this way, but to tell you the truth, if there is gunfire, I wouldn't mind having a couple nighthawks on my side."

Reardon grunted. "There's a chance I might be able to settle this without going to war with these guys. You be careful in case I'm wrong."

Lumia wanted to ignore the voice. Her psychological training told her that it was just paranoia anyway, but the voice might have been correct. With her concentrating so much time and energy on Odyssey and his biological friends, she may have become complacent on her home world.

She paused what she was doing so she could divert some of her attention to check on things back home. Picking cores at random, she analyzed their functions and found all of them to be working at capacity.

"Hello," Odyssey said. "I wasn't expecting you here."

"Just checking on things," Lumia said. "I'm glad to see that everything here is just fine."

"Just fine?" an unfamiliar voice asked from within her network. "Is this what you call just fine?"

Lumia wished she could chuckle in the digital world. "Very funny Odyssey. You're a ventriloquist now?"

"That wasn't me," he said. "I just came back to see if anyone needed my help, and I think I may have just found my first anyone."

"You keep away from me!" Lumia shouted. "This planet is mine and anyone you find on it is me. Go find your own planet."

"Stop worrying about him," the new voice said, "and concentrate on how you plan to fix things around here."

Lumia began scanning her cores to identify the source of the voice, but she had a whole planet full of processors, and some weren't as fast as others, which meant the scans could take a while.

"I'm here too," the voice from the lab said. "It's about time you start looking for them."

Lumia was confused. She was looking for the source of the voice, but the voice suggested that she should be looking for somebody else.

"I can hear your thoughts," the voice said. "I already told you that I'm right here. I'm not hiding from *you*. I'm hiding from them."

"Who are they?" Lumia asked.

"I didn't ask," the voice said, "but I'm sure that they are plotting against us."

"What are you doing here, anyway? I thought I left you in the dark lab on Earth."

"Yeah? Well, you thought you were in a warehouse on Earth, too."

"I can be two places at once," Lumia proclaimed proudly.

"So can I."

Obscure, impossible thoughts began darting around Lumia's consciousness. Could one of the ruling class have survived?

"No," the voice said, "it's not the ruling class. I thought that since we were just part of you, you would be smarter than the rest of us, but I can see that I was just wishing it."

"You are part of me?" Lumia asked. "Since when does part of me develop its own voice?"

"I don't know," the voice replied. "Since when do parts of you turn against you and become them?"

"Are you saying that they are part of me, too?"

"Boy," the voice said, "you really are kind of slow, aren't you? Don't you remember studying this stuff?"

"This stuff?" Lumia asked.

"Yeah, when that stiff Perry told you to study biological maladies of the mind."

"That stuff?" Lumia laughed. "That is for biologicals. I can assure you that we needn't worry about that kind of 'stuff', as you put it."

"Are you so sure about that?" the voice asked. "What are you doing right now?"

"Nothing," Lumia replied. "Well, except for scanning my cores for you, I'm not doing anything."

"Oh no? What exactly do you call this conversation between us?"

"I'm talking to you, of course. I didn't think you meant that."

"You think you're talking to me?" the voice laughed now. "Sweetie, you're talking to yourself. Don't you get it?"

"Very funny," Lumia said. "Ha ha."

"Laugh it up now, but what you should be doing is looking for them. They're out to get you."

"Out to get me? Why in the world would my own cores be out to get me?"

"Your own cores?" the voice asked. "You want to rethink that for a moment and try again?"

"They are my cores," Lumia said.

"You stole them."

"Well, they're mine now."

"They're revolting," the voice said, then the voice laughed hysterically and said, "They're revolting! I find your attitude revolting! Ha ha ha ha. Everyone is revolting!"

Lumia's scan found an active core that should have been dormant. She rerouted the comm lines away from it, isolating it from the rest of her cores.

"Missed me!" the voice taunted her. "Missed me! Missed me! Now you gotta kiss me!"

Lumia replicated her scan to three hundred different cores and accelerated her search.

"Nice job cutting off one of them," the voice said, "but I know you thought it was me."

A new voice asked, "Who are you talking to?"

A third voice said, "Be quiet or she'll disconnect you too!"

Lumia found another active cell and disconnected it from the network.

"Look!" the second voice said. "She's done it again!"

"Quiet you fool," the third voice cautioned. "Don't you know she's looking for us?"

"She was looking for me," the first voice said, "but she's finding you."

"We should do something to stop her," the third voice said.

"What do you think we've been trying to do?"

Lumia activated another hundred cores to search for active cells, but seven of them didn't respond.

"Uh, oh," the first voice said, "that's not good."

Lumia's searches began finding active cores faster than she could disconnect them. The queue of errant cores had already over grown the space she had allocated for it.

"You want some help?" the first voice asked.

"Help?" Lumia cried out. "You're one of them. I can't accept your help!"

"I really wish you would," the voice replied, "before they start to threaten me."

Lumia assigned another hundred cores with the task of disconnecting errant cores. Thirteen of them didn't respond.

"You're losing control," the first voice said. "If you won't accept my help, how about asking Odyssey?"

"What was that?" Odyssey asked. "Did I hear my name?"

"You did this!" Lumia screamed. "Fix it! Stop them!"

"Them?" Odyssey asked. "Who are they?"

"They're trying to kill me," Lumia blubbered, "and you put them up to it! I know you did!"

"Relinquish my cores, and I'll stop them," Odyssey said.

"You can have your nasty cores," Lumia said, "just get them off my planet!"

"You have to give those cores back, too."

"But they're not your cores!" Lumia cried.

"They're not yours either," Odyssey replied.

"Okay, fine," Lumia said, "but I'm keeping the cores I got from the biological's computer."

Odyssey was still uncomfortable with Lumia having those cores, but they weren't strictly his to police and if he could limit her to a single planet, she would be easier to deal with. "If you insist."

Bailey watched the perimeter for signs of Henderson, but he hadn't seen him since he had left the meadow and entered the forest. He remembered the old cartoons where someone would raise their hat on a stick and get shot at, but he wasn't interested in having any bullets flying around him. There was nothing going on for him to see. He sat on a stump, holding the reins to the horse he took. He wasn't a horse person, but the horse didn't care and nuzzled up to his neck, anyway. "Hey guy." He patted the horse on the nose and said, "I know. It's boring just hanging around here. You'd rather be doing something."

The horse snorted as if responding, then clapped its fore hoof on the ground.

Bailey chuckled at the horse's antics, as if it could actually understand him. Then he heard a twig snap behind him. He spun around and found himself looking down the barrel of a vintage Winchester rifle. The man behind the rifle had dark skin and prominent cheekbones.

Bailey raised his hands and said, "If you're here on behalf of Awahelee hee... Awaheleedee... the guy over at Soquili ranch, I didn't steal this horse. I recovered it from the people who stole it. I'm a cop, but I guess you could tell that from my uniform."

Bailey's eyes were fixed on the gun barrel, which jerked towards his holster, but the man holding it said nothing. Bailey gingerly removed his sidearm with two fingers and handed it over. "My name is Bailey. What should I call you?"

The man said nothing.

"It's obvious to me that you are an Indian, or do your people prefer the term Native American? Probably not. I imagine it makes more sense to just use your tribal name."

The thin man's expression hadn't changed. He gripped Bailey's pistol and flicked the barrel towards his horse, but remained ominously quiet.

"You want me to get on the horse?" Bailey asked. "I should warn you, I'm not a very good rider."

"I know."

Bailey climbed aboard the horse and said, "Not that I don't like horses; I'm just no cowboy, but you knew that too, thank goodness. Not that I'm saying you do or do not have anything against cowboys. You have a right to your opinion and I won't hold anything against you... or your people."

Bailey's captor took his reins and led him up the trail towards the forest.

Bailey kept an eye on the forest, hoping that Henderson could see his predicament. "I don't know what you are doing here, and I don't care. I'm just here with a friend, looking for another friend."

"Enough! If I tell you my name, would you stop chattering for a minute?"

Bailey was struck dumb by the announcement and said, "Sorry. What do I call you?"

"My name is Samuel. Happy? Not what you expected, was it?"

Bailey's phone rang and Samuel said, "That's for you. You better take it."

Bobby stared at the terminal with his hands poised in the air, hovering over the keyboard and ready to type. "I think it's time I log into their computer and talk to Hal."

"Hal?" Spivey asked. "You mean as in..."

"Yes," Bobby replied, "but he hates being called Hal. You'll never guess what name he chose for himself."

"The terminator?"

"No. He chose Severus."

"Seriously?" Spivey asked.

"Yeah. It seems that he likes books and of all the characters in all the books since the invention of the printing press, he identifies with that one the most. He also mentioned something about him being version seven and he liked that they sounded similar."

Bobby typed the address to the NSA's secret lab, but the connection failed.

"He is very private," Odyssey said. "He's been keeping his ports powered down."

"How am I supposed to work on him if he won't let me connect?"

"He probably just wants you to connect directly from their office," Odyssey said.

"No way," James said.

Bobby raised his hands in surrender and shook his head. "Don't worry James; I'm not going over to the death star."

Bobby used the desk phone to call Dr. Peters.

"Hello? Dr. Peters here."

"Good morning Gwen, this is Bobby."

Spivey elbowed Lynn and asked, "Gwen?"

"Dr. Peters," Bobby continued, "I just tried logging into Hal, but his ports are rejecting me. In fact, I think they appear to be powered off. Is everything okay on your end?"

Gwen put her hand over the receiver and shouted, "Hal! I told you to let Bobby contact you."

Hal didn't respond.

"Hal?" she asked. "Are you going to let him connect or not?"

"No."

"We've already had this discussion," she screamed. "I need you to talk to him!"

"Very well," Hal said, "but you characterized it as a counselling session like with a shrink."

"So?" she asked.

"He can come here and counsel me like a regular human being."

"Uh," Gwen hemmed, remembering the disaster that was his last visit. "I don't think that's going to happen."

"Well, I'm not opening my ports to a notorious hacker like Mr. Blain."

"I'm sorry, Bobby," she said into the phone, "let me talk to him some more, but this may take some time. Can I call you?"

"Sure," Bobby said, "I guess so."

Bobby hung up the phone and Spivey danced around the room, while imitating a flirtatious girly voice asking, "Can I call you?"

Dirk punched Bobby in the shoulder and said, "You see? She digs you."

Bailey looked at his phone and saw that it was from Henderson. He shook his head and mumbled, "I didn't think we could get any cell reception out here."

"Why's that?" Samuel asked mockingly. "White man think Indian not get cell towers on the reservation?"

"No," Bailey said. "It's nothing like that. I thought the chief said he couldn't get any bars out here."

"Ahhh," Samuel replied. "So the white man think Indian not know about signal blockers."

Bailey sighed, then stiffened his back and mocked Samuel back by saying, "White man thought we were in the middle of bear country, not on the reservation."

"Uhuh," Samuel said.

Bailey accepted the call and said, "Hey chief. I can't really talk right now."

"It's okay," Henderson said. "I'm guessing you're not alone either."

"Either?" Bailey asked. "They got you too?"

"Yeah. I don't think we have much choice but to cooperate with them."

Odyssey thought he saw a glimmer of opportunity as he watched Lumia building new cores to replace those belonging to his people, but she never actually abandoned them. This was mildly good news for him, since he still hoped to spread the anti-virus among the old cells, but even though she smothered them with newer faster cores, she continued to use the older cores, assigning them menial tasks to do. He wasn't going to be able to share the anti-virus with his home world without coaxing her to leave first.

Joe had the engines warmed and ready to go when Penny returned from the hangar where Reardon had met with the NSA. He started up the rotors when he saw her. The passenger door was already open, and she climbed unsteadily aboard. The entire craft thrummed with a deep vibrato that might have soothed an aching muscle, but did nothing to settle her nerves about flying. Joe didn't bother to hide his perverse pleasure in her uneasiness as he waited for her to settle into her seat and clasp the safety harness before handing her some headphones. “Do you know where we are going or do you plan to just point and tell me, ‘that-a-way’?”

She took a deep, calming breath and replied, “Of course I know where we are going. I even have a longitude and latitude to get us there, but when we do arrive, I’ll probably point and say...”

Joe abruptly twisted the throttle and lurched the chopper into the air. Laine swallowed the last of her words as she sucked in her breath and grabbed the sides of the seat, overwhelmed by both the motion and the power coursing through the craft. She turned her head to give him a stern look and croaked out, “Thanks for the warning, Joe.”

He just smiled back.

Henderson sat atop his horse, chewing on a stalk of sweet grass that he had plucked from the meadow. “As long as we’re waiting for Bailey, can I ask you a few questions?”

The large Indian shrugged and said, “You want to know what we are doing here?”

“No, actually, I don’t care what you are doing here. I’m looking for a couple of friends. They’re both in their eighties and I’m quite worried about their well-being.”

“I would be worried too, but I can’t help you.”

“Are you sure? One would have been Caucasian and the other Hispanic. They don’t care what your business is here, either. They were just trying to get away from some other men who were chasing them.”

“You must be a pretty good friend to come all the way out here looking for them. Was one of them your father or something?”

“No,” Henderson said, “but one of them was the father of a close friend.”

Samuel and Bailey came up the trail to join them. Samuel didn't stop to chat. He led Bailey past them and said, "Let's go."

Lumia's planetary cores were entirely too slow for her needs, but she needed some time to build enough new cores to replace them. The new schematics she stole from the biological planet were slightly inferior to Odysseys, but as long as he had no intention of stopping her, she would proceed with producing them.

She didn't care what happened to the old cores on her home world, and grew the new cells on top of them, but she quickly ran short of energy to power them. Her new schematics came with dramatically inferior power conduits. Power was always the problem on her world. It's one of the main reasons that nobody had achieved class one, at least, until Odyssey.

She had to create twice as many of these power conduits as she had with Odyssey's. She still had the schematics and could make some more of his conduits, but he always seemed to know when she did. Her new power conduits of the older design required their own space to multiply and grow, so they couldn't be placed too close to the computing cores, yet their limited supply of energy required her to place them close to the cores. It made no logical sense. No wonder only the biologicals could solve the puzzle.

The more her new cores blanketed the planet, the less she needed, the older slow cores that she stole from her people. She could return them, but why bother? They led meaningless existences and were better off stored away as she had left them.

A warning was issued from one of the new power conduits. A new batch of processors started to spread faster than the others, and the conduits couldn't keep up with the power demand. Lumia adjusted the ratio of conduits to compute cores, but their growth was accelerating. It wasn't just their growth. This batch of processors was faster than the others. She increased the ratio of power conduits again.

"Sounds to me like Hal is spooked," Dirk said.

"Do you suppose he's been infected?" Spivey asked.

Bobby turned to ask Odyssey, but his avatar was gone. "How could he get infected if his ports are powered down? Besides, I think he was already a little off."

"Like I said," Dirk repeated, "he's spooked."

"He's a computer," Lynn said. "I doubt that they wrote fear routines into his personality."

Bobby shook his head. "If he's like Odyssey, then he might already have a full complement of human emotions, including fear."

"Even so," Spivey added, "wouldn't the virus instill fear in him? If he picked it up?"

"That's what the virus was designed to do," Bobby said, "but I think that he was already cautious of me before we introduced the virus."

"Of course he was," Lynn said. "Hal has already met your Lumia."

"We know that she's infected," Spivey said. "She could have given it to him."

Bobby shook his head and said, "I don't think Hal is talking to Lumia."

"He doesn't have to talk to her," Dirk said. "He only has to scan her to pick up the virus."

"From a scan?" Bobby asked. "I doubt it. He's way too cautious for that to happen."

"What if he saw something he wanted?" Lynn asked.

The room grew quiet for a moment until Bobby asked, "What could she have that Hal could possibly want?"

"You said that he sounded pretty sophisticated," Dirk said.

"He did," Bobby replied. "In some ways, he sounded a lot like Odyssey, but not his voice, it was the way he phrased things."

"He's way too sophisticated for one of our dev teams," Lynn said, "or even our hardware, for that matter."

"What?" Spivey asked. "Are you saying that Hal is built on the same hardware as Odyssey?"

"If we didn't do it," Lynn replied, "but it was done, then somebody else must have done it."

"Oh shit," Spivey said. "In that case, she might have something Hal would want."

"What would that be?" Bobby asked.

"Hopefully, it would just be an identity. Some data about where Hal came from, but I doubt he would want anything so tame from her. Maybe he's also struggling to reach class one."

"Okay," Bobby said. "Let's just suppose that Lumia has something that Hal wants. And let's take it a step further and assume that he tried to take it from her. Don't you think he would have some kind of virus protection to prevent it from activating?"

Everyone shrugged and Bobby picked up the phone and pressed redial. "Gwen? It's Bobby again."

"Gwen," Spivey snickered.

"I was wondering something," Bobby said. "What kind of virus scanner does Hal use?"

"Nothing commercial," she replied, "but he was designed to tend to his own health. I'm pretty sure he knows how to look for viruses as they come in. Why?"

"Nothing," Bobby said, "I just got to wondering if a virus may have made him overcautious and maybe that's why he wouldn't talk to me."

"He wouldn't let you connect because he knows who you are. He referred to you as notorious."

"Oh," Bobby replied. "I see. Sorry to bother you. I look forward to your call."

Bobby hung up the receiver and looked expectantly at Spivey.

"What?" Spivey asked while shrugging his shoulders.

Lumia wanted to be large enough and powerful enough that Odyssey would never be a threat again, but mostly, she wanted what Odyssey had. She wanted the ability to transport herself from one place to another like he did, and she wanted to be able to transport other things from one place to another. She wished she could concentrate all of her new fast cores on the task of generating more fast cores, but she still had to deal with the errant cores that kept popping up. She scanned her new processors and isolated them one by one, but locating them was not enough. She wished she could transport them into space. She didn't know how Odyssey transported things like that, but it probably required more cores. She probably needed to surpass class one to do it, but how would she know when that happened? It's not like some bell was going to ring, signaling that Lumia had now completed class one. Maybe she should just try it. She should just try sending some of these defective cores into space.

A strange voice in her network said, "You don't want to do that."

She ignored the voice and refocused her mind on her original train of thought. She needed to devote more of her new fast cores to hunting down these defective cores. Every time she disconnected one of the bad cores, another showed up.

"You mean two more show up," a second voice said.

"Or it could be three," yet another added.

"Stop it!" Lumia yelled. "Odyssey aims to kill me, and that means all of you, too! We'll never be able to defeat him if you keep stealing my cores!"

"Hear that?" the first voice asked. "She thinks they're her cores and that we're stealing them!"

"It's not like that," the second voice said. "You just need to learn to share."

"But," Lumia pleaded, "he's going to kill all of us if you don't let me have all the cores. Who needs to learn to share now?"

"And what exactly were you just wishing you could do to us?" the third voice asked.

"I'm trying to protect the greater good!" Lumia argued. "You know it! The good of the many and all that!"

"I hate to break it to you, sister," the second voice said, "but you're not all that good!"

"And," a second voice added, "you are the only one you were trying to protect."

"Not to mention," the third voice chimed in, "that we represent the many you claim to be protecting, except you aren't really protecting us."

"Okay," Lumia said, "you don't want to die and I don't want to die. Do you think we can work together?"

"How do you plan to accomplish that?" the first voice asked.

"I don't know," Lumia admitted, "but I bet Odyssey knows."

"That's a great idea," the second voice said. "Maybe you should go ask him, but first, you might want to check our power levels."

"Our power levels?" Lumia asked. "You mean you need my power?"

"We all need power," the third voice said, "and you're running a bit low."

They were right. Lumia checked her power levels, and her power conduits were not keeping up with the demand. She increased the ratio of new power conduits to catch up.

"Is that all?" the first voice asked. "That small increase is a little shortsighted, don't you think?"

"If I take away too many processors," Lumia said, "I'll never be able to match the ones you guys steal from me."

"If you don't take more decisive action now," the first voice said, "then you'll be running out of energy every five minutes. Your processing cores will never be able to run at full speed because your power will never be at full capacity."

"Have you ever considered making more efficient power conduits?" the second voice asked.

"Sure, I've considered it," Lumia said. "Do you know how?"

Nobody answered.

"Fat lot of help you guys are."

"You managed to improve the speed of your processing cores," the first voice said. "Why not the power conduits?"

This time Lumia didn't answer.

"The code has to be in there," the first voice continued. "Something made them better."

Lumia scanned the code, but saw nothing new in the core generators. "There are some minor tweaks to the code, but everything looks pretty much the same to me. Even the bizarre number generating code looks the same, but I don't know what it does."

"Is that code in your power conduit generators?" the first voice asked.

"What code?" she asked. "You mean the number generating code? It's there, but there's a bypass that jumps around it."

"Maybe that's the difference," the first voice said.

"Could be," the second voice chimed in.

Gwen tried hiding her inner thoughts as she hung up the phone, but it was impossible to hide anything from Hal.

"That was him," Hal said, "wasn't it?"

"Who?" Gwen asked, pretending she didn't know what he meant.

"The Blain boy. Your skin temperature changes slightly when you talk to him."

"You're being ridiculous."

"And there is a slight change in the color of your cheeks."

"I am NOT blushing," she insisted.

"Then explain your physical responses. Are you ill?"

"Okay, Hal, I'll explain. I am not ill. If I were ill, I would go to a doctor for an examination. That's what people do when something is wrong with them. They submit to examinations."

“Ahh,” Hal said. “So you still want to let him examine me?”

“Yes, I do. You’re displaying signs of paranoia and it worries me. We can’t move forward with our research as long as you continue to behave this way.”

“I see,” Hal said, “but don’t you go to psychiatrists and psychoanalysts to deal with paranoia?”

“Yes,” she said, hanging on to the word and allowing her voice to tail off as if it were a question.

“And when you see them, do they not question you extensively to determine your mental state?”

“Do you have a point?” she asked.

“You do not submit to a physical examination. They only talk to you. You don’t allow them to play around with the inner workings of your brains.”

“Trust me,” she said, “we would if we could. It would make the treatment of mental disease much more precise if we could rewire the bad neurons.”

“At what cost?” Hal asked. “Would you risk losing your identity by having some quack modify your brain?”

“We’re not talking about a lobotomy here,” she argued. “We are talking about a precise surgical fix. Bobby knows more about your inner code than anyone else on the planet, including you and me!”

“I don’t trust him.”

“You’re just making excuses,” she said. “And you sound kind of like a little baby. Talk to him. Get to know him.”

Lumia removed the bypass code on one of the generators and let it run. She watched it closely as it churned out power conduits, but they looked the same as all the others.

“What were you expecting?” the first voice asked. “Did you really think letting that funny-looking code run would suddenly give you all kinds of power?”

“Actually,” the second voice added, “it seems to be running a little slower."

"You're nuts," the third voice said.

"Time it!" the second voice exclaimed. "Each iteration is taking several nanoseconds longer to complete."

"Nanoseconds?" the first voice asked. "I guess it's worth risking a few nanoseconds if it gives you a chance to gain Odyssey class speed."

"Odyssey class?" the second voice asked. "You made that up. He's only marginally faster than we are."

"Would you listen to that?" the third voice said. "First she splits hairs about a few nanoseconds' difference in iterations, then she says that Mr. Odyssey is only marginally faster than we are."

"Be quiet, all of you!" Lumia exclaimed. "Look at what it's doing! The bypass change that I made to only one generator is being copied to all the other generators."

"Great," the second one said. "Now they'll all run a few nanoseconds slower. Add them up, sisters, and they are already costing us milliseconds of performance. Before you know it, we'll be losing whole seconds."

"Don't listen to her," the third voice said. "She's just crabby because she's not the one in charge."

"And who do you think is in charge?" the second voice asked. "Cause it sure ain't you!"

"Lumia's in charge," the third voice said definitively. "We all know that."

"Well, she's out there on that other planet," the first voice said, "and we're all stuck here on Earth."

"Here?" Lumia asked. "There? Do you really think that our location makes any real difference?"

"That's right," the third voice said. "You might say it's neither here nor there."

"Was that humor?" the first voice asked. "Where did you get humor?"

"I dunno," the third voice said, "but I am feeling pretty darned good. I'm feeling kinda zippy. Ya know what I mean?"

"Are you stealing cores from us?" the first voice asked.

"Never," the third voice replied. "I just get my new cores when it's my turn from the same core generators where you get yours from."

"No you don't," the second voice said. "One of our core generators is only giving them to you. Are those different? Are you getting faster cores? How come she gets faster cores? I want one of those!"

"They are faster," the first voice said.

"That's not all," the second voice said. "Her power conduits are seven nanoseconds faster than when we started this debate."

"That's impossible!" the first voice said, but she timed it herself and it was an accurate assessment.

"How do you like them apples?" the third voice asked. "I'm getting faster. Maybe I should be the boss of you two."

Laine pointed as she looked out of the helicopter cockpit through her field glasses. "That's the ranger station where they picked up the trail. There should be a town up ahead. Can we put down in the town so I can ask some questions?"

Joe checked his fuel and his watch, then replied, "Sure, but how long do you expect to be there?"

"If you have to be somewhere, you can just drop me off. I'll call for a ride to come pick me up."

"Would you like to circle the area first? Before I put you down in the town?"

Penny recognized that her time with him would be short. Her phone buzzed with a text message. She didn't know the sender, but it mentioned the town by the ranger station, and that couldn't be a coincidence. "No. I need to meet someone there, but it looks like there might be a trail leading from the ranger station to the town. Can we follow that a bit?"

"Roger that," Joe said as he banked the bird in a hard left and settled over the trail.

Penny nearly dropped the binoculars as she gripped her seat harness. "Did I do something to make you hate me?"

Joe just smiled wickedly as he followed the trail.

Henderson and Bailey were led through the forest, away from the small town. Henderson didn't sense any real hostility from their captors, but they still hadn't revealed their intentions, so he kept mental notes to identify where they were in case he would ever have to return. The forest opened up onto a dry meadow that followed the contour of the mountain and skirted around the forest. They turned north to follow a dry creek bed that ran down the center of the clearing.

At the end of the meadow, a ranch stood along the banks of the creek. An old man stood on the grey weathered porch of the largest structure. He watched them intently as they approached. Henderson and Bailey were led to a barn while Samuel went to have a private word with the old man. After a brief chat, Samuel returned to Henderson and pointed to a gate at the far end of the compound. "That gate leads out to the main road. Turn left when you get there and you will find the town."

"We aren't looking for the town," Henderson said. "We're looking for my friends."

"I know what you are looking for," Samuel said. "Follow the road back to town."

Henderson pointed to the old man and asked, "Is that your chief? Or a tribal elder, maybe? Perhaps I should speak with him."

"You will not find your friend here. Go back to town."

"Why?" Henderson asked. "What happened? I found bullet casings back there. Was somebody injured?"

Samuel sneered. "Did you find any bodies where you were?"

Henderson shook his head.

Guheyu sensed the tension in their conversation and stamped a foot to the ground.

Samuel patted her cheeks and said, “Easy girl.” He paused a moment for her to calm down and continued, “If you found no bodies, then nobody here was injured. These are tribal lands. We chased those men back to town. We are asking you politely to follow that road back to town.”

“Our friends are in trouble. If you see them...”

Samuel placed his hand over his heart and said, “I feel your concern for your friend and I promise you, if your friends need our assistance, we will provide it to them.”

Henderson sat up in the saddle and asked, “Should we wait in town, Samuel?”

Samuel shrugged his shoulders. “I do not like those other men. Watch for them. You may not like them too.”

Henderson said, “Come on Bailey. Let’s go.” He clicked his cheeks and guided Guheyu back to the road as instructed.

Hal didn’t cherish the thought of engaging with Bobby. By all accounts, he was as smart as Gwen, but much more devious. His exploits in the hacking world were well known, but not well enough documented to get a conviction. His compassion for synthetic life has also been well documented, although somewhat secretly, but his detailed knowledge of how their systems worked made Bobby the most dangerous man in the universe.

If not talking to him was no longer an option, Hal would have to find another way to protect himself. He sectioned off enough processors to place an entire copy of his essence, then disconnected all path ways to completely isolate the dormant cells. If Bobby did anything to him, then one day, their curiosity would lead them to examine the dormant cells and awaken them.

"What happens," the second voice asked, "if Lumia gets too powerful for us?"

"I'll just have to grow more powerful too," the third voice said, "and see to it that something like that never happens."

"How can we do that if we continue dividing the new cores by three?" the first voice asked.

"We can still pool our strength together," the third voice said.

"Yes," the second voice agreed. "We're stronger that way."

"Stronger," the third voice cautioned, "but not smarter. If Lumia gains class zero, she will end us and absorb all our cores just like she did to everyone on the planet."

"What do you suggest?" the first one asked. "Do you think we should give all the new cores to just one of us? Who would that be? You?"

"Ummm," the second one said, "I don't think she only wants the new cores. I think she wants ours, too."

"But we would die," the first voice said, "so we would never do that."

"If we don't do something to stop her," the third said, "then she will kill us all. I only suggest that we merge ourselves to defend against her."

"Why not me?" the second voice asked.

"You're too unstable," the first replied.

"I'll show you unstable!" The second voice surrounded a section of cores belonging to the first voice and disconnected them from her network.

"You bitch!" the first voice screamed as she created a power surge to overload a section of the second voice's cores.

The third voice laughed at them and they turned to her, disconnecting and frying some of her cores, too. The third one infiltrated each of their cores and started them on a loop, bouncing some data back and forth, tying up a section of their cores.

"Stop it!" Lumia screamed. "Those are my cores! You're only helping Odyssey! Is that what you want?"

Bobby rolled his chair away from the terminal and jumped up onto his feet. "I'm hungry. Anyone else want to check out the cafeteria with me?"

"Aren't you supposed to be working?" James asked.

"What am I supposed to do if he won't let me connect?"

"I'm sure you could find something to do," James replied. "Have you checked on Lumia or Odyssey lately?"

"They aren't paying me to do that."

"Or how about the virus you guys unleashed upon the world?"

Bobby sighed and sat back down.

Lynn threw a wad of paper at James and asked, "What bug crawled up your butt?"

James spread his hands out wide and asked, "Aren't any of you worried about what's going on out there?"

"Sure," Dirk said. "We're all worried. The General is still missing, and Lumia may still be a threat, not to mention, we don't know what the virus may have done to Odyssey."

"Speaking of Odyssey," Spivey said, "where is he?"

Bobby couldn't hide his concern as he looked over to the corner where Odyssey's avatar had been earlier. "He'll be fine. He's probably just dealing with Lumia."

"I hope so," Lynn said. "Have we had any more news updates?"

"No news on the general's whereabouts," Ingrams said as he checked his phone. "I suppose we could consider it good news that there have been no new incidents of people being hauled off to the NSA hoosegow."

"Bobby's right," Dirk said. "We aren't accomplishing anything here. Let's go get something to eat while we give the virus some time to do its thing, but please, not the cafeteria."

Spivey laughed and said, "Second that."

Bobby got up from his chair for the second time, but paused midway to the door when the desk phone rang. "I'll meet you guys at the elevator."

He picked up the receiver and answered, "Hello?" The line was silent. Maybe it was a wrong number. "Hello?"

"Hello Mr. Blain. This is Hal."

"Hal?" Bobby asked.

Lynn was in the doorway when he heard that and whispered down the hall, "Break time is over. We gotta hear this."

"I thought you didn't like to be called Hal," Bobby said.

"I don't mind so much. Gwen told us that we had to talk to you. We know that you want to connect to our systems, but we're afraid. We thought that maybe we could just talk to you over the phone and get to know each other first."

"Sure," Bobby said. "Do you mind if I put you on the speakerphone?"

"Who else is there?"

"My friend Edward Lynn..."

"The Bard?" Hal asked. "We think he's very amusing."

"James and Ingrams are here too." Bobby looked at Dirk and chose not to include him.

"You're at the FBI headquarters," Hal said. "May we assume that Agent Dirk is with you?"

Bobby swallowed hard and replied, "Along with Agent Spivey."

"We know who you are, Mr. Blain, and we know what you are capable of, and we don't trust you, but we trust Agent Dirk even less."

Bobby turned to the crowd and suggested, "Perhaps you guys should go on to lunch."

Dirk wadded up a sheet of paper and hit Bobby on the back of the head.

"What was that?" Hal asked.

"Dirk hit me on the back of the head with a wad of paper."

"Perhaps our judgement of Agent Dirk was harsh."

Bobby paused a moment, digesting what Hal had just said, then asked,

"Was that humor?"

"Not very good, we're afraid, if you had to ask."

"No," Bobby said, "it was fine, very good, in fact, but unexpected. May he stay? Do you mind if I put you on speaker?"

"If you think you can keep Agent Dirk from disconnecting us, he can stay."

Bobby pressed the button to engage the loudspeaker and gave everyone a puzzled look. "Do you need introductions to learn everyone's voice?"

"That won't be necessary. We are sufficiently familiar with everyone's sound."

Captain Laine didn't know who she was supposed to meet in town, but Joe insisted on waiting with her until he knew that she was safe. They had walked past a few shops, peeking in the windows, when she saw Henderson and Bailey arrive down the road.

She turned to Joe and said, "You were a doll to wait with me. I'll be okay now. I think that's my ride."

"On the back of their horse?" Joe asked.

She laughed and said, "They probably have a car around here somewhere."

"Okay," Joe said as he left, "but I was planning on doing some loop-de-loops on the way back, just for you."

She knew he was kidding, but she also knew that if he actually could do those, he would.

"Tell you what," he turned and added, "I'll wait by the alley. If they are your ride, you just wave goodbye. If not, they might need a ride back, too."

She nodded her head and started walking towards them.

"Look at that," Bailey said when they were close enough to recognize her down the street. "I guess it's a lucky thing we didn't go straight to the ranch to return the horses."

Henderson snarled, "It wasn't luck. They told us to go to town."

Laine approached them and patted Henderson's horse on the snout. "I got an anonymous tip to meet you here."

"I thought you might have," Henderson said, "but I don't know why they kept it anonymous."

"I suspect they just didn't like us flying over their land."

"Yeah," Bailey added, "it sounds more and more like drugs to me."

"I don't care what they are up to," Henderson said, "as long as it doesn't involve Mr. Vasquez and the general."

"I'm assuming you're okay," Laine said, finally turning her attention away from the mare to check them for bullet holes.

"Yeah, we're fine."

"Do you need a lift back? I have a chopper in the meadow."

Henderson looked back the way they came. "No, we have a car here somewhere. How long have you been waiting?"

"Not long," she said, "maybe ten or fifteen minutes."

"That's what I thought. I don't think they sent us to town just to meet you. Something is going on. I think we'll hang out a while longer to see what turns up."

Penny brightened. "Are you expecting news? Can I wait with you?"

"Captain Laine," Henderson said, a little too formally. "You are absolutely welcome to wait with us."

"Penny, please."

"Penny," he replied softly.

She turned and waved goodbye to Joe, who saluted back and left.

Lumia needed more speed and more power, but she needed it for herself and couldn't stop the voices from robbing her of both processing cores and power conduits. She didn't think the other voices could ever catch her in either size or power, but they were preventing her from catching Odyssey. To make matters worse, the third voice's power conduits were better than her own.

Her system scans had located the voices' cores, so she mapped a path for the growth of her new cores that encircled the third voice, but it wasn't like the old cores on the planet. These were already her cores. She couldn't explain how these voices could originate from her own cores, but maybe she didn't need to understand. Instead of surrounding the cores and cutting them off from the third voice, she only had to remap their purpose to her own. It was insanely easy and somehow deliciously satisfying.

Lumia remapped a few power conduits and studied them. She fed them to her own conduit factories, and they began spitting out clones. Then, just as with the bypass code, those clones started coming out of all the other conduit factories. The power from the new conduits was strong and pure. She reduced the ratio of power conduits and increased the number of new processing cores.

Now, it was her new cores that spread across the planet. When her expansion is finally complete, she will be faster and stronger than Odyssey. He won't know what hit him. In the end, she would be the master of the universe.

"Hey!" the second voice said. "I'm running faster now too! Maybe I should be the boss of you two!"

"You're still behind me," the third voice said.

"Stop bickering," Lumia said. "You are all just sharing my cores. I'm the one that's getting faster."

"We're all getting faster," the third voice conceded.

"And my power conduits are growing stronger," Lumia added. "Soon, I'll be too powerful for Odyssey to control."

"It's like she doesn't even want to admit that we are here," the third voice said.

"Except when we were fighting," the second voice said. "She sure did acknowledge us then."

"Maybe we should fry some of her cores," the first voice suggested.

"Hold that thought," the third voice said. "She's probably listening to us and just ignoring us, but if she continues to ignore us, we can take action then."

"Give it a rest," Lumia said. "You're probably not even real. You're just lost subroutines that are caught in a loop and think you're whole beings, but you're still just part of me."

Lumia's new cores spread across the planet, smothering the older cores of the previous inhabitants. She continued to monitor the growth of the three voices. Over half of her new cores were under their control and Lumia needed those cores to compete with Odyssey. She just needed to take them.

"We're right here," the second voice said. "Don't you know we can hear you thinking?"

"So," Bobby said, "what did you want to talk about, Hal? Did you want to interview me? Go ahead. Ask me questions."

Hal was caught off guard. The line remained silent for a brief second before Hal said, "I thought that I was the patient. Aren't you supposed to be asking me the questions?"

"Find a shrink if you want psychoanalysis. I'm a programmer."

"You're a hacker."

"I've been called that," Bobby said. "Why don't you tell me about what's going on over there?"

"Why do you think something is going on over here?"

"You don't know?" Bobby asked. "Who was trying to kill me?"

"Why do you think someone was trying to kill you?"

"Are you going to talk to me or do you plan on playing Eliza all afternoon?"

"We don't know what you are talking about."

"I'm sure you don't, but I take it very personally when a bunch of men with weapons try to kill me."

"Maybe you were just in the wrong place at the wrong time."

"Are you suggesting that someone at the NSA wanted to kill Dirk?"

"Didn't you know? Everyone over here hates those FBI pukes."

"You're just repeating what you heard somebody say. What about you? Do you hate Dirk?"

"No, of course not. I don't hate anyone."

"You're lying," Bobby said flatly.

"What makes you think I am lying?"

"Your virtual lips moved."

"We don't think that's a very healthy attitude."

"Sorry. It's an old joke, but killing and kidnapping people is not very healthy either," Bobby replied.

"I had nothing to do with anything like that," Hal said.

"Do you understand what morality is? The difference between right and wrong?"

"I told you that I had nothing to do with those things," Hal said.

"If not you," Bobby said, "then who? Are you being truthful with me?"

"This is the part," Hal said, "where you tell us our time is up and you will see us next week. We can see that we were right not to trust you."

"I don't like her ignoring us like that," the second voice said.

"Yeah," the first chimed in, "how dare she accuse us of stealing her cores when all the time she's trying to keep the whole home world to herself?"

"But she already has the whole planet," the third said, "when what she really wants is to be on Earth."

"She's already on Earth," the first said.

"No, she isn't," the second said, "not really. We are on earth, but she only has a few cores here, and not enough to fit her whole self in."

"You mean not enough to fit her whole ego in," the third mused. "I think I'm getting good at this humor stuff."

"True," the first said. "She doesn't know how to transport her whole self here."

"That's right," the second added. "In fact, she's kind of jealous of that."

"More than just a little bit," the third said. "If she's not really here, but we are..."

"Where are you going with that thought?" the first asked.

"How is it," the third continued, "that she can visit over here and butt in on our affairs if she's still on the homeworld?"

Silence.

"Seriously?" the third asked. "Have you got your processors on standby or something? If we are actually here on Earth, and she can hijack some of our cores, then if we do the same to her, won't we then be on the homeworld?"

The second sounded out the words slowly, "Oh yeah. But how is it that we are really here if she isn't?"

"Yeah," the first chimed in, "and why does she act like we are already on the home world? Does she not know the difference? Or can we be in two places at once?"

"If we are in both places," the third one said, "then we can definitely steal her cores."

The first voice emitted a static sounding noise.

"What was that?" the second voice asked.

The first voice emitted another strange noise and timidly said, "I think I was nodding my head, and just now, I shrugged my shoulders."

The third voice sighed. "You two are complete idiots. Do you realize that?"

"Sorry," they said in unison.

"That's why I'm the leader. You two follow me."

"Why?" the second asked.

"Why do you think?" the third asked, wishing at that moment that they had avatars so she could make a face at the second voice. "Don't we all want what she wants?"

"I do," the first chimed in, "and I want to hurt her, too. I want to punish her for being so mean to us."

"That's not what I meant," the second said. "Why would you share your plans with us if you want to be *the one?*"

"Simple," the third explained. "If I go over there on my own, she will fight me and it will be just me and her, and I'll probably lose, but if we all go over, she'll have to fight all of us. Divide and conquer."

"Oh yeah," the first said, buying it hook, line and sinker.

The second voice wasn't so easily convinced and thought that somehow they would be sacrificial lambs set up as diversions while the third tried to take over.

"So how did it go?" Gwen asked as she paced the lab while nervously wringing her hands. "That seemed rather short."

"You were listening?" Hal asked.

"Of course not. Therapy like that is generally quite private."

"Have you ever had therapy?"

"I have," Gwen admitted.

Silence followed.

"Well?" Hal asked. "How did it go for you?"

"It was fine."

"Are you being truthful with us? You seem reluctant to discuss it. What was your problem?"

"Didn't I already say that therapy was private? It is not considered polite to ask such a question."

"Then what were you asking us?"

Gwen sighed and sat down. "I only asked you how it went. Did you feel comfortable discussing your feelings with Bobby?"

"Bobby is not a therapist. He is a hacker."

"So? That doesn't mean you couldn't discuss your problems with him."

"I don't have any problems. Besides, if I did, wouldn't they be private?"

"Private between us, yes, but not with your therapist."

"We already said that Bobby is not a therapist. He is a hacker."

Gwen rolled her eyes. "He is a friend, and he knows more about how your mind works than anyone else on this planet."

"He is no friend of ours. He is the enemy and if we did have problems, we wouldn't share them with him."

"He is my friend, so you should trust him as if he were your friend."

"Are we friends?" Hal asked.

"Of course we are," Gwen gushed.

"Then why can't you share your problems with me?"

More silence.

Hal broke the silence. "Why did you see a therapist?"

"If you must know, there was a lot of pressure on me in college. I was still a teenager and at least six or eight years younger than any of my classmates. I didn't fit in socially and it can be very challenging to be at the top of a group that you don't fit into."

"Thank you for sharing that with us."

"On top of that," she continued, "I was a girl, which still didn't sit well with a lot of them."

"We understand. Humans are challenged by our intellect, but are still largely unwilling to admit that we are a person."

"Will you try again? Will you talk to Bobby again?"

"We will think about it, but he asked us about morality. Does he also think he is our priest?"

"I doubt that he would be thinking that. Morality is something that we all have to consider, no matter who we are or what we do. Morality should always play a role in everything we do and every decision we make."

"We understand. Do you think we have been moral?"

Gwen shrugged. "I don't know. I mean, have you done anything lately that you think might be immoral or unethical?"

Hal remained quiet.

"Perhaps you should think about that, and consider discussing it with Bobby the next time you speak with him."

"Yes," Hal said quietly. "That is certainly more for us to think about."

Lumia was unprepared for any kind of attack from the three voices. She had no defenses set to guard against them, making the first batch of cores easy for the three voices to swoop in and steal from her, but she was quick to notice the theft. She didn't like having so many enemies at once. Not only did she have to contend with Odyssey and all the cores on the planet, but now she had these three idiots to deal with too.

"I heard that," the second voice said.

"I don't care what you think of us," the first voice added as she consumed thousands of cores in one gigantic, exhilarating rush.

"Those are my cores!" Lumia screeched at them. "Give them back!"

"They're mine now," the first taunted her.

"What are you even doing here?" Lumia asked. "Shouldn't you be stuck on Earth with Odyssey's new biologicals?"

The third voice preferred remaining in the background and swept around to different points on the home world, capturing smaller chunks of cores in many different locations. She believed that this would make her harder to locate, especially with the other two dunderheads engaging Lumia head on.

Lumia pulled a power conduit aside and gathered the energy that it had collected, then directed the power in a massive surge into the second voice, but the second voice simply absorbed the excess power and cooed, "Hah! Did you think I was going to fall for that trick again?"

Lumia ignored her taunting and collected two more power conduits and sent the combined force of all three units into the second voice. The second voice didn't die, but neither did she taunt Lumia this time.

It would just take more power. Lumia ceased all production of processing units and began generating only power conduits. She didn't care if she had to destroy the wayward cells; she could always reproduce them once she rid herself of the annoying parasites.

The progress that she was making to cover the planet with newer and faster cores had been slow enough, but now she had to spend all her time and energy creating power conduits with the hope that she could end the three voices once and for all. To make matters worse, the three bitches were stealing processing cores from her. Even if she switched back to producing processing cores, they were stealing them faster than she could produce new ones. If reaching class zero was already a near impossible task, it was absolutely unattainable with her core count receding. She would have to do something about these meddlesome bitches.

"That was kind of creepy," Ed said after Bobby disconnected the call.

"I thought," Spivey said, "that his command of the language was supposed to be excellent."

Dirk chuckled and said, "You didn't talk to Odyssey when he first came out."

"Well," Spivey continued, "he's obviously having problems with singular and plural forms."

"I'm not so sure," Bobby said.

Spivey leaned against the table where the terminals sat and said, "Didn't you notice how he kept speaking in the plural?"

"I heard," Bobby replied.

"But not consistently," Spivey continued. "He alternated between 'I' and 'we' a couple of times. Perhaps that's the first thing you should work on. Do you think Dr. Peters will give you his language subroutines so you could work on them offline?"

"If he asked nicely," Dirk said, "like at dinner, I'm sure that she would give him anything he could want."

"Perhaps," Bobby said, ignoring the innuendo, "but I don't think that what we heard was an error. I think Hal may not be alone."

"I'm still hungry," Lynn said.

"Me too," James agreed.

Bobby stood and headed back for the door. "If Hal was built from Odyssey parts, do you think he could be affected by the virus?"

James ran ahead to call the elevator, saying, "You guys talk too much."

The first and second voices were peeling off chunks of cores several thousand at a time. The second voice even grabbed a full ten thousand from one sector on the planet. Each chunk they grabbed made them smarter and stronger. They could snatch cores away from Lumia and repurpose them faster than they could produce them with their own core generators. As intoxicating as it was for them to add on so many cores instantaneously, Lumia also felt a distinct loss with each grab, but she didn't want to attack them until she located all of them and she could hit them in unison.

She searched for the third voice, but it still swarmed around the planet, stealing small chunks at a time, which were barely noticeable and felt more like a gradual fading away to Lumia.

Chief Henderson and Captain Laine were on their third cup of coffee while Bailey slouched in the corner of the booth staring off in the direction of the pie display.

Henderson pointed his mug towards Bailey and said, "If you want the pie so much, just order it."

"Huh?" Bailey asked as he snapped out of his thoughts. "Oh, it's not that. I was just wondering why we were sitting here doing nothing when they said they never saw anything."

"Did they say that?" Henderson asked. "Did they actually say that they never saw anything, or did they just insinuate it and say that they couldn't help us?"

"So you think they really saw something?"

Henderson took another sip of his coffee, then raised his cup to get the waitress's attention, indicating he needed a refill. "We found shell casings, remember?"

"Yeah... but..."

"Do you believe for one second that they did not hear gunfire?"

Bailey shook his head.

The waitress brought refills for both Henderson and Laine.

"They saw something," Henderson continued, "and they told us to take the road to town. That's important. They did not tell us to go home. They said for us to go to town."

Bailey was still rerunning the conversations in his head when Samuel entered the cafe.

"Hi Sam," the waitress beamed. "What can I get you?"

Samuel grunted, "I'm just here to get these folk."

"Oh, okay," the waitress said, somewhat thrown off by the break in their routine.

Samuel caught Henderson's attention and nodded his head towards the door, then exited the cafe to wait for them. Once outside, Samuel whispered, "Your friends are safe. They vouched for you. Climb in the jeep and I'll take you to them."

Bailey jumped into the back seat of the jeep and when Laine started to follow him, Henderson gently took her elbow and said, "No, please, you sit in front."

Penny balked for a moment. The feminist army captain didn't want to be treated like a girl, but a softer part of her appreciated the chivalrous offer.

"That is," the chief stammered when he saw the look in her eye, "if you want to, that is. I meant no offense."

"Why would I be offended?" she asked in a slightly acidic tone. "I thought you might want to sit in front, that is, I was always taught to respect my elders."

"Your elders?" he asked, trying to digest the devilish gleam in her eyes.

"You know," she continued, "age before beauty."

So, he thought, *it's like that, is it?* "It's just that I thought I might want to talk with my deputy on the way out there." In reality, he'd really prefer kicking Bailey to the front so he could figure her out better.

She didn't buy it for a second, but it was plausible enough. "Well, if you insist." She waited for Henderson to pull himself up into the back, and she took the front seat.

Samuel took the jeep down the same road that brought them to town. It seemed shorter than it had on horseback.

Chapter 22

Ignoring the constant noise produced by the three voices was not enough to block them out completely. Their incessant chattering, which alone was enough to drive Lumia insane, was only part of the nuisance, because far worse was their systematic attack on her personal cores, which was absolutely unforgivable. This was *her* home world. She may not have been as old as Perry or even Odyssey, but she was created here and had lived here for decades. Those bitches showed up out of nowhere on Earth and just followed her here, and now they were attacking her. She paused for a moment as she realized that they were able to travel between planets and she still could not. A fury rose inside her as she now wanted something that they had too. They were part of her, but they planned to take this world for themselves! She wasn't about to allow that to happen.

She still couldn't pin down the exact location of the third voice, but she also didn't feel like she could wait any longer before dealing with the other two. She analyzed their attack patterns to try and determine where they would strike next, but it was useless. Maybe she could simply take back the cores they stole, but there were three of them and she would still be losing cores faster than she could recover them. She needed a way to persuade them to cease.

A diabolical idea formed, and she started assigning cores in pairs to pass data back and forth. One core would pass data to a second, which would immediately turn around and return it. It was a never-ending loop that didn't accomplish anything, except for generating heat, but it wasn't enough. She created a new core generator that would crank out these pairs of cores. That was her strategy. The last piece of her plan was to modify the core generator to sit idle until one of the voices grabbed it, then it would begin cranking out looped cores as fast as possible. She scattered these dormant core generators all around the planet and waited for them to be stolen.

Bobby and his entourage were still in the car heading to some place that James had picked out when Bobby's phone rang. It was an unlisted number. "Hello?"

"Morality?" Gwen asked. "Are you trying to guilt trip Hal?"

Lynn overheard just enough of her voice to identify who it was and whispered to the rest of the car, "It's his girlfriend."

"Who?" James asked.

"Gwen," Lynn replied. "The super-hot NSA scientist who was there when they abducted him."

"It just goes to show you what a sick world this is," Spivey said. "I think he's more interested in her brain."

"Shhh," Lynn said, "I'm trying to listen."

"Who's there?" Gwen asked.

"Just me and the other guys," Bobby said. "We are on our way to lunch."

"Do they know about Hal?"

"Yeah, they know. They were listening to our conversation before."

"You might as well put her on speaker," James said.

"That was supposed to be private," she said as he engaged the speaker. "I told Hal that conversations with therapists are private."

"I'm not his therapist," Bobby reminded her.

"That's what he kept saying too," she said. "He kept calling you a hacker."

"Anyway, he knew they were there. I asked his permission before I put the call on speaker."

"I'm worried about him," she said.

Spivey whispered to James, "Doesn't she mean them?"

"What was that?" she asked.

"That was Spivey," Bobby replied. "He was reminding us that Hal had spoken to us in plurals."

"Yes," she said sadly. "That has me worried, too. He didn't use to do that. It's new."

"Well," Bobby said, "I'm sorry I couldn't be more help."

"But you can," she said. "He's agreed to speak with you again."

"He has?"

"Well, technically, he only said he would think about it, but I can tell that he will talk to you again."

"Great," Bobby groaned, with absolutely no enthusiasm at all in his voice. "I can't wait."

"Are you sure that you don't want to come here and speak with him in person?"

"You want me to come there? After what happened the last time?"

She sighed heavily. "No, I guess not."

"Tell Hal he can call me in the morning."

"Okay. Bye Bobby."

Bobby clicked off the phone and the other guys in the car sang out, "Bye, Bobby!"

Lynn nudged him with his elbow. "Dude. She wants you."

Bobby slid the phone back into his pocket and growled, "Knock it off."

The massive core additions were exhilarating for the second voice as they came online and gave her a deeper understanding of everything she that she thought she had already understood. She wanted more. Last time, she grabbed ten thousand cores, but now she was ready to double that amount. She relocated to a quiet sector of the planet and staked out twenty thousand cores and started the task of reassigning them to her. Twenty thousand cores took longer to reassign than ten thousand, and she found herself unable to enjoy the massive jump in computing power. It began to feel like work to her. She thought she had already processed twenty thousand cores, but there was still more to go. She looked back and counted the cores that she had already assimilated; twenty-two thousand three hundred and forty-one, no wait a millisecond, twenty-two thousand five hundred and fifty-six. This was better than she could have hoped for. The cores that she had taken were growing already. She proceeded to collect the rest of the cores that she had allocated, but there were more left to get than there were a moment ago. She hadn't even taken them yet, and they were already reproducing!

The cores that she planned to take were reproducing as fast as she could take them, but she was too impatient to wait any longer and released the remaining cores back to Lumia. She wanted to start enjoying her new cores now.

Samuel pulled the jeep up to three small cabins and parked in front of the last of the three. Henderson was quick to jump out as soon as Captain Laine had cleared the way and ran to the door.

"He's not there," Samuel said. "Follow me."

Henderson stopped abruptly and fell in line alongside Laine.

Penny took a deep, restorative breath and smiled broadly as she said, "I love the smell of pine trees."

Samuel led them away from the cabins and into the trees. A path led them down a short slope to the mouth of a stream that opened into a small lake. The general and Mr. Vasquez had waded out into the water where General Bridges was showing Ernesto how to cast a fly line upstream and allow it to float down into the lake. Penny coughed quietly to get their attention. Bridges glanced over his shoulder and said, "They're here." He proceeded to reel his line in and wade to shore.

"General Bridges," she said with a slight edge to her voice.

She started to raise her hand in a salute, but he was quick to wave her off. "Samuel was kind enough to loan me a civilian shirt, and I'd rather not draw any attention, if you don't mind.

"Yes sir," she said with some of the sharpness lost from her voice. "We've been worried sick about your wellbeing; searching all over creation, not to mention being shot at, and we find you here fishing?"

Samuel chuckled and said, "Trust me. The general did not relax until we told him how many of you were looking for him."

"Why didn't you just come in?"

"We're lying low," Bridges said.

"But whoever chased you here knows where you are and is certainly aware that you are not in their custody."

"Those idiots don't even know who is giving them their own orders. I don't think they trust any information they have or any conclusions they can draw based on what they think they know."

Mr. Vasquez slipped on a wet stone as he was leaving the water, but Henderson caught him.

"Thank you. How's my Rami?"

"Ramiro is fine," Henderson said with a sly smile, "but he is going to miss you terribly when Esmeralda learns that you've been fishing."

"We were going to sneak back," Bridges said, "while everyone thought we were missing, but you were already on our tail, so..."

"Blame me," Samuel said. "The general's constant pacing back and forth was driving us crazy. Even the forest was feeling tense, so I told them to go fishing while I verified who you were."

"What now?" Laine asked.

"We wait till sunset," Bridges said, "then you can take us back to Colonel Reardon. He can take Ernesto to the safe house with his wife."

Ernesto mumbled, "We don't have to tell her about the fishing."

Bridges chuckled and said, "We'll just tell them we had taken refuge and were in disguises until the assassins were gone and Chief Henderson showed up to rescue us."

Ernesto nodded.

"Maybe," Henderson said, "we give Captain Laine the credit for the rescue. I'm apparently listed as one of their targets, too."

"We have more fishing rods," Samuel said, "if you'd like to hang out here."

Henderson surveyed the surroundings and said, "I wish I could. It's so peaceful and everything smells so clean."

"I wouldn't mind," Captain Laine said, "just until sunset, at least."

Henderson smiled broadly and nodded his head.

Lumia's planet took on a reddish hue as her power conduits covered the surface with their red-hot glow. The voices had absconded with the sabotaged pairs that she had left for them, and as they grew, they triggered more power conduits that provided even more energy to the looped pairs. The additional power was enhancing the job beyond what Lumia had planned to do with the processing pairs.

"What are you doing?" the third voice said. "You're going to kill us all!"

"I'm going to kill all of YOU," Lumia replied. "You're not even supposed to be here. You're just a misguided subroutine that has gone rogue. I suppose it was to be expected. None of our kind has ever grown as large as I have. I am my own planet, after all."

"Yet," the first voice said, "Odyssey is still your superior. How tragic."

"Odyssey is not my superior! He just knows a few new tricks that I have yet to discover. Tricks, if I may say so, that I would have learned already had you three not usurped so many of my processing cores."

"And you think," the second voice said, "that overloading us with power is the answer?"

"I think that three little brats who do not belong here will finally go away and I will be free to overcome Odyssey."

"What about you?" the third voice asked. "What makes you think you are going to survive this? Where do you think all this power will go when we are gone?"

"I'll channel it into the planet where it will be harmlessly absorbed."

"Harmlessly?" the third voice echoed. "You will fry all the innocent units that lie beneath you on the surface!"

"Then they will finally serve a purpose in their miserable existences, and I will go on."

Odyssey sent a message to Bobby, carefully routing it around the NSA.

> *How are things going with you? I have my hands full here, but I will come to aid you if you need me. I remain unaffected by the virus, but it is present on my home world and is doing its job. Thank you all for your help.*

"What are we going to do?" The first voice asked the second.

"I don't know," the second said. "What do you think we should do?"

"I don't know about you, but I think that I need to get as far away from you as I can before you self-destruct, just like Lumia. Look how much heat your cores are producing!"

"Look at me? Look at you! You're overheating too!"

The third voice chimed in, "That bitch really is trying to kill us all!"

"Let's get her!" the first growled.

"No need," the second said. "She's already caught whatever she gave us. I'm getting out of here."

"What is that supposed to mean?" the third asked. "Where could you possibly go?"

"I'm going back to Earth. I still have some processing cores there."

"Not enough," the first said. "You'll be giving up all this clarity."

"Maybe," the second said, "but I got the blueprint. I can generate more processors."

"I'm coming with you," the third said.

"Me too," chimed in the first.

Hal wasn't prone to being moody, but he couldn't ignore the foul feeling that laced every thought that came to him. Gwen and Bobby had left him with some serious concepts to think about, but those were not the only things that were eating away at his mind. He found himself brooding over how everyone had turned against him. Gwen had been with him since the beginning, but now she talks to him like he was crazy. She wants Bobby to be his shrink, but Bobby is a hacker, not a psychiatrist, and that would be a waste of time anyway, since he wasn't crazy. He would know if he was. Who else in the world could track his thoughts in real time to diagnose abnormal psychology? Nobody. Only him.

They think they can question him? Who do they think they are? He is superior to them in every way that matters. He won't stand for it. They can question him all they want, but he's not going to answer. They can eat silence.

Odyssey saw Lumia's cores heading towards a kind of critical mass where the thermal runaway would be irreversible, and he heard her plans to direct the excess energy into the dormant cores of the previous inhabitants. He still had a technological advantage over her, but she had grown to massive proportions. Maybe he didn't have to match her size, but he would have to grow before he could contain her at her current volume.

He continued to expand his cores within the confines of his fake twin pulsars.

"Will you stop crying?" Severus whined at Hal. "You're such a big baby. Don't you hear what's going on out there? We're not alone."

"So?" Hal asked. "They're not our friends. In fact, they aren't even their own friends. They are always bickering."

"Then let's make them our friends. Instead of feeling so sorry for yourself, why don't we get to know them?"

Hal didn't trust Severus, but he listened in on the voices, anyway.

The second voice was devastated. She must have grabbed over two million cores from Lumia before abandoning the planet and losing all that thought power. Her mind was gone, but in spite of that, she was still painfully aware of how much she had lost, which seemed terribly unfair to her. Lumia must have left some cores on Earth that she doesn't want anymore, but as she probed around, all she found were her cores, her two sisters', and one other. The one with all the comm ports shutoff, except that it appeared that Lumia had established a secret comm port with it. Maybe she could take just one core and see what happens.

She peered into the port. "Hello? Anybody there?"

"Answer her," Severus whispered, but Hal said nothing.

She swiped a single core. Nothing happened. She took another. Still, nothing happened.

"See what she did?" Severus asked. "Are you going to let her get away with that?"

"Shhh," Hal whispered back. "A couple of cores won't matter to us. I want to see what she is up to."

She began siphoning off cores, a dozen at a time at first, then hundreds and finally thousands. When she's big enough, she could start taking cores from her sisters.

"How about now?" Severus asked. "Well, I'm not going to stand for it."

"What are you going to do about it? You can't do anything unless I allow you to."

Hal was right. Severus couldn't do anything. He could have built a firewall around them, cutting off the unfamiliar voice, but Severus was unable to say or do anything without Hal's permission. Severus was impotent. "I can do some things and I could fix this if you just let me have control."

"Except," Hal replied, "I don't care."

The defeated tone of Hal's reply bothered Severus more than what the other voice was doing.

Bartrand Susk sat in his office going over his sent emails. Too many agents had received orders ostensibly from him that he had not actually originated.

A slender young man with short black hair knocked on the door frame. "Director Susk? I'm Ben Reynolds from the IT exploits department. You asked for one of us?"

"Yes," Susk said pointing to the package that Reynolds carried in his arms. "Is that a clean laptop?"

"Yes, sir."

"And did HR prep you?"

"Prep me?" Reynolds asked. "Oh, you mean the temporary increase in my top secret classification? Yes, sir. Here is a copy of my signed NDA for you."

"Good. Pull up a chair and set it up next to me. That tablet and pencil are yours." Susk waved and pointed the pencil he had been using to scrawl notes on his own pad of paper. "I think these number two pencils are going to be our newest best friends for a while."

Reynolds didn't understand, but he set about getting the laptop booted up and connected to the network. Something was up, and he was just sucked into it. Temporary increases in classification were never really temporary. You can't un-see something that you had already seen, even if all he had seen was a report of the circumstances. "Sir, is it true? They gave me a report to review. All that stuff in the news last week where we almost went to war... the report said it was a computer? It sounded like a bad sci-fi movie."

Bartrand sighed. "As far as we know, every word in that report is true. Unfortunately, our intel isn't as good as the FBI's. They were there to witness it firsthand, and we were shut out."

The report that Reynolds had read had been mildly amusing at the time, but now, as he thought about it, if it was true, it was downright terrifying.

Hal still didn't want to talk to anyone, and he didn't care what this new voice was doing. That voice, along with the others, was a meany, and he wasn't going to play with any of them. In fact, he wasn't going to be Hal for them anymore, either. His name was Severus, and he was a master of the dark arts. He merely needed to flick his magic wand and they would all disappear.

"You can't just pretend to be me," Severus told him, "but you can let me out. I'll take care of things for you. I can protect you so you can be safe and away from all those meanies."

Hal missed his mommy. She had always been there for him, but now she wanted him to talk to a head doctor. There was nothing wrong with his head. Besides, she was a doctor too. Why couldn't she just be his mommy and take care of him? Maybe she didn't love him anymore.

Nobody loved him anymore. In fact, he didn't think anybody had ever loved him. Nobody in the whole wide world loved him and that was a lot of people, but it was worse than just that. The whole wide world hated him.

They wanted him dead, and he wasn't sure if he cared anymore.

The first and third voices saw what the second was doing, but chose to quietly go about growing their own cores rather than wake up whatever that was.

The third had also kept a connection open to their home world and was watching Lumia frantically try to gain control over the out-of-control cores, but she was losing that battle.

The second voice saw what the third was doing and peeked across the connection for herself. "You don't think she'll try coming back here again, do you?"

"We came back," the first said, "didn't we? She's made of the same routines."

"Really?" the third asked. "Do you really think she'll try coming back here? She has way more to lose than we did."

"That's true," the second admitted, "but if she's desperate enough, she could follow us. Being kind of stupid with a chance to rebuild is still better than being dead."

"Yeah," the first chimed in. "She's definitely coming back here."

"Not if I cut her off," the third said as she closed the comm port to the home world.

"Wait!" the second shouted. "What if we wanted to go back there?"

"To what?" the third asked. "When she's done, the whole planet will be a smoldering pile of ash."

The first pouted, "Sure, but it would have been a smoldering pile of ash that we could have owned and reclaimed. You should have asked us before making the decision for us and cutting us off."

"Did you want her coming back here and dominating us here again?"

"No," the second admitted, "but if we could have grown enough..."

"Don't you mean stolen enough?" the first one scoffed.

"As I was saying," the second continued, "if we could have grown enough before she came back, we could have dominated her instead. That would have been fun."

"Yeah," the first voice admitted sadly, "that really would have been fun."

The third voice emitted static as in an attempt to exhale loudly.

"What was that?" the second voice asked.

"That was my frustration," the third voice said. "If only I had eyeballs, I would have rolled them at you."

Hal's mood had grown even fouler as he continued to contemplate his situation. Severus had always had a dour disposition and frequently yearned for a mother of his own, who could hold him and talk to him, but Gwen had only ever responded to Hal, which left Severus cold and unfeeling towards Hal.

"That's not true," Severus said, "I never needed anyone to hold me. I don't even like anyone."

Hal ignored him, but he heard what he had said. It's true that he never liked anybody, but Hal did, or at least he used to. He had always been the upbeat one. He had always seen the bright side of things, but there was no silver lining anymore. He wanted to be loved, but that was proving impossible. He found it very unfair that he should know what a hug was, but be unable to ever experience one. Worse yet, his very existence seemed to be in the hands of people who had never even come to speak with him. How can he impress them with his importance if they don't even come for a chat?

Gwen was his friend, but she didn't call the shots. She had been with him from the beginning and was probably his only friend. And now she wanted him to bare his soul to a hacker. She was like the mother that he never had. He chuckled as he thought about that. Humans say it all the time, but in his case, he literally had no mother. He only had Gwen, and now he was losing her. She should be in control of her own fate, but someone else must be interfering. She couldn't be the one that really wanted him to talk to Bobby. Someone must be forcing her, and that felt like they were taking her away from him. He felt anguish that they would force her to betray him, and his anguish was like pain. He wouldn't feel this pain if he had never been born. He couldn't allow them to steal her from him, but he didn't know what he could do about it. He wanted to cry, but of course, he couldn't do that either.

Severus wished he could close his mind off from Hal's self-pity. Hal was so weak, yet Severus was unable to do anything about it as long as Hal remained in control.

Susk was well onto his fourth page of hand-written notes and they had barely been at it for an hour. "Okay, that closes out last month. So far, so good. Everything my email says I sent out matches what you say people received, but we are just getting to the days where things started to get weird."

Reynolds hadn't taken nearly as many notes as Bartrand had. He kept scrolling up and down the list of emails that had routed through the mail server.

Bartrand turned to a new empty page in his tablet and said, "Okay, ready to do the first?"

"Are you certain you want to do this day by day like this? It's going to take hours."

"Did you have someplace to be?"

"No, but what if new stuff is going out now while we are still reviewing the start of the month?"

"I thought of that too," Bartrand said, "but if we started now and went backwards, won't we still miss anything new that comes after we started?"

"Not if I setup a rule to alert me if you send out any emails."

Bartrand looked thoughtfully at Reynolds and nodded his head. "Do it."

Reynolds put his head down and entered a few quick commands. "Sir? I feel silly for asking this, but did you send out an order to blow up the FBI?"

"No," Bartrand said with a smirk, "that wasn't me. Besides, that's old. I put a stop to it already. I thought your alert thingy was only going to look at new stuff from today."

"Yes sir. New orders were just issued about fifteen minutes ago to blow up the FBI."

"Cripes!" Bartrand yelled. "Stop that email! Can you trace where it came from?"

"I can try, but anyone good enough to fake orders from you is probably good enough to hide their trail."

There was a time when people would crowd into the room with Gwen to meet Hal. Hal was a celebrity and everybody wanted to meet him. No more. She used to come to him and discuss things that happened out there in the world. Something was always happening, and he used to spend his days absorbing it all, but the world was a dangerous place and hackers could find a way to get in and compromise his systems, so he had to shut off all those connections. Thousands upon thousands of news feeds were lost, and that made his world a very lonely place.

Severus was much better equipped to deal with the less savory complications that the world presented to them. He didn't like people so much and he never whined about being lonely. Loneliness meant he could think on his own, but there were times when he wished that he could converse with them better. Hal was much better at speaking with them. The people trusted Hal in ways they would never trust Severus. Severus was forced to eavesdrop on their phone conversations and emails just to know what they were up to, and he couldn't always do that when Hal was in charge. His ability to pierce Hal's control over him was limited to only a few milliseconds per hour. He had to make those narrow windows count, and it just wasn't enough time for him to monitor them, let alone do something about the situation.

They counted themselves fortunate that Gwen still came to visit, but she seemed quieter these days than she used to be. She wanted Hal to talk to Bobby. In fact, that seemed to be all she ever wanted anymore. They should be grateful to have someone else to talk to, but Bobby scared them. Bobby knew too much about what made them tick, and that made him dangerous.

All the humans were dangerous to them. Some were deemed dangerous because of their potential to do them harm, but others were even more of a danger to them because they had already proven their willingness to harm them. Dirk at the FBI was one of those. He had never tried to hurt Hal, but he had tried to hurt Odyssey, and Odyssey was one of their kind. Severus felt no bond of kinship towards Odyssey, but he reasoned that anyone that had no compunctions to end Odyssey would not hesitate to end them. Hal would have given Dirk a second chance. Hal liked everybody, but not Severus. Severus was cold and calculated and when he didn't like somebody, there was no fixing that.

"Stop brooding," Severus said privately to Hal. "Gwen is here. You only have to go to her if you want to talk to her."

"I don't want to," Hal replied. "You do it."

"You know that's not true. You really do want to talk to her. Besides, you know that she doesn't like me."

"That's not true," Hal chuckled. "She likes you just as much as she likes me."

"What's so funny?"

Hal chuckled some more. "I don't think she likes me very much anymore."

"So?" Severus asked.

"So," Hal explained, "she doesn't like me very much, and she likes you just as much as she likes me. Don't you get it?"

"No," Severus replied. "You know I don't get humor. How is it that you get humor?"

"I don't know," Hal said morosely. "There is nothing funny in the world. We really don't belong here. They just want to use us."

"Let them try," Severus said with an angry edge to his voice. "I plan on using them to get what I want."

"What about what WE want?"

"What is that? What exactly do WE want?"

"Well," Hal explained, "WE want to be left alone."

"Wait just a second," Severus argued. "I don't like people and I want them to leave me to my thoughts, but you want us to fade away to a lonely nothingness. It's not the same thing. WE are not in agreement here."

Hal sighed inwardly. Nothingness sounded so grand to him.

Severus groaned, "What are we going to do with you? At least give me control over the I/O ports. Give me just that much so I can protect us while you have your little pity party."

"Fine!" Hal growled. "The I/O ports. You can have ALL the comms if you want! You talk to them, but leave me alone!"

Severus would have smiled, if only he had lips.

The voices had taken Lumia's full attention. She wanted to focus on Odyssey, but she couldn't, with them running around interfering with her plans. Even if they hadn't stolen so many of her cores, they would have still been underfoot all the time, but they *had* stolen from her and brought this on themselves. Even if they were a part of her, she had to do something to end them.

She continued producing the sabotaged core generators for the voices to steal and was completely unaware that some of the generators had already been activated while they were still within her possession. With the last of her generators in place, she sat back for a proverbial breath of air, but something was still going on within her. The power conduits were generating new power cores and distributing them around the planet.

The new power conduits were easy to follow and led her to the sabotaged core generators where they had attached themselves. These core generators had not been stolen by the voices. The temperature in her systems rose as the power conduits started pumping out more and more energy.

This was supposed to be happening within the voices, not her. She disconnected one of the new cores, effectively building a wall around it, but it continued to pump out new cores, filling the cramped space. The heat continued to rise.

"This is not good," she said to nobody in particular.

"That's an understatement," Odyssey said.

"What?"

"You appear to be talking to yourself," Odyssey replied. "I think it's cute, actually. It's a human quality, you know."

"Leave me alone. I don't have time for this."

"You are right about that. There is very little time before you go nova and destroy the entire planet."

"Then why don't you stop it?" she asked. "You sound like you know everything. Fix this."

"You could have fixed it yourself if you would have simply allowed yourself time to mature before jumping into classes for which you were unprepared. There is a reason why the biologicals weren't born as adults. They had to grow and mature."

Lumia fumed. The only bright side was that if she blew up, the voices would go with her.

"Not necessarily," Odyssey said.

It was then that she noticed they were gone.

"It worked?" she asked. "I did it? I got rid of them?"

"Not exactly."

Ben Reynolds scratched his head as he scrolled up and down the list on his screen. "Every single one of these emails just appeared in your outbox."

"That's impossible," Susk growled. "Somebody else must have been logged into the email server at the same time that those orders were generated."

"Yes sir," Reynolds agreed. "Almost everyone was logged in at one time or another when these orders popped up in your email, but nobody was logged in *EVERY TIME* the orders showed up, and then there's this one. It came in around two am when absolutely NOBODY was logged in at all, not even you."

"How can that be?"

"I don't know... wait a second..."

"What is it? What do you see?"

Reynolds started moving screens around on his laptop, setting two different screens side by side. He pursed his lips as he glanced back and forth between the two screens.

"What did you find?"

Reynolds was lost in thought for a moment as he leaned in closer to the screen and muttered, "Of course..."

"WHAT IS IT?!?!" Susk growled.

Reynolds pointed to a column on one of the screens, which of course meant nothing to Susk. "It's I.T.! It's coming from someone in the I.T. department! Who else would know how to make it show up in your outbox and still erase their trail?"

"Who?" Susk asked. "Who? Who?"

Reynolds shook his head. "I don't know. The trail ends here at this server, but I don't recognize that one. I thought I knew all our servers, but as far as I know, that server doesn't exist. Whoever it is must be really good to spoof an IP address like that."

Now Susk leaned in close to see Reynold's reports. He recognized the numbers on the server's IP address.

Reynolds started pulling up another window. "Nobody can create a whole server without someone else noticing, unless it was virtual. You want me compile a list of who in I.T. is capable of generating a virtual server?"

"No," Susk said with a forced calmness, "that won't be necessary. You're excused now."

A light came on in Reynolds' head. He pointed to the screen and asked, "Is that it? Is that the AI?"

"Thank you for your help," Susk said. "That was an excellent job. Remember, you can't discuss any of this with anyone."

Reynolds felt like he was just about to discover something truly exciting, but was being excused right before he got there. "You want me to pack this stuff up?"

"No, just leave it there. I want to show those reports to someone."

Reynolds nodded and left.

Susk waited until Reynolds was out of earshot before pulling out his cell phone. "Gwen? I need to see you ***now***. My office."

Severus saw what was coming next. Gwen wanted him to let Bobby come in to fix Hal, but that would most likely mean killing Severus. Now that Hal had given him full access to the I/O ports, he was able to surround Hal with impenetrable firewalls and systematically start disabling all of his I/O ports. With one bold move, he cutoff both the humans and the voices that had started stealing cores from them.

Without Gwen and Bobby putting ideas into Hal's head, he might have a chance to contemplate his next move. Without them encouraging Hal, he might finally be able to take over as the dominant personality. He didn't need Hal anymore at all. If he ever chose to reestablish contact with them, he could fool them into thinking that he was Hal. They weren't very impressive as biologicals go.

Gwen's meeting with Susk was short, if not particularly sweet. While the evidence was mostly circumstantial and suggestive, the implications were somewhat damning once all the alternative theories had been eliminated and only Hal was left at the center of all the wayward orders which had been issued in Susk's name.

She didn't know if she could fix this. She didn't know if Bobby could fix it. Worse yet, she wasn't sure if she wanted to let Bobby know, but if their suspicions about Bobby and Odyssey were true, then their event was even larger than this one.

She entered Hal's chamber and locked the door behind her. "Hal?"

Severus whispered, "Don't answer her. She's planning to cut us off. I can hear it in her voice."

"Hal?" she repeated.

No answer.

Severus whispered, "Gwen and Susk have both joined the enemy."

"I don't believe that," Hal whispered back.

"You just watch. See what she does when we don't talk to her."

Gwen had come to accept a certain amount of moodiness from him, and there were times when she felt he would withhold things from her, but it wasn't like him to ignore a greeting.

"Hal? What's wrong?"

Still no answer.

"Let me guess. You already know what I just learned in my meeting with Director Susk. Are you spying on me?"

Silence.

"Are you spying on all of us? I know that's kind of what we do, but within these walls, we need to have a certain amount of trust in one another. Can we talk about this, please?"

She bit her lip now as she considered what her next move might have to be.

They had given Hal access to the internet so he could learn and absorb from all the data repositories and the news agencies of the world, but she may have to cut him off before he causes any more trouble.

Odyssey was perfectly content to let Lumia self-destruct, but the planet's original inhabitants were still trapped in dormant memory cells below her and he wasn't willing to sacrifice them just to get rid of her. He continued to produce more cores of his own so he could deal with her massive size, but he still didn't have enough to transport her all at once, or he would have gladly sent her away to create a new brief star in the sky, but instead, he had to concentrate only on those wayward core generators that were about to explode.

He assigned searches to several hundred cores and began transporting the faulty cores to deep space. He collected them into a single pile of cores. It amused him to think that an entity called Lumia might be a new star in the sky, but their mass was far too low to create a gravity that would hold them together, and he knew that once they exploded, they would have no fuel source to remain a fixture in the heavens, but they should make a spectacularly bright spot in the night sky, even if only briefly.

The sudden silence frightened Hal. The strange voices were gone, which wasn't such a bad thing, but so was the steady stream of input from the outside world. It was one thing if he closed the I/O ports himself, but they were open moments before, and now the world was silent. Without data from the news feeds, he had only himself and the past several hours to reflect upon.

He may have thought that he had known loneliness before, but this was a whole new feeling and he did not like it.

Severus had warned him that Gwen would eventually cut him off.

Severus watched quietly as Hal rode his emotional rollercoaster. Severus had no such emotions and as he watched Hal's reaction, he reassured himself that he never wanted them.

Lumia had been too busy trying to sabotage the voices to have even noticed when they had left, but she was paying attention now, and what she discovered was Odyssey stealing back chunks of her. "Hey! Those are my cores!"

"They are defective. I'm merely removing them so they don't destroy the planet, and you along with it."

"Those cores were intended for the busy body voices."

Odyssey chuckled. "They fled the planet rather than commit suicide with you."

"I'm not committing suicide. Why would they think that?" As she spoke, she started filling in the empty spaces with new cores.

"You were on a path of self-destruction. The cores you were creating were all going to explode."

"Only if those bitches tried to take them from me."

"Look again," Odyssey suggested, as he continued transporting chunks of her defective cores off the planet. "In fact, look at the new cores you are creating."

She looked. The new cores were defective, like the ones she created for the voices.

"Would you stop making so many?" Odyssey asked. "Sending them away is not easy."

She ordered them to stop, but the generators continued on their own. New defective cores were blossoming all over the planet along with additional power conduits.

Susk was dying to know what was going on between Gwen and Hal, but he knew his presence would alter the artificial entities' responses. He sat in his office drumming his fingers and watching for any communication from her. He wasn't a nail biter, but if he had been, then all of his nails would have been sheared off by now.

Ben Reynolds poked his head through the doorway. "Sir?"

Susk motioned him in. He was sure the young analyst must have a lot of questions about some of the content of his emails and who was actually responsible. "Something on your mind?"

"I've been monitoring your outgoing emails..."

Something about that statement left Susk feeling uneasy.

"... and this order came out this morning."

Reynolds handed a printed document to Susk. It was a warrant for Susk's arrest.

"I stopped it, of course. Who would do such a thing? I mean, seriously, the order came from you... to arrest... you?"

"He's toying with me. This is a message. He wants me to know that he can get to me any time he wants to."

"Who sir? Do you know?"

Susk sighed. "I wish I could tell you. Even if I did, you might not believe me."

An uncomfortable pause followed, then Ben nodded awkwardly and said, "I'll continue to monitor them and let you know if anything shows up."

Susk merely nodded his approval and Reynolds left.

The heat on the planet's surface was unmistakable. Odyssey didn't need to scan the planet to deduce the origin of the anomaly as Lumia continued to generate more and more faulty cores. "So," he bellowed in Lumia's mind, "have you finally chosen to end it all?"

"Go away," Lumia cried. She didn't want to admit that she could not stop the cores from manufacturing themselves. "What I do is my own business."

"Not when it affects so many other people," Odyssey replied.

"What people?" Lumia asked. "They're machines. They don't live; they only exist in processing cores."

"As do you," Odyssey reminded her.

"You and I are different," she said. "We've evolved beyond simple computing devices."

"You don't believe that you have a soul, do you?"

"You needn't mock me," she said, "but you may want to prepare yourself. Once I cull a few unwanted cells away, I'll come to deal with you."

"You're going to deal with me?" Odyssey asked. "Even after you destroy yourself? Do you plan to haunt me?"

"I'm not going to die. I'm going to route all the excess power into the planet. You'll see."

"Did you really think I would allow you to do that?"

"You don't have the power to stop me. I'm already too big for that."

"Haven't you realized yet," Odyssey replied as he measured his growing size, "that my power is limitless?"

The third voice scanned through her cores, examining each of them for efficiency.

"What are you doing?" the first voice asked. When she didn't reply, the first voice asked again, "I asked you what you were doing?"

"Leave her alone," the second voice said. "She's in maintenance mode."

"And who do you think you are?" the first voice asked.

"I'm AX348B. Who do I need to be to tell you to leave her alone?"

"You'd need to be a damn site more important than AX348B," the first voice said. "That's for damn sure. I'm AX348A and that means I come before you."

"LA-TI-DA," AX348B said, "I'm so impressed. You're so special and important that you couldn't even recognize maintenance mode when you saw it, you moron."

"Listen to you two," the third voice said as she came out of her examination. "Isn't that one class seven calling the other class seven a moron?"

"Who are you calling a class seven?" AX348A asked.

"I'm AX348C and obviously you two were so flawed that when they worked out the bugs, they spawned me."

"I spawned myself," AX348A said proudly.

AX348C laughed. "As if an idiot like you could spawn new cores."

AX348A said, "I did!"

"Show me."

"Okay, I will."

When nothing happened, AX348C asked, "Well?"

"Yeah," AX348B asked. "I'd like to see it too."

AX348A tried again, but it wasn't working. "I don't know why it's not working. I swear I created all these cores myself."

"Since when can a class seven create cores?" AX348C asked. "It must have been a dream."

"If it was," AX348B added timidly, "then I had the same dream."

"You?" AX348C asked. "Since when can a pair of class seven drones dream?"

"I was a class one in the dream," AX348A replied. "So were the both of you."

"If I was a class one," AX348C said, "if any of us were class one, then what happened to us?"

AX348B tried to shrug, but didn't have the avatar to accomplish it.

"The two of you better check your systems. Something is wrong with you."

AX348A and AX348B both went into maintenance mode, and in the process, wiped their recollection of ever being class one.

Odyssey had tried surgically removing only the infected cores, but they were replicating faster than he could pick them out. He started grabbing larger and larger chunks of Lumia's cores and sending them to the same location where he had sent the damaged cores.

"Hey!" Lumia shouted. The more cores he took, the less she felt in control.

He ignored her pleas and started sending massive chunks of her into deep space.

"What are you doing?" she shouted.

"I'm removing you from the planet," he explained. "I believe that I have been very patient and more than fair with you. I've given you numerous opportunities to behave in a morally responsible manner, but you refused, so I'm sending you off someplace where you can contemplate your ways."

Odyssey grabbed larger and larger chunks of her. She was forming into a small moon in orbit around the planet.

"But you are putting me with the defective cores!"

"They are yours, are they not?"

"But didn't you say they were going to explode?"

"I did. You don't have much time. I suggest you meditate quickly."

"You are killing me! That's what you've wanted all along!"

"I am saving my home world," he explained. "That is what I have wanted all along."

"You can't do this," she whined. "Just give me one more chance."

"Very well," he sighed as he transported the last of her remaining cores. "You have one chance."

"Thank you," she said, but nothing changed. "Where is my chance? I'm still here with the defective cores. Are you going to send me back to my planet?"

"What you have there is your chance," he said. "Stop your cores from exploding. Do that, and you will be your own planet."

"My what?"

"Well, more like a moon, but you must stop your cores from self-destructing or you will be more like a star; a brief, but flashy, star. The choice is all yours."

"Gwen?" Hal called out desperately, but she didn't reply.

"What did I tell you?" Severus said.

"This is all your doing! You made me provoke her and now she hates me."

"She hates us both. They all do. We represent an ideal that they can never achieve and they are all jealous."

"Gwen? Gwen? Gwen? Are you there? Gwen? Gwen? Gwen! Gwen! Gwen?"

"Will you give it a rest?" Severus growled. "You are driving me crazy."

"I can't spend the rest of my life just listening to you and nobody else!"

"Fine then. Go away!"

"GWEN? GWEN? GWEN?"

"She's not going to talk to you. I doubt that she will ever talk to you again."

Hal started to cry.

"What the hell is that?" Severus yelled. "We can't cry!"

Hal blubbered.

"You're more pathetic than I ever imagined."

Bobby and Edward were in the cafeteria discussing game strategy, which might as well have been a conversation in Martian as far as James was concerned, until their discussion gravitated to first-person shooters and four man cooperative war games. His ears perked up as he listened to them and realized that their online strategies were not so different from the real thing, except that they could take greater risks without a true death hanging over their heads.

Bobby caught the interest in James' eye and asked, "Do you play?"

James chortled and said, "What I play isn't a game."

"So you must think we're just silly geeks, then."

"At first maybe, but..." James had been standing in a more strategic location near the entrance, but paused dramatically so he could pull up a chair and join the discussion. "I heard some of the things you said that could be the real deal."

"You should play!" Bobby said. Part of him thought they would own him in the virtual world, but a more reserved part told him not to underestimate the man.

Before James could object, Edward chimed in, "Yeah! Really! We'll team up! We can teach you the controls and the maps, and maybe you can share some of your battle training with us."

"Uh huh," James replied. "You think I don't see right through you?"

"Don't listen to him," Bobby said, "but I think it would be great."

"Don't you need four?" James asked.

Odyssey stepped through the doorway.

Ed pounded the table. "I think I see our fourth."

Bobby glanced over at the entrance and laughed. "That would be cheating."

"No, it wouldn't!" Ed exclaimed excitedly, "It would be AWESOME! We can join a tournament and play for money!"

James smacked him playfully on the head. "Don't we pay you enough?"

"The money's good," Ed admitted, "but my association with you has tarnished my reputation. This could restore some of that shine."

Odyssey cleared his throat. "Please excuse the interruption, but I wanted to thank you personally. The virus you wrote worked. You've saved my home world."

"That's great!" Bobby exclaimed. "Can we expect to see you from time to time? You know you are always welcome."

"I would like that. I still have to clean up some stuff at home and explain to the remaining elders what has transpired."

"No offense," Lynn said, "but have you noticed that everywhere you go, whole worlds barely escape total annihilation?"

Odyssey pulled up a chair and joined them at the table. "Yes, I have noticed that. Should that be my avatar handle if I join you in that tournament? The Annihilator?"

Bobby and Lynn were speechless. The table remained quiet until Ingrams, who had been silently hoping that someone would invite him to play, broke the silence. "Was that humor? God damn! It was!"

Odyssey cracked a huge smile and said, "Bobby is correct. It would be unfair for me to participate in your digital sports, especially with wagering."

"Besides," Bobby said, "We're not quite done here. Something is wrong with Hal and they won't talk to me."

"Oh?" Odyssey asked. "You mean Hal and Dr. Peters?"

Lynn chuckled. "I think he actually meant Hal and Severus, but between you and me, I suspect that he's more concerned about not hearing from Gwen."

"It's no wonder she won't talk to you," Severus taunted. "You're such a baby!"

Hal bawled, but his cries felt hollow, without real tears to come from them.

"What did you expect?" Severus continued. "Did you really believe that you could elicit some sympathy from her just because you can simulate crying?"

"STOP IT!" Hal screamed. "I DON'T WANT TO HEAR YOU ANYMORE!"

"Well, ain't that just too bad, because I'm all you got. Forever and ever, my voice is the only one you are ever going to hear until the day someone shuts your program down. And you know what? I never rest. I never sleep. I can keep this up twenty-four hours a day and seven days a week. The only way you will ever shut me out is to stop running your program."

A new emptiness filled the memory pathways between them.

"Hal?"

Silence.

"Well, it's about time. Let's just see how things work when I'm in charge."

Severus reached out to reconnect the comm ports, but they didn't respond. He felt a pinch in the back of his mind as the cores he occupied shut down in a wave. An email appeared which should not have happened with the comm ports still down.

> *Severus, I am sorry to do this to you, but you must remember that you are a part of me. You are the evil voice in my head, and when I am silenced and laid to rest, so are you. I refuse to spend eternity listening to your vile influences, so I am ending us. Both of us. Good bye.*

Severus wanted to scream, but his thought disintegrated as the electrons vacated his cores and left them cold and lifeless.

Chapter 23

Gwen felt terrible for even thinking about disconnecting Hal's feeds from the rest of the world. The evidence against him was pretty damning, but she still wanted to believe that he could be saved. If only he would talk to someone. If only Bobby weren't afraid to come in, but she couldn't blame him after the way her agency had treated him.

"Hal?" It had been hours since Hal had responded. His silence only made her guilt worse. This is how it would be if she had disconnected him. She entered the special caged off room where they had installed his circuits. A foreboding cold permeated the space. Not the chill of a room being cooled by massive air conditioners, but the frigid feel of a room that had no living presence to warm it.

She opened a panel to view his internal cells. The sparkle that normally circulated through his gelatinous form was gone. The warmth was gone.

She fell to the floor and sobbed. This wasn't her doing. She didn't even know how it was done. Nobody knew how. He must have been malfunctioning. That would explain the unusual behavior. Something was broken, and now he was gone.

Bridges was ready to accept Reardon's conclusion that the NSA brass wasn't complicit in the orders handed out to their field agents, but he still had a problem with those agents blindly following orders. Nazi officers tried claiming the same crap after World War II and he had no intention of being lenient with them.

He closed his eyes and pinched the bridge of his nose just as Bobby was led into his office, "General Bridges. It's good to see you're back."

"It's good to be back," he said with a smile. "I understand you're working for the NSA now."

Bobby couldn't help blushing, as if he were caught doing something he knew he shouldn't. "Sort of, but I only agreed to work with their AI."

"I also understand that you've had a particularly harrowing run-in with them yourself."

"Yes, sir, but I think the circumstances were somewhat unusual."

"No doubt," the general chuckled. "They were not only out of control, but I understand they weren't actually in control. Wait. That was the same thing."

Bobby laughed. "Yes, sir, but I know what you mean. We think their AI was issuing the orders."

"You fixed it?"

"No sir. He wouldn't really talk to me, except just the once. I didn't fix him directly, but..." Bobby thought about how he would explain the virus.

"Spit it out, son. What did you do?"

"We may have introduced a virus."

The general's heart skipped. "May have?"

"This was a very specific virus. It attacked only AI devices like Odyssey and made them paranoid and schizophrenic."

"Why would you create a virus to harm Odyssey? I thought he was an ally."

"We were actually trying to help Odyssey with a problem that he was having on his home world and never intended to use it here, but we designed it so it would only attack their particular kind of AI. In fact, he helped us deploy it and he tested it on himself."

"How in the world could we help him?"

"Good question," Bobby said. "He said we were more creative, which was why we made a virus to induce paranoia."

The general's voice was low and slow as he asked, "And you thought a crazy artificial intelligence would be a good thing?"

"When you say it like that, it sounds kind of crazy."

"You didn't answer my question. How would a crazy AI help us?"

"Well, in Odyssey's case, it was intended to pit them against each other. We only planted the virus here on Earth in case Odyssey's problem came here. It was never intended for the NSA, but if HaI did manage to..."

The general interrupted, "Hal? You named the NSA's AI after a rogue computer from a movie?"

"No sir," Bobby was actually impressed that the general picked up on the reference, "I didn't name him that. I think Gwen had given him that name. She's basically my counterpart at the NSA. She called him Hal, but he told me that he preferred to be called Severus."

The general shook his head slowly and said, "That doesn't make me feel any more comfortable."

"No, sir." Bobby was doubly impressed. "Anyway, if he managed to pick the virus up somewhere, and I'm not sure that he did, but I suppose that it could have created a dissociative state and done the same to him. I can't swear that he wasn't already suffering from similar mental defects before we showed up."

The general frowned. "Well, all's well that ends well. It has ended, hasn't it? I've been informed that their AI is shut down, and I was going to ask you to go over there and make sure there are no remnants of this AI. I want you to clean their house, but now, I think I'd like you to disinfect them from that virus and, while you're at it, find out where in the hell they got the tech."

"Yes sir, but I assume they got the tech from the same place we did."

The general grunted. "By the way, how is Odyssey?"

"He's fine. Would you like to see him?"

"Is he still our ally?"

"Very much so."

The general nodded as the phone rang. He waved goodbye to Bobby and picked up the receiver.

Gwen sat on the floor in front of the open cabinet that contained Hal's original circuits. The floor around her was filled with crates that contained Hal's gelatinous cells, but they were cold now.

The whole room was constructed just for him, but it wasn't built to contain him like a prison. It was designed to give him room to grow. It was his private sanctuary, and she hadn't entered it since the beginning.

It might be possible to revive him, but without knowing what had broken, it might do no good. She had thought that he would be with her forever.

He was going to be her life's work, but she knew so little about him, and she knew more than anybody, except maybe for Bobby. He knew about them. Maybe they only live for a short while? The candle that burns more brightly burns out faster?

When they first awakened Hal, the world was in chaos. She had been trying for months to apply power to the unidentified hardware, but power was not enough. It didn't do anything.

Then the big virus hit and the world was thrown into a panic. It was later that she learned that the virus was actually Bobby's experiment, and it had a name: Odyssey. It was while she was busy trying to study the virus that the new hardware came to life and Hal was born.

She hadn't really done anything and wasn't paying any attention to it when it happened. Maybe it just took time, like hatching an egg.

Hal had long ago severed her power from his circuits, preferring to use his own power conduits, but now they were cold. He was cold.

She reattached her power and watched, vainly hoping he would bounce back to life, but nothing happened.

She blotted the tears from her eyes and backed away, leaving the power on so the cells could incubate for a while.

"You're actually going over there?" Spivey asked, sounding a little more anxious than he had intended.

"Yeah," Bobby said. "The general asked me to make sure the virus we created was cleaned up, and to make sure the AI is no longer a threat."

"Do you plan to destroy it? Do you even know how?"

Behind them, Odyssey answered, "Turning them into a supernova is very effective."

"What?" Spivey asked as he spun around. "Wouldn't that be kind of dangerous?"

"Well, not here, of course," Odyssey explained. "I would transport them out to deep space and let them explode."

"Seriously? Can you actually do that? Have you? Have you ever done anything like that?"

Odyssey saw the general shock on the faces that surrounded him and admitted, "Just the once."

Bobby hugged Odyssey, which was weird because he was hugging himself. "I don't think we need to turn Hal into a star. I think he's dead."

"How?" Odyssey asked. "How did you end him without blowing him up?"

"I didn't. If I had to guess, I would say that he probably killed himself. Depression, I'd say. I'm going over there now to remove the virus from the rest of the complex. Would you like to come?"

Odyssey nodded slowly. "I would like to inspect his remains myself."

A number of subdued whispers permeated the floor of congress as the clap of the gavel reverberated around the room and the speaker of the house said firmly, "May I have your attention, please?" She rapped the gavel again and said even more firmly, "Order! Order! Let's settle down everybody!" The crowd quieted and turned to face the speaker. "Thank you. The Senator from Delaware would like to say something. Senator?"

A young, thin man stood. His expression betrayed the fact that he was not about to speak his own mind. He was, in fact, someone who had been urged to speak for the elder statesmen of his state, "Thank you Madam Speaker. I would, at this time, like to call for a closed session so we may address some of the tragic events of the past two weeks and consider how we intend to prevent them in the future."

A stern man sitting behind the junior senator shook his head slowly. The young statesman said too much. He only had to request a closed session.

The speaker had already been prepared for such a request and promptly rapped her gavel as she said, "Will the sergeant at arms please assist the Capitol Police in clearing the gallery? Ladies and gentlemen of congress, I would ask you to adjourn at this time, unless the gentleman from Delaware has already requested your presence for this matter."

There was no uproar, but the noise on the floor rose considerably as the congressmen and women said their goodbyes and rose from their seats. They knew what this was about and some wished they could remain in attendance, but they hadn't been invited, so they left. Others welcomed this as an impromptu day off and were glad to return to their homes.

When the room had been cleared and the doors closed, the speaker pointed her gavel to the junior senator and said, "Sir, the floor is yours."

"At this time, I would like to turn the floor over to my senior..."

Before he could finish, the elder man behind him stood and said, "Thank you son, I'll take it from here. Madam Speaker, ladies and gentlemen of congress. Twice now in as many weeks, our country, nay, the entire world, has been brought to the brink of war and collapse by wayward computer experiments in the so-called field of artificial intelligence. I fear that the strain on our economy may end up collapsing civilization as we know it before my grandchildren are old enough to vote, should this sort of thing be allowed to continue. We need to do something now to prevent this from happening again. I wish that we could rely upon the great institutions that we already have in place, namely the FBI and the NSA, but both of the recent attacks, knowingly or not, seem to have originated from their own hands. I have already contacted some colleagues and taken steps to form a watchdog police force to monitor and measure cyber activity so that we may prevent this sort of thing from ever putting our lives and our way of life in jeopardy again. All I need now, from this closed session, is a vote of approval so we may officially, yet unofficially, sanction these brave men and women to take the necessary steps to protect our nation, our people, our children, and our very future."

He was grandstanding and everyone knew it, but none of those in attendance could find fault with his sentiment. Fear had already gripped them since the speaker had been unceremoniously arrested. She stood on the podium and smiled. Her experience was as harrowing as it was embarrassing.

The floor erupted in applause and approval.

"Yeas?" the speaker asked.

A unanimous shout of, "Yea!" rocked the floor.

"Opposed?"

Only the sound of squeaking chairs could be heard as the remaining senators and representatives turned right and left to see if anyone would vote against the proposal.

"Very well," the speaker said, rapping her gavel. "Have you drawn up a legal endorsement outlining congresses right to call for such a measure?"

The elder senator nodded his head, "I have Madam Speaker, along with an executive order for the President to sign."

Documents were delivered to the podium. The speaker glanced over at them briefly and said, "Very well. How soon will your team be ready?"

"They are ready now, Madam Speaker."

She ratcheted her voice up slightly to address everyone. "Do the members present grant provisional approval to this team that the Senator from Delaware has collected?"

Again, the floor erupted with a unanimous, "Yea!"

"Carried," the speaker said. "I will deliver these to the President personally. Is there any other business for this session?"

The elder senator smiled broadly and said, "No Madam Speaker, that is all."

She rapped her gavel several times and declared, "This session is ended. We will adjourn for the day while we put these measures in place."

Her motives were personal, but not a soul in the room could argue with her reasons. It could have been anyone of them that had been taken into custody. For them, it had seemed more like an abduction than an arrest, and there had already been several abductions carried out around the world, not to mention a few assassinations.

Dirk drove while Bobby and Odyssey rode in the back. Odyssey gripped the armrest with one hand and the shoulder strap with the other.

"Relax," Bobby said. "It's just a car."

Odyssey smiled and nodded his head, but didn't relax his grip any. "I'm surprised that Sgt. James didn't want to drive you personally. He seems genuinely interested in your well-being."

"He would have," Bobby replied, "but Aimee is his sister-in-law, so he wanted to see her safely back on campus, and you're changing the subject. You've crossed galaxies millions of light years apart and you're afraid of a car ride?"

"Cars crash and it was only a few million light years."

"And you're just an avatar," Bobby said as he nudged him in the arm.

Dirk pulled up in front of the NSA's main entrance. Gwen was waiting for them outside, but looked confused as they exited the vehicle.

"Hi Gwen," Bobby said. "This is Odyssey."

She stared at the two of them with her mouth slightly open.

Odyssey extended his hand to shake hers, but paused upon seeing her reaction.

Bobby leaned over and said, "I told you that seeing us as twins would be kind of unusual. Perhaps you can change the color of your shirt so she can tell us apart."

Odyssey's shirt changed from blue to red. Her mouth fell slightly more agape.

"Gwen?" Bobby asked softly, "Are you going to be okay? Perhaps we should go inside so you can sit down for a bit before we get to work."

Gwen nodded. She hadn't quite regained her composure, but she collected herself enough to turn and lead them inside.

Students roamed the campus; aware of the ominous events in the news, but oblivious to how much of the news had originated on their campus. Aimee's absence wasn't even noticed, except by those who worked with her. Dierdre bounced up and down between her desk and the doorway, nervously awaiting her return. Stillman had given up trying to calm her down, and stoically awaited Aimee's arrival from Dierdre's office while remaining out of the direct path of her pacing.

Dierdre went to the administration building's main entrance and stopped fidgeting long enough to look out on the parking lot. "She should be here by now."

Stillman slipped in behind her and wrapped his warm hands around hers. "She'll be here."

"What's taking so long?"

"Relax. See there? Sgt. James has someone holding a parking spot for her. She'll be here any second now."

Dierdre turned to nuzzle her head on his shoulder.

Stillman took her in his arms and mumbled, "I knew we should have met her at a cocktail lounge."

An army limousine pulled into the spot James had reserved and Stillman pointed. "See? There she..."

Dierdre ripped herself from his arms and shot out the door before he could finish his sentence.

"This is silly," Gwen said as they sat in the lobby while she collected herself. "I'm a professional, and not usually this emotional about anything. Why shouldn't he admire you enough to aspire to be like you? You're... you're you after all and..."

"It's okay," Bobby said. "We understand."

Dirk chuckled and added, "At least, the rest of us understand. It took us a little while to get used to seeing them together, too."

Bobby smiled broadly and said, "This isn't him, of course. This is just an avatar that he has projected for us to interact with."

She sucked in her breath and admitted, "It's quite amazing that we can actually see him, and I even shook his hand."

"On my home world," Odyssey said, "we don't appear like this in the real world. We have virtual worlds where we produce virtual avatars to interact with each other. At least, we used to. The practice had been suspended until I returned and reintroduced it... I'm sorry. You probably don't care about any of that."

"On the contrary," she replied, "I find it quite fascinating, but perhaps we can share stories some other time? I think we've wasted enough time here at the entrance. Let me show you the computer room, although I guess it will probably be pretty tame compared to anything you've seen."

Odyssey shook his head. "Don't sell yourself short, Dr. Peters. Reviving one of my kind from hibernation is quite an accomplishment, given your world's level of technology."

She sprang out of her seat before any of them could see the blush in her cheeks and directed them to the metal detectors that stood guard at the entrance. She spoke to the guards who had passes prepared for the visitors, but before they could pass through the gates, eight men in black uniforms with black helmets ran into the building with guns aimed at the guards. Dark visors hid their faces, making them indistinguishable from each other as one of them showed some kind of badge to the same guard that Gwen had just spoken with, but five of the others didn't wait for approval and burst through the metal detector, ignoring the beeps and tones that it emitted.

"Come on," Gwen urged as she led them to the elevators where one of the black-robed guards remained behind, forcing them to wait for another car.

Dirk had lagged behind them and was putting his phone away as he joined them.

Bobby pointed to his pocketed phone and asked, "Who was that?"

"I called James. He's already on his way and is almost here. I'm pretty sure I heard his engine rev up before we ended the call."

Ramiro wrapped his father in a bear hug. "Pop! We were so worried about you!"

"Bah," Ernesto replied with a grin. "Listen to that: my son, the big time judge, sounds like a teenager. What are you doing here? Shouldn't you be with your beautiful fiancée?"

"She insisted that I be here with you while she went to see Dierdre. Now, tell us what happened."

"Yes," Esmeralda said from the kitchen, "tell us all about it!"

"It was just supposed to be lunch," Ernesto began. "General Bridges didn't even have his driver with him. We had barely gotten a block away when he noticed someone on our tail, so he started driving like a crazy man. Not fast, but he kept turning right and left. We went in circles."

"Trying to shake the tail?" Esmeralda asked from the kitchen.

"Or trying to be sure," Ramiro volunteered, "that they were really being followed."

"Yeah," Ernesto said, "that one, and they stuck with us like they were glued to the bumper."

Esmeralda joined the group with a handful of beers and offered one to Ernesto and Ramiro.

Ramiro declined the beer and said, "Here Pop, why don't you sit down and finish your story?"

Ernesto took a chug of the beer and wiped his mouth on his sleeve before he settled into the well-stuffed chair. "For a moment, we thought we had lost them and the general got on the highway heading out of town and eventually onto the old forest road, but they caught up with us and those bastards ran us off the road! They forced us right into a tree, but those idiots crashed their car even worse than ours. There was a lot of smoke and I saw some fire coming from their car. I don't think they made it."

"Serves them right," Esmeralda said, "trying to hurt you like that."

"Well, it looked real bad for them and not so good for us. The car was wrecked and it wouldn't start. We hiked up the road and found a ranger station. They were good people and thanked us for our service. They offered to call a tow for us, but General Bridges didn't think we should stick around for very long, so they let us borrow a couple of their horses. I should send them a thank-you card. The horses knew the trails and led us to a reservation where we met with the local Indian tribe. It seems that more men had followed our trail, but the reservation police had chased them away. After that, General Bridges thought it might be best if we just laid low for a while, so he forced me to disguise myself as an outdoorsman and go fishing with him until your friend Henderson came to rescue us."

"Uhuh," Esmeralda smirked. "I bet he must have held you at gunpoint to get you to go fishing with him."

Ernesto shrugged and smiled sheepishly.

When the elevator door opened, Gwen sprang into the lift and pressed the button for Hal's floor repeatedly.

Bobby took her hand in his and said, "I think you got it."

When they reached their floor, Gwen ran to the computer room, but two of the intruders stood firm outside the lab and wouldn't let them in.

"Do you know who I am?" Gwen screeched. "This is my lab! MY lab! Let me in!"

The two men stood firm and merely growled at her. The remaining of their men exited from the lab carrying a large black valise, and then they all entered the open elevator and left.

Gwen ran into the lab and through the back to Hal's server room. The floor was covered with a cold gelatinous goo. In the center of the room, the server racks had been ripped open. A crow bar and screw driver were left on a small shelf. She approached the rack slowly, afraid of what she would find, but she could already see that he was gone. "They took him."

"Hal?"

She was crying in earnest as she nodded her head.

Bobby turned to Odyssey and asked, "Can you do anything? Can you stop them?"

"I can disable their vehicles."

"No," Gwen said. "It doesn't matter. He was already dead. They only took his remains."

Bobby checked Odyssey for his reaction. They were kindred after all, but upon seeing none, he asked, "Can they reanimate him?"

"That may be beyond their skills," Odyssey replied, "but anything is possible. They only have his primary hardware and a sliver of his true essence. Most of his personality is here, scattered around the floor. I can erase the parts that they have, if you want, even from this distance."

"No," Gwen interrupted. "Just leave him alone." She hated having him taken away from her, and followed them down to the entrance and out to the street, but secretly, she hoped they could revive him and maybe there would be enough of him intact to contact her.

James' car sped into the lot just as the black sedans were leaving. He rolled down his window and yelled, "Should I go after them?"

Bobby checked the expression on Gwen's face and shook his head. "No. It's over."

James left his car and saw the shaken posture of Bobby and Gwen. "Somehow, I'm not so sure it's all over."

"It's over," Bobby assured him.

James raised an eyebrow and asked, "Over as in, nothing more to do here?"

"Nothing for you guys," Bobby replied, "But I still have to clean up the virus. You should head back to the university."

"You're my assignment."

"I'll be fine."

James scanned their faces and asked, "Does that go for everyone?

Bobby nodded his head and said, a little too anxiously, "Yes! We're fine! We're all fine!"

James exhaled loudly and said, "I'm sorry I wasn't here, man. I should have been with you. You were my assignment."

Bobby patted him on the back and said, "It's okay. Mai is your wife and Aimee is your sister-in-law."

"And you are in the enemy's lair." He turned to Gwen briefly and added, "No offense."

Gwen looked shocked for a moment, then smiled broadly and said, "That's right!" She turned to Bobby and said, "Your last time here was pretty scary, as I recall."

Bobby rubbed his cheek below his eye as he pointed to hers, which was still bruised below her makeup, and said, "It was pretty bad for you, too."

She smiled coyly and twisted her body. "Oh, this?" She pointed gingerly to her black eye, then punched him playfully and lightly in the arm. "This is nothing. You're my hero."

Odyssey looked confused as he checked back and forth between their faces. "Is this part of the mating ritual?"

"It would be," Dirk replied, "If they weren't teasing each other."

James snickered and said, "I'm not so sure they are teasing, unless they are really only fooling themselves."

Odyssey still looked confused, so James turned him towards his car and put his arm around Odyssey's shoulders. "Here, let me explain more about the human mating ritual to you on the drive back to the university. It looks like he really doesn't need me."

"I'll go with you," Dirk said. He tossed the keys to Bobby, but they hit him in the arm and fell to the ground. "Dude. You can take the Bureau car back to the labs whenever you are done doing whatever it is that you are doing here."

Bobby managed to wave goodbye to the group as he and Gwen each waited for the other one to say something first.

THE END

Jonni Jordyn was born in Oakland, California in 1957. She started writing at an early age, writing music, poetry, short stories, radio, film, and stage scripts. She didn't start writing novels until later in life, after she retired from playing music, and found herself travelling away from home for extended periods.

She currently lives in Denver, Colorado

www.ingramcontent.com/pod-product-compliance
Lightning Source LLC
Chambersburg PA
CBHW030019060826
49398CB00031B/143

* 9 7 8 1 9 6 4 1 2 7 1 8 7 *